Critical Acclaim for *The Last Spy:*

★ *Kirkus*
★★ United Press International
★★★ *Boston Sunday Herald*
★★★★ *Booklist*

"Crackerjack spy yarn about an ultra-deep Soviet agent trying to come in from the cold. High-velocity action plus clever interlude—as when Ash confesses to his girlfriend that he's a spy—add up to a smart, taut thriller, Reiss' best by far."

—Kirkus

"Very readable . . . This well-wrought tale perfectly captures the undercover agent's sense of paranoia, the inability to trust anyone or anything, and the consequences of that terrible loneliness."

—Publishers Weekly

"This is an action-paced, suspense-filled tale with plenty of surprising plot twists and just the right amount of romance. A good read that will probably be quite popular among fans of the genre."

—Booklist

"Sparkling and fast-paced . . . A thoroughly engaging thriller . . . that explores how humans behave when their world collapses around them, leaving only doubts amid the rubble."

—Boston Sunday Herald

"Bob Reiss's sparkling and fast-paced thriller . . . Thoroughly engaging."

—Washington Post Book World

Ash crunched across the white gravel driveway, feeling utterly naked. The front door was opening. David waited in the open doorway, grinning, in a running suit of white cotton and tennis sneakers, bathed in stark light from inside the house. A voice inside Ash's head urged, turn around, get back in the car, you still might have time to get out.

But Ash had to try this. He was powerless against his need. He forced his legs to move, fighting off a premonition that he was walking to his death . . . .

THE
LAST
SPY

BOB REISS

ST. MARTIN'S PAPERBACKS

Published by arrangement with Simon & Schuster

THE LAST SPY

Copyright © 1993 by Bob Reiss.

Cover photograph by Michel Del Sol.

Library of Congress Catalog Card Number: 92-31808

ISBN: 0-312-95231-7

Printed in the United States of America

Simon & Schuster hardcover edition published 1993
St. Martin's Paperbacks edition/March 1994

St. Martin's Paperbacks are published by St. Martin's Press, 175 Fifth Avenue, New York, N.Y. 10010.

10 9 8 7 6 5 4 3 2 1

A very special thanks to: Ted Conover, Ann Hood, John Irving, Andy and Angela Long, Alice Mayhew, Esther Newberg, and Irene Webb.

THE LAST SPY

Prologue: 1967

THEY WERE LAUGHING at him again. The whole class. Howling. It made his face burn, his ears pound. He wanted to crawl into a closet and lock the door. Wanted to be invisible. He dug his fingernails into his palms, under his desk, where the other kids couldn't see. In his head, the boy repeated, I won't cry.

"A camera," giggled the fat girl, Glorie Haines, in the first row, sending the class into paroxysms of laughter. "He thinks you can put a camera in a . . . *bomb.*"

"It wasn't a stupid question!" the boy cried from his seat in back. It was no use. Even his teacher joined in. "That's quite a notion, James," she chuckled, half covering her smile with her fingers. Concealing nothing.

"Your head is on the moon!" someone shouted.

"Moon Boy, Moon Boy!" The chant grew louder. "Mooooooon."

The boy tried again. "Why can't you put a camera in a bomb? Then you can make it go where you want! Like a model plane!"

To his right, one of the McNeil boys curled in the aisle, holding his stomach, gasping for breath, he was laughing so hard. A spitball flew by the boy's head and struck the bulletin board and the OUR TOWN, SMITH FALLS, MASSACHUSETTS sign. Laughter seemed to draw the walls in, to suck away air. Everything was whirling: the American flag by the row of windows, the TRAFFIC SAFETY IN FIFTH GRADE bulletin board, the *Berkshire Eagle* photo of President Johnson and Premier Brezhnev at a conference, the Russian pounding his fist on a table, the science corner filled with dioramas of local black bears and deer.

"Like a model plane, *hahahaha!*"

Miss Dietz leaned back against the board to maintain composure. She smudged the "Where is Vietnam?" she'd chalked beside the unrolled map of Red China. It was current events hour. They'd talked about Communist gains, like guerrillas in Peru. And how Communist guerrillas in Southeast Asia were beating Americans and South Vietnamese troops, how they attacked and retreated into the jungle where the Americans couldn't find them, couldn't fight them with bombs. The boy had asked, "Then why not put cameras in the bombs, so as they drop, you can see where they're going and guide them to the target?"

He wanted to close his eyes. Wanted to leave this place. The worst part was, *she* was laughing. He knew if he looked at her, he would feel worse, but he couldn't help it. He turned and she was right behind him, one seat away. Corinna, he thought. Her face so beautiful it made his knees weak. Now it was twisted, mouth contorted into a hole, skin blotchy with laughter, long blond hair bouncing as she shook. Her voice usually made him feel like someone was caressing his neck. Now an animal squeal came from her. As if she had someone else's voice, someone crueler who could not possibly be her. Her lips pulled back, showing little white teeth. Her blue eyes had a glazed, shiny excitement, turned toward the boy beside her.

Toward Cabot. The tall, dark-haired boy named Cabot. The boy everyone looked up to, even Miss Dietz. The boy who earned straight A's, who captained the softball team, who seemed older than ten already, whom everyone admired, everyone loved, nobody questioned, nobody called Moon Boy. Cabot could have stopped the laughing. All he had to do was look at them quietly, and they would stop. But Cabot had started it.

Doesn't *he* ever make mistakes? the boy thought. Doesn't he ever do anything wrong?

Even now Cabot stared back, braying, but something besides humor was in his black eyes. Something hard and appraising behind the laughter. Something malevolent.

"Dumbest question I ever heard," Cabot said softly, just for the boy. But that was when the boy noticed it. The slightest tapping of the end of Cabot's index finger, not a movement really, or even a motion. More like a whisper of activity in the air, a feint, a twitch. Almost not there. It was the kind of thing the boy was good at detecting. The little giveaway.

He's lying, thought the boy, puzzled. He liked my question. Then why is he making them laugh?

For the boy the world reduced itself to the triangle of faces. The lovely blond girl in the yellow sundress. The tall, slender, dark-haired boy with the button on his pressed paisley shirt that said MCCARTHY! And himself. The freckle-faced target in the white polo shirt, crew cut, and rolled-up, baggy jeans, looking longingly at the others who wouldn't let him in.

"Why don't *you* get blown up by a bomb," someone growled. It was Danny Minsky, the short, angry kid who followed Cabot everywhere.

"No, don't leave us, Jimmy! Who would ask the stupid questions then?" Ira Stowe cried.

"Calm down, class," said Miss Dietz.

The boy stood up.

Miss Dietz said, sharper, "James!"

The boy walked toward the door.

"James, sit down," the teacher commanded.

He wasn't going to give them the satisfaction of seeing him run. He moved calmly.

Miss Dietz cried, "You need a permission slip to leave the room!"

The boy turned left into the wide, empty corridor and shoved his hands in his pockets to brake his speed. He heard laughter welling after him. *"Now* what's he doing?" Cabot's voice shouted. He walked past rows of lockers, one with Joe Namath throwing a football pasted on front, out the double elementary-school doors, and under the THANKSGIVING '67 sign, with its pilgrim and strutting-turkey cutouts. He was alone in the school parking lot. Pumpkin- and apple-colored leaves blew against the whitewalls of the Fords and·Chevys. A cold wind blew from the west.

When he looked up, laughter echoed down from the second-story windows, lined with heads above the ivy.

"James, come back! Why can't you be like Cabot?"

But then they were gone and he was running. Down the long driveway to Main Street, past a windbreak of evergreens obscuring the school. A small boy running through Smith Falls. Past Hanson's Five 'n' Dime and the white colonial facade of Lester House, where tourist skiers ate steaks on December nights. Past the tattered signs on the community bulletin board from last summer's theater festival, and the Price Chopper where house-wives peered out at him as they shoved shopping bags into station wagons.

"Jimmy! School out early?"

"Out for the track team, pal?"

He almost ran into Sergeant Curtis as the policeman left Mo's Clip 'n' Shave, fresh from his two o'clock. Smelling hair lotion on his hands. The sergeant called, "You!"

But he didn't stop. He breathed harder, gasping. After the firehouse he stumbled into a field, crisp dead leaves trapped in weedy grass, and the oaky smell of woods came to him. It was hard to see now from tears.

He nearly ran into the barbed-wire fence.

The boy stood, gasping, nose an inch from the cold, rusty wire. The strands were so high they seemed to cordon off the sky when he looked up.

Ten feet away, on the other side of the barrier, a soldier lumbered toward him with an old World War Two Thompson slung over his half-buttoned tunic. Troops in this part of Siberia always got new-issue weapons last.

The soldier looked down at the boy, dwarfing him. He took

off his cotton cap with the red star on it and wiped his hands over thinning straw-colored hair.

"Now you've done it," he said gently.

The tone released the boy's anguish. Weeping, he cried, "I want to go home."

The corporal pulled a shiny apple from his pocket and offered it through the wire, but the boy shook his head. "I don't care if I cut myself going over. Just tell me which way to go," he begged. "Walk away and I'll climb over. I'll never tell anyone you helped."

"You're going to get me in trouble," the man sighed, "coming here all the time. They'll transfer me and then who will I have to talk to on Sundays?"

They sat crosslegged on the grass, barbed-wire between them. Behind the soldier the boy could see a flat vista of knee-high grass, waving slightly, severed by a single dirt track rutted by carts. It led toward the empty horizon, which rose rather than fell, implying vastness, giving the feeling of being lost in an immense shallow bowl. The trees out there were different from the ones in town; shorter white Russian alders instead of American maples, already dying in this climate.

The soldier spread a crumpled handkerchief on the grass, yellow cheese on red cotton. He sliced the cheese in thin strips with his bayonet knife. He handed a slice through the fence. He smiled when the boy chewed it.

"How proud your parents are of you," the private said.

"I don't remember them. Why'd they send me away?"

"They're important or you wouldn't be here." The soldier's voice grew hearty, but it was clear he felt sorry for the boy. "Cheer up. You get meat every day. You get milk. You have other children to play with. It's not so bad."

The boy said, "If there's a road, there are people. I'll get away and never tell anyone you did it."

The soldier laughed at that, but frowned at the growl of the inevitable search car. A cloud of advancing dust marked its approach. "Sure, they'll never guess," he said, slicing cheese.

"My mother sent this from the Ukraine. A hundred times better than the pig fat they call cheese here."

"It wasn't a stupid question," the boy blurted. "It wasn't."

The soldier nodded thoughtfully as the town police car came into view, Sergeant Curtis at the wheel, the principal and Miss Dietz in back. "If you asked a question, it couldn't have been stupid," he said.

The soldier dusted himself off and groaned as he rose, standing to attention. He stayed near the boy until the principal and Miss Dietz got close. The principal, Mr. DuChamp, was a wiry, nervous KGB major in a gray suit. He hated pretending he was an American all day. He thought the whole facsimile town was an idea doomed to fail. He turned his wrath on the trooper first.

"I've warned you not to encourage him. I'm going to get you transferred!"

He turned on the boy. "Into the car. Now."

None of them spoke on the ride back. The technique was supposed to intimidate him, but he liked the air on his face through the open window. Liked the idea of being free. The illusion ended when they pulled up to school. And then he was in the principal's office, on the leather couch, listening to Du-Champ and Dietz in the office on the other side of the cinder-block wall, with its color photo of dead President Kennedy. They thought he couldn't hear them.

"He doesn't fit in here," the principal said.

"He asks questions he shouldn't. He disrupts the class," said Dietz.

"It was a mistake to bring him here."

"I'll say."

"He should go back," DuChamp said.

The boy leaned forward, scarcely breathing. Please, please, please, please, please, he thought.

"Absolutely," Miss Dietz said.

"Then we're agreed. Write up the report and in a few weeks he'll be gone and we can concentrate on the others."

In the pause that followed, the boy's heart began to sink. Then Miss Dietz said with a low, crafty tone, "I think it would be better if you write the report, Comrade Principal. After all, you are in charge of the school. You carry more weight."

"But you're his teacher. You know him more intimately," coaxed the principal. "You can describe his problems in the strongest possible terms."

The boy imagined the two adults looking at each other. Miss Dietz said, "You know who his parents are? It is really your job."

A few moments later they returned to the office. DuChamp beamed. "We've decided to give you another chance, James. We know how important it is for you to be here, and I know how hard you'll work to fit in. To make your parents happy. And Uncle Yuri. You don't want to disappoint him, do you? That's not asking much, is it?" Broad grin. "Hmmm?"

The principal wagged a finger at the boy. He sat down at his desk as if he had important work to do, as if this matter had distracted him for as much time as he could spare. He was thinking that he wished he were back in Moscow. That the kids in his charge had a horrible fate in store for them. That even Hitler, whom he had fought against twenty-three years before, wouldn't have done this to kids.

"I know you'll behave from now on," the principal said.

ONE

HORACE CRAGG, A U.S. State Department clerk who regarded his job as unimportant as the report he was pirating, cleared the last security barrier in headquarters and stepped onto C Street on a warm August Washington evening. At seven thirty, the sky glowed coral above the oaks on Constitution Avenue and the Lincoln Memorial to the south. The air smelled of tidewater river and auto exhaust.

Clutching his little brown briefcase to his damp chest, the bureaucrat hurried to his car. He regarded its parking sticker as his most impressive reward after fifteen years of government service. The backseat of the Honda was littered with McDonald's wrappers his wife hadn't cleaned away. The faint smell of baby shit came to him as he started the engine and drew cautiously into the stream of post-rush-hour traffic inching past construction toward the Roosevelt Bridge and the really big jams near Rosslyn.

Fifteen years, he thought, and now the department was being stripped by budget cuts. A federal job was supposed to be secure, but for the first time he could remember, clerks were being fired. What did they call it? "Temporarily laid off?" Thank God he still had his job, but they were working him so hard he had to stay late and sneak work out at night just to stay afloat. To pay his stupid mortgage in Reston. To pay for his wife's tennis club. To keep up with repair bills on what had to be the only lemon of a Honda in the continental United States.

His intestines burned from the strain. He had to do something about the tension.

I won't go home right away, he thought.

Immediately he felt better. He took ten minutes to change direction, to make a U-turn and get back to Fourteenth. He made a left turn and traffic broke up. Driving north now, he spotted the still-unlit marquee of the new strip place on G Street a few minutes later. Cragg felt his heart slow down, then begin to race with a new kind of excitement.

Cragg loved looking at prostitutes. Not actually buying them, or touching them. That was too risky. What if he caught a disease? Or got robbed and the police called his wife? Better to just eye them from the safety of the car. He loved the little short skirts that lengthened their legs, the high heels that lifted their asses, jutted them out just for him. He licked his lips. The idea that at any second he could stop, no chance of those old rejections, nobody saying you're too short, too bald, too pasty, too flabby. All you had to do was call them over, just unlock the door. It filled him with a delicious sense of imminency. The tight blouses that accentuated their young breasts. The notion that they came without the burden of responsibility, bills, a wife who wanted him to tell her how much he loved her—to hell with her. To hell with not sleeping with her. Tonight I'll do it, he thought. Then he laughed at himself. That's what I always say. His little safe game.

I should lock the briefcase in the trunk, he thought. What if I do it and the briefcase gets stolen with the report inside?

Stupid report. Six pages of satellite photos over Malaysia. Numbers showing the commercial timber-cutting in some who-gives-a-damn Sarawak forest. He'd be up till three copying, analyzing, writing a report nobody would ever read. Nobody appreciated how hard he worked. If they found out he'd taken the worthless thing from the office, he'd be crucified. Angrily, Cragg switched on the radio. Nothing happened. He hit the dashboard. A wave of earsplitting rock music blasted out at him.

"I'll kill that kid," he shouted, envisioning the spiky, dyed-black hair on his fifteen-year-old, punching the control button, lowering the sound, sinking back hearing the oldies station, The Doors. Jim Morrison wailing "Touch Me." A wave of nostalgia washed over Cragg. The Doors, he thought. At the University of California, Berkeley, 1969, who could have imagined, in their wildest dreams, that Horace Cragg the longhair would end up a GS 12 in Washington.

He pushed the Honda past L Thomas Street, around Sheridan Circle and into the seedier area of apartment buildings and small stores adjacent to downtown. The sun was almost down. Drivers switched on headlights. Horace slowed, began looking side to side, scanning the pedestrians in front of the fried chicken stores, auto supply shops, and sagging apartment houses, looking·for the flash of high heels.

Dumb report. The NORAD satellite's mission hadn't even involved forestry data to start with. The pages Horace had been handed by his smirking department head at four forty-five this evening had started with number 204. "You don't need to know the rest," the man had said, rubbing it in. Two hundred and four, Cragg·thought angrily. That meant there were 203 other pages of military information, weather information, biological research information, all kinds of goddamn important information before, as an afterthought, NASA had programmed the photos from Sarawak. Of some out-of-the-way forest being logged over by the Japanese. Probably the only people in the world who knew the information even existed were Cragg and some *Washington Post* reporter named Ash who'd been bugging him all day for a look at the thing, as if he'd ever give it.

Nothing on Thirteenth, but Ah! at P and Fourteenth Cragg spotted a really foxy black girl in a short red skirt and black stockings, high heels that shone in the lights, hair, probably a wig, in a wave. He slowed, passing, eyeing her as she beckoned him over. Oh, my God, he thought. His heart sped up. Oh, my heaven.

And now two of them, walking between Q and P. Another black one, tall and skinny in black hotpants and silky white blouse unbuttoned near the top. A wave of luscious weakness swept over Cragg. This is really sick, he thought happily, his hands slick on the steering wheel. When he made love to Nora tonight or next month or whenever she decided to allow him, he'd have some really nice images to think about.

"Yeah, yeah, yeah," Cragg said out loud, with The Doors blasting and the tall girl smiling, hands on hips as if to say, "You like it? Take it. You stopping or what?" Horace heard himself breathing. Pull over, he thought. This one time. Do it. Unlock the door and she'll slide in, long legs on the seat. What you want, mister? What you want me to do? Cragg moaned, feeling free.

He caught her eyes, slowed, but sped up as always and kept going. His heart was really going. My god. Another one. This one white, that pale West Virginia complexion, with too much eyeliner and hair that had to be dyed, deliciously slutty. He bet she smelled like a perfume counter. Once he'd actually stopped, rolled down the window, and one of the white ones had stuck her head inside and god, if that smell hadn't stayed in his head for weeks, kept him going. At his desk, lingering over report after report, eyes burning, fingers cramped, his world a parade of thousands of pages, that smell had just come over him, bathed him, gotten him hard as he was now. Cragg felt his nostrils flaring. He bit his lower lip; he was especially horny tonight. Something wild rising in him. He eyed the white one receding in the sideview mirror before he snapped his attention back to where he was going.

Cragg turned down one of the narrow little streets off Fourteenth, drove between a gauntlet of brownstones with lots of black people on stoops. He turned right on Kingman Place, a one-block-long link between P and Q. Ahead, standing in the middle of the street, a girl—young kid, had to be a teenager—was blocking the road, flagging him.

The perfume memory was still strong. Maybe she'd be wearing some, give him a really good whiff. He felt his right foot shifting to the brake. He leaned over and rolled the passenger window down a few inches, checking the rearview mirror for cops or hoodlums. These little streets were terrific ambush points.

Up close she was younger than he'd thought, fifteen maybe, impossibly skinny, so thin she might be sick. A black girl with high cheekbones, T-shirt, tight jeans, not dressed like the other prostitutes, the ones who probably had pimps. There was no perfume smell, but with the girl so close he could barely think. Still, he was surprised because she lacked the come-on look. Nothing coy or brassy. Actually, there was a plaintive quality, a waifishness in the girl. Maybe it was the rip in the jeans. He was aware that his mouth had gone dry.

"Mister, can you buy me a sandwich?"

A sandwich, he thought. Weird opening, but the game was, you pretended you were just passing through, not ogling everything in high heels in the neighborhood. He said, reverting to his bureaucratic tone of disapproval, "I don't want to go with you. I'm just lost here." Meanwhile he feasted on the closeness of her, her thin lips, the way her chin curved down to the hollow below her neck. The soft sheen of sweat on her skin.

"Mister, I no prostitute," she said. "I don't sell myself." It struck him that she was telling the truth. It was crazy but he felt the truth of it, and an unexpected wave of shame washed through him. Plus, he'd misjudged how thin she was, she was awfully skinny. He was off balance with the lust buffeting him and slow to say "Wait" when she surprised him again, reached in, unhooked the door, and she was in the car and he wanted to say, "Get out," but he didn't say it. I'm still in control, he told himself. I can kick her out anytime. He wanted to see what was going to happen. He could scarcely breathe.

"I want a sandwich," she said. He nodded, like he owed her, considering the satisfaction she was giving him. "Ham and cheese is only a dollar fifty at McNeil's," she said. "The other places charge too much. Is a dollar fifty too much?"

He started driving, telling himself a patrol car might notice a stopped vehicle. He was going to ask her to get out, but not yet. What the hell am I doing? he thought. Get out of here. He glanced at her placid face and thought, she's simple. That's got to be it. A sandwich? Who stopped a car and asked for a sandwich? A dollar fifty? Then he thought he heard her say, "I'll satisfy you, don't worry."

"Excuse me?" said Horace Cragg.

"I'll satisfy you. I mean, you don't want anything hurty, do you? I won't do anything hurty."

"No. Not hurty," he whispered.

"Turn left here. There's the store. Do you want a sandwich? Or a pop?"

This wasn't happening, Cragg thought. He gave her two dollars and she went into the store. That broke the spell. He felt ridiculous, exposed, bald, old, sitting outside the store. She'd fooled him, he saw. She was just a street person, hustling. She knew why he was in the area. Horace started the ignition and began to shift from park to drive, but suddenly she was tapping at the window again, a puzzled expression on her face.

"Where you going? There's a basement here. I mean, all the people go there. You satisfy me, I satisfy you." She had a brown bag in her hand. The sandwich, he guessed. "Don't worry, mister. The bad people are on Fourteenth." Like a little girl, seeming hurt, she said, "Don't you want to come?"

Heart pounding, Cragg watched himself getting out of the car. Walking down some basement steps with this girl he'd just met, thinking, this isn't happening. I'm going to turn around and drive off. I won't do anything down there. I just want to see what's going to happen. Cragg, feeling the crazy wildness in him rising more than it ever had, pounding in him. Fuck it, he thought. Cragg, seeing the smashed circle of condoms on the concrete floor at the bottom of the steps. Watching her unbutton the jeans. The slit of black flesh growing. Cragg, finally not thinking anything, pulling at his clothes, looking into her shut little-girl's eyes as they jerked against each other and she mewed, lost in another world. "Billy, Billy, Billy."

The sex was greater than anything that had ever happened to him. His breathing came back to normal. He smelled urine at the bottom of the steps. He realized what had just happened.

Horror filled him. He rushed back toward his car.

Oh, shit, oh, shit. The car won't be there. Oh, shit, I caught something.

He went dizzy with terror. Someone leaned against the car.

A man in a seersucker suit, he saw. A man who didn't look dangerous, but who watched him approach, pushed himself off the hood, burgundy tie askew, somehow, despite the clothes, blending in on this seedy block. A white guy in a suit. Hands visible. Blue eyes turned to him, fixing on him.

"Hi, Mr. Cragg," the man said politely, stretching out a hand. "I'm Ash from the *Post*. Tried to reach you this afternoon."

Horace Cragg stood absolutely still. It was dark now. Boys with baseball caps turned backward on their heads rode by in a pack, on bicycles, screaming, "Zowsa," or something like that. Think, Horace thought desperately. The man in the suit acted as if they were in an office, or at a reception. But Cragg knew he'd been present the whole time he'd gone down the steps with an underage and probably AIDS-infected simpleton.

Ash stood quietly, hand poised to shake. "You know, I called about the report," he said.

It was the word *report* that got to Cragg. Horace Cragg drew himself up, reached past the reporter, and inserted the Honda key in the lock. He got in and rolled the window down. He could act as if he were in the office, too.

"Mr. Ash, I told you on the phone, I'm not permitted to talk to press. Call the public relations department if you want an interview, or a copy of whatever this report is you want to see. I don't know anything about the report. We're not allowed to talk to you. Nice meeting you."

Cragg started the car. Cruised up the block, turned back on Fourteenth Street, toward the bridge to Virginia.

Forty seconds later he made a U-turn and returned. Ash was standing under the trees, where he'd left him.

"Please don't tell," Cragg said.

They sat in the front seat together, the sounds of whooshing traffic and crickets and screaming bicycle riders around them. On

Cragg's oldies radio station, Mitch Ryder sang "Devil with the Blue Dress On."

"Please don't write anything," Cragg said.

Ash said nothing.

"I have a wife and sons. I've never done anything like that before."

Ash just watched him.

"You won't write it, will you? I was driving and I saw her. She wasn't even a . . . I mean . . . I didn't pay."

Cragg's head sank into his palms. "Oh, God. What did I do?"

The reporter said, "I don't know what you're talking about," in a way that let Cragg know that he did. "I just wanted to ask about the report."

Cragg raised his eyes. "I can't give it to you," he said.

But a minute later he went to the back and got the little brown briefcase. He pulled out pages 204 to 209. "I'm begging you, don't use it. They'll know where you got it. It's not important. Mr. Ash, I've never met you, but please, I'll be finished there. Please, Mr. Ash."

In the half-light from the overhead, Ash scanned the pages rapidly. "I can't promise anything. I'll see what I can do. I want a Xerox of this," he said.

"I'll do anything else. I'll owe you one. Someday there'll be something important, more important than this. I mean, I'm not important but sometimes I hear things. I'm not supposed to have this out of the building. They'll fire me, Mr. Ash."

Horace Cragg started to cry.

"There's a Xerox place on Connecticut Avenue," Ash said. "I meant what I said. I'll see what I can do."

"Then you don't need to take the copy, do you?"

Ash just looked at him. Cragg started up the engine. Twenty minutes later they parted outside the late-night copy place on Connecticut and R. Horace Cragg headed south over the Fourteenth Street Bridge. I caught AIDS, he thought. He's going to print it. Oh god, prayed Horace Cragg, make it okay.

* * *

Ash entered the *Washington Post* building on the L Street entrance, nodded to the guard watching the video monitor of other parts of the building, and took the back elevator to the fifth floor. At 9:00 P.M. only one writer hunched over a terminal in the Book Review section, and Ash passed the Sports, Outlook, and Style areas, to emerge into the big, brightly lit city room.

The night people were punching in stories or working the phones. Ash wove around desks until he reached a lone man writing in red pencil in the inside curve of a U-shaped desk. The man was a few years younger than Ash, maybe thirty, with baby fat still on his cheeks but hard green eyes framed inside round wire spectacles.

"Get it?" he said.

"Nope."

"Well," the editor said, leaning back in a steel swivel chair, rolling the pencil on his knuckles, "you gotta miss sometime. First time in eight years. You're human."

"Nine years," Ash said.

The man laughed. "Call the *Guinness Book of Records*. Ash's famous intuition finally fails. Don't worry. Jap cutting in Malaysian forests is no big deal. But we might have a juicy fuck-up at USAID." He was holding a manila file toward Ash. "By the way, you hear what's going on in Moscow tonight? Country's breaking apart, breaking apart. Who would have dreamed they'd collapse so fast."

"Not me," Ash said. "By the way, congratulations on your raise."

The editor sat up a little. "Nobody knows about that. Who told you?"

"Ah, Watson, you never lean back in your chair unless you have good news."

The editor laughed. "Svengali. USAID. Money supposed to go for disaster aid. Mexico earthquake. Instead the guy who runs it has a new house, car, hell of an electronic security system, costs a few thousand. Want to look into it?"

"Why not?" Ash said.

The editor leaned back toward the desk, lowered the pencil,

began circling words on a computer story printout in big red circles. "Bring back bodies."

"Pervert," Ash said. "How do you want 'em? Pickled? Roasted?"

"Naked."

There were no windows in the city room. Ash sat, loafers up on his desk beside his computer console. Frowning, ignoring the report the editor had handed him, he went over the satellite information again. There were a couple of infrared shots from miles up, red for deforested areas, smaller blue-green for standing forest. It was mostly red, with harsh black lines showing logging roads between the jungle and the aqua-colored South China Sea.

A bucket line of wedge-shaped dots led from the big island toward the northwest. They were ships bringing timber to Japan, the logo said.

Big deal. Ash strolled back to the library, barely manned at this hour, and had the wheelchair-bound attendant pull up everything on the subjects of Sarawak, Malaysia, Asian logging, timber in general, and Japan, on the Nexis information line and in the old clips. That covered every major publication in the United States. Bleary-eyed, an hour later he muttered, "Nothing."

Back at his desk, he spread the six pages like poker cards, propped forward on his elbows, and said, to the pages, "What am I really looking at?"

He sat there, going back over the information, waiting for an idea to hit. There was a magazine photo of Dwight Gooden taped to the side of his computer, and another of the old Dodger player Maury Wills. A World Wildlife Fund coffee mug on his desk. Some news clips tacked to the bulletin board marking his cubicle, reading, "Three at Commerce Indicted after *Post* Investigation," "More Arrests Expected in Commerce/Drug Connection," "Ash Runner-up for Pulitzer."

One more try. Checking his Rolodex, he punched a private number in Potomac, waited through three rings, and said when a groggy male voice answered, "Charlie. Ash. Quick question, okay? . . . Is World Wildlife doing anything on logging and

Malaysia? Any legislation pending? Big World Bank loans going
through? U.S. businesses involved? . . . Not at the moment?
That's all Japanese there, right? Anybody else there? . . . Go back
to *Rocky.*"

It was almost ten when Ash locked the other report, which he
had not read, in his desk, along with a second Xerox copy of the
satellite information. He took the original back to L Street,
where he retrieved his Saturn sports coupe from the parking
garage across the street and headed across the Fourteenth Street
Bridge into Virginia. He drove northwest. Georgetown glowed
with red and yellow lights across the Potomac, and under a full
moon he could make out the towers of the Healy Building
between gaps in maples lining the George Washington Memorial
Parkway and Palisades. On the radio, an announcer said the
Soviet Union was breaking up, more republics declaring freedom, breaking away from Moscow.

"The KGB might even be dissolved," the news announcer
said. "The once feared Soviet secret police may be absorbed into
regular military units, its power broken."

Ash yawned and changed to a music channel. A light Mozart
minuet played. He hummed along with it, driving slightly above
the speed limit, shifting easily and admiring the way the Tennes-
see-made car took the turns. At a light near McLean, after he left
the main road, he turned to see a cute redhead in a Rabbit
convertible staring at him openmouthed. "That's *you* singing? I
thought it was your radio," she said. "You have a beautiful
voice."

The grassy median strip dropped away and the four lanes
merged into a two-lane country backway. The night began
smelling of rain. Clouds were coming in, although a few stars
were still visible. On one side was Virginia state land, thick
Southern pines alternating with streams. On the other, spaced
more and more apart, he passed big homes, mansions almost,
some antebellum, some new. All of them had fences blocking the
long driveways. A few had floodlights illuminating the highway
in front.

At length he slowed before a spiked iron gate that was opening for a car coming from the other side, low slung from the look of the headlights. He glimpsed the driver as she shot past, long blond hair already streaming behind her. Just a quick vision of a head staring straight ahead, silver hoop earrings, the lapel of a white cotton business suit, a flash of his own headlight on a bracelet.

Ash caught his breath. He watched the taillights receding as the gate slid shut in front of him. It's her, he thought. He felt numb for a few moments. Then the pain started up in the back of his head.

After a few moments he felt the cool night again, heard the crickets, heard himself breathing. When he pushed the intercom button at the gate, he looked directly into the closed-circuit camera and said, "It's Ash."

"Ash! My god! Ash! This is wonderful!" The gate was sliding open again; it moved with a smooth whirring sound and stopped with a clang. It began closing the instant he passed onto the grounds. It took a few moments of driving up the white gravel driveway before he even saw the house, a big log fort of a place more suited to the Shenandoah Valley than this semisuburban part of Virginia.

Lights glowed from small windows set into the massive timber edifice, a two-story rectangular frame with one-story wings jutting from both ends. From the outside, it was ungainly. Ash drove around to the front, which faced woods beyond an extensive lawn and hedgerows. He parked in a circular white gravel drive and barely touched the Irish-wolfhound-head knocker when the door swung open.

"Ash! Son of a bitch! You shouldn't be here," the man who answered the door said, grinning.

"David," Ash said. He had to look up to see the face, model handsome, smooth shaven even at ten thirty P.M. The owner of the house wore an argyle crew-neck sweater, gray cords, and Top-Siders showing new socks at the worn seams.

"I thought I'd come and investigate you, ruin your life," Ash said. "Publish your deep dark secrets. Strip you of all you hold dear."

Laughing, the man swung Ash into the front hallway, his fingers strong on Ash's shoulder. The rich smells of evergreen and expensive cigar tobacco came from the hall. Despite the rustic elements—thick plank floor, gaslit hallway, log wall—the house had a cool, clinical feel that could only come from air-conditioning. Ash caught the sharp odor of Polo cologne off the man. Plus something slightly raunchier underneath. A hint of sweat mixed with perfume.

He noticed the dogs. Two big rottweilers had come up silently, materializing in the hall at David's feet. They didn't growl. They just stared at him.

"This is Jeremy and Jeff. My buddies," David said. "Are you Jeremy?" he cooed, scratching hard behind the first dog's ear as the stumpy tail jerked back and forth. "Are you Jeff? Sure you are," he said, patting the other one. "They'd tear anyone's head off snuck in here. Watch. . . . Lemon."

The dogs suddenly went stiff, tails out, ears up, mouths parted. They didn't take their eyes off Ash.

David laughed. "Okay, okay, guys, enough." The dogs relaxed. To Ash, David said, "Never mind the attack word."

"I'll be sure to knock next time," Ash said. He guessed in his head what went with *lemon*, what would make the dogs attack. *Jello? Pudding?*

The host brightened. "Are you hungry? I'm starved. I'm making myself a sandwich. Come into the kitchen." Ash followed him through a hallway with teak rafters and an antique brass coatrack hung with a Baltimore Orioles baseball cap and an Armani raincoat. The prints on the walls were old London, 1880. In the remodeled kitchen Ash sat on a stool at a counter while David built sandwiches.

"Fresh Virginia ham, honey mustard, gherkins on black pumpernikel. You hungry, big guy?"

"Plenty. You got any beer?"

The floors were all heavy planking. There was a vague pattering noise and Ash realized rain was falling on the skylight taking up half the ceiling. "Sam Adams," David said, plunking two frosty bottles on the counter. "None of that foreign stuff in this house. My god, the last time you were here was, it had to be the inauguration party, right? What are we talking, ten, twelve years ago?"

"Younger days," Ash said, a twinge of pain coming as he remembered the woman in the car outside. Ash loosened his tie. The beer tasted good. "Undersecretary of state," Ash said, shaking his head in admiration. "When you were a kid, did you ever think you'd actually get to be an undersecretary of state?"

"When I was a kid I wanted to be king," the man laughed. "Anyway, retired undersecretary now. Private D.C. consultant. Come here, I got to show you my gym. Just put it in. Take the beer."

Ash felt the folded-up satellite report rubbing against his chest in his breast pocket. Almost time, he thought. The living room, which they passed, was decorated with travel trophies, Oriental rugs, Chinese vases, a samurai sword in a glass case, a bust of President Reagan, and an antique upright piano. There was a dying fire in a granite fireplace, hunting prints, and floor-to-ceiling bookshelves filled with leather-bound originals, and sets of presidential papers. The gym had a wall-to-wall wrestling mat, Gravitron machine, barbells, bicycle ride, and parallel bars. The study, at the back of the house, was a masculine room in dark paneling and burgundy leather chairs, with a desk used by Thomas Jefferson, a crystal humidor filled with Havanas, and oils of Benjamin Franklin and President Jackson. In the painting, Jackson was in his office greeting a line of well-wishers, average people who looked like farmers, after his inauguration.

"Another Sam Adams?"

"Sure."

"OJ for me. Got to work later. That's the bad part about going private," the man joked. "You make your own hours." He opened a small refrigerator in the study near a rolling bar and took care of the drinks. Then they sat looking at each other.

David, draped on a couch, sighed. "You really shouldn't come here. You're not supposed to."

"I know. Here," Ash said, taking the report from his pocket, never taking his eyes off David's face.

"You never know who's watching the place," David said. "Next time do it the regular way." He sipped orange juice from a crystal glass and Ash heard the ice shift and tinkle. The rain hit harder against the window. David picked a pair of reading glasses off the top of the desk and leaned back.

"Hmmmm. I see. Good job. How'd you get it?" David glanced up and laughed. "Why even ask."

"Look at these pictures," he added. "It's amazing, I'll never get over it, a camera so high up. Miles up, and you get these great shots I can't even get from twenty feet away. I was in China last month, I must have spent a thousand dollars on camera equipment. Lenses. Film. Flash. Meters."

"David?"

"Wait. We're at the Great Wall of China with the premier, for god's sake. Am-azing place. Two thousand goddamn miles of wall, and all I want to do is take a shot of him standing still." David shook his head. "Forget it. Comes out looking like one of those photos of attack dogs leaping." He laughed. "A lot of blur. Teeth, or at least that's what they looked like."

"I want to ask you a question," Ash said.

David made a pistol shape with his right hand and "shot" Ash by pressing his thumb against his index finger. He said, "Bang-o."

"Why do you need this stuff?" Ash said.

The wall behind the desk was lined with eight-by-ten framed photos. David shaking hands with President Reagan. David teeing off at golf with President Bush. David in a circle of Supreme Court justices, everyone caught laughing, everyone holding drinks. David sitting on a couch with General Noriega, with Willie Brandt, the man's hands folded, acutely aware of the camera. David with Robert Redford. Charlton Heston. David hanging over the side of a sailboat as Robert Rockefeller worked the tiller. David shaking hands with Colin Powell under a banner that said WELCOME HOME FROM SAUDI ARABIA. David always looking equal to whomever he was with. Always as handsome, always as present, never diminished by the powerful people filling his trophy wall.

Ash rose and went to the wall and saw his reflection moving over the still-fixed smiling countenance of the president of France. Saw David, more vividly, reclining on the couch sipping orange juice in the reflection.

"Why?" Ash asked again. "I don't get it. Malaysia? What do they want with Malaysia, and besides," he said, turning, "what the hell are we even doing here anymore? The country's falling apart. The premier's out. There's no cold war anymore, no conflict anymore, maybe not even any KGB anymore. So who are we? For the last year my assignments have been getting very weird. David, why are we still doing this?"

The man on the couch had raised his brows, amused. He put his glass down, licked a spot of juice off his lip. "Oh, Moon Boy," he said, chuckling. "You never changed. You'll ask Moon Boy questions till you die."

Ash said, "That's not an answer. I'm not just talking about that." He flicked a finger toward the report in David's hand. "But the last two you wanted, too. Mexican soybean futures? Who cares? U.S. position on World Bank loans to Uruguay? Uruguay, David? When have we ever had an interest in Uruguay? Moscow's letting Eastern Europe go, we're risking exposing ourselves over Uruguay? What's going on?"

David went to the rolling bar. Poured more juice in his glass. "How do I know?" He shrugged. "You think they tell me why they want things? Listen to yourself. There's peace now. But who knows what'll be happening a year from now. And even if there is peace, real solid peace, unshakable peace, you think the Israelis don't have guys in Washington? The French and Germans and Japanese? Come on, Ash."

David sat down and crossed his legs, one worn Top-Sider moving casually up and down. On the side of his glass, almost too subtle to be noticed, Ash saw the tip of his index finger begin shifting. It left a smear mark on the condensation the size of a tick.

"You'd think journalists would be the most savvy people," David said affectionately. "They're the most naive."

He leaned forward, looking a little more serious, more concerned. "You saw Corinna out at the gate, didn't you. Is that why you came?"

"This isn't about Corinna."

"Ash, I'm sorry you saw it."

Ash shook his head heavily, fighting off the sluggish feeling clogging him. "It was you she wanted all along. The divorce went through three years ago. It was never a marriage. It was just what they ordered. She never wanted to do it. This isn't about her."

"All the same," David said compassionately, "it's one thing to know something, another to see it." They eyed each other. David sighed and rose, signaling the night was over. "Next time you don't need to see me. Next time use your drop. I can forgive one infraction after all this time, and it's good to see you, but"—David shrugged—"bad policy. You don't want to get sloppy after all these years."

"How many of us are left?" Ash said softly.

David whistled, low and long. "Oh, Moon Boy," he said. "We were having such a nice time."

"Where are the others? I wonder about them. Are they even alive? Will we ever have another reunion? Were any of us ever caught?"

David shook his head, an affectionate gesture, leading Ash back down the hallway. The dogs, which Ash realized were not permitted to come in the study, materialized again out of the shadows. It was eerie the way they made no sound. He sensed their muzzles following behind his Achilles' tendons as David escorted him to the door.

"Every system has kinks in it," David said. David Kislak now. Not David Cabot since they'd come here. "Those marriages— bad idea from the start."

Ash tried for the last time, knowing he wouldn't get a verbal answer, watching the finger. "What does Moscow care about forests in Malaysia?"

"Good question," David said. "Maybe one day we'll even find out." He laid a hand on Ash's shoulder. "Things will work out at home. We're all concerned. I have an early day tomorrow. Clients. Ciao, guy."

Outside, Ash climbed into the Saturn and drove back toward the gate. The rain had stopped. He noticed more closed-circuit cameras in the trees, as well as some sort of black boxes, which he guessed sent out an infrared alarm system through the grounds. During the Reagan years security precautions had been beefed up even for undersecretaries. The gate slid open as he reached it and he steered through, headed down the road, stopped a quarter mile later, where he was not visible from the house, and got out. Ash stood in the road, looking back. The forest was filled with the sound of dripping. The moon broke out from between racing clouds. Ash looked back toward the house for a long time.

While inside the house, David Kislak let the curtains fall back across his living room window and leaned down to pet the dogs. "Jeff, gooooood boy, goooooood boy. Do you guard your daddy? Do you guard your Jeremy? Yesss, yessssssss."

Kislak walked back to the study and punched a number into the phone. "Concerned is right," he said to thin air.

"We have a problem," he said when the receiver was lifted on the other end.

He hung up and sat a long time looking at the bank of pictures on the wall, finger tapping on the satellite report.

TWO

"**I**T'S ELEVEN-THIRTY, and the world is for lovers," the beautiful voice said. "Nothing else matters. Lovers toasting each other. Lovers in each other's arms, whispering secrets in the dark. Lovers without partners, seeking the light. I'm alone in this room with the mike and a coffee cup that says WLLO. The phone has eight buttons, but none have lit up yet. I don't care about Russia or the housing market or the Orioles or the weather. I care about the real thing. I'm Jennifer Knowles and I want to talk to you. I'm the Night Owl. Tell me your secrets. Whisper your dreams. Call me, now."

Ash drove slowly across the Key Bridge back into the District. The night was humid, the river smell washing through the open windows from the Potomac. He barely heard the words on the radio, but the voice was low and pleasant. He hadn't seen David in person in almost ten years.

"David is your big brother. We're family, all we have is each other," came another voice in his head, an older voice, the voice of Uncle Yuri. "We have to protect each other. Look out for each other. And never, never do bad to each other. That advice will keep you alive."

Ash reached the Washington end of the bridge and turned right onto M Street. As usual, by eleven-thirty Georgetown had lost its veneer of respectability and deteriorated into a carnival of drunken revelers and fraternity boys. The vagrants came up from the river towpath to beg. The streetlights fronting the bars made cars crawling along M Street shine. Rap music poured from a Mustang to his right, filled with underaged adolescents with beers in their hands.

In his head, he saw an old man with a white goatee, silver glasses, a small feminine hand shaking with slight palsy, filled with Chuckles jellied candies. He was sitting in the "town square" in Smith Falls, Massachusetts, which wasn't really Smith Falls, across from the police station. The old man was saying, "Come on, kids. Eat up. Candy!"

Ash turned left by White Castle and bounced up a cobblestone lane to Prospect Street. He drove up to Thirty-sixth and over to P, where he found a parking space under the maples. Other than a couple of students leaning against each other and stumbling back toward the Georgetown University dorms, the street was empty. He walked half a block and mounted the steel steps leading to a brick town house. Curtains covered the French windows, but light bloomed behind them. Ringing the bell, he thought, it's not your job to think about this. David is right.

"Jimmy, perfect timing," said the woman in the doorway, moving back, letting him in, backing into the light of her living room in her brown silk dashiki. Ash looked down at the high ebony cheekbones and happy eyes and opal pendant nestled in shallow cleavage above the translucent silk. She spoke with a French accent. The combination living room/study had a deep white pile carpet; bright pillows lay bunched for sitting. Mahogany bookshelves were filled with French and English editions, with woven baskets as bookends. Near a small, cluttered antique French desk in a far corner, and the still-humming computer with the green screen, Ash saw an array of wall photographs from the Cameroons. Market day. A rhino looking at the lens. An elderly couple in front of a hut. A man in a white linen suit behind a big desk, looking important.

"You're the sexiest woman I've seen all day," said Ash.

She jumped up, wrapped her legs around his waist, and they were kissing as he carried her into the adjacent bedroom, steering by memory and the flicker of a half-burned candle that filled the room with a sandalwood smell. She tasted of a spice he had eaten but could not remember. When she was naked, her jewelry still brushed him. The long silver earrings sliding up the inside of his thighs. The smooth gold of her anklet riding his calf and later, the hollow of his neck. The bright pool of candlelight reflected in the opal, swimming in sweat beads between her breasts.

"Oh, Ash. Oh, Jimmy. Oh, Jimmyyyyy."

He'd met her at the World Bank three months before at a cocktail party. A Cameroonian economist bored with the officiousness of the bank. It was just physical at first, and then they'd started to like each other. Which meant a bad time was coming. And might even be here. Tonight she was even fiercer than usual, her nails probing his back and buttocks. The urge to burst huge in him. He buried his face in her mound, licking. There was something about the way she used her fingers that made him feel them everywhere, even when they were somewhere else. In the back of his throat. In his groin. The candle snuffed out; bright moonbeams bathed the bedsheets. At the end they slammed against each other and said each other's name, and she said, "Don't stop ever, Ash, ever. Don't stop."

It was the catch in her voice that told him. Tonight would be the last night.

They lay, breathing hard, her index finger tracing directionless lines on the muscles of his chest.

"Jimmy," she said at length, making it sound like "Jee-mee." "It's not that you come here so late. It's not that you work all the time. It's not even that you don't tell me what you're doing."

Ash sat up in bed and looked down at her. Her eyes were black and almond shaped and enormous. On the dresser, the moonlight rippled when the curtains covering the window blew. There was the whoosh of a passing car on the cobblestones outside. She wasn't crying yet, but she would be soon.

"You're not even going to ask me not to say this, are you?" she said. "That's what the problem is."

Ash kissed her belly. He ran his hands through her hair. It was downy with a springy softness. At times Uncle Yuri's voice could come to him as fresh, as close, as if he were sitting at the old man's knee. "If you think you're getting close to someone by telling them who you are, you're wrong. You're selfish. You're killing them," the voice said.

The woman on the bed turned her head away, gazed off at the painting above her dressing table. A still life of red orchids. The opal, askew, lay in the hollow of her throat. She said, "First I thought you were just quiet. Men . . ." She paused a moment, wanting to say it right, not wanting to refer to others she had been with. "Men don't need to talk as much. Then I thought it was because I was from another country. Different customs. I can't expect an American man to be like a Cameroon man. Or did you pick me for that reason?" She turned back, looking into his face. "Because you knew I wouldn't see you were different?"

"You picked me," Ash said.

She laughed softly. "I did the talking, Jee-mee. But that's all it was. I don't want to see you anymore," she said. "I really don't know who you are. There's something . . . wrong there. Not bad. Something inside. Something too private."

Ash saw that she was waiting for him to reveal himself. Not expecting it, but hoping enough to give him the chance. He said, "I have eleven different wives in different cities." She didn't laugh. He said, "Okay, I'm a murderer. I killed eleven people." A week ago she would have laughed. He said, "But I had a good reason." It wasn't working. Ash got out of bed and went into her bathroom. He turned the shower on hot, so it steamed up fast. Everything here was so feminine, so beautiful. The smells of shampoo and perfume. The way the steam seemed a mist when they'd showered together. The little pink shaver for her legs. The loofah he'd soaped her with. The glycerin soap from Cameroon. He dried himself when he was finished washing. She never came in the whole time.

In the bedroom she sat on the bed, legs akimbo. She wore a robe of peach-colored terry cloth, an inch open at the hip.

Ash sat on the bed with her, stroked her cheek. "I don't have any secrets. I don't have any big revelations to share. I like to have fun, is that so bad?" He smiled. "Nobody raped me when I was a kid."

"That's not what I'm talking about. When you're with somebody, things get . . . deeper naturally," she said, watching him. "It just happens. Little things do it. Somehow they don't happen with you."

"Little things," he said, as if he had no idea what she was talking about. "Little things."

She sighed. "I guess you just don't want to," she said. Ash dressed quickly, not wanting to drag out the rest, the pain in the room palpable. You don't want to know, believe me, he thought. He told her that the woods in Virginia had been pretty today. She said, playing along, that she liked to hike in the woods.

"I'll call you later," he said, waiting for the no.

"No."

He leaned to kiss her but she gave him her cheek. They'd kill you if they ever found out. She linked an arm through his and walked him to the door. She punched him lightly, on the chest, before she unlocked the door.

"American man." Her eyes seemed a little teary. "You Americans."

Outside, Ash smoothed back his hair and told himself he didn't love her, it was temporary. That much was true, but it was always temporary. He liked her a lot. Sometimes he wanted to scream out the truth in the middle of the street. Just stand up in the office and blurt it out. But then what? Uncle Yuri's voice in his head said, "You're responsible for each other. Protect each other. If you hurt yourself, you hurt the others. Give yourself up, you give up the others. Even kill the others. And your parents, believe me, those bastards would hurt them to teach you to be loyal. They'd even kill me. I love you, children."

The lights went out in Dara's town house. Ash shoved his hands in his pockets and walked toward Wisconsin Avenue, its lights and bars. Uncle Yuri's voice said, "You're not sharing with them, you're dooming them. Not loving them, just indulging yourself."

At Wisconsin Avenue the lights seemed brighter. He passed a traffic cop ticketing a double-parked Monte Carlo in front of a movie theater where the midnight show was getting out, then went into a corner bistro called Au Pied de Cochon. He seated himself at a long, curving bar in front of a mirror that reflected a smattering of tourists, insomniacs, lovers, and late diners in the well-lit room behind. Above the bar was a painting of a butcher on the cobblestone streets of nineteenth-century Paris, a struggling pig in one hand, a long knife for killing in the other. At the far end of the bar, beyond a man in a three-piece gray suit who seemed to be sleeping, a small woman in a Georgetown University sweatshirt stared back at him in the mirror, not looking away when their eyes met.

David was lying, Ash thought.

He kept seeing the finger moving, twitching, on David's glass.

David was lying. No, not lying, Ash thought. Lying, after all, was the wrong word. Lying was David's job. Lying would never make David uncomfortable. David could tell a normal lie without giving himself away. And even if he did lie, that wouldn't make Ash uncomfortable. So why was the finger moving? Why had he needed the satellite data? What was different?

Ash cast back in time. To the little classroom where they'd had lessons like American kids during the mornings. Real lessons from America. Long division. Colonial times. Who's the governor of Massachusetts? The Spanish-American war. Each year the lessons getting harder as they kept pace with their counterparts in Smith Falls, Massachusetts, seven thousand miles away. And then, after the American lunch, franks and beans, macaroni and cheese, hamburgers and fries, the opposite lessons. Why we love the party. Why the morning lesson was a lie. Movies about slavery in the United States, slavery that continued even in 1960 with black people shut up in slums. They'd see newsreels of strikes at factories where rich people put breadwinners out of work. They'd see films of U.S. troops in Europe threatening the peace-loving Soviet Union, or helping the French in Vietnam. Third grade becoming fourth, fifth, junior high school.

Ash looked into the mirror and remembered the manila file Uncle Yuri had given him when he turned twelve. "This is a famous American journalist, but a bad, bad man," Uncle Yuri had told him, just the two of them in Ash's dormitory room. The old man in his tweed jacket with the pipe smell, with his awful posture, sitting on the edge of the iron bed. The boy thrilled to have Uncle Yuri to himself. Staring at the picture of the *Washington Post* columnist. Drinking up Uncle Yuri's words, filled with love for the man. "He pretends to help the poor but he is paid by the rich ones. Study him. Learn about him. All my children are seeing photographs of people they will meet. Learn what he likes, what he hates. Learn how to make him like you. One day you will be a reporter at the *Washington Post*. Don't look so scared, Jimmy. You can do it. You can live there. You children have each other. No one is smarter than my children. Nobody matches you in intelligence. Don't be scared. David will work with a politician, and Corinna, my sweet Corinna, will be an intern with a very important lawyer who works on treaties. And you will depend on each other there, just like here. And David will be my eyes and ears."

Uncle Yuri had smiled, reached into his jacket pocket, and brought out Chuckles candies. "Now look how good a reporter you are already, Jimmy. I'm not supposed to tell you these things, but you got it out of me. There's a reason why you ask questions all the time. A purpose, even if the others laugh at you sometimes. It's your destiny to ask questions. One day your questions will help the Soviet Union stay safe. But now you'll keep my secret, won't you? I can trust my children and you can trust me. Who else do we have if not each other? And you'll always listen to David, you'll never doubt David. Because David speaks for me. Now, enough seriousness for one day, eh? Come on, it's May Day. There's a celebration outside."

Ash shook himself back to the present. In the long mirror behind the bar, the girl in the sweatshirt still looked his way.

He ordered a Sam Adams and sipped and caught sight of himself reflected in the polished mahogany of the bar. The lines of his seersucker jacket pointing to the undone collar. The narrow chin and long nose. The deep blue of the eyes. He hadn't even heard from David in a year until last week. You went along, forgot a little, just enough to feel the outer edges of comfort. You pretended. You took longer breaths. You told yourself they wouldn't use you anymore. And the phone rang one night.

"Fuck it," he said to his reflection softly.

"I said, you look like you're pondering very weighty matters," a voice said. It was the girl in the Georgetown sweatshirt, seated next to him now. Ash looked into a small, crooked face brimming with intelligence. Green eyes boring into his despite the relaxed attitude. Girlish pageboy haircut with bangs falling askew by a tiny, upturned nose. Smile open on one side, appraising on the other. The bartender put a drink in front of her with orange juice in it. She hadn't asked for it.

"Here's the question," she said, rocking slightly on the swivel seat. "A girl gets off work late at night. She likes to hang out at the local restaurant. There's a very interesting-looking man at the bar who clearly doesn't want to talk to anyone." She hunched her shoulders, looked down at the bar. She was a bearish imitation of Ash and he laughed. But it was the voice that got to him. He knew that voice. Low and beautiful, he felt it in his gut. Ash chuckled inwardly at his bottomless appreciation for women.

"The girl wants to meet the guy. Worst that happens, her curiosity gets satisfied. Best"—she smiled, showing white even teeth—"these days, who thinks about best. So what does she do? Girl doesn't want to be too forward. Looking needy, that's a big no-no. Stupid conversation never gets anybody anywhere. What do you think the starting point is, or shall I go away?"

"I'd call Jennifer Knowles, the Night Owl," Ash said, impressed by her straightforwardness. "She seems to know what to do in social situations like those."

"Jennifer Knowles," the girl said, swiveling and tapping her drink with her index finger, "always knows what to tell other people to do."

This was the way it had started with Dara. A cute meeting at a World Bank party. A woman's smiling face. The open, happy facade of opportunity. And then that scene at the town house half an hour ago was how it always ended. A face turned to a wall. A voice telling him to open up. Ash didn't even think about it anymore.

"Your voice," Ash said, not coming on to her, simply saying what he thought, "is beautiful."

"When I was a teenager, my teacher said to me, 'Radio, Jennifer. You've got to go into radio.' Translation: you're not pretty enough for TV."

"Well, you're not the TV type," he said. "Flashy."

"That's teaching me to fish," she said, laughing. The bartender refilled her glass from a gallon jar of orange juice, without being asked. He flashed Ash an angry look.

"She never talks to anyone," he said. He looked jealous.

"Boyfriend?"

"No."

"He wants to be," Ash said.

"What's got you so blue tonight?" Jennifer Knowles said.

"I thought you stopped these questions when you got off the radio."

"Oh," she said. "I never stop it. I'm doomed to repeat it. By the way, that's a very expensive perfume you wear. Joy, isn't it?"

Ash laughed. "I thought I washed it off."

"Well, she's rich, whoever she is. Uh-oh. I made you sad. Change the subject, Jennifer. Let's see. Music? I think Madonna's on the way out. Sports? How ya like dem Redskins? Life history? Shut up, Jennifer. You're babbling."

"You talk a lot," Ash said. "You should be on the radio." Then he pushed the bad part away. Dangerous to show it in public. He liked Mozart and she liked Mozart, as it turned out. He preferred baseball to football. She played tennis in Georgetown each morning.

"Life history then," she said, settling close. "I'm from western Massachusetts, little town, Lenox. You know western Massachusetts?"

Ash's heart started beating faster. He kept smiling. He thought, get out of here.

"Me, too," he said.

"No kidding. Really! I thought I recognized the accent. Which town?"

"Smith Falls."

"Ah, the Wildcats. You beat us in the county championship. Where in Smith Falls? I know it a little."

Ash made himself look embarrassed. He watched her very, very carefully. "Not really in town, more in Becket," he said. "It was a . . . um . . . home for kids. No parents. It was called DuChamp."

The girl gasped. "The place that burned down?"

"Yeh," Ash said. "But they farmed me out before that. To a family in D.C. And I stayed."

"I remember that fire."

"Luckily, all the kids were out," Ash said.

"It just exploded, didn't it? I mean, the boiler."

Ash nodded. "It wasn't so bad there. But you didn't really mix with the kids in town much. We stayed on the grounds a lot. Had teachers. Hiking. Fishing. They used to take us to Tanglewood in the summers. That's where I first heard Mozart. Boston Pops orchestra." He blew out air. "They'd bring peanut butter sandwiches. And cherry Kool-Aid. Vile stuff." He grinned. "They were big on dental hygiene."

"You want to go hiking with me sometime?" she said.

"Sure," he said, and thought, no way.

"Eastern Shore isn't like home," she said. "Too flat. But it's nice, the shore birds. Hey! Remember Smith Falls Day? I always loved Smith Falls Day."

He was waiting for the phony question. The trick question. Who was she? FBI? David? Uncle Yuri? Just a woman in a bar? "Smith Falls Day was good. We got to ride on the fire truck. That and vanilla shakes at McKay's."

"Yeah, McKay's," she said, a dreamy look on her face. "Hey, wha'd I say?"

Ash had stood up. "Nothing," Ash said. "Long night."

"If you're going to go hiking with me, I have to know your name. Otherwise my mother won't allow it," she said.

What the hell, he thought. If she knows it already what difference does it make? He told her. She said, "Jennifer," and shook his hand seriously, like a lawyer, and burst out laughing. The bartender should have been glad Ash was leaving but glared at him instead, making sure he hadn't hurt the girl's feelings.

Outside, the evening was cooler. He wouldn't come back to Au Pied de Cochon for a while, not that she wouldn't come at him again if David had sent her. He still remembered how nice her voice had felt. It made him feel as if he were kissing her, even when he was walking away.

THREE

ASH, TERRIFIED, felt the station wagon rock as it rushed south toward the U.S. border. It was the middle of the night. He was seventeen. David and Corinna sat beside him on the backseat, fingers twined. Ahead, beyond the heads of the two adults who had picked them up in Montreal, and the rain battering the windshield, headlights burned into their faces from cars coming from the south. More cars than Ash had ever seen. An assault of dazzling floodlights that lit up the interior every few seconds; the stiff, frightened teenagers in back, the camping equipment the driver had smeared mud on to make it look used. The greasy hamburger bags scattered in the car to show a family "on vacation."

The woman swiveled, her big moon face over the backseat, under her kerchief. "This is going to be easy," she said too gaily. "Believe me. Borders here aren't guarded like they are where you come from."

The man jerked the wheel, muttered, "Raccoon," and the wagon skidded, righted itself. More lights slid across his red plaid collar and drove shadows over the bunched muscles on his hairy neck. "And besides," he said, "the guards hate to work outside in the rain." He tried to sound light but his voice was scratchy. "Don't worry, we'll go right through," he said.

Then why are you driving so fast? Ash thought. Uncle Yuri had told them, teary eyed on the dock in Riga, "You'll land in

Canada as diplomats' children. You'll get new American passports in your own names. Our good friends will drive you in groups to Massachusetts. If anything goes wrong, you know to get yourself to Canada or Mexico. And remember," he'd whispered, "if your back is to the wall, if there are no other options, if you are in trouble and desperate with nowhere else to go, come to the embassy in Washington. Give the code. I'll be contacted. But we don't *want* you to come to the embassy. If you come, the FBI will have your picture, check you out. You'll be brought home, and if you don't have a good explanation for exposing yourself, your life will not be pleasant. If you come to the embassy, you will be finished in the United States. You will not see the other children again. So use it as a last resort. Only as a last resort.

"I'll miss you so much. I'm proud of you," Yuri said.

Now David told the driver, "We trust you." Buttering adults up like always. They never saw through it.

"One more mile," the woman said, reading a sign.

The tight, closed feeling grew stronger in the car. Ash joked, watching a neon green BAR go by, "No sweat. Ethel and I fool 'em every time." At once the driver snapped, "That isn't funny, kid," and the woman gave a little gasp and glared at him. Ash was quoting from *The Rosenbergs,* a film they'd seen before leaving, black-and-white footage of a man and woman, "Soviet spies," the American announcer said, "walking to the electric chair."

"They're strapping down Julius Rosenberg," the announcer had said while the cameras showed a long gray building. "They're fitting the steel cap on his head."

"They burned to death," Principal DuChamp had told them. "That's what will happen to you if you're caught."

David spoke up beside Ash. "Don't mind him, sir. He's got a sick sense of humor."

Ash's stomach rose as he felt the car slowing. He was helpless in the backseat. The solid white line in the headlights broke into strips battered by rain. They joined a line of cars, shining red brake lights ahead, inching toward a white glow around a booth.

"This is it, kids," said the driver, who had introduced himself as DuChamp, shocking them with the same name as their old principal. Now he said, "Relax, okay? We were camping. We're heading for Smith Falls. We cut it short because it's raining. But I'll say it. Martha, give them the food."

As the woman rummaged, Ash rehearsed the line they'd given him to say if the guards ordered them out of the car:

"Come on, man. It's raining. Give me a break."

Be petulant but not obnoxious, the woman had told him. Do you know that English word? *Obnoxious?*

The car moved forward one space. The woman handed out saran-wrapped sandwiches, mustard smeared on brown crust. "Who wants Kool-Aid," she said. Her eyes looked enormous and distorted by too much mascara, and the cherry drink was so sugary it made Ash's teeth throb.

David rehearsed his line with Corinna. "She's pokin' me, Ma."

The big woman in the passenger seat turned, smiled at them, motherly. "Leave your brother alone!"

They rolled a few feet. Now Ash saw the guards, two men in yellow slickers and gray hats under clear plastic, with wide, dripping rims. Leaning into both front windows in the Ford pickup ahead of them. Vermont plates. Walking slowly around the truck. Shining a flashlight in the cab.

"Good," said the woman to David.

The bologna tasted like sandpaper. The woman pulled an apple out of her bag. When she bit into it, a tangy, fruity smell came into the car.

Ash shivered. Close up, as they rolled into the cone of light, the booth looked cramped, with a peaked wooden roof that kept the guards dry as long as they never moved three feet from the building. They didn't seem to mind standing in the rain.

"Ma, she's pokin' me," David said. "Ma, she's pokin' me."

The driver rolled down his window. "Some vacation," he told the guard. "You get one lousy week and look what happens. It hasn't stopped raining since I got off."

"Ma, she's pokin' me," David said.

The guard's face swam into the window; narrow and open, shiny shaven, with a silvery emblem of an eagle on the collar. The woman turned toward the backseat. "Leave your brother alone!"

"Where you folks from?" the guard said. Funny accent, Ash thought. He'd never heard English with a Southern accent. The driver said Smith Falls, Massachusetts. Best little town in the Berkshires. But the guard was staring at Ash. He wouldn't take his eyes off Ash. Ash's head started pounding. "Who are you?" the guard said. "You're not Ash." Suddenly Ash realized he wore his red scarf, the scarf they donned back in Smith Falls for afternoon lessons. His fingers fumbled with the knot. He couldn't get it off.

"What's that?" the guard snapped.

Ash sat alone in the car. He couldn't reach the ignition to get away. He couldn't remember his line. He stuttered, "Gimme a . . . gimme a . . ."

The guard reached through the window, clutching at Ash. Suddenly Ash couldn't breathe. Cold fingers wrapped around Ash's wrist.

Ash shot up in bed, sweating.

Through gray morning light the red digital clock read five-thirty. He was in his bedroom in Dupont Circle. He hadn't had the dream in years, but seeing David in person had jumbled him up. He still saw the hand reaching for his face.

Tail swishing softly, Ash's tiger cat Tyler sat at the end of the bed, eyeing him. The cat crept up the quilt and nuzzled his hand, wanting to be petted. Ash scratched him behind the ears. What a dream, he thought.

Usually he loved waking early, when the world was private. Downstairs in the duplex, the Mr. Coffee was perking on automatic. He poured steaming vanilla French blend into his big china mug and padded on thick pile into his living room. Seventeen years, he thought, in Washington. He broke them into compartments, the way he did with everything else in his life. First the "new" years, quiet all the time, hesitantly testing what he had learned, always afraid when the phone rang, when there was a knock at the door, when he saw a police car. Living with the couple who had "adopted him." Dreaming at night about that Rosenberg movie. Realizing that people really believed he'd been born in the U.S. Then the "beginning of working," the internship at the *Post*. Someday he'd learn how it had been arranged for him. Passing along little bits of information, things that you learned at the paper but were never printed. Who was having an affair with whom. Who was probably taking money, but the paper couldn't find enough evidence to confirm it. Things Moscow didn't need evidence of to start investigating. "Leverage," Uncle Yuri had said.

Ash sipped slowly, lying on the long sofa, legs dangling over the side. After that period, he thought, the "doubting" time. After he ended his marriage, never mind orders. Told Corinna to go. What was the point of keeping her against her will? What am I doing here? he'd asked himself. I want to get out of here. This country isn't the way they told us it would be. It's better. Freer. The poverty isn't as bad as they said it would be. The police aren't as frightening as they said they would be. There aren't riots all the time. You can go anywhere you want.

Once, after the separation, he'd driven up to Massachusetts, to the real Smith Falls, to spend a weekend there. He remembered rolling up Route 8 through the real Berkshires, his heart hammering as he saw the Otis and East Lee signs, passing beneath the real Massachusetts Turnpike, driving past the real strip of Friendly's and McDonald's and pizza stores. Parking across from the real Lester House, except in the real Smith Falls, it had been a little different. The sign had been in black, not red. And Hanson's Five 'n' Dime had been smaller than the one back home. And the real town cops had worn Sam Browne belts across their chests, not just gunbelts, like they had at home.

Ash shook his head. It hadn't felt like home. At the time, drinking beers at Lester House that night, all the people around him laughing and sipping beers and watching the Red Sox on television, he'd known finally that home for him wasn't a physical place. It was the other kids. How could he feel disloyal to a country that would imprison him if they found out who he was?

Turn himself in? He'd have to turn the others in, too. Go back to Russia? He'd be killed for desertion. Go away? Where?

And then one day, as if David knew what Ash was thinking, he'd found the newspaper article at his drop. He couldn't even tell from what paper. Just a photograph and a news clipping in an otherwise empty Band-Aid box. "Hit-and-Run Accident." He never knew if all of them had gotten it, or just him. It was a photo of sad-looking Lewis Pell, the quietest of them, the kid at the back of the classroom in Smith Falls, the kid who was some kind of math genius, Uncle Yuri said. The kid Ash had always figured was working with a defense company somewhere.

Ash lay on the couch now, smelling the coffee, the dream fading as he remembered opening the Band-Aid box, unfolding the paper, slightly brown, as if David had been waiting for the right occasion. He saw himself standing in a copse of maple trees in Rock Creek Park, his drop every other month that year. The sun hot on the back of his head. Staring at the clipping.

Ash still felt cold thinking of it. It was inconceivable to him that David could actually have sent someone after one of them. That any of them would harm another.

Lewis must have tried to turn them in. It was the only reason that made sense. That David hurt one to save the others.

Gray light edged into the apartment through the ground-level windows, past the curtains. Ash had spent a lot of time fixing up the place. "You will have a difficult life so you must love little things," Uncle Yuri had always said. "Food. Music. Sports. Literature. Comforts you control." On the wall was an Elliot Porter clouds photograph, white clouds in blue. An old-man sketch by Dali in yellows and black. Beads, "tears of joy and sorrow," he'd picked up on a South African assignment, before the government there banned his return. "Too liberal," the customs man had said to him at the airport after his series on life in the black townships. "Fascist," Joe Slovo, secretary of the Communist Party, had snapped at him during an interview. The memory made Ash laugh.

Today I'm going against David, he thought.

Ash changed into his running sneakers and a POST SOFTBALL

TEAM T-shirt and headed out into the cool morning at a brisk pace. At 6:00 A.M. traffic was almost nonexistent around Dupont Circle, and the homeless people were lumps under blankets near the fountain, or on benches. The smell of fresh baking bread came from up Connecticut Avenue. He headed toward Georgetown on P Street, then ran down to the dirt towpath after Thirtieth. Breathing easily, running hard, Ash passed other runners, concentrating only on the muscles working, the fresh morning smell of the Potomac, the morning breeze on his face, the crunch of pebbles or earth underneath.

Ash ran faster, through the red-brick Georgetown mall and between the big rock retaining walls onto the flat path that ran all the way to Virginia. Carp were rising in the glassy canal that ran parallel to the Potomac. The sun topped the trees ahead and cast bright shadows on the packed-earth path, the old towpath for mule-pulled barges. Ash turned back at the four-mile marker and headed home.

The morning *Post* lay outside his door when he got back. He showered and made an enormous breakfast. French toast and well-done bacon, two scrambled eggs, and more coffee. He ate on a stool at the kitchen counter, studying the paper. The power struggle in Russia was all over the front page. "Yeltsin and Gorbachev Head to Head," one headline read. There was a picture of the Soviet premier addressing the Politburo. And another of his rival Boris Yeltsin addressing a packed rally in Moscow.

"Military Said to Be Uneasy with Change," read a page-two story, "Opposes Empire Breaking Up." There was a big map of the Soviet Union broken in pieces. Little arrows ran from magnified parts of the map to explanations in italics. The Baltic republics of Latvia, Lithuania, and Estonia would declare independence, their boxes predicted. The republics of Moldavia and Ukraine might follow. "Ethnic Tension," read the box listing problems in the southern republics.

On the editorial page, a columnist had written, "What will the changes mean for the Soviets in Washington? The diplomats? The members of the Communist Party? Let's face it, the spies?

Nervousness sweeps the Soviet community."

Ash checked the time, went upstairs, and dressed in jeans, running shoes, and a green khaki shirt with button-up pockets. Green would blend in with where he was going. He took binoculars from a dresser and, before leaving, grabbed a plastic groundsheet from a closet and filled a thermos with coffee. He left food for Tyler in a dish that said THE PRESIDENT. A wave of guilt swept over him. Uncle Yuri's face came into his head. Those gentle gray eyes regarding him fondly. Ash fought the feeling off.

He was almost out the door when the phone started ringing. Ash grabbed it.

"It's me," Corinna said. The pain started up between Ash's eyes. "I figured you'd be up."

"You looked good last night," Ash said, seeing the woman in the car at David's gate. "Do you live there now?"

"No. I knew that was you, but I didn't know what to say to you. It's funny, isn't it? You're married to someone and then you have nothing to say to them."

Ash shrugged. Tyler, jealous, jumped up on the coffee table and rubbed against Ash's hip. Corinna had a breathy voice; her sentences tended to tail up at the end. Strangers usually needed a second to realize she had finished talking.

"How are you?" Ash said. Mundane words dropping into a void. No matter how much time passed, he felt hollow inside when he talked to her.

"I need to talk to you."

"You do?" he said. "Or he does?"

"He doesn't know I'm calling. I have a problem."

Ash smiled into the phone. She said, "Stop smiling like that. I'm serious. He didn't ask me to call. Well, he did ask me to call, but I'm not calling because of that. Well, it is that, but not *that* that."

Tyler meowed and bumped his head against Ash's hip. For a little animal, he could produce a lot of pressure. "Tell Tyler he'll have you back in a second," she said. "I always thought he was a girl in a tom's body."

"He knows when the competition's stiff," Ash said.

"Please," Corinna said. "What time?"

"Two?" He had a flash of her belly, hard and flat and just above eye level, pumping up and down. She'd been like a narcotic. He couldn't get enough of her. Like she brought ten million nerve endings he'd never known existed to life. Ash saw her hair whipping across her bare shoulders. He saw his fingers squeezing her nipples while she whipped back and forth. All in a second. The spiky pain in his head grew.

"Where?" she said.

"Filomena's. You can watch me eat ravioli and I can watch you eat nothing."

"Girlish figure," she said before she hung up.

Ash picked up Tyler and said, "Sometimes you're a pain in the ass, Mr. President." Outside, he unlocked the Saturn and headed back toward Virginia. It was seven-thirty when he reached the stretch of road near David's house. The birch copse was where he remembered it, far enough from any driveway on the private-land side of the road so that it was out of sight of the big houses, thick enough to conceal the car in, accessible from a gap in the lead trees. Ash left the car and walked a hundred yards through the woods until David's front gate came into view through the low branches. He found a grassy spot still dewy from last night. He spread the groundsheet and opened the thermos. He shook off a twinge of guilt at what he was doing.

Eight o'clock became nine and nobody left the grounds. Traffic picked up on the two-lane road, all the lawyers and government officials heading downtown in their BMWs, Volvos, and Mercedes. A Virginia state trooper drove by slowly, pausing at the gate. Ash finished the coffee. It was warm in the woods and he loosened a button on his shirt. He told himself it was silly to be here, but he stayed anyway. He didn't know exactly what he was waiting for, but the words of his old *Post* mentor came back to him. "Good journalism isn't just good questions. It's doing nothing sometimes. It's waiting around. It's giving your instinct a chance to catch up with your thoughts."

At 10:30 a red sunbird pulled up to David's gate. Ash

watched through binoculars as the driver got out: a tall man with a slightly unkempt appearance. Brown summer-weight jacket. Slacks a little too bunched at the cuffs. Graying hair just long enough to start to look unkempt, springing from both sides of a long bald pate and bunching around the ears. Ash took in the trimmed black beard and squarish nondescript wire-framed glasses. There was something familiar about the slightly pigeon-toed steps.

Son of a bitch, Ash thought, catching a glimpse of the odd way the man's right arm hung when he moved. It's Price. A wave of affection swept over him. So Price was still around too. Price, the hero-worshipping Kislak sidekick. Price, the chess genius who'd followed Kislak everywhere back in Smith Falls. Who'd broken his arm in two places in a sledding accident one December, and the doctors had not set it right. Ash memorized the Virginia license as the gate opened and Price drove into the grounds, known by a new name like all of them in America, but to Ash he would always be Price.

Half an hour later when Price pulled out of the estate and turned right, Ash was behind him, far enough back so Price wouldn't see. There were no intersections of consequence coming up for at least twelve miles, so Ash took a chance and hung back, catching up with little spurts, getting glimpses of the car before falling away again.

Price brought him back to Route 123 and the George Washington Memorial Parkway. Ash used traffic as a shield. He figured Price was heading into the capital, but just before the Roosevelt Bridge Price got off the highway, reentered going back the way he came; Ash cursed and dropped back. But then Price's right blinker went on and he made a quick turn into a parking overlook for Roosevelt Island park. You could only enter the park from the northbound lanes.

Ash cursed because he had to swerve across lanes to reach the entrance. But if Price noticed it, he didn't show it. On a weekday morning only two or three cars were parked in the lot, which led to a footbridge to a woody/swampy area of little Roosevelt Island. Excited, Ash thought, it's a drop.

Price, unhurried, followed the bridge to the island and stepped off onto the dirt path in the woods.

Ash kept following but it was harder now without traffic to shield him.

The path grew thinner and curved along the outer edges of the island. It was a brushy, ugly park of stunted trees and thorn bushes. Planes coming into National Airport roared overhead at three-minute intervals, and through occasional gaps in the cypress Ash glimpsed the Washington Monument's tip, across the river. Bees flew everywhere. Near a bend in the path skirting a patch of skunk cabbage, Ash glimpsed Price slipping right into the brush. Ash moved into the trees. A minute later Price reappeared and strolled past him, heading back toward the lot.

Ash waited a few minutes to make sure Price didn't come back. His own instructions had always been to get away fast after making a drop. He didn't know how much time he had until the next courier arrived to pick up whatever Price had left here. Probably a half hour at most. You didn't want messages lying around.

Moving quickly, Ash entered the woods where Price had, then stopped and considered, cataloging the potential drop areas in the thick brushy bog. Dead log on the ground. Knothole in tree. Big rock that didn't look like it had been moved. Trickle of a small stream. Maybe Price had left something in the water. Or under the skunk cabbage leaves, in a little hole. There were no footprints in the mud. No disturbed twigs to indicate where Price had gone. For a slovenly guy, Price moved with grace.

Ash found it under the second cabbage. A three-inch patch of disturbed earth. He dug a little and found a plastic bag with a couple of pages folded inside. His heart started ticking. It was the satellite report.

Ash put it back where he'd found it.

Now he needed a place to watch what would happen next. The only spot where he could conceal himself and still see was thirty feet off, up the straight path, behind a patch of thornbushes. The bees had found it a marvelous location, too. They swarmed all over. Ash squeezed behind the bush, feeling the thorns scratching his pants, and the back of his hands. A bee crawled on his scalp. Great, he thought. The nest was in the next bush over.

What Ash heard in his head was an old man's voice, a soothing, melodic voice, the voice that had been an island of love. Trust David. Love David. David is my eyes and ears. Hearing it, he felt ashamed of himself. Felt a hot flush coming over him. What am I doing? he thought. Of course David is moving the report. Why would he want it if he wasn't going to do anything with it? It was just a stupid finger moving on a glass. I'm just edgy because of what's happening at home.

Ash told himself, if it's nothing, I'll go home and nobody will ever know I was here.

He caught his breath. Price was on the path again.

The man moved differently now, carefully approaching Ash's spot, coming up the path, looking around, right hand low near his hip. Price looked directly toward Ash's bush. Another bee crawled on Ash's head. He waved it away.

Price stopped five feet from Ash.

His fingers touched the bottom of his jacket.

Price turned abruptly and moved off.

Ash was sweating now. He realized what he had thought were bees crawling on him was sweat.

At noon a small girl, about ten years old, ran toward his hiding place up the path. A big Labrador retriever followed. The dog dug around playfully in the cabbage area. Ash kept his eyes on the girl. The dog paused, looked up, sniffed the air, nose pointed in Ash's direction.

"Chummy, get over here!" the girl cried, running back.

An Oriental man carrying a bird guidebook walked up the path, stopped when a crow called, looked around, and walked away.

At twelve-twenty an elderly couple meandered down the path, the man leaning on a walking stick, moving with a slight limp, red bandanna around his head. The woman's face was hidden by the brim of a wide straw hat with a floral pattern of roses on a cloth tied around the brim. They sat, resting, on the fallen log near the skunk cabbages. Ash heard the woman exclaim, "Look, the Monument, Joe!"

The couple left.

At one-fifteen a park ranger came down the path carrying a hammer and some nails. She bent over the fallen log. She hammered what was probably one of those stupid and obvious plaques on the log. Something saying LOG. She sat down, pulled a candy bar from her pocket, chewed it, then sauntered off.

The bees were driving Ash crazy, and the sun shone directly on his head. The swampy heat seemed to rise out of the earth here. The park smelled like rotten sauerkraut.

At two, the Oriental man came back.

He still had the bird book, but he moved more briskly now when he saw nobody was present. Looking both ways, he slipped into the forest exactly where Price had disappeared. He emerged two minutes later and hurried off.

By the time Ash reached the bridge to the parking lot, the man was pulling out of the lot. He drove some kind of metallic blue foreign car with diplomatic plates.

Japanese? Ash thought, following. Malaysian? A Japanese-looking man could be American, except the diplomatic plates meant foreigner. Ash was aware of an odd mixture of elation, disappointment, and relaxation as he drove. Animal joy at the thrill of tracking Price, disappointment because for once in his life he would like to find a flaw in David, and it was starting to look like this wasn't going to be it. Relaxation because with the appearance of the Japanese man, the whole thing became possibly logical. The Japanese had an interest in how much the U.S. knew about their timber operations. Moscow was doing a friend a favor or maybe even had a man with the Japanese.

Ash turned combinations over in his mind as he drove. The important thing was, the fundamentals looked less alarming. Sure enough, the Toyota headed up Massachusetts Avenue to embassy row and turned into the Japanese embassy. Ash, at a light, watched the driver get out and bow to another man in a gray suit, who took the car to park it. Ash quickly found a parking spot a block from the embassy, illegal, a diplomatic zone, but he left the Saturn there and walked back to the building. A plainclothes guard in the lobby stood beside a glass barrier.

Ash held out a $20 bill. "Excuse me, but the man who just came in dropped this."

The guard looked surprised, pleased. *"Thank* you," he said.

"Blue suit. Wire glasses. White shirt."

"Mr. Humasaki," the guard said.

"Okay," Ash said as the guard reached for the telephone, a grin on his face. "It dropped out of his pocket when he got out of his car."

"He'll want to thank you," the guard said.

"No, I'm in a rush," Ash said. The guard was speaking rapidly in Japanese into the receiver. Ash heard the word *Humasaki.*

A ticket was on the Saturn when he got back to it. Ten fucking minutes and he got a ticket. Might as well leave it there now, he thought. He found a pay phone on the corner and called the Japanese embassy. Ash asked for the press office. He identified himself as Ash of the *Post.*

"No need to bother Mr. Humasaki," he said. "I'm just checking the spelling."

The press attaché gave it to him, glad not to have to bother someone.

"And his official title?" Ash said.

"Commercial attaché."

Ash hung up the phone, feeling better. The commercial attaché would be exactly the person to safeguard Japanese interests here against any lobbying, legislation, or bad press coverage of their environmental strategies. Mr. Humasaki was building up his reputation as an effective force in Washington by coming up with the satellite report. If Mr. Humasaki was connected, as he undoubtedly was, this meant Moscow's man was more solidly in place.

Ash felt the glow of suspicion dying, and then it was gone.

* * *

An hour later it was back.

Ash leaned back at a table at Filomena's restaurant in Georgetown. It was a sprawling ground-floor garden of a place where the food was excellent, the lights low, and the ferns and potted palms separating tables accentuated the air of privacy. There was a half-eaten portion of ravioli and prosciutto on Ash's plate. Corinna drew a sip from her glass of San Pellegrino water. She left a lipstick *O* on the rim.

"I'm worried about David," she said.

He had always had trouble concentrating when he was near her. What had been girlish beauty in the teenager had grown into elegance without losing allure. She wore a low-cut sea-blue dress and a single strand of small white pearls. The candlelight sculpted her high cheekbones and slightly jutting, oval lips. She dug the long nail of her pinky into the tablecloth, leaving little dig marks.

All Ash could think was, you are so beautiful.

"I know I can't ask you why you came by last night, but he couldn't have asked you to because I was . . . um . . . there," she said, digging the nail in. "He's not sleeping. Not eating. He pretends it's nothing. Pressure," she said. "Going private, but something else is bothering him."

Ash took a bite of ravioli. Behind his pounding heart, a little warning went off. "You want to ask me about him?" he said.

"Oh, Ash. Who else? You went to his house. Why'd you do that?" She sounded a little desperate. "You must know something. David takes care of us but nobody looks after him. He's always so cool, but inside you don't know him. He doesn't show everything he feels."

"David will take of himself." Breaking off a breadstick, Ash watched her blue eyes. He wished he knew what it was that his instinct was telling him to be wary of.

"He's always a big eater," she repeated. "You wouldn't think it looking at him. He's so fit. I think it has to do with what's happening back home. He's worried about something."

"Home," Ash mused. "Do you really think of it as home, still?"

"I think of us as home." Blushing, thinking Ash thought she meant David and her, she clarified the obvious. "All of us."

"Home." He nodded. "And David's not eating," Ash said, annoyed at her concern for David despite himself. "Well, I'm no doctor." There was a certain logic to her coming to him. Even sitting with her, aware of how much just her presence could still hurt him, he felt free of the deception that was so much a part of his daily life. She knew who he was. She knew where he came from. The same had to be true for her. Yes, he could see her coming to him independently. He could see David sending her here. David was overconfident enough to do something obvious like that. Ash could see it both ways. The question was, which was it?

The waiter materialized at the table. He'd been hovering too much. "Does the beautiful signorina want more water?"

"You're so attentive," Corinna said. The waiter beamed. "But I'm interrupting the lovers," he said.

"Last night," Corinna said, "I made his favorite." Ash was surprised. She'd never cooked for him. He never knew she cooked at all. It was funny how little things could still bother him. She said, "Chicken with basil. He loves chicken with basil. He eats mounds of it. He can't get enough."

Ash chewed his ravioli. "Who would have guessed that."

"There's no need to be nasty," she said. "You knew all along I didn't want to marry you."

"Touché."

"You think David liked telling us we had to do it? Yuri made us do it."

"Oh, yeah, I forgot," Ash said, kicking himself for being churlish.

"David and I always loved each other. You know that as well as I do. I didn't come here to go over old ground. You were always the perceptive one," she said, and he thought, that's just the way David would say it. "You would have seen something last night if it was there. Help me." Corinna started to cry. She really did love David. "Please, I have no one to talk to," she said.

Ash reached across the table and took her wrist, tried to

ignore his galloping heartbeat. It was some crazy chemical reaction over which he had no control. The waiter, coming toward them again, veered away, seeing how close they were. Ash said, "I was there only half an hour." He laughed. "Half an hour in ten years."

"You see more in half an hour than other people do in five years," she said. "Remember back in Smith Falls? You'd say, Danny stole something again. He's looking at the ground. Maureen helped David with his homework. See how she's looking at him?' And we'd laugh. And in the end you were right. Always right. I guess that's why they used you."

"And you could make a boy feel like he was about to be king of the universe. Like he was the only person in the world. Like he was sexy, powerful, important. All you had to do was look at him."

She blushed. "That was just you, Ash," she said.

"It's still me," he said. "But it's every man, too."

"Then I guess that's my talent." She pouted, still young enough to pretend she didn't like compliments. "Never mind my job."

Ash pushed the plate of ravioli away. "I went there because I have a lot on my mind, too. What's really happening back home? What's going to happen to us? Don't you ever think about that, Corinna?"

"No, it's not my job. David thinks about that for us."

"That's right, and that's probably why he's so tense. Meanwhile," he said, squeezing her hand, "trust him. He's done a good job." Ash sighed. "I was wrong to go there last night. I didn't accomplish anything. It was selfish. I endangered everyone," he said, using the words Uncle Yuri used to drum into them. "I just wanted to ask him a question, that's all."

"You broke the rule to 'just' ask him a question? What question?"

"Whether he thinks Doc Gooden has a better fastball than Roger Clemens."

Corinna blew out air and drank some water. "You really think nothing's wrong?"

"You know him better than I do." He smiled. He patted her hand. "Nothing's wrong that David can't fix."

She smiled. The tears looked real. "You used to say, 'Uncle Yuri's foot is tapping, that means he's nervous. Carol's not saying anything, that means she's scared.' You could always read people." She sipped the mineral water. "I hope you're right."

"Of course I'm right," he said. "How about some *tartufo*? If you die of anorexia, you'll never get anywhere with David."

"No, I have to get back. We've got a big restraint of trade case on a Manila company. Philippines," she said. Corinna was a lawyer with the Justice Department. She was usually working on investigations into corporations.

In Ash's head, Uncle Yuri's voice said, "No one suspects interns. Interns are college students. It's amazing the lapses in security at the bottom. You'll start out as interns. You'll end up in positions of authority. You're the smartest, bravest children in the world. Your parents are so proud of you. The premier himself knows about you. One day you'll be famous."

Ash paid the bill and they parted out on M Street. "Give me five minutes, make sure I'm gone, then call him." Ash grinned. "Oh Ash," she said, slapping him on the arm, "I'm not going to call him." Corinna watched Ash walk away. She went back into the restaurant. The pay phone was downstairs, near the silver bowls of mints. She dialed a D.C. number and let it ring once. She hung up and gave David five minutes to reach a pay phone. David said, when the phone rang, "I want you now. I'm hard thinking of you. Come to the office."

"I told you there was nothing," she said.

"Nothing?"

"He's the same as always. Pesty."

"Not even a little twinge? Think of who we're talking about here. Not even one little question?"

"David, he's with you," she said. "In his own way."

"That's a relief," he said. "A lonely guy like that. He never liked me."

"I've always felt that even though he's in left field half the time," she said, "more than any of us, he needs the others. The rest is an act."

David had a wonderful laugh. "Thank you, Dr. Freud. Come to the office and I'll pay your bill."

Two hundred miles north, a man did push-ups on a woven throw rug in a Staten Island apartment. There was the sound of a ship's horn blowing outside the window, and each time the man pushed himself off the floor, he glimpsed, through the window, a crane hoisting crates half a block away. A color Zenith broadcast the midday news on a coffee table of Scandinavian teak. The screen showed tanks in front of the Kremlin. A voice said, "Pressure mounts in the Soviet Union. Gorbachev may have to share power with the republics."

The man frowned, grunting. A hundred and six. A hundred and seven. Straining, his cheeks bulged in half-moon shapes pushing into creases near his mouth. His legs were thin for his bulky torso, his black hair was cropped close and full over his squarish head.

What the neighbors knew about him was, his name was Danny Morgan, not Danny Minsky, his old name in Smith Falls. He'd lived in this apartment twelve years, with his wife, Maureen. He worked as an engineer on the Staten Island ferry, worked hard, seven days a week, accumulated vacation for trips he and Maureen took every few years. The poor couple had had a child once, before they came to Staten Island, but it had died at birth. Now Maureen couldn't have kids. They were a quiet couple. They kept to themselves. They liked Kevin Costner movies, always had stickers for local Democratic candidates in their windows. Once, four years ago, some toughs on the no. 103 bus had tried to mug Maureen when Danny was on the other end of the bus, on the way home from work. He'd broken the jaw of the lead boy, and the wrists of the other two. He'd used the switchblade he'd taken off one of them to cut off the leader's thumb. "Try mugging someone now," he'd said to the writhing, screaming teenagers.

None of them had pressed charges. The passengers and bus

driver had told police they hadn't seen anything. The police, who knew the boys, hadn't made a big deal out of it.

The phone on a small coffee table rang. The man stopped his push-ups, not even sweating, reached for the receiver, and said, "Yeah?"

"I need you," a voice said.

The man hung up, showered quickly, and left a note for his wife that said, "Tell Eddie I got sick. I'll let you know when I'm coming back. Remember to water the coleus." He packed a small suitcase. Inside, with his shirts, wigs, and makeup, he included a snub-nosed steel .22, a retractable knife, and a double-strength glass vial of a thick amber liquid. He was careful, with the liquid, to pack it so it wouldn't bounce.

The man took the ferry to the no. 1 train and the 1 train to Penn Station. Amtrak ran Metroliners to Washington so regularly he was in the capital four hours later. David was always so considerate and had his favorite foods waiting in his hotel room. Salted lox and bagels with capers on the side. California plums so fresh the juice ran down his chin. It was just like home the way David, whom he never saw or talked to personally unless there was a specific job, had gifts arriving a few times a year, just to let them know he was looking after them. Them and Howie Granger and his wife, Estelle, investment bankers who made up the other couple in Danny's cell. After he ate he used the pay-phone system to make contact with the man who had called him, going from booth to booth as he got instructions in pieces, and finally, at the third pay phone, recognizing David's voice on the other end. It always filled him with nostalgia inside. Sometimes he mixed up David's voice and Uncle Yuri's, but Uncle Yuri had always said, "Think of David as me." He was sorry to hear that Ash was the target. He remembered Ash as a small, confused boy who asked silly questions. Teasing Ash had been lots of fun before Ash had grown older and the other kids had started liking him and he'd become to Danny as uninteresting as the rest.

But by the time he reached the *Post* building he was already musing about logistics. Danny took up position across the street, in a yogurt dessert shop, ordered a vanilla cone, and licked it, waiting. He had Ash's address but Ash wouldn't be home during the day. Danny sighed, watched, finished the cone, and ordered an iced tea. He spotted Ash coming finally, bigger and older but the face looked the same. If David told you to kill someone, that was what you did.

FOUR

ASH RAN THROUGH THE FIELD, fleeing for his life. The wheat whipped his thighs, sprayed kernels into the air. He was a good athlete and he breathed easily, pumping his arms. But the heavy footfalls behind kept pace.

"Thief," came the cry, too close for Ash to turn around. He'd barely glimpsed the peasant rising from the field, club in hand, barely managed to turn away. More voices joined in from farther back, from the village. "He's heading for the forest!"

Ash was thirteen.

"Congratulations, your first solo," Principal DuChamp had said this morning as they stood at the "Smith Falls" gate. Except DuChamp hadn't been smiling. Neither had the instructors: Miss Dietz, the classroom teacher; a lieutenant named Martini, who taught scouting and self-defense; an Uzbek named Kazanjian, who taught shooting.

DuChamp had bent close, eyeing Ash grimly, his gray jacket smelling of wet wool. "This isn't a game. It's preparation. Someday it'll be real. There's a village four kilometers from here. Find it. Go into it. Come back and tell me everything about it. But do it secretly. They're not friendly."

Around them, in an envious circle, the other kids glanced at the fields beyond the fence. Only David and Price had been allowed out of the compound alone until now. Neither had told what they'd seen.

"Are you listening, Jimmy?" DuChamp had demanded. "I want to know how many people live there. The breakdown between children and adults. Condition of houses. To see if you can do this kind of work. I want to know the answers to questions I haven't even thought of yet."

DuChamp tended to narrow his eyes when he was reconsidering a decision. Suddenly Ash was terrified DuChamp would cancel the exercise. "You're thinking how much fun it's going to be, aren't you," the principal said. "It's not going to be fun. Without your friends you're unprotected. You're nothing. There's nobody to help you if something goes wrong."

Sure, sure, Ash thought. Open the gate.

He was dizzy with delight when DuChamp signaled a guard to unlock it. He watched the wire strands swing away. A wave of fear washed through him, leaving his knees weak. "I warn you," DuChamp said, "get caught in that town, there'll be no help."

"Ivan! Leonid!" Now the cry rose behind Ash. "Get him!"

Ash ran harder, feeling the muscles pull in his hips and calves. Behind him, he knew, his pursuers had spread out in a ragged oncoming line. A fan shape of grimy, screaming farmers plunging through the wheat. Ash almost tripped into a gopher hole, but the waving stalks revealed it at the last instant and he twisted away, his Keds coming down hard on the lip. He monitored his bearings. He was moving southeast, the sun told him, away from the village, up a bowl-shaped rise toward granite outcroppings fronting a line of white birches a hundred yards ahead. The forest border. Safety. The sun flashed in the leaves up there. The barnyard smell from the village was gone.

I can keep going when I reach the trees, Ash thought. It wasn't the kind of thought he'd had in a long time.

But the hoarse breathing behind him seemed closer. Sweat ran in his eyes. I'm faster than them, he thought.

The morning had started pleasantly enough. Humming "A Hard Day's Night," from Western-music class, he'd strode up the cart-track he'd always gazed at from inside the fence. The fields smelled of daisies, the sky was clear. Clouds of dragonflies flashed copper above wild grasses on both sides.

Notice everything, Martini had told them in class. Something unimportant one day can be crucial the next.

If he didn't perform today, Ash had known, they might not let him out again.

He'd hidden in the field when he saw a cart coming. A scrawny gray mare struggled past, twitching flies away with her ears, pulling a two-wheeled cart loaded with straw and ax or sledgehammer handles, he couldn't see which.

The driver is old, Ash told himself, older than Dietz but younger than Yuri. She's thin and pale and coughs, so she's sick. The cart is freshly painted but she's hitting the animal with a switch. Anything special? She cares more for the cart.

He used a compass Yuri had given him to aim across meadows smelling of lilies, then through hemlock and spruce forest where little brown seed cones lay scattered on the pine-needle floor.

He caught his breath when the woods ended and the village came into view. It looked like one of those photos in his textbooks, at least from half a mile away. Beyond a flock of noisy, wheeling ravens, gently rippling wheat spread away from him, down a shallow bowl of earth, lapping to a rust-colored river meandering to and from the town.

Across the river more wheat flowed to a crest where the woods began. "Observe things in layers," Martini had taught them. "First the general picture. Then details. Never wait until you're on top of an objective before you start studying it. You'll miss things."

There are people here, Ash exulted. Other people. He wanted to walk boldly down the hill and introduce himself. Sneaking around seemed stupid. But what if DuChamp had someone watching? Ash kept going. A quarter mile later, creeping through the wheat, he heard children's laughter. Then a whiff of animal smell and something viler, like the toilet overflowed in the dorm. He realized that despite himself he was starting to get excited. There was something he liked about the challenge of this game.

A hundred yards more and he realized the buildings weren't

so picturesque after all. The barns forming a jagged ring for the village were practically falling apart; the homes inside the ring looked like squat, weatherworn plank or timber edifices set into the earth, some leaning sideways, unpainted. Ash was struck by the difference between the way things could look far away and close up. He was surprised because in school Miss Dietz gave a more prosperous picture of the Soviet Union. Ash supposed this village was an aberration.

Ash's heart beat quicker. How close can I get?

He dropped to his belly and wriggled through the wheat.

Corinna will be proud of me.

Pay attention. Memorize things, Ash thought. He noted the freshly painted red house with a white fence. The timber shack with broken shutters, pig rooting up the yard, woman in a brown cotton dress singing while she hung wash from a basket. And a bigger house beside the church, with a red star painted on the siding, and real windows. It had a double swing and poppies in a flowerpot on the porch. No men yet.

Ash circled the village, smeared dirt on his face, and dashed twenty feet to the side of a house after a woman disappeared inside. He inched to the open shutter. He was looking into a bedroom, he saw. He memorized the double bed with red-and-black quilt; vase of flowers; men's leather, backless, brown slippers on an oval woven throw rug; egg-shaped wire spectacles on a wooden reading table beside a half-burned candle, daguerreotype of a man in a fez on the wall. Anything special? There were little horizontal red pencil marks on a wall near a mirror. Three sets. But the marks looked faded. Maybe the kids were grown.

For the next two hours Ash crept through the village, avoiding the women and children, keeping to the shadows and hedgerows, lucky enough to attract only one friendly dog. The thrill was wearing off. He wanted something more challenging. He felt frustrated that even though he was so close to these people, something essential was missing. He reached the house with the real window. Slipped beneath a crawl space underneath, hearing a record playing from up top, and a man and a woman laughing.

The record was Wagner, he recognized from the school's regular Tanglewood nights. The crawl space was filled with the ammonia odors of goat piss and bits of fleece. A dog crawled in beside him, wagging its tail as clouds of fleas rose with each swish. Ash petted the animal.

A minute later he heard people running up there. Two sets of boots, one big and heavy, one light, hurried off from the back of the house. Minutes after that, three more sets of boots, men coming in from the fields, passed by the space.

"Nobody stole your pig, Igor," a man's voice mocked. "Knowing you, you ate it. You've put on a gut."

The men began roaring. The word *stolen* gave Ash an idea. I'll take something from the house, he thought. Instantly all his senses seemed acuter and he felt hot. When the men passed, he eased from the crawl space, crept up the steps, and tried the door. It opened. He slipped inside. A delicious sense of terror enveloped him. His breathing sounded thunderous.

Ash moved through the house, looking for the right trophy. The curtains were white lace. Oriental carpets covered the floors. There was a fireplace with a half-empty bottle of wine on the mantel, and a boar's head above.

The owner could come back any minute.

Ash found what he wanted in the study: a piece of paper half rolled in a typewriter. A letter, he saw. It started, "Dear Comrade Commissioner, I am writing with great joy to inform you that our harvest has exceeded our wildest expectations."

Ash folded the paper into his jeans.

DuChamp will go crazy when he sees this, he thought.

He crept from the house, down the steps, ran toward the wheat.

The peasant had been waiting for him.

"Thief!"

Ash could barely understand the accent. The man had appeared from nowhere. Just risen out of the field. An ambush. It was crazy. "Expect unexpected things," Yuri had always said. A pig? What did Ash know about a stolen pig?

Ash splashed across the shallow river, scattering trout. He was heaving.

He risked a glance over his shoulder. The lead man was only twenty feet back, big knees pumping, red vest bouncing, club practically pulling him forward. Didn't the man ever lose his breath? Behind him, two more peasants were coming on while a handful of others dropped back, bent and gasping. Thirty feet to the rocks. If I can make the rocks, Ash thought, I can reach the trees.

As Ash passed the rocks, two more peasants came at him from out of the trees.

They were right in front of him, boys a little older than himself, in mud-smeared breeches and soiled T-shirts. Flanking him in a pincer movement. A tall boy looking angry. A red-haired one smiling in anticipation.

Ash veered right, felt the tall one's fist grip his shirt, broke free, but stumbled back into the belly of the lead peasant.

A voice cried, "Hold him!" He started to say, "I didn't take your pig!" A blow exploded on the back of his neck. The ground came up. Ash smashed into it. He gasped, rolling away, "Someone else . . . someone else!"

"Someone else? *Who?*" red vest said, hauling him to his feet. The man's strength was enormous. Up close, his green eyes blazed and his thick, rubbery features were twisted, and the thick odor of garlic roiled off him. The other men were swarming up the hill; even the peasants who had stopped running were now energized by the capture. Then the red-haired boy sneered, "Liar! You were running!" Their eyes met and Ash had an instant of clarity. *"You* did it!" Ash said.

A flash of horror burst in the red-haired boy's eyes.

As the boy raised his fists, a voice in Ash's head—Martini's voice—cried, "Pressure points! Vulnerable points!" Ash ignored the closing circle of peasants, forced all his attention on the hands gripping his shoulder. He relaxed and twisted and drove his bunched fingers into red vest's eye. The man howled and fell back. The others roared and they were on him. Ash drove his knee up into red-hair's groin. He bit someone's arm and heard a howl of pain. Wriggling, he kicked out, felt his foot drive into something soft, heard an "Ooof!"

But there were so many of them, hands everywhere. The tall boy angling in, delivering a roundhouse punch into Ash's stomach. Ash fell. "Shut out pain, feel it later," the instructor had always said. "Use it to make you angry!"

Easy for you to say, Ash thought.

I don't feel it.

"He . . . ," Ash gasped, pointing at the red-haired boy. "He . . ."

Then they were moving on him, but red vest seemed to stumble backward, fall away, and Ash realized someone had leaped on the man's back. It was David.

David! Ash could have wept with joy. And Price came into view now, swinging a stick at the tall boy's knees. And Danny Minsky, the kid who liked to torture animals, tying rocks to cats. The kid who excelled in football and liked to run his helmet into weaker kids during games. Minsky was there, too, and the tall boy had taken two steps backward, hand on his forehead, streaming with blood, as the rock Minsky had thrown rolled on the ground.

They were yelling, "Ash, get up. Run!"

Ash crawled to his feet. The red-haired kid stood three feet off, staring at him. The red-haired kid looked confused.

The red-haired kid ran away.

Ash knew he had only a second before the peasants recovered. They were bigger, stronger. Red vest was lumbering in a circle, David clinging to his neck, hammering him on the back of his shoulders. "Leave Jimmy alone!" David shouted. The tall boy was starting to get up. It wasn't going to work. Ash found Minsky's rock, a sharp edge, charged red vest, and smashed it over and over into his belly. Blood spurted from the vest.

There was a glint to Ash's left and he spun. Minsky had a knife out. A big knife. The two groups faced each other. The other peasants from the village were huffing toward them, still too far away.

Minsky smiled. Everything seemed to stop.

"Thief," red vest said sullenly.

But the men didn't chase them when the boys ran into the forest. They ran a long time, at first in fear and then with giddy triumph when they realized they'd escaped. They collapsed, laughing, where a big spruce had fallen across a stream. They pounded each other on the shoulders.

"Did you see his face!"

Minsky imitated red vest, clutching his back, jeering, "Ow!"

"Yuri sent us after you," David said. "He had a fight with DuChamp. He said DuChamp had given you something too tough to do." A wave of love for Yuri and David swept over Ash as he lay on the big log with the others.

"We saw those bastards chasing you," David said. "We hoped you'd make the trees."

"We should have cut their heads off," Danny Minsky said. "Like frogs."

"Hey, Ash," Price teased in that old mocking classroom voice, "DuChamp'll kill you for getting caught."

"Shut up," David snapped. "DuChamp'll be glad we stuck together. That's what they teach us, isn't it?" Ash couldn't believe it. David was defending him. Price looked as if he might cry and Minsky grinned, looking from face to face. Minsky was happy anytime someone got chewed out.

David sat beside Ash on the log. Their bare feet dangled in the cool water. Price, eager for forgiveness, produced some of Yuri's Chuckles. They were more delicious than anything Ash had ever tasted.

"You're a good guy, Jimmy," Price said, buddying up to him.

"It's us against everybody," David said to all of them fiercely. "Never take sides with anyone against us. Even with DuChamp. Or Uncle Yuri." Price gasped but nodded; David had grown taller in the last three years, his voice was deeper, he seemed to know things the others didn't. "Only we care about us," David said. "Jimmy, DuChamp'll be proud that we stuck together."

DuChamp had warned him to tell nobody what he found in the village, but to hell with him, Ash thought. David was right. And the boys were awestruck when Ash produced the stolen letter. And then David and Price told what *they* had done when they had left the compound. Scouting work, that was all. In the forest. David put his arm around Ash's shoulder on the way back. "I'm proud of you," he said.

Back at Smith Falls there was a dance that night, after the "I Love Lucy" and "I Dream of Jeannie" TV shows. All the girls wanted to be Ash's partner. Once, when Ash was standing on the far side of the gymnasium, telling the story for the fourth time to a bunch of boys, after the Twist, Corinna came over during a "girl's choice" selection. She was wearing heels that made her taller than him, and her hair was washed and fell in waves past her shoulders to the center of her back. Her eyes were gleaming. Like headlights shining into the middle of him. She took his hand and led him toward the dance floor. He walked inside a cloud of her perfume. He could feel where her soft skin touched the smooth roundness of her fingernails. She said, "Oh, Jimmy, Jimmy, you must have been so *scared.*"

"Are you in a coma or something?"

Ash snapped back to the present. The *Post*'s intern librarian was standing by his desk, looking amused, holding four envelopes stuffed with newsclips toward him. Ash could read the lettering on the top flaps. They said HALLOWEEN, KISLAK, SUPREME COURT, and STOCK CAR RACING. The only subject Ash was interested in was Kislak, but he didn't want to call attention to that.

The librarian leaned her jeaned hip against his desk, near the Dwight Gooden photo. She said, "I give up. What's the connection?" She was a pleasant Bostoner named Grace, a Harvard graduate student who dreamed of being a reporter one day, and usually Ash joked with her when he used the library. Now Ash shrugged. "You're not going to believe this," he said conspiratorially.

"What?"

"The Islamic Brotherhood plans to drive stock cars into the Supreme Court and run over the justices on Halloween."

"I'm going to drive stock cars on you," she said.

"In heels?" he said hopefully.

Grace shook her head, grinning, and walked off. Ash called after her, "Why do you want me to tell you things if you don't believe them?" It was like some kind of disease, not being able to let go of a question. His throat felt raw and he felt throbbing in his temples. Even if David never found out what he was doing, Ash felt low and disloyal. Uncle Yuri's voice in his head said, "Never talk to anyone about the others, even casually. You'd be surprised how much people remember."

He upended the files and spread the clips on his desk, making a mess so no one would see what he was concentrating on. The Kislak file was disappointingly thin, but then again, he would have expected no less of David. Only a handful of carefully folded newsclips slid out. Most were already yellowing with age. The oldest, five years old, was entitled "New at State." There was a photo of the new secretary and four of his undersecretaries, David among them but the least prominent, hanging back, face half-hidden behind the others.

"David Kislak, from Smith Falls, Massachusetts, worked with the Secretary at Yale and helped write some of his most influential papers on relations with Third World countries. He will concentrate on Latin American affairs," the caption said.

The next three clips weren't actually about Kislak, but any article that mentioned a person was cross-referenced in his file. Kislak was quoted on Chilean loan defaults and Panama Canal policy. Another piece two years later listed position changes at State, mentioned that Kislak was being moved to Western European affairs.

Ash couldn't stop going over the lunch with Corinna. Any contact with her was unsettling, and it usually took hours before he could calm down enough to see what he might instantly have noticed with anyone else. He tried to slow his heart. Corinna expected people to cooperate with her and grew testy if they didn't fall in line immediately. A beautiful woman's weakness, Ash thought. But she hadn't grown exasperated when Ash teased her, which meant she'd been on a job, not her own. She had no patience when she was on her own.

Ash toyed with a pencil, frowning. Okay, David had sent her. Nothing wrong with that, especially after Ash had broken the rules last night. Not checking on Ash would have been a lapse, he supposed. Then what was bothering him?

Ash let his mind drift, seeing what would come into it. It was his wedding ceremony. Ash had a vision of slipping the ring on Corinna's finger, glorying in the silkiness of it, all his friends from the *Post*, all her friends from Justice, behind them at the civil ceremony in the Old Inne in Annapolis, beaming, Ash filled with joy until he'd seen her eyes burning out at him through the lace. He'd been fooling himself those days, telling himself he'd make her love him, and suddenly he was looking into pupils wide with horror, reflecting himself in his wedding jacket leaning closer, opening his mouth.

Ash closed his eyes.

That was it. For all Corinna's professional skills, in personal matters she was a bad actress. Where David was concerned she couldn't hide a thing. Which meant when she'd said David was acting strangely, she'd meant it. Ash shook his head in frustration. With Corinna all his senses went out the window.

Ash blew out air. Two opposite certainties. It didn't make sense.

He began putting the clips back into their folder but noticed a last article stuck to one he'd already read. It was datelined six months before.

"Former U.S. Officials Go Private," the headline announced. Ash read, "Want to make a million dollars? Get a job in the Administration and become a lobbyist when your term is up. At least five officials have joined scores of others making the transition from public service to private consultant, catering to corporations or countries they used to regulate."

The piece listed half a dozen high officials of the recently departed administration who had set up lucrative private practices acting as liaisons between their new clients and old friends still in government.

Kislak was mentioned midway through the piece: "David Kislak, a former Undersecretary of State, now represents countries including Japan, the Philippines, Uruguay, and Mexico."

Ash sat up a bit.

"Critics of this professional merry-go-round are pushing for legislation to ban former Administration officials from using their knowledge against the country they once served," the clip said.

Ash thought, impossible.

"Amen." Sheperd's voice startled him, coming from directly behind. Iced tea in hand, the editor was leaning over Ash's shoulder, peering at the clip. Sheperd looked weary. "Hypocrites," he said. "These guys sell the country to the highest bidder. If anyone else did what they do, they'd be arrested as spies."

"Damn right," Ash said. He thought, David's gone private? But it felt wrong. He couldn't imagine David doing it. Moscow would never let him do it.

Ash said, "Aaah, you purist. What's wrong with making a buck?"

"You coming to the roast for Kenneally?" Sheperd asked, mentioning an editor who was retiring. Sheperd was Ash's best friend at the *Post*. They played outfield on the softball team. They drank together after work at the Post Pub. But in ten years, he'd only been to the man's house five times.

"Make up something funny," Sheperd said. "We need speakers. By the way, Lisa asked if you wanted to come for dinner Sunday. I think she's got another prospect."

"Oh, god," Ash said. "Not again. That English professor, where did she dig her up? Two hours of penis symbolism in Solzhenitsyn."

Sheperd laughed. "Lisa finds 'em at the health club. I'm under orders to ask."

"Tell you what. You and Lisa come to my place without the new prospect. I'll grill burgers. The Orioles are on."

"I won't tell her the Orioles part," Sheperd said. "And Ash, get your ass in gear on that disaster-aid story?"

Ash shrugged. "Give a guy a raise, he turns into Heinrich Himmler."

"I'm serious." Sheperd lowered his voice. "Don't tell anybody about the raise."

"Too late. I distributed letters."

"Sunday," Sheperd said.

"Sunday," Ash said.

Ash's smile faded when Sheperd walked off. He looked back at the clips. Japan was one of Kislak's clients. The man who had picked up the satellite report worked for the Japanese embassy. Uruguay was one of Kislak's clients. Ash had passed along defense information on Uruguay last month.

David wouldn't do it, he told himself. None of us would do it. It was too crazy. It was against everything Yuri wanted. It was dangerous. Moscow would never allow it. Unless Moscow ordered it. But why would Moscow order it?

The phone screamed and he picked it up. As soon as he heard the low, liquid voice, a vibration seemed to start up in his gut. "Want to go to a Ku Klux Klan rally?" said Jennifer Knowles.

"On the first date?" Ash said.

"Well . . ." Jennifer Knowles said, and Ash had a vision of her leaning back in a swivel chair, bare feet on a desk, pageboy hanging to her shoulders, a little animal in a Georgetown sweatshirt. "I could tell you liked me, even though you hid it. I figured, Jennifer, this guy is still in love with somebody else. You've got to intrigue him with the invitation. Don't just rely on your fantastic charms. Skip the movie and dinner. Go right for the firelight. Hooded men burning crosses."

"I don't usually go to Ku Klux Klan rallies until the fourth or fifth date," Ash said. "And then I really have to like the person. Besides, who says I'm in love with someone else?"

"I'm a very intuitive person," she said.

"You are, are you?" Ash thought, wait a minute, I've got to stop thinking about Moscow as one faction. What if this has to do with the breakup in Moscow?

"Yes. That's always been my problem," she said. "I get feelings about people."

"You mean men." Ash smiled, flirting while all his warning bells screamed.

"They're usually included in the category," said Jennifer. "Although I've known several who aren't." She'd looked cute in that Georgetown sweatshirt.

"Deep dark secrets," Ash said. He thought, but what faction would be interested in Uruguay? And anyway, what connected Uruguay, Japan, and Mexico besides the fact that they were David's clients?

She had the perfect laugh for her voice. It seemed to bubble out of the receiver. "Feelings that turn out to be right."

"And what do your feelings tell you about me?" Ash said.

"Nothing."

"Ah," he said, "that wonderful attractive nothingness, so appealing to women." He thought, say you have to go.

"Well, it's intriguing to me," she said. "You have such a strong presence and you send out nothing."

Ash said, "Didn't you used to work with the Amazing Kreskin? You were the woman in the audience with the microphone in her blouse."

"I'm glad you're coming," she said. "We got a news release from the KKK, at the station. It's a recruiting rally, in Hagerstown. The general public is invited. Aren't you curious? I am. I've never seen a Ku Klux Klan rally."

Ash was more curious about Jennifer Knowles. "My sheets are at the laundry," he said.

"It's very informal, not like the usual Klan soiree. Sevenish okay? Do you know you look like Baryshnikov?"

Everything she said threw him. "You're taller than he is," she said. "But you have the same kind of round face. Slavic cheekbones drive me wild. I have a poster of him in my bedroom. I bet everyone tells you you look like Baryshnikov."

"Especially when I'm in tights," Ash said.

On his desk, peeking out from the little pile of folded newsclips, was the edge of David's brow, some black hair, one eye looking up. What are you up to? Ash thought.

"I always had a crush on Baryshnikov," she said.

Ash said he would go to the Ku Klux Klan rally. "By the way," he said, "how did you know I worked here?"

"I'm so glad you're coming! I'll take you to the Dan-Dee Motel," she said.

She hung up.

The U.S. Department of Commerce building, a seven-story Depression-era monstrosity, occupies a huge rectangular block on the west side of Federal Triangle. Ash strode through the empty marble lobby and told a guard reading *Outside* magazine where he needed to go. As he got into an empty elevator, another man pushed inside. Ash figured they were going to the same floor since the man didn't push a button. Instead he leaned against the far corner and studied Ash. The man looked unfamiliar. Thin legs. Big torso. Lots of turquoise and silver jewelry. Too pasty to be from the Southwest, Ash thought, nodding hello. An East Coast cowboy.

They went in opposite directions when the doors opened, Ash strolling to the click of the man's receding cowboy boots down a long linoleum corridor in government green, passing door after door marked by black plastic plaques saying things like DIVISION OF MIDWEST SOYBEAN PRODUCTION. DIVISION OF EASTERN SEABOARD MARITIME GROUP. B-o-r-i-n-g. Each office was the same; small and crammed with typing secretaries. The tinny sound of a Jennifer Knowles show drifted from one office. A taped show on the radio, he figured, since she was on at night. *"I love you,"* Jennifer was saying. "How many times have you said it? How many times has someone said it to you? What does it mean, anyway? I want to talk about *I love you."*

At the end of the corridor Ash reached the doorway of the DIVISION OF REGISTERED LOBBYISTS, until recently at the Justice department. It was a surprisingly pleasant library of a room; a row of polished wooden desks beneath twelve-foot-long fixtures hanging down, and beside long windows flooded with sunlight from Constitution Avenue. A couple of lawyerly looking men studied thick volumes at one table. A swarthy-looking clerk in a worn maroon jacket ran a cigarette back and forth beneath his mustache, behind a gray steel counter and beside a sign in red that said NO SMOKING!

Up close, Ash saw the derivative state of Washington creativity reflected in the man's cardboard coffee cup. It had a red, white, and blue drawing of Thomas Jefferson on the side, the caption over Jefferson, in little red stars, reading, "Monticello! You've Tried the Rest, Now Try the Best!"

"Do I tell you what to eat? Do I say to you, 'No meat'?" the clerk demanded of Ash, slamming the gray volume Ash had signed for on the counter. "No! So why do you tell me I can't smoke?"

Ash took this as a rhetorical question. The clerk, shaking his head, said, "You can't answer, can you, because I'm right!" He sighed. He had a foreign accent, Eastern European, Ash guessed. "It's alphabetical," the man said. "You look up the name of the lobbyist group. Then it's simple. See?" He randomly ran his finger down a list of countries beside the name of one consulting firm. "You get the clients on the left. Are you a lawyer or journalist."

"Journalist," Ash said, taking the volume.

"That's all we get in here." The clerk looked agitated again. Nicotine fit, Ash figured. "Just once I'd like to have an average person come in. You put street robbers in prison in this country but not the real criminals." Ash guessed Poland or East Germany. "Does anybody care about these men? Selling out your country?" The man shook his head. "No. What paper do you work for? You're not good-looking enough to be on TV."

"The *Post*."

The clerk snickered. "The *Post*," he said, rolling the word around. "I'm from Latvia. You know Latvia? The little country. . . . Well," he said, when he saw Ash nodding that he knew Latvia, "I stood on Sixteenth Street for ten years, holding a sign that said 'Free Latvia,' every Friday. Five of us, alternating Fridays, holding signs. In the rain. In the snow. Those Russian bastards from the embassy, they used to drive by in their Ladas, laughing when I held that sign." The man smiled grimly. "Now they'll be called back to Moscow, hanged."

"That's a little extreme, isn't it," Ash said, "even if they get called back?"

The man grinned. "You don't know Eastern Europe. Well, those Russians are finished everywhere. Those bastards will be kicked out of Latvia soon. It's all going to turn around."

Ash thought, David is getting orders from somebody new now.

"In Latvia people understand freedom because we don't have it," the clerk ranted. "If you had a room like this in Latvia, there would be lines ten miles long to find out who was making money selling us out."

"Sometimes," Ash said, "chewing gum can help you stop smoking."

The man waved his unlit cigarette. "I don't want to *stop* smoking," he said. "I want to start."

Flipping pages at one of the empty tables, Ash found KISLAK ASSOCIATES. The clerk hurried from the room, unlit cigarette in his mouth as he flicked a lighter on and off. Immediately the man from the elevator strolled in, sat across from Ash, stared at him.

Ash found Kislak's firm in the book. Clients: Republic of Poland. Uruguay. Japan. Mexico. Iran. The Philippines.

"Hey," the man whispered.

Corinna had said she was working on a case involving the Philippines.

Ash looked up. "Don't let them know," the man said.

Ash frowned. "Excuse me?"

The man leaned over the table. One hand lay on the desk, near Ash's book. The other was under the table. "Come outside. I have to tell you something."

"What are you talking about?" Ash said.

As the man half rose, Ash fixed on the frayed collar of his jacket, the dirt under his fingernails, the dark, unshaven shadows spouting on his Adam's apple, the caked plaque between his brown front teeth.

"I have to show you," the man whispered.

The clerk strolled back into the room. He seemed happier but frowned when he glanced toward Ash's table. "Are you here again!" he cried, rushing over. "I told you," he snapped at the man in turquoise, "leave!" The man got up and smiled slyly at

Ash. "Matthew, Luke, and John," he said, flicking his finger at Ash's volume. "The money changers in the temple."

"He's a nut," the attendant said. "He's been coming here for weeks. He's an outpatient somewhere, supposed to be on medication. He talks to everybody. Get out!" he said, and followed the shuffling man from the room. The attendant hung out of the doorway, watching the man go. "Next time," he called after him, "I'm going to call the police!"

Uncle Yuri's voice drifted into Ash's head again. "In the years to come you might be puzzled sometimes at what you're asked to do," came the warm, avuncular tones. "But I'll tell you a story, children. About blind men and an elephant. Do you know this tale? Has your teacher told it to you?" Ash instinctively relaxed, picturing Yuri. The funny tufts of white hair on both sides of his bald pate. The thick lenses that exaggerated the watery green eyes. The pipe he was always stuffing, cleaning, sucking at, smoking, during his monthly visits. "Well," the voice continued, "three blind men go to a zoo and touch an elephant—they want to know what it feels like. The first slides his hands down the trunk. 'Ah,' he says, 'elephants are long and thin.' The second touches the leg. 'No,' he says, 'elephants are straight and thick.' The third blind man gropes upward, feels the ear. 'You're both wrong,' he says. 'Elephants are thin and wavy, and they create a cool breeze when you stand near them.' Children, how could any of those men even begin to know what the whole elephant looked like? When they were blind to start with, and then only touched a little piece?"

Ash closed the book. Corinna had said she was working on a case involving the Philippines. Ash's headache was back. Three out of four, he thought.

"You are the blind men," Uncle Yuri said in Ash's head. "Never try to guess why you are being asked to do something. You won't be able to. That way, if you are caught, not that you *will* be caught, because you are my geniuses, but if you are caught, you will not be able to hurt the others. And if they are caught, they will not be able to hurt you. Knowing only little parts helps. Blindness is good. Always listen to David. He knows what you should do."

I'm going to forget this, Ash thought. I never went to David's. I never saw this book. Corinna never told me she's working on a case involving the Philippines. The only reason I started this was because I knew I was going to be convinced I was wrong. I'm sorry, Uncle Yuri, he thought, as if the old man could actually see him.

"Ignorance is safety," Uncle Yuri said, smiling in.Ash's head.

Quite unexpectedly, a wave of rage broke over Ash. I could have had a normal life. I could have been a kid. I hate all of you, I didn't ask to do this. Uncle Yuri, fuck you, bastard, bastard, bastard.

He was weak with hatred. He hadn't felt like this since he was ten, trying to get out of that compound.

The vile, stupid bastards had destroyed his life.

The walls seemed to expand and contract with the pulse in his head. His skull could shatter in a million pieces. Ash gave the book to the attendant, smiling. He wanted to scream.

I'm going home, Ash thought. I'll drink a beer. I'll put on Chopin. I'll work out and take a bath and read a good book.

"You wait. Those KGB bastards . . ." The man drew his finger across his neck. "Wherever they are, they're going to get what they've been giving people all these years," he said. "And they won't go down without a fight."

It's not my business, Ash thought. For once, I'll leave things alone.

He got up.

"You call this a free country?" the attendant called as Ash walked out and spotted the man with the turquoise jewelry waving to him, from down the hall. "Even in Latvia they let you smoke."

FIVE

MANFRED LIGHT, "America's Cold Warrior" to his fans, sipped warm V-8 juice in his glassed-in office in the *Washington Post* city room and studied a stack of summer-intern applications. It was May 1978. Light's syndicated column, "Calling a Red a Red," ran in eighty-two newspapers around the United States and was famous for calling the Carter administration a patsy for the Communist bloc.

Liberal bastards, Light thought, eyeing the reporters rushing by outside, in the big room. They would have fired me years ago if I didn't bring in so much money. Light, original name Lichtenberg, was a Czech refugee who'd fled Europe after World War Two, who loved to identify Soviet espionage operatives in Washington in his column. They were men and women, attachés, secretaries, even janitors, who remained in the country because of diplomatic immunity. Everyone knew they were agents. Nobody did anything about it. Light made them all uncomfortable with his prodding.

Now Light glanced at a phone number on his desk and frowned. As soon as he picked his intern for this summer, he'd start checking a tip he'd gotten last night at a party at the Indian embassy. The Russians, a Turkish cultural attaché had told him over gin and tonics, were considering sending troops into Afghanistan if the pro-Soviet government there couldn't contain Islamic rebels. Not right away but within two years.

Light lifted his index finger to let his secretary know to send in the next applicant, James Ash. Scanning the application, Light saw the kid was an orphan. He sympathized. Straight-A student. He admired that. And a journalism major at American University, right in D.C. A third plus. The paper tended to pluck employees from the Ivy League schools. Snobs, Light thought, lowering his reading glasses so he could peer at Ash.

Ash, at twenty-one, sat legs crossed so his ankles showed. He was thinking, I don't know why David made me buy pants so short. But Light nodded approvingly. The boy was well groomed, blond hair brushed, nails clean . . . the undersized trousers told him the kid didn't spend too much time on his appearance, unlike the parade of preppie liberals who generally assaulted him at intern time. Manfred was uncomfortable with people who looked like they'd just stepped out of a fashion magazine. They made him feel, well, short.

Manfred studied Ash for the first few minutes, as part of what he thought of as "the Manfred test." Seeing if Ash would get uncomfortable. The kid looked back pleasantly, knowing when to be quiet, not babbling to show off, intrinsically understanding that quiet at this point was part of the Manfred test. Very, very big plus. Light noticed Ash's Timex. Sensible and essential, a good watch. Just last week Manfred had spent fifteen minutes ranting at his Thursday-night poker group about the overstylized clothing foreign correspondents wore. Safari jackets. Rolex watches. Give me a Timex every time, he'd said. In fact he'd rejected an applicant this morning, a kid from Bel-Air, because the kid wore a Rolex. An eighteen-year-old with a Rolex. Eighteen-year-olds should have better things to do with their money.

"Ash," Light said.

"Yes, sir."

Sir, Light thought. Good.

"So you want to work for me."

"Yes, sir."

"You know what I do?"

Ash smiled. "You write things people can't read anywhere else, sir," he said.

Well! Pleased, Light leaned forward. "That's right. Things you can't read *anywhere* else." He flashed on his newest target, a recent arrival at the Soviet embassy, number two man in the Ninth Directorate. Sergei Akromeyev. As a rare reactionary presence on the *Post*, Light was constantly fed information by foreigners in Washington who opposed the Soviets elsewhere in the world. In this case a Chinese diplomat's wife had sidled up to him at an art gallery opening and mentioned that Akromeyev was an old-style KGB butcher. A man with a sordid history in a camp near Vladivostok. A comer who'd risen through the KGB by cleverly accusing rivals of disloyalty and getting them arrested or executed with manufactured evidence. A man whose arrival in Washington probably signified a new aggressive wave of Soviet espionage attempts.

Ash, in the chair, was thinking David's thoroughness had long ago ceased to amaze him.

I want this job, Ash thought. All his training, all the preparation, all the years, had been geared toward this moment.

"Four reporters. Four important people. If you work for any of them that would suit us," Uncle Yuri's voice said in his mind. Ash and Yuri were in Yuri's house, which the old man used on his monthly visits to the compound. Cans of cold Budweiser sweated on the coffee table. A taped broadcast of a Washington Redskins–New York Giants game ran on TV. Yuri's fingers pushed tobacco, smoothed it, wedged it into his old cedar bowl.

"You'll get one of these men to hire you. Then you'll 'break' some stories with our help, so they'll keep you on after your internship is over. Then you'll start feeding them things, things we want them to know, true things about other people in Washington, things that will ruin them," Yuri said.

Now, in the glassed-in office, Manfred Light said, "Do you mind working long hours? Do you have a girlfriend?"

"She'll have to understand what's important," Ash said.

Light nodded vigorously. "That's what I used to tell my wife," he said. "She never understood." In fact she was now his ex-wife. Light sipped the V-8 juice. The kid was looking good. But there was still the political aspect. Every year there were a handful of polite but empty-headed flatterers angling for the job. Light wanted his intern to regard the work as more than summer employment. He wanted a future journalist. He wanted a kid with his head in the right place. He wanted someone with good inclinations in place at the *Post*.

"James," Light said carefully, "what do you think the biggest danger to our country is right now?"

Light sat back. The kid before Ash had paused a minute too long before answering. The girl before that had said, "Selfishness." Almost right. The boy before that had said, "Overindulgence." Not bad either, but not perfect.

"This is going to sound corny, sir," Ash said after a suitably short pause to allow for phrasing, "but I think the greatest power of evil, and I consider Communists evil, is the fact that good people don't really believe it exists."

Light pounded the table. "My god!" he said. "Exactly what I always say." Light peered at him harder a moment, and Ash saw the thin light of suspicion enter his eyes. But the man liked flattery too much to entertain it seriously.

Uncle Yuri had said, three years ago when Ash had first seen Light's picture, "Let him do the talking." Uncle Yuri had said, "Don't volunteer information unless he asks." Uncle Yuri, sucking on his pipe, blowing scented tobacco smoke in the little room, had said, softer, "You know you can tell me anything, Jim."

"I know, Yuri."

"More beer? I mean," Yuri said delicately, rising and strolling in his living room, pausing by the poster of the Grand Canyon, "you could tell me if you had a problem with me. If you were angry at me."

Horrified, Ash said, "Angry? You?"

Yuri sat on the hassock, in front of Ash. One by one, each student had been invited to his house as part of graduation. Yuri said, "If you hated me."

Ash rose, filled with panic he didn't understand. "I could never hate you!"

"Don't worry." Yuri nodded. "Even if you did, even if any

of my children did, I'd forgive it." On the screen, Redskins tight end Jerry Smith danced in the end zone after completing a touchdown. The crowd in RFK stadium roared. All the Skin ends leaped into the air and slapped their upraised palms together.

Yuri continued, as the scene on TV switched to an electric-shaver commercial, "You have a very schizophrenic existence here. In the morning you're American. In the afternoon Dietz teaches you why everything you learned in the morning was a lie. Doesn't that confuse you?"

"Sometimes."

"Only sometimes?" Yuri said. "Remember when you used to try to run away? You always had the most spirit. Always interested me the most. Deep inside, do you still want to leave?" On the screen, the shaving commercial switched to men in a bar staring at a blonde who looked good, but not as good as Corinna. "Tell the truth," Yuri urged.

"Sometimes," Ash said.

"Good. Jim, you bind people together in different ways. Some with love. Some with deception. You, with knowledge. You know why I'm telling you this? Because you already know it, maybe not here"—he said, tapping his forehead—"but here." His yellowish fingertip rested lightly on his heart.

"Don't get upset," Yuri said, "but I'm trying to figure out if we should send you over or not."

"Not send me?" Ash said, stunned.

"I could release you," Yuri said, staring into his face. "Send you out there." He nudged his head toward the wall, and beyond that, the town, fence, tundra. Ash was suddenly afraid of being rejected by Yuri.

"Not all of my children are"—Yuri cast about for the right word—"strong enough to go. Once you get there you'll make friends with people. American people. You could start to feel other . . . loyalties. You'll only see one or two others from here, not the whole group. You'll be lonely. Does that frighten you?"

"Yes," Ash said.

Yuri smiled. "I'm glad. The truth is," he said, packing his

pipe, "you're not all going. A few of you might not be able to stand it. The only way to combat that pressure is to know what you are loyal to in the first place. You'll get there and see Dietz and DuChamp exaggerated about how bad it is. You'll have to remember, when you have success there, and you're paid a big salary, and you have a car, house, things, you must never lose sight of the greater good."

"You mean the poor people who paid for them," Ash said.

Yuri laughed. "Well, that's what Dietz would have you answer, but I don't mean that. I mean your family. Us. Ash, you do hate me, don't you?"

"No!"

"Not on top, where you're aware of it. But inside. It's natural. I don't mean all of you. I just mean part of you." Yuri lit his pipe and the room filled with the aromatic odors of tobacco. "We've got to get past this, it's part of graduation," Yuri said. "Remember those times you wanted to leave. All we had to do was open the gate and you could go. Don't you hate me just a little bit? Aren't you just a little bit angry?"

"Well, what are you loyal to?" Ash said.

Yuri started laughing. He was delighted and he sputtered, the pipe bouncing in his hand, "There's my Ash! Just when I have you, just when you're down, up he comes, fighting. Me? Games," he said. "I'm loyal to my children. And I'm loyal to games. But Ash, answer my question."

Ash looked down. "Not for a long time."

"I'll still like you, Ash, still respect you. If we aren't honest with each other, there's no one to be honest with. Let's look at this feeling. Believe me, I'm expecting it. You have to admit it. Just a little."

After a while Ash was crying, saying, yes, yes, I hate you. He caught sight of Yuri's reflection in the front window. The TV announcer screamed, "Fifty-two yards! The Skins win it!" Yuri was nodding, patting Ash's hair. Murmuring, "See? Get it out."

And in Manfred Light's office the columnist asked Ash the final question, about world trouble spots. "In your opinion, where will trouble break out next?" And Ash, according to script, replied, "Not for a year or two, sir, but Afghanistan. The Russians are having trouble there, and this might sound far-fetched, but with Carter looking weak I think they might go in."

Manfred, grinning, rose and stretched out his right hand, the one with the Timex. Light shook hands, grinning. "James Ash, I hope you're at the *Post* a long, long time."

At twilight, Jennifer Knowles left her 1965 Mustang convertible, the only car she had ever owned, in the makeshift parking area in a field in Hagerstown, Maryland, next to a Ford pickup with an IF GUNS ARE OUTLAWED ONLY OUTLAWS WILL HAVE GUNS bumper sticker. Ash and Jennifer joined the knots of people moving slowly toward the larger group milling in the wild grass, near a podium set up in the middle of the field, and three wooden crosses set into the earth. Two small ones flanking the big one, twenty feet high.

"I asked you to come. I'll pick *you* up," she'd said when Ash wanted to drive. "What is it about guys? They never want the woman to drive."

"It's in the instruction book we get when we're twelve," Ash said. "Rules we have to follow the rest of our lives. Not letting women drive. Not asking for directions when we're lost."

"Not telling women what bothers you."

"That's a key one," Ash said. "We can't reach puberty unless we get that one straight."

Once, when Ash had sprained an ankle playing basketball, he'd gone to a doctor who'd treated him with ultrasound, a machine that sent a soothing vibration through his limbs. Whenever Jennifer spoke, her voice was like ultrasound, penetrating his body.

He was aware, as they swished through the grass, of her hand bumping against her thighs inches from his own. On the ride up he'd kept glancing at her fingers on the steering wheel. Small fingers that rubbed the wheel as she drove, shifting expertly, zipping in and out of traffic on 270 north.

Most of the men at the rally wore jeans and workshirts, the women were in jeans or cotton dresses, and some couples had

brought children. There had been three or four state trooper cars
by the turnoff and a cardboard sign that said K MEETING. Uniformed men whom Ash had first mistaken for national guards-
men stood, arms folded, around the fringes of the field. Except
when he'd passed, he'd realized they were Klan storm troopers.
KKK insignias on their shoulders. Trousers tucked, military
style, into boots. Truncheons dangling from Sam Browne belts.

"Gives me the creeps," Jennifer said.

"They're just for show," Ash said.

She looked at him sideways, cute in a gray sweatshirt tonight.
It said UNIVERSITY OF FLORIDA. She also wore white hightop
sneakers and smelled faintly of roses. He had a vision of a
wardrobe closet filled with university sweatshirts in cream, black,
maroon, pink. She said, disgusted, "People brought kids."

The ride up had been pleasant enough, with Ash holding his
questions about Jennifer in abeyance while she entertained him
with funny stories about calls she got at the station. The Baltimore housewife who called herself the Goddess of Love. The
retired postman from Cleveland Park who insisted Jennifer was
the phone teller from NatWest bank.

Jennifer had asked him how he'd gotten such a coveted job
at the *Post*. Ash had answered, "I lucked out when I was an
intern."

Now light faded and the storm troopers drew in from the
edges of the field. Two more troopers escorted a man in a black
suit and tie through the grass, to the podium. Jennifer nudged
Ash. "Fashionable spring hoods," she said, eyeing four or five
Klansmen in white, black, and red hoods, off to the side, twenty
feet from the podium.

The man in the suit took his place behind the podium. He was
skinny and quite pale.

"Friends," he began, "I'm deeply pleased at the turnout
tonight. These days we hear so much about Americans not
caring about our country anymore, but your presence here
proves that's a lie."

There was a smattering of applause. Some people looked at
the crosses, nudged each other, waited for the fires. Jennifer

scanned the crowd. Ash turned to see a man sitting behind him on the ground, with a "Duke for President" button over his plaid woolen shirt. Black cap that said DIESEL POWER. Toothpick in his mouth. The man nodded at Ash, half listening to the speaker, half scrutinizing Ash.

America was still great, greatest country in the world, the speaker said, sounding as harmless as congressmen Ash had met at dinner parties. But "some people" were undermining our way of life. "Some people" were leeches sucking the good in the country away. The speaker never named who "some people" were. "You know who," he said. They were the doomsayers. The selfish ones. Ash was starting to get angry. All the knights of the Ku Klux Klan wanted, the speaker said in reasonable tones, was to get a little power back to average people, real people, people who did the work, drove the trucks, got food to the city, fought in the army, voted. Was that so bad? Think about it.

If Ash had closed his eyes and not seen the uniforms, crosses, or hoods, he might have been at a standard political rally.

The speaker finished by inviting the audience to stay for a little ceremony. The hooded figures arrayed themselves in front of the podium, but behind the three crosses. They lit the two small crosses. The flames rose quickly. Jennifer looked transfixed. Then they formed a circle around the largest cross, and one man in black doused the base with gasoline. This time the flames shot up really high, toward a quarter moon that had risen over the trees. Somewhere in the woods a dog started baying. Within a few minutes the fire died to embers, the crosses glowed, and most of the audience began drifting back across the field to their pickup trucks and station wagons. A few stayed, getting into conversations with the Klan troopers or the hooded men. Ash spotted the man who had been sitting behind him, now in spirited conversation with a man in a hood. The man waved Ash over, but Jennifer tugged his sleeve and they went the other way.

Ash and Jennifer circulated, listening to snatches of conversation. In the dark, with the speaker gone, the talk got uglier.

"It's coming, it's coming soon, they better watch out," a man's voice warned from the darkness.

"There's gonna be a race war," said a storm trooper to two men in bib overalls, while they nodded and said, "Good."

At a table near the podium, a half dozen men and women filled out Klan applications to the light of a kerosene lamp. "Mister, hey," the trooper taking forms called jovially to Ash. "Want to sign up? Big guy like you, we could use you."

"My grandfather, Rabbi Plotnick, wouldn't like that," Ash said.

The people at the table swung around to look at him. Another trooper, a fit-looking man with a VanDyke beard, came up from the side. The man was holding his truncheon. He looked into Ash's face, trying to decide if he was joking. "You don't look Jewish," he finally said.

Ash nodded. He felt out of control. "Only one side of the family was Jewish," he said. "But my grand*mother* used to say, 'Never forget, son, we were slaves when we came from Africa, no matter how white you look.' "

Jennifer said, "Let's go," as the guard moved up to Ash. Their faces were two inches apart. The people who had been filling out applications watched. Ash looked right into the man's eyes. They reminded him of the eyes of the red-haired boy in Russia, a long time ago. A deep rage was surging in Ash. Baiting this man was against all his training.

The man wouldn't do anything, Ash saw it in the eyes. He took Jennifer's hand and they strolled back to the car.

Back at the Mustang, Jennifer said, "You are crazy, you know that?" But she looked happy about it. She put the top down. Across the field they could still see the glow on the big cross, and shadowy figures moving in the moonlight. Ash still felt his heart beating. He was disappointed the guard hadn't attacked him. "Boy, were you right," he said. "Not even an hors d'oeuvre."

Jennifer burst out crying.

"I hate them," she said, balled up near the door, bony shoulders shaking beneath the sweatshirt. Ash realized that was why he had wanted to fight: they'd upset her. Her face was shiny with tears. "Let's get out of here," she said.

She bumped off the field, turned onto rural highway 15 and eventually got back on 270 toward Washington. Whatever the Dan-Dee Motel was, Ash guessed they weren't going there anymore.

She drove in silence, cool evening air washing through the car, the hum of traffic around them. Ash got a tight feeling in his throat, glancing again at her fingers on the wheel. He had a flash of her fingers sliding on his penis. He shifted position because he suddenly needed room on the seat.

Moving in silence toward the capital, they passed through Washington's think-tank corridor, rolling hills housing satellite and weapons contractors. To Ash, some of the complexes represented assignments he had completed. Passing the COMSAT sign, he flashed to a small, willowy man in a gay bar in Dupont Circle, a married engineer with a secret life, whom he'd interviewed for a series on gay life in D.C. No names in the article. But names passed to David.

Ash blew out air, watched the broken lines on the road flash by.

"When I was a girl," Jennifer said, "I did something I'm the most ashamed of, in my life. There was a girl in my class. Helen Wu. From North Korea," she said falteringly, seeing what had happened then in her mind. "Her family had gotten out during the Korean War. Opened a restaurant in Pittsfield—why Pittsfield I don't know. They didn't have relatives in Pittsfield. Her father said the mountains reminded him of home. She sat behind me in English. We got to be friends and I invited her home."

Between the air rushing in the car and the sudden softness of Jennifer's voice, Ash had to strain to hear. "We were at the kitchen table, eating Reese's peanut butter cups. We both loved them. We were stuffing 'em in our mouths. Her father had given her a box. And my father came in. He put his lunch box on the counter. He froze when he saw Helen. She didn't see him yet, he was standing sideways past her shoulder, and I remember his lips, the way they twisted back. I'd never seen an expression like that on his face. Like some dirty animal had gotten in the house."

Jennifer blew out air. "He didn't say anything. He just turned and walked out of the room and I heard him go down to the basement, to work on his fishing flies. But I kept thinking about his face. I thought I'd done something wrong, but I couldn't think what. Playing wasn't fun anymore. And after she left—I mean within seconds—he was up in the living room. He looked furious. I was terrified. 'Is that why Uncle Tommy died in PuNang?' he said. He called her a 'chink.' He had names for everybody. 'Kike.' 'Nigger.' 'Wop.' But I'd never met any of the kinds of people he hated before. He hated everybody. No more talking to her, he ordered."

"What did you do?" Ash said, knowing the answer.

"I listened to him," she said. She turned off 270 onto Wisconsin Avenue and began the slower, stop-and-start drive through the Maryland suburbs toward the District. She didn't say anything for a while. "I was thirteen. I couldn't stand the idea of him looking at me like that. The next day Helen came over in school. She asked me to come to her family's restaurant for dinner. She said it was her birthday. I was her best friend, she said, and she wanted me at the dinner. I think she knew something was wrong. Christ, what a jerk I was." Jennifer was crying again. "I just walked away."

"You were a kid," Ash said.

"I was afraid," Jennifer said. "Of him. Not that he would hit me. But what he would think of me. It was so . . . twisted."

Ash nodded, "Yeah, that was pretty bad."

She smiled. "Thanks for not pretending it was a little thing. Tonight that meeting brought it back. I think that's why I go to those things. So I don't forget." She stopped for a light. "My husband was like that, too," she said.

Ash was surprised at the stab of disappointment. "To Rick," Jennifer continued, "everybody had a label. Black. Communist. Rich. I can't live like that."

"Sounds like overly theoretical grounds for divorce," Ash said.

"We didn't get divorced because of that," she said matter-of-factly. "He just stopped sleeping with me. He said he wasn't attracted to me anymore."

Whoever the guy was, Ash found himself angry at him. "My good luck," Ash heard himself say, wanting to be rid of her, wanting the night to go on longer, wanting to leave.

Uncle Yuri's soothing, warm tones came to him. "Don't confuse liking with trusting."

Jennifer brightened. "That was quick," she said. "And kind. I didn't see that in you before. Kindness. What's the worst thing *you* ever did?"

Ash made himself look contrite. "I hijacked a TWA 727 and flew it into the Potomac. Maybe you heard of me. The Butcher of Bethesda?"

She burst out laughing. "Sooner or later you'll talk."

Ash twisted his arm behind him, as if someone had him in a full nelson. "You'll never get it outta me," he growled.

In a month or two when he kept deflecting her with jokes, she'd get quiet, then a little moody, even though she'd try not to, then depressed. Once or twice Ash had tried actual lies, making up stories, but he felt like he was tricking women when he did that. Better to be honest enough to admit he was hiding things. It wasn't perfect, but it was better.

What am I thinking? he thought. Somebody sent her.

He had another flash of her fingers on him, sliding on his skin, just the tips of them, tracing little lines. Ash shifted on the seat again.

What the hell is going on inside me? he thought.

"Sorry we skipped the Dan-Dee Motel part," she said, heading up Reservoir Road, "but I couldn't eat after that."

"You said you'd tell how you knew I worked at the paper," Ash said.

She smiled coyly. "I read the *Post*," she said. "When you said your name, I recognized it. I called the *Post* and asked for you. And you turned out to be you."

"I always turn out to be me," Ash said. "I'm starving."

"No problem. But I don't feel like going to a restaurant. You need fancy?"

"No."

"Okay," she said. She drove up MacArthur Boulevard and out to the Potomac Palisades. She had a one-story cottage a block from the river. Inside, there were dance posters, lots of Baryshnikov, Martha Hayes in midair, an old one of Ted Shawn dressed like an Indian. There was an old upright piano beneath a painting of autumn colors in Massachusetts. Fresh flowers everywhere, and the house smelled like roses. Jennifer took off her hightops and socks and left them on a throw rug. "Feel free," she said. She had small feet and beautiful arches, which made him guess she'd studied dance, and tiny toes that seemed to grip the polished wood floor when she padded from the living room. Her toenails were painted a pearly color. Ash watched the crack of her ass under her jeans as she left the room. His throat was dry. He called out to her, eyeing the poster over a bookshelf, "I don't think I look like Baryshnikov."

There was the sound of a door slamming. Ash peeked into the kitchen to make sure she was gone, then he hurried back to the living room and quickly opened drawers. He didn't want to be doing it, he wanted to relax, but that was impossible. There were some letters from Massachusetts with a Smith Falls postmark—good, good, maybe she really was from there. He took one and put it in his back pocket. He had to know who she was. There was a Mexican-recipe book and a Victoria's Secret catalogue, some dried flowers, pencils, an address book he flipped through, spotting nothing official. There were a few quarters, a bill for fixing a washing machine. Then the kitchen door slammed again and he shut the drawer.

Ash poked the piano with one finger, humming a Chopin nocturne as he heard water running in the kitchen. She entered the room carrying a hickory tray with a chilled bottle of white wine on it, a whole round black bread, which smelled fresh, a long carving knife, and a bowl stacked with tomatoes, onions, cucumbers, carrots, and a squash.

"Fresh from the Knowles garden," she said. There was dirt on her bare feet.

She put down the tray on a coffee table and tossed him an egg tomato. "Check it out," she said. Ash bit into it. It was sweet and the juice ran down his throat. Jennifer was eating another one, the red juice smearing the right corner of her mouth.

"I just picked them," she said. Legs akimbo, she sat next to him on the couch, its saggy cushions nudging them together, thigh to thigh. The feeling was electric. He heard her throat working at her tomato. She said, "You like onions, they're sweet, just bite into it." She was breaking off chunks of the black bread as the bitter, hot onion taste filled his mouth, backed up his nostrils, seared his throat.

The wine was cold and they drank it from the bottle. The carrots snapped when he bit into them, and the cucumber juice ran down his chin. He liked the way she'd not felt compelled to put on music. He liked how she didn't run into the bathroom to use Scope or Listerine or brush her teeth every time she took a bite of onion. When he glanced at her, she was looking at his lips. Some sort of pressure was building in the room. When they were finished eating, nothing was left: no wine, no vegetables. Jennifer stabbed up the last bits of bread with her index finger and Ash watched her Adam's apple bob as she swallowed the crumbs.

She said, rising, "I always liked October the best in Massachusetts. My family and I used to hike on Mt. Greylock. In October the shadows were always clearer, and the light was hard and orange, and there was always that one weekend, last weekend of fall, when the moisture would rise out of the ground as mist, and there would be no more leaves, and after that it would be winter."

"I loved fall, too," Ash said. He was thinking that reports he had received about the real Smith Falls had always described stores or events, but had never dealt with light, mist, leaves.

"I liked Halloween best," Ash said, which was true. It was the one time they could dress up, throw eggs at DuChamp's house, smear shaving cream on Yuri's house. Things they could never do the rest of the time. Things they would be punished for the rest of the time. "Stupid American things," Miss Dietz had said.

"Halloween," Jennifer said, smiling. "My mom always had bags and bags of Chuckles. Just bags of them. The kids would know, they came to our house, we were the Chuckles House."

Ash stared at her. Why had she said Chuckles? Yuri had always given out Chuckles. It was a coincidence, he thought, trying to hold on to the good mood. He was being paranoid. No, she was trying to tell him something. Or she'd slipped up. Ash thought, idiot, millions of people eat Chuckles.

The mood in the room had changed. They both looked at the clock. At the same time, he said, "Well, I better go," and she said, "I'll drive you home."

Did she look hurt? He couldn't tell. Ash said, "I can take a cab."

Jennifer laughed. "Oh, no, I said I'd drive, that means I take you home. Would you put *me* in a cab?"

In the car Ash made mundane conversation. The *Post* city-desk editor had played a practical joke on the sports editor, he said. Jennifer said, sure, the engineers at the radio station played jokes on the manager all the time. But the spirit was out of the conversation. Ash thought, am I falling in love?

Jennifer found a parking space on P Street and insisted on walking with him to his door. Nobody else was on the street. Neither of them said anything and Ash thought his footsteps sounded loud on the pavement. "Well," he said, "of all the Ku Klux Klan rallies I've ever been to, that was the best. That second act really made it."

"I thought the climax was too short. They didn't milk it enough."

"The third act, when they brought the camel onstage, that really got me," Ash said.

"I did like the camel," Jennifer said. "Or was it a drome-dary?"

It was going to be all right, at least for the moment. Ash put the key in his lock, the hair was in place, and he pushed the door open.

Then abruptly he heard footsteps behind him and whirled to see a man holding a pizza box five feet away, on the walk. "Your name isn't Repetto, is it?" the man said hopefully. He had short, cropped hair and a round face that looked nervous. The night was cool but Ash noticed that no steam rose from the box.

"No," Ash said.

"I've got to find this Repetto guy," the man said. "He ordered this an hour ago. It's my first night, they're going to kill me. He said Dupont Circle, this address. Do you know someone named Repetto?"

The man took a step closer. Ash said, "No, there's no Repetto here. I know the neighbors." In Washington, he thought, midnight was late to be delivering pizza. Ash looked beyond the man and saw no delivery car. "Can I come in and use your phone?" the man said, taking another step. Jennifer backed to the side, smiling. Ash saw he was hemmed in by Jennifer and the deliveryman, the half-open door at his back. Suddenly Ash thought, where's Tyler? Where's the cat? The cat should have come out by now.

Then everything seemed to happen at the same time. Jennifer was looking past him, into the apartment, and Ash was starting to move, head coming down for the rush, and Jennifer was saying, "Oh, my god," and the pizza man was saying, "Holy shit," and Ash, stopping himself with the greatest effort, saw they were both looking behind him, into the apartment. Not pretending. Ash turned, too, to see the cone of moon and streetlight on his white carpet, the edge of an overturned lamp in the light, and a large irregular, dark stain on the smooth white expanse.

"Tyler," Ash said.

Ash flicked on the light.

From the interior of the apartment he heard a door slam. Running through the living room, into the kitchen and toward the back door, Ash was peripherally aware of more smaller stains leading away, toward the bathroom, of a table moved an inch, of a pillowcase bulging with weight against a wall, where he'd never left it.

In the kitchen the back door swung on its hinges. He stood in the alley out back. Nothing.

Ash looked at the lock on the door. It was a dead bolt. Steel. It had been cut.

He felt cold now. Jennifer was on the phone in the living room, saying, "Yes, P Street," and, "Hurry," and, "Knowles, my name is Knowles but I'm not the one who lives here." Ash thought, shit, police. No police. And the man with the pizza was coming out of the bedroom, shaking, saying, "Mister, there's a dead animal in there."

Ash, fighting the crazy, wild grief rising in him, found Tyler on the bed. The trail of blood led right to Ash's pillow. The animal had somehow crawled there, collapsed, died.

Ash thought, no, no, no, no, no.

Ash picked up the warm carcass and spread it on his thighs. Tyler's head had practically been shattered by a blow. Bits of white bone protruded from his gray fur, an ear had been sheared off, and his face seemed more blunt. There was an odor of blood in the room. Blood came off on Ash's hands when he ran his hands through Tyler's fur.

"Tyler," Ash said.

He saw it. The intruder had come in and Tyler had attacked him, and the robber, fighting off the cat, had knocked over the lamp. No, Ash knew. Not a robber. Ash felt arms slide around his chest from behind, smelled Jennifer's rose smell amid the sweet blood odor, heard her gasp, "Oh, your cat. I'm so sorry."

Ash was thinking, yes, my cat. All these years when there was no one to tell things to, real things, he'd told Tyler. Tyler had sat there and Ash had talked. Ash thought, I was too slow, I got old, I should have sensed it. The faint sound of sirens came to him, getting closer. The deliveryman held his box, stupidly, in the doorway. "Shit," the guy said, awed by the violence perpetrated on the animal. "He must have smashed its head. What kind of sadist would do that?"

Ash knew what kind of sadist. Jennifer was saying, "The poor cat." The sirens were coming closer and soon police would start asking questions. Ash should be collecting himself, getting ready, getting prepared. But inside he was wailing over Tyler. Tyler had saved his life. Without Tyler there would have been no overturned lamp, no stain, nothing to alert him that someone was waiting for him in the apartment.

What kind of sadist had killed Tyler? Ash had seen cats killed like this before. A long time ago, thousands of miles away. The pieces of fur clinging to the blood. The faces stripped of animation. Usually, back then, there had been a small boy grinning nearby. A boy holding a club. A boy Ash had grown up with, who had come to this country with him seventeen years ago, whom he had not seen in all that time but whose signature was as obvious as a fingerprint. A boy who had been sent by David. A boy named Minsky. Ash thought, racked by grief, I'll kill him. Ash cradled the cat and rocked back and forth and petted Tyler, and Ash said, "Tyler, Tyler, Tyler."

SIX

POLICE MOVED THROUGH Ash's apartment, dusting for fingerprints, peering in closets, examining the sliced lock on the back door. The medical examiner kneeled on the living room carpet, scraping Tyler's blood onto a microscope slide. The pizza man stood by the Dalí old man, repeating his story to two detectives. He held the delivery box in front of him, like a shield.

Ash sat on the couch with Jennifer, a steaming Orioles coffee mug on the end table, Jennifer's fingers icy in his own. Pulsing squad-car lights from P Street swept over the curtains, flashed in her eyes. The *Post* police reporter had left twenty minutes ago, promising to keep the robbery out of the paper. Alerted by the writer, Sheperd had called to make sure Ash was unhurt. "I hope they get the bastard," Sheperd said. "You want to sleep at my place tonight?"

Now Ash watched a squat, wide man in a Lacoste tennis shirt, gold chain and pendant, and pleated Italian pants amble from the bedroom, coming his way. No cop dressed like that, but he was holding out a badge. "My kid has a cat," he said. He looked more suited to Las Vegas than a robbery investigation in Washington, D.C. Everything about the man, the incline of the head, the pressed lips, the way he held his hands, palms to Ash, spoke of sympathy. Except the eyes didn't. Ash's warning bells went off. He looked into a flat, observant stare.

Ash was thinking, David tried to kill me.

The detective introduced himself as Allegretti, Paul Allegretti. Ash noted the thick, curly hair, the shine on his face showing a recent shave, despite the hour. Thirty years old, Ash guessed.

"I'm sorry to go over this again," Allegretti said, and Ash had the feeling he wasn't sorry at all, "but nothing was stolen, you say."

"Just the stuff in the pillowcase," Ash said, nodding toward the bundle against the wall. "And he ran off without taking it. I must have startled him."

"Lucky for you the pizza guy slowed you down. You might have walked in on him," Allegretti said, squatting down and looking at one spot on the floor.

"Very lucky," Jennifer said, squeezing Ash's hand.

Did she take me to the rally to get me out of the house? Ash thought.

"What I'm trying to figure out," Allegretti said, making eye contact again, "is sometimes people don't realize how much they notice. You didn't see the guy, so why do you know he was a guy?"

Ash shrugged. "I assume he was a guy," he said. But it had been a mistake. He'd known it was a guy because it was Minsky. "I'd like to get my hands on him."

Is Minsky at her house? Ash thought.

"I would, too," Allegretti said. The pendant around his neck was a St. Christopher, Ash saw. The other detective to interview him had written notes in a book, but Allegretti didn't want to lose eye contact. "You figure it was a robbery, you surprised the guy, he runs out back."

"Don't you?" Ash said.

"Well, excuse me, I got to get up. Circulation," Allegretti said, huffing to his feet. He was so short Ash didn't have to look up very high to see his face, but the effect he projected was concentrated power. The forensics man was going out the front door. "I used to play baseball, in high school. Catcher. Man, I could crouch for hours." Allegretti sighed.

Ash thought, I can play this. "I was in the outfield," he said.

"What position?"

Ash flashed back to Smith Falls. The white arc of the ball coming his way against the blue. Ash running, glove outstretched, the ball impacting against leather. "Left."

"You must have been good."

"I was fast," Ash said.

"I can't believe you're talking about baseball," Jennifer said.

Allegretti laughed, turned serious. "It looks like a robbery, okay, but one thing bothers me. He cut the dead bolt."

When Allegretti shifted his gaze, it was like a floodlight moving. Now he was studying Jennifer. Ash said, "And?"

"Well, a robbery, I mean, these guys come up from Fourteenth Street. They want something fast. They don't have time to cut a dead bolt. They don't have the right kind of tool either. They certainly don't have the time. They go down the alley, check the lights, listen for sounds, maybe break a back window, reach in, if they can't get in, they move on to the next house."

"Too bad he didn't do that," Ash said.

Allegretti rubbed his cheek. "I robbed plenty of houses in the old days. And you don't cut a dead bolt. You look for a different place."

Ash stared. Allegretti nodded, grinned at the effect. "You never heard of me at the *Post*? No?" He sighed. "Fleeting fame," he said. "It was you guys that saved me. Bad childhood, addicted father, blah blah blah." Allegretti looked serious. "But when I got arrested, Carl Lockheed went to town for me. Did a whole series on me. And the mayor read it, figured, give the kid a chance. The commissioner made an exception for me, brought me in against rules. Special program, turn convicts into cops. I'm the only graduate." Allegretti laughed. "So I owe the *Post*. If it weren't for Carl, I'd probably be in Jessup now."

Allegretti rubbed his cheek again. "I want to pay the debt. I don't want anything to happen to you. You said you can't think of anyone mad at you." He looked skeptical. "Come on. You're a reporter. You piss people off for a living. You working on something that would piss someone off?"

"Believe me," Ash said, noting that Jennifer's hand had tightened at the question, "nothing that important."

Allegretti nodded but looked utterly unconvinced. Ash had the feeling the man was a bulldog. He wouldn't let go. "You're not going to tell me what you're working on," the detective said. "Well, I don't think this was a robbery. 'Cause of that lock. And because if what you've told me about the timing . . . I mean . . . the front door is open, the guy's inside, he can hear three people are out here, because they're talking. He has a minute, maybe more, to leave. But does he leave? Not right away. Not the instant he hears the door unlock. Not when he should have left if he was just robbing the place."

"Why does he do that?" Jennifer said.

"Ah," Allegretti said, leaning down again so their faces were close together. Ash smelled Opium cologne. "Ask your boyfriend. Why?"

Boyfriend, Ash thought. "Maybe he was finishing off Tyler," he said.

"Touché," Allegretti said. "Was that before or after he turned on your computer?"

Ash started. Allegretti, nodding, said, "Yeah, it's on, and it's on menu. Maybe you left it on, six, seven hours ago when you left. Or maybe he switched it on. If he switched it on, we have an intruder who saws through a dead bolt and doesn't just steal your computer—how much is it worth, a thousand? But he takes time to switch it on, looks for what's in it. He's got the little TV in the corner, he's got silverware, he's got your watch, but does he leave? No. He putzes around with the computer. What's he looking for? Nintendo?"

"I'm not working on anything that would have people breaking into my house," Ash repeated.

Allegretti said, "I'm not saying he *is* more than a thief, but *if* he's more than a thief, then the cat, well, suppose it's a kind of warning."

"I can't believe anyone would do that to a cat," Jennifer said.

Allegretti held up his palms. From the big calluses Ash saw, he liked to work with his hands. Allegretti caught the look, glanced at his hands, glanced back at Ash. Ash thought, he's fast.

Allegretti said, "I put in a fence this weekend.

"If I leave him alone," Allegretti explained to Jennifer, sensing protectiveness, "next time it might be worse." Then, to Ash, "My kid's got a calico. I got it from the pound. People ought to spay their cats; they have kittens, it isn't right to do that to a cat. She calls him Felix."

"I left the computer on," Ash said. He didn't care if Allegretti thought he was lying as long as the detective thought he was doing it to protect a story.

Allegretti pulled out a thick wallet, extracted a card, and wrote something on the back. "This is my home number. Office is on the front. I can keep your article secret. Think about it. I wouldn't want Diaz to be scraping you off the carpet instead of a cat next time. I'm not going to let anything happen to my buddies on the *Post*. Ask Carl about me. I can keep your secrets. By the way, where you going to sleep tonight?"

"You can stay with me," Jennifer said.

Ash looked into her clear green eyes, thinking, did she bring me home at a prearranged time? Did the pizza guy screw up their plan? Is Minsky at her house?

"Don't bother," he said. "I'll stick around, wait for the locksmith, lock the place up. I can stay here."

Allegretti played with his ring. Ash guessed he'd spotted the detective's tell. "If you don't mind, I'd prefer you didn't," the cop said. "We'd like to come back tomorrow, look the place over in daylight. Don't want to miss anything. If you stay here, you'll move things, maybe erase something. Would you mind sleeping someplace else?"

"Not at all," Ash said. "And thanks. Get the guy."

Allegretti winked. "If that's what you want." To Jennifer he said, "My wife likes your show."

"He didn't believe you," Jennifer said when the detective joined the other two men questioning the pizza man. She was indignant.

"I'd rather he worked too hard than not enough." Ash ran his index finger across her palm. He wondered if it was always this cold. "Jennifer, why don't you go home. It's late. I'll call you tomorrow."

"You don't want to stay at my place? Where are you going? A hotel?"

"A friend's," he lied. He could see her wondering, what friend? "Thanks for staying," he said. "I'm glad you did. I'll call tomorrow."

"Do you want me to drive you somewhere?"

"Go home," Ash said, steering her toward the door. "Get sleep. Even the Night Owl needs sleep."

On the walk she turned back to him. Her pupils looked enormous, shiny. Her brows dipped and her lower lip edged out so he could tell how cute she'd looked when she was nine.

"You told the truth, didn't you?" she said.

"I lied," Ash whispered, glancing both ways. "I hid the plans for the MX missile in my vase."

Jennifer slapped him lightly, on the arm. "Clown."

He waited until she drove off, and after a while the cops left and so did the locksmith who installed a new dead bolt. Ash kept a 9mm parabellum near his bed, behind the night table. He went to shooting ranges to practice with it, but he'd never fired it at a person. He pocketed it and drove to the *Post*. There would be people at the *Post*, even at two A.M. He left the Saturn near the L Street entrance and finally relaxed inside the building. He took the elevator to the fifth floor. His heart was beating crazily. He had to reach David right away. Had to tell him it was a mistake. He knew what he had done wrong now, what had upset David. It wasn't that he'd asked about the satellite information, even though that was a breach. It was that he'd asked where the others were. David, who had to protect all of them, had lashed out right away.

Ash told himself that had to be it. Because if David were thinking properly, he had to know Ash would never, in a billion years, betray the group.

Even at this hour the city room blazed with light. The night skeleton crew moved sluggishly; reporters had their feet on desks, sat bleary-eyed at computer screens, leaned into phones and used long-distance lines for freebie calls to lovers on the West Coast.

The night city-desk editor, a recent arrival from Trenton, called over, "Jim, we heard what happened. Close call."

"That son of a bitch," Ash said.

Other reporters looked up, called out condolences, came over, concerned. The editor said, "Are you okay?"

"I'm fine. I was lucky. A guy was delivering pizza to another address, he was lost, he kept me out of the house asking directions. That saved me." The reporters shook their heads. Ash said, "The guy ran out to the alley."

They went back to work. Ash found a Virginia phone book and looked for David's number. It was unlisted. It had always been too dangerous for Ash to have it. He drifted from empty desk to desk in the foreign section, deserted at this hour, looking through reporters' Rolodexes. He flipped to *K* for Kislak, *S* for State Department, *D* for David. There were always interesting numbers in the dexes. Woody Allen. Margaret Thatcher. Boris Yeltsin. Idi Amin. One card had Kislak's office number. In the end, Ash found nothing.

His eyes burned and his nerves were screaming. He kept seeing the door swing open, the cone of moonlight on the carpet, the dark burgundy stain leading to the bedroom, Allegretti's questioning eyes staring into his own. Ash sighed and went back downstairs, said good-night to the guard on duty, and stepped outside into the night. He felt exposed, vulnerable. The stars glowed bright above the parking garage across the street. In the artificial streetlights parked cars shone as if recently washed. A block north, across Sixteenth Street, a woman carrying an umbrella walked away from him. No one else was visible. That didn't mean Minsky wasn't around.

Ash walked to Fifteenth Street, turned left, and hurried toward the Mayflower Hotel. A few cars drove by; they made him feel better. He glanced at the drivers' faces to see if he recognized them. At the hotel the bellboy looked puzzled that he had no luggage, but the room was comfortable and, more important, had a phone. Ash couldn't use the one at the *Post* because even late at night the switchboard operators could tune in to conversations. Not that they would do it on purpose. But they might do it by accident.

Ash dialed a number by heart. Two rings. He heard Corinna's answering machine switch on. "Hi, it's me," she said to the soothing guitar tones of Joe Pass playing "Blues for Sammy." *Me*, he thought. That's just like her. Not *Corinna*. Just *me*. Like the whole world should know who *me* is. "I'm not here, but leave a message. I'll call you back."

Ash felt desperate. At the beep he said, "Corinna, it's Ash. It's import—" There was a click and she said, utterly awake, "What?"

"We've got to talk about us," he said. It was code. It meant emergency. She inhaled sharply and said, "If we have to. But we're not going to get back together. We've been over this." Ash had always hated how stupidly appropriate the code was. He said, "I need to talk to him now." This time there was a long pause. That wasn't code. There was no code for talking to David. She said, "You're not home?" Ash gave her the number.

After they hung up, he checked the time and paced. There was a TV with a cardboard sign above it advertising the late pay movies. There was a refrigo-bar that he opened but he didn't want a drink. He pushed the curtains aside and looked down on Fifteenth Street, staying to one side so he wasn't visible from below, scanning the sidewalks and parked cars. What would Minsky look like after eight years? Even if he looked the same, he could be wearing a hat, a phony beard. But there was nobody.

Ash paced. The other problem was once David knew his phone number it would take about two minutes to find his location. All he had to do was to check a numbers directory and match the digits to the Mayflower Hotel. Two more minutes to contact Minsky. Five to ten minutes for Minsky to reach the Mayflower. Ash fingered the gun. Outside, in the corridor, he heard laughter. His knob turned. A woman's voice said sharply, "That's not our room, Al. You're drunk, give me the key!"

The phone rang.

"Hey, how you doing?" said a cheery voice. It wasn't David.

It was the voice that gave him assignments, and he had a feeling it was Price on the other end.

"I need to talk to him," Ash said.

"No can do," the voice said. Ash cursed inwardly.

"Now," Ash said. He pushed it. "It's about Minsky," he said, using the old name.

The voice sighed. Ash heard a hand pressing down on the receiver. The caller was talking to someone else. Then the voice said, "He's busy until Thursday. The Thai Room. Six o'clock."

Ash, recognizing the code, the place, the time, started to say no, but the phone went dead. It was an easy code. Subtract one day from the one mentioned, three hours added to the hour, and Thai Room meant an old drop Ash had used two years ago, a deserted picnic area in Rock Creek Park, the last place he wanted to meet anybody.

Today. Nine P.M. Rock Creek Park.

He tried calling Corinna back to move the meeting place. The line was busy. Ten minutes later it was still busy. It would be busy all night. It would be busy all day tomorrow. She had call-waiting service, so a busy signal meant the phone was off the hook. Ash went back to the front desk. The lobby was deserted. "You call that a quiet room?" Ash snapped at the bewildered clerk. "I'm checking out."

He took a cab to the Omni Hotel, turning, every few moments, to see who was behind. The driver joked, "You a spy? Somebody following you?" Nobody was. An hour later, checked in under the name of Merrill, Ash was asleep.

In Ash's dream there was cold wind on his face and it was night, and high above, stars rushed by. He couldn't move his arms when he tried, they seemed to be bound to his sides. But it wasn't unpleasant, just strange, and every few moments came a soothing, "Mmmmmmmmmmm." And rich-smelling smoke. A gentle voice said, speaking Russian, "Are you a smart boy? Are you a genius boy? You'll do very, very well, little Jimmy."

Then the scene changed and there was a metallic, screeching noise as a man's silhouette rushed toward him, legs dangling and arms outstretched as Ash crouched and fired until his finger hurt. It was a drawing with David's face. Ash smelled cordite. The figure stopped a foot away, suspended from a wire, drifting back and forth, black holes punched through the chest. Behind Ash, the same pleased voice said, still speaking Russian, "You killed him. Good shooting."

Ash woke up. He was soaked with sweat. It took a moment to remember where he was. The sun streamed through the thick open curtains. He was tangled in a big double bed. He looked at the clock. Six A.M. He'd slept three hours. I better feed Tyler, he thought. Then he remembered what had happened to the cat.

Grief flooded him and for a few moments he didn't move. He saw Tyler as a kitten, chasing rolled-up paper balls. Tyler running around the living room and crashing into walls, high on catnip. Tyler late at night, after Corinna had left him, climbing on his chest, knowing Ash needed comfort.

He pushed it away. If he was even a little distracted today, it could kill him. He needed to clear his mind, focus on what he needed to do.

Ash always started the day with calisthenics. They cleared his senses. He would make himself do them now. He would push the questions to the back of his mind and make sure he was in control of himself before bringing them back. With effort he rang the front desk and asked if the gym was open yet. When the clerk said it was, Ash asked if there was somewhere he could buy shorts. Sorry, said the disgustingly perky voice. Not till eight. Ash tried the laundry. Had anyone left an extra pair? He tipped the bellboy who brought them and took the elevator to the fifth floor. Ash spent two hours on the machines, starting off with slow, light weights, then the Gravitron, increasing the load he was carrying, then the leg press, rowing machine, sit-ups on the board until his stomach ached. Then a good forty minutes on the running machine. As he worked, his mind eased and he ran plans over in his head. He would rather have jogged outside, but that seemed dangerous today.

Finished, muscles aching, he showered and ordered a huge breakfast of four eggs, toast, cereal, fruit, Danish, and two pots

of coffee from room service. The hard edge of anger returned,
but now he was in control of it. In his mind he saw his back door
swinging inward from the alley, saw a man's form coming into
his apartment. Saw Tyler, unafraid, hissing from one of his
favorite perches, the counter or the stool.

Tyler the watch cat, Corinna always called him.

Ash saw Minsky as a kid, kneeling in a field in Smith Falls,
outstretched hand offering a piece of raw hamburger. Other
hand behind his back, clutching a stick. "Oh, cat . . . ca-at,"
Minsky purred, the stick swishing where he could use it quick.

Anger makes you sharp, Uncle Yuri's voice said. Anger is a
tool.

Ash called Detective Allegretti's office to see when the police
wanted to recheck his apartment. Would nine A.M. be conve-
nient? Fine, Ash said. He finished his coffee, forcing himself to
sip slowly, giving his mind a chance to surprise him, to come at
him from a direction he hadn't considered yet, as he watched
sun-drenched N Street and commuters walking to work, the
crammed buses heading downtown, the lawyers and World
Wildlife Fund staff trickling into the glass buildings flanking the
Omni. And his mind did surprise him. Instead of going back to
last night it brought up the questions that had been bothering
him before that. Why had his assignments changed so radically
lately? Why had Corinna said David was so tense, so strange?

The detectives found no new clues at the apartment. When
they left, Ash packed a gym bag with things he'd need tonight.
Rolled-up jeans, a green T-shirt, binoculars, the American war-
surplus compass Uncle Yuri had given him almost twenty years
ago, running shoes, a loop of clothesline, a carton of grape juice,
a ham and cheese on seeded rye, extra hot mustard, and the
parabellum.

Nine P.M., David had said. Yuri's voice in his head said, "No
matter what happens to you, no matter how upset you ever get,
never neglect your job. Never put your position in jeopardy."

Ash went to work.

He'd been compartmentalizing himself so long he forced
himself to do it now, it was good discipline. But Ash needed his

concentration to complete mundane tasks. His mind kept running over his plan on its own. Don't use the Saturn, rent a car, he thought while he unlocked his drawer and read Sheperd's memo on the graft story at USAID, which he'd been ignoring for the last two days. The memo had originally come from a young metro reporter. It said:

I live in Virginia and after work I usually stop off at the Blue Knight near Reston for a beer. Over the last two months I've become friendly with a regular, a heavy drinker named Alsop, who told me he works at USAID. Alsop is an economist who checks the figures on deliveries of disaster aid abroad against dollars Congress allocates for the aid. He told me over the last three months there's been a mysterious drop of materials delivered although funding has actually gone up. He says a field man who went to eyeball earthquake relief work in Mexico came home and said Alsop was wrong, the figures matched. But the man soon started appearing in new clothes, car, house, etc. Please let me work on this. The Reston School Board is driving me crazy.

Ash stared at the memo, his heartbeat picking up. Mexico was one of David's clients, he thought.

Ash called the library for newsclips on USAID, but his mind flashed to the meeting place David had chosen. Ash had used it often as a rotating drop for information. It was a small, generally deserted clearing in the park, twenty yards through woods beyond the road, fifty yards from a bridle path, invisible from the road. It was perfect for an ambush.

Sheperd phoned to see how Ash was feeling. Carl Lockheed, acting editor in chief, came by and said he'd heard about what happened last night. "Move to the suburbs," Lockheed advised. There was a message, "Call Jennifer," with her home number. And one from someone named Horace Cragg, underlined, "Call home, not office," with a checked box "important." Ash couldn't place the name at first, then he remembered the little clerk from the State Department who had passed him the satellite report two nights ago. Probably calling to beg him not to publish it. Ash didn't phone.

He wished the meeting were right now. Ash strolled over to the metro section and found Sheperd's memo writer: a kid with bottle-bottom glasses, a crimson crewneck sweater against the air-conditioning, and Phi Beta Kappa pin from Cornell. He looked like he wasn't even out of high school yet, let alone college. "I know who you are. Wow, I always see you here," the kid said when Ash introduced himself. "I've been reading your stuff since high school. That car-theft-ring story was so cool. Weren't you scared when the thieves found out who you were, in the junkyard?"

"Who wouldn't be?" Ash said, sitting on the kid's desk, noting the envying glances the kid was getting from the other metro reporters, making himself concentrate on the kid and the story. "You leave anything out of the memo?" Ash said.

"Can I work on it with you?"

Ash liked directness. "I can ask Sheperd, but I wouldn't hold my breath. He doesn't like people outside the department."

"Mr. Ash, this school-board stuff is driving me crazy," the kid pleaded, glancing at piles of suburban newspapers on his desk, all with headlines like "School Superintendent Charges Local Watergate" or "War in Iraq Nothing Compared to School Board Fight, Moms Say." The kid sighed. "So much bullshit."

Ash laughed. "I'll see what I can do. But tell me, does Alsop know you're a reporter?" The kid said no. Ash frowned. "We've got to tell him without scaring him away. He's bothered by what he tells you? Or he's just making conversation in a bar?"

"It bothers him a lot. He keeps talking about the villagers in Vietnam, how poor they were. The whole thing makes him mad."

"He was in Vietnam?"

"Yeah. Is that important?"

"Well, it gives him a feeling for the area. We can use that. How well do you know him? Well enough to introduce me?"

"Sure, I buy him beers all the time."

"And what's the name of the inspector who went to Mexico and came back with the new car?"

The kid's face fell. "I didn't want to ask him yet. I was afraid he'd get suspicious."

"No, that's good," Ash said, suddenly seeing Tyler in his head again, keeping the rage off his face. "Let me think about it. I'll see if Sheperd can get you off the school stuff and with me, okay?"

The kid looked apoplectic with gratitude. "Thanks."

Ash wrote a computer memo to Sheperd asking that the kid be assigned to him. That would show he was on the story. When he finished, last night burst in on him again. He sat before his reflection on the green screen. They'd tried to kill him. After seventeen years, out of the blue, they'd sent Minsky to kill him. No, he reminded himself ruefully. Not out of the blue. *After I asked where the others were.*

Or was there more to it?

At one, eight hours before he was to meet David, Ash left the Rent-A-Wreck place on Connecticut Avenue and drove the old Escort he'd rented up Columbia Rd. to Adams-Morgan where he took side streets into Rock Creek Park. The Saturn was too recognizable to use. He'd changed from his suit into the jeans, T-shirt, and sneakers in the rental agency bathroom. He took the northbound lane toward Maryland, checking his rearview mirror, making sure no one stayed behind. He kept the windows open; the heat was searing. At any other time it would have been a pleasant drive along the meandering two-lane road that bisected the park. On news radio the announcer said tensions were at the breaking point between ethnic groups in the Soviet Union's southern republics: "Shooting reported between Armenians and Azerbaijanis. Three dead in Lithuania as troops fire on crowds demonstrating for independence. Gorbachev, in the midst of the turmoil, is reported to be leaving for a vacation at the Black Sea."

With the announcements, Ash again began going over the questions that had been bothering him before last night. He made a list in his head. Why did so many of David's clients match up with assignments both he and Corinna had had? What could the potential breakup of the Soviet Union have to do with the new direction their work was taking?

Ash came up blank.

Ash cruised in light traffic through Rock Creek Park, past woods, meadows, picnic and softball areas. He rolled the windows down. Summer heat baked the inside of the rented Escort. He didn't want to lose his edge by turning on the air-conditioning. The temperature kept him alert.

Amid the green, the park was filled with students on summer break, cyclists, lovers, tourists, day-camp classes.

He went over the meeting area again. There would be a quick right turn into a parking area, big enough for half a dozen cars. A narrow footpath disappearing into the woods, cutting off his view of the road, zigzagging between oaks and maples to provide hikers with privacy. It would also give David a potential ambush point. The path would take Ash to a triangular clearing hemmed in by more trees, with a single picnic table. Charred-stone grill. Log stripped of bark, serving as a chair. Rusty wire trash barrel.

By nine P.M. there would be no people.

Imagining the landscape, Ash knew behind the clearing the woods thickened again, but it would be possible, by slogging through bushes, to reach a bridle path fifty feet up the hill. That would give David, or whomever he sent, another possible entrance route.

I'm not going in the front, Ash thought.

He passed the parking area without slowing. It was empty at the moment, but there was no way he would leave the Escort in view. Rental plates were a giveaway. Instead he continued another mile. The road curved up a steep hill wooded so thickly it might have been the country, not the city limits. At the top of the rise the woods opened up to a softball field and large parking lot, which Ash steered into. It was filled with cars. On the sidelines of the field teenage boys in red jerseys were screaming, "Go, Huey!" as a fat kid lumbered around third base and stumbled toward home. A catcher in green blocked the plate.

Ash parked in a back corner of the lot behind an Isuzu pickup with a Labrador retriever eyeing him sadly as he tried to wedge his nose out the driver's window. No one could spot the Escort from the road. By night the other cars would be gone, but the dark blue Escort would blend in with the shadows.

"Always have at least two exits from a drop. Animals have two exits in their dens. If they can remember it, so can you," Martini had always cautioned. Ash would double back to the meeting place and give himself this extra escape route if things went wrong.

The problem was that David had had the same training he'd had. If Ash would come early, so would David. Ash was banking on David's not coming *this* early.

Ash checked the clip in the parabellum, made sure the safety was on, and hiked into the forest. He looped the clothesline over his shoulder. He needed to hurry even though the meeting was hours away.

Martini had always said, "Never go to a meeting blind."

Walking quickly but sweating from the heat, Ash took ten minutes to reach the bridle path and fifteen more to get close to the clearing. He slowed down. Listened. A few steps and stop. More steps and pause. He passed no one. The picnic area was empty, just as he remembered it, the grass a little brown this late in summer, the feeling of isolation strong despite the hum of occasional cars fifty feet away on the road.

Ash needed a hiding place where he could see the road, clearing, and bridle area. He studied the oaks hemming the clearing. None looked high enough to give him a view, and none had branches where he could conceal himself for hours and stay comfortable enough to move fast after all that time in one position.

Searching, Ash followed the slope of the hill back up into the trees, toward the bridle path. He stayed in grassier areas to avoid leaving footprints. When he paused to survey his surroundings, he went up on his toes so he wouldn't depress footprint-sized areas of grass. Then he saw the tree.

It was a huge old oak bulging out of a split boulder near a ledge, separating into two trunks ten feet up, each large enough to hide him. Both trunks were smooth at the bottom but gnarled enough ten feet up to give him footholds if he climbed that far. The best foliage started fifteen feet up. He couldn't even see if there was a place to sit up there.

Satisfied, Ash tied one end of the clothesline to a rock, stepped on the boulder, used his left hand to steady himself on the trunk, and with the right tossed the weighted end of the clothesline up until it looped over a thick lower branch. He let out slack. The rock dragged the rope down to him. Holding both strands together, he hauled himself hand over hand to the lowest branch, pulled himself up, then tugged the rope after him. Up here he had toeholds and didn't need the rope. Ten feet higher Ash found what he needed. He stretched along the length of the branch, back against trunk, legs out, ankles crossed. Pulling the foliage a little closer, he could hide his face from below.

Now he had a view of the road and parking area. He could see patches of ground below. No glimpse of the bridle path from here, but he had a feeling this was the best he would get. Martini would have said it was stupid to cut off escape by climbing a tree. Ash figured Minsky and David would do things Martini's way. They wouldn't spend a lot of time looking for him up here. And he was pretty high up even if they did.

Ash flicked the parabellum safety on, off, on, making sure it moved without making a sound. He watched traffic on the road, cars or an occasional bicycle, for a view of the drivers. Traffic was light and nobody looked familiar.

After an hour he ate the sandwich and drank the fruit juice. Good mustard, he thought. He was enormously hungry. He folded the sandwich wrapper and juice carton and put them in his pocket. He heard a skittering sound behind him, in the leaves: a squirrel. Ash could hear himself breathing.

Would they give him a chance to explain? Or come after him right away? He wondered if messages had gone out to others this morning. Were they getting their families into cars, driving to safe houses, waiting for David to send an all clear?

He remembered sad little Lewis Pell at the reunion years back, in a corner, drinking gin and tonic after gin and tonic, making too many references to his work at some kind of military aircraft plant, grabbing Ash's arm, saying, "I want to go home. When will they send us home?" And then the article at Ash's drop about Lewis's "accident." Had David invited Lewis to a meeting like this, when the engineer grew dissatisfied?

By four-thirty traffic was increasing, the afternoon people going home, the evening picnickers arriving. The sun lowered enough to shine into Ash's face, making it harder to see. It burned his eyes. He sweated freely. Nobody stopped at Ash's area. An hour later the light was growing brittle, and through the branches the lower rim of the sun lowered enough so it stopped hitting him. Jennifer Knowles's voice came into his head. It said, in those low, throaty tones that made his mouth dry, "You want to sleep at my place?"

Ash sat up. A red Sunbird was sliding into the parking area. It was Price's car, which Ash had followed yesterday. The sun blinded him when he tried to see inside. But the driver's door opened and Price got out, wearing the same khaki, epauletted raincoat. Ash felt the weight of the 9mm parabellum in his pocket. He turned his attention to the man getting out on the passenger side; he was small but compact, with long arms and a bulky torso that seemed light when he moved. Even though Ash knew Minsky was in Washington, seeing the man brought all his rage back. Unlike Price, who was dressed for an office, Minsky wore loose-fitting, olive-colored military trousers and a chamois-colored, button-down shirt that blended in with the forest. The face—dark mustache, sideburns, and thick brows— was unfamiliar. Ash wouldn't have recognized Minsky if he hadn't been expecting him. United again.

Ash tensed as Minsky moved toward him, into the forest. He caught glimpses of the man coming up the slope, moving and stopping. There was a cry from a crow and the swish of a car going by, but Minsky himself made no sound. He disappeared in the forest. He reappeared a few minutes later over on the left. He was making slow circles around the picnic area, scouting the woods, working his way higher.

Sure enough, he was going for the ledge.

Ash brought the gun out quietly. He released the safety. He'd made no noise, but Minsky, thirty feet away, paused, hands on hips, looked in Ash's direction.

Minsky closed to within fifteen feet. He was below Ash's tree and between Ash and Price, on the ledge. He looked toward Price, who shielded his eyes, trying to find Minsky, but having no luck. Minsky looked back at the oaks, the brush. Ash had the gun ready; he didn't know if Minsky was pretending. He didn't know if he had been seen.

Minsky went back to the car, conferred with Price. They opened the trunk and Minsky bent inside, straightened, armed now, probably. That made Ash feel better, although the trunk dug into his spine. If Minsky hadn't armed himself until after checking the woods, they weren't concerned about Ash's being here early, they were worried that he'd alerted the police.

Price got back in the car alone and drove off.

Minsky walked into the forest again.

Straight toward Ash he came, the strategy the same since the training had been the same. Find the high point. Hunker down. Wait for Ash. Price would be getting the car out of view, or going to get David. Maybe doubling back through the forest. Ash fought away an image of his cat lying on his pillow, bleeding. Ash envisioned Tyler dragging himself away from Minsky, the life spurting out of him, struggling to reach Ash's pillow. To reach my fucking pillow, he thought. The cat knows I'm not even there and all he can think is to get to my pillow. The gun shook in his hand.

The leaves blocked Minsky and Ash cursed inwardly. Then he saw him again, closer to Ash's tree. Minsky had smeared dirt on his face. Ash glimpsed the length of a gun barrel, too long to be natural; it had to be a silencer. Minsky slid his head left to right, nose up. Ash tried to remember if he had put on cologne. Minsky reached down, examined something near the ground. The broken-off tip of a twig on a sapling. He rolled the fresh cut between thumb and forefinger. He kneeled to study the ground where Ash had swept away footprints.

Ten feet. Ash had him cleanly in his sights now, impossible to miss. He pressed back into the crook of the branch. Seemingly unconscious of Ash's presence, Minsky walked behind a tree.

At length Ash heard Minsky moving again and risked a look. Minsky's back was to Ash; he had chosen a spot on the ground, at the edge of the ledge in a brushy area. He was squatting on his haunches, looking toward the road.

By six traffic picked up with rush hour. By 7:30 the evening picnickers, hikers, and volleyball players were clearing out of the park. Ash's muscles ached from immobility, but he didn't want to risk a noise if he moved. Don't think about the pain, he told himself. Minsky didn't move either. It seemed impossible that a human could squat for so long.

The clearing darkened and at eight-ten the red Sunbird came back, parked, and shut off headlights. David, Ash thought. He watched the driver's door open. In the dark he could barely make out the man shape emerging, a wide-brimmed hat low over the head. He felt better until he realized the size was wrong. Not tall enough. Or regal enough. Not that David posture. It was Price. Ash went cold. In the dark it would have worked. If he hadn't followed the car yesterday, hadn't gotten here early, they would have had him.

Now Price picked his way to the picnic area and sat at the table. He checked his watch.

Ash stayed put. He didn't know how much time had gone by. His thigh muscles were screaming. At length he heard stirring in Minsky's direction, and the barely visible form rose and made its way back down the slope. Minsky came into view below. The two men conferred. They got back in the car and drove off.

Ash sat in the branch, hollow ache in his heart. For all his training and knowledge, all his acuity in acting, all his intuition in moving through his adopted world, at that moment he couldn't help feeling an overwhelming terror at being cast out. For all his logic, the boy in him had believed that David would come, and he was lost. They can't think I would betray them, he thought. Uncle Yuri rose in his mind, but it wasn't the pipe-smoking, gentle countenance he was used to remembering. It was a sad, hurt face. Like Ash had hurt it.

Ash climbed out of the tree. They were his family; Corinna and David and Price and Yuri. The reporter in him reminded him there was more to it than that; things had seemed wrong even before Minsky came after him. But Ash, almost thirty-five years old, felt lost, the darkness thickening around him. The sensation came as a memory so strong he could swear he was back in Smith Falls, one of the night exercises. He was six years old, in the woods where DuChamp had left him. Utterly lost and trying not to cry. A small boy beneath immense trees, listening to animals, praying the others would find him.

Ash headed back toward the car. The gun felt like it weighed a thousand pounds. His mouth was dry. He was immensely tired. The radio, coming on when he turned the ignition key, seemed to broadcast tinny gibberish from another planet. Ash drove slowly into the District, the trees of Rock Creek Park giving way to the homes of Adams-Morgan. He needed time to think. He couldn't go home. He couldn't go to the police. As if he'd really turn the others in. Faces flashed through his mind. Dara. Jennifer. Allegretti. Sheperd. Forget it. Corinna. No, by now Corinna would be out of reach, too.

He drove aimlessly, for no reason. Found himself cruising along K Street, down I, H, Fifteenth, Constitution. He drove past the Jefferson Memorial, around the Tidal Basin.

Ash pulled over across from the *Post* and looked up at it, nine stories in yellow brick, lit at night. Just leave, a voice in his head said. Start over.

Ash laughed. Whatever David and the others had become, they were what he had. All he had.

And with that thought a new idea came to him. It was risky, but he didn't have a lot of choice. It would be tricky, very tricky. He felt fresher as he steered the car across the Teddy Roosevelt Bridge into Virginia. He would need all his senses, all his abilities.

It took twenty minutes to reach Route 123, and ten minutes

later he was in front of David's iron gate. Ash pressed the intercom button, heart hammering. David's voice sounded testy when it replied, but maybe that was just distortion on the line. "Who is it? It's two in the morning." When Ash said his name, there was a pause, then a chuckle, then David said happily, "You turd, I was worried when you didn't show up before."

Ash spoke quietly, radiating warning. "David, are you listening?" The gates were sliding open.

"Come in! I'll make coffee, guy!"

Minsky might be there, so might Price. The gate clanged open, and the driveway disappeared through the woods, in the floodlights. Ash said, "Before I come in, I want to tell you something. I wrote it down. David? *I wrote it down.* It's at the paper. If I don't get back by tomorrow, they'll find it. It's in their boxes. And there's a letter to the police. Are you listening? I told the editor I was coming here." Silence. "David?"

Silence.

"David?"

"What are you so excited about?" came the cheery voice. "Come in!"

"They'll open the envelopes tomorrow," Ash said.

"You like espresso? I got some great espresso from Venice," David's voice said. "What are you waiting for? Get in here, you dog."

Ash drove up the driveway, watching the iron-spiked gate closing behind him in the rearview mirror. This time he studied the grounds as he glided toward the big log house. He saw closed-circuit cameras in the pines. Floodlights. Sprinkler system. Copse of birches providing concealment. More cameras. Were the dogs out? Anything more? Anything extra? Tool shack, but it looked locked. Cabana by the swimming pool. Single power line going to the slanted log roof.

Ash crunched across the white gravel driveway, feeling utterly naked. The front door was opening. David waited in the open doorway, grinning, in a running suit of white cotton and tennis sneakers, bathed in stark light from inside the house. A voice inside Ash's head urged, turn around, get back in the car, you still might have time to get out.

But Ash had to try this. He was powerless against his need. He forced his legs to move forward, fighting off a premonition that he was walking to his death.

SEVEN

"**J**AMES, YOU DOG," David said happily as Price walked out of the living room, pointing a .38 at Ash. David pressed his index finger against his lips to order quiet. "It's two A.M. Don't you ever sleep?"

Ash halted just inside the front door. His senses were screaming. He thought, stay calm, look calm. Price wasn't shooting so he might have a chance. "If you ever have to kill someone, don't hesitate," their instructor Kazanjian had said. "Don't give them time to react."

To Ash's left, a large oil of a Shenandoah fox hunt dominated the foyer, the Blue Ridge mountains in the distance, the fox in the foreground, shivering in a tree as dogs bayed at the base. The gilded frame brought out the blues and greens in the forest. The hunters had not reached the quarry yet. The paint was cracking with age.

David regarded Ash ruefully from two feet ahead, in his running suit of white cotton and tennis sneakers. Close up, Price surprised Ash in how badly he had aged. The washed-out pallor was accentuated by the gray chest hair visible beneath the open V neck of his shirt. Magnified beneath thick lenses, one eye seemed wider than the other, as if Price had suffered a stroke or some other facial disorder. There was a sucked out, beaten down look to Price. A spark had been drained from him. But the brown eyes held Ash's, and Ash knew he would shoot in an instant if he had to.

More paintings stretched at intervals down the long central hall toward the interior of the house.

"When's the last time I saw you, ten, twelve years ago?" David said, using the same greeting as last time. Standard Kislak opening. "At the inaugural? Calling me up out of the blue—this better be good, guy. But business later. Let me show you around the place. There's a lot to see."

Price gestured Ash to stay still. On the gun, his fingers seemed thin and almost feminine. Everyone in the group had been taught to shoot.

Beyond Price on the right, Ash saw a small fire in the fireplace, and above the mantel, President Madison seemed to look his way. The eyes were enormous. David's two rottweilers came up behind Price. One looked adoringly at David. The other licked its penis.

"Still at the *Post?*" David said. "I get so little time to read the paper anymore."

At a nod from Kislak, Price handed his .38 to David, approached Ash, and slid his hands across Ash's shoulders, into his armpits, down the front and sides of his torso, probing and patting. Up his thigh. Into the pit of his back. David was saying, "This painting's an original Chesire, 1820, can you believe it?"

Price found Ash's parabellum. David's brows went up. He said, not breaking his beat, "Look at Madison's face. Chesire never even met the man, he painted it from description and it's so realistic. He was a genius! Come closer!"

Price backed into the living room. He must have put the gun down because he returned without it. Ash heard his steady, hoarse breathing as he stepped close again and fingered Ash's shirt buttons, studying them. He stepped back and mimed unbuttoning motions, ordering Ash to strip. Ash shook his head no. David said, "A lot of people thought Madison was a coward, the way he fled Washington when the British attacked." He sounded bright and cheery, but he shook a finger to indicate that refusing Price was a bad idea. As Ash began undressing, David said, "But he's underrated, even as a general. Who did we have? Washington was dead, the Revolutionary War staff retired or dead. A good general knows when to give up."

Ash was down to his socks and underwear. It was cool in the hallway. He glanced into the eyes of the treed fox in the painting. The animal was backed against a high branch of the tree, muzzle swiping sideways, the lead pursuing dog caught four feet in the air, leaping as it howled. One of David's rottweilers groaned. Price gestured for Ash to strip the rest of the way.

David said, "You like this sword? Incredible, isn't it! It's a real samurai sword! Four hundred years old. Yomo Tashimeri, head of Tashimeri electronics, is a client, and his great-great-grandfather was a samurai. I'm in Tokyo a couple months ago, and Ash, you wouldn't believe his house! The garden! Bonsai trees! They don't have a lot of space there, but what they do with it is art."

Price's fingers felt moist and hard, probing Ash's navel, under his arms, beneath his scrotum. Disgusted, Ash felt the cooler nails dragging against his skin. He jerked away. David pushed the gun at him. "Yomo gets up after the tea ritual, and he says, David-san! San, can you believe it! Touch the blade!"

The plank floor was cold against Ash's bare feet. The fingers, spreading Ash's buttocks, seemed to linger. Ash wasn't imagining it. Price was pushing one finger all the way into him. Behind him, the breathing seemed to quicken.

Ash swung his elbow back. Heard a grunt, heard Price's footsteps as he fell back. David looked beyond Ash, an annoyed look crossing his cupidlike features. But he seemed angry at Price, not Ash. His brows furrowed as if to say, do your work.

Price stepped around in front of Ash, glaring at him, rubbing his chest where Ash had struck it. David continued, "He hands me the sword. He says, 'This has been in my family sixteen generations.' "

Price made an open-handed gesture to David. It meant, I didn't find anything. David said, "Now I want to show you a lute I got in Germany. The chancellor gave it to me. He knows I like music." He dismissed Price with a wave. Price again disappeared into the living room, this time returning with a blue and red running suit he handed to Ash. He gathered up Ash's clothes and shoes and moved down the hall. A door slammed. Ash heard Price's footsteps as he brought everything upstairs.

David lowered the gun, nodded at the running suit. "Put it on. Sorry about the search. Believe me, if there's a hole, you can hide something in it."

"Price is a little enthusiastic," Ash said, using the old name with David. Inside, he crawled at the memory of the probing fingers.

"He's loyal. Man, I was worried about you. What happened? I waited in the park over an hour for you."

"You didn't wait an hour. You never came."

David threw back his head and laughed. The rottweiler jerked up, emitted a long whine. It inclined its muzzle toward Ash.

David scratched the dog as Ash donned the running suit. It was flannel and it made the house too warm. "Did I wake you, Jeff?" David crooned to his pet. "Were you dozing? Were you dreaming doggy dreams?"

David turned to Ash, still patting the dog. "Where were you? Up a tree?"

"Yeah."

"Up a tree." David laughed, shaking his head. He started back down the hall, Ash falling into place at his side. "I told those guys to go early," David said. "Did they even do that?"

Ash gripped David's wrist. The muscles underneath the cotton jacket were surprisingly powerful. David must work out all the time. "David," Ash said, "I want you to stop Minsky. I didn't tell anyone anything. It was just an innocent question the other night."

David smiled sadly. "When was there ever an innocent question?" he said. It was darker in this part of the hallway, but each painting had a small light mounted over it and David's frown was illuminated by this soft light. The oil over his right shoulder showed a square dance by a country inn in colonial times. The men wore breeches and tricornered hats, the women balloon dresses. Holding hands, they ran in a circle, the whole party dwarfed by mountains and purplish clouds.

"Then what was that crap you said on the intercom?" David demanded. "You wrote things down in a letter? You left it at the *Post?*"

Ash caught David's shoulder to keep him from walking away. "Stop fucking around," he snapped.

He'd forgotten the rottweilers, but he didn't let go when he heard the growling behind him. He heard the clicking of dogs' claws on the hard plank flooring and something bumped the back of his knee. Ash was furious. "What would you have done?" he said. "I wrote those letters *after* the park."

David exhaled softly. "Price told me when Minsky's finished putting on all his stuff, nobody would recognize him." He bent to the dog, patting. "You're my big buddy, aren't you? You're my protector. Yes, you are."

He said to Ash, as they started walking again, "So how'd you know it was Minsky?"

"He killed my cat."

David looked puzzled. Ash said, "Like he used to do in Smith Falls. My goddamn cat, David."

David repeated, "He killed your cat?"

Ash felt hollow inside. They'd reached the kitchen. Ash saw a glass of milk and a pie wedge on a plate on the counter. Cherry or strawberry. David seemed to eat a lot for a lean man. He must have a high metabolism, must be burning himself up inside. "It crawled on my pillow to die," Ash said.

"I didn't tell him to do that."

"No," Ash said, amused by the idiocy of it. "Just to kill me."

"That's right," David erupted suddenly and passionately, face twisted with rage. "You want to talk straight? You think I wanted to do that? Ash, you come here after ten years, to my house. My fucking house. You're never supposed to come to my house. But you do, so I'm thinking, trying to come up with an explanation on your side. It's Moon Boy, Moon Boy asks questions, he always has to ask questions. Do you think I wanted to believe it was more than that?"

For the first time, Ash saw the tension in David's face. The confidence was gone. In an instant he'd aged ten years. This is what Corinna had been talking about. David slumped onto the stool near the uneaten pie wedge. "But then you want to know where the others are. How many are left? Where are they?"

Galvanized by the memory, David pushed off the counter. He was so close Ash looked into one big eye. "What the fuck would you do in *my* place?" David said, using Ash's own words. "Tell me. Why did you come here in the first place?"

Stunned, Ash said, "I didn't realize."

David mimicked him. "I didn't realize. I didn't realize. Am I a mind reader? I have thirt—I have other people to worry about."

Ash thought, unable to help what came into his head, thirteen left.

"Even tonight, you're back again," David said, looking disgusted, although Ash wasn't sure with whom. "You give that speech at the gate. You left letters for other people, you say. Did you really leave letters, you *wrote everything down?* You told your editor you're coming here?" David was so furious he actually pushed Ash, pressed his hands into his chest lightly.

"Come on, Ash, what am I supposed to think?" The dogs, who had calmed down, shifted uneasily. They were living meters for David's moods. They thought Ash got David too excited.

"Are you wearing a wire?" David said, driving at him. "Is the FBI across the highway? Why do you think I have Price upstairs, looking through your clothes? For a microphone." Ash smelled a meat odor coming from David, beneath the smell of Lavoris. "Tell me, Ash. *Have* you turned? What are you doing here? Why are you asking these questions? Moon Boy, what am I supposed to think?"

Ash looked down, mortified. He's right, Ash thought. I've endangered everyone for an idle question. "I would never do anything against us," he said.

They stared at each other. It was the moment when things would go one way or the other. David was sizing him up. Then the anger seemed to ease from the room. Like pressure going out of it. David sighed, propped against the counter. Ash could see the terrible weight on him.

"Danny was always a sadist," David said. It was the closest he would come to contrition. "You have that cat a long time?"

"Nine years."

David and Ash walked out of the kitchen and down the dark, long hall, toward the study. They didn't seem to be going anywhere in particular. They just needed to be moving.

Ash said, "I'd like to do that to him."

"Never mind that," David said.

"I know."

"You'll leave him alone?"

"Yeh," Ash said.

"You started it. It's over now. You're responsible as much as he is."

Ash made a noise in his throat; it wasn't a word, it was just grief coming out.

"Okay, enough of this," David said. He put the gun on his desk, looked at it in disgust, wiped his palms together. "Look at us. We only get to see each other once every ten years and we waste it on this. Come with me. I want to show you something."

The dogs came into the study after them. One lay on the floor by the door, blocking it. The other padded to the long, leather couch and jumped on it and lay down. He scratched his hindquarters.

With the fight over, Ash felt weak. He sprawled in an easy chair as David bent behind his desk, opened a drawer, brought out two Sam Adams. He brought Ash's beer to him. He said after a long draft, "Seventeen years. Who can be perfect for seventeen years?" To Ash, David had always been the coolest one, unflappable. But nobody could be like that all the time. David looked exhausted.

David took another drink. He lay beneath his trophy wall with the photographs of himself with world leaders. He didn't talk for a long time. Ash felt ashamed he had added to David's troubles. Then David said, "It's what's happening at home, isn't it? It has everybody jumpy. It has *me* jumpy. It's why you came here the other night. You don't know what's going to happen from one day to the next. What they want. Who's even in charge anymore."

He spoke so softly Ash had to strain to hear. Almost as if David were talking to himself. And then Ash understood that the group was in danger. All of them. The back of his throat was dry, and a pinpoint pain began throbbing in the back of his head.

"I'll tell you, Ash," David said, and to Ash they were boys again, on a log in the forest, bare feet swishing in the water as they told each other secrets, "I have no idea why we've been getting these weird jobs. I can't blame you for asking. I asked, too." David frowned, finished his beer. He went to the desk. Ash thought, I'll do whatever he wants. David slid a drawer open. "I didn't get an answer either," he said.

"How about my clothes?" Ash asked. "Price has had time to check them."

David glanced at the ceiling. "You want the truth? He's going through every button. Every pocket. You'd be amazed what the FBI can do with microphones these days."

"He didn't look so hot," Ash said.

"I know. He was in a head-on on the Beltway a couple years ago. His insides are all smashed up. In pain all the time."

David threw a fat envelope on the desk, next to his plate. "See? I broke the rule, too. I couldn't help it. Look."

Ash gaped. It was pictures, photos of the reunion eight years ago. Utterly forbidden souvenirs that would prove they all knew each other. Ash's heart beat fast. They were so precious. Forcing himself to go slowly, he went through the pile. He didn't remember David having a camera at the party. Of course. It had been hidden. He could tell because the angle of each photo was always the same. The camera had been in a wall, or behind a table. As a result many of the shots didn't show people's faces; just backs, sides, profiles. He didn't care.

The world reduced itself to the tiny three-by-five photographs; each shot's background the cheap basement paneling in David's old New Haven basement, when he had been anonymous enough to invite them home. Their first and only reunion.

"Remember when we were going to have one every two years?" Ash said.

"But that was too risky, so we planned it every five."

"Then none, but I don't think anyone could stand that," Ash said.

So there had been one. First and last. Ash remembered coming into New Haven in a rented car, no licenses allowed to show home states. No real names. No mention of employers. No talk that could be used against them later if one of them turned.

But somehow that had made it more magical. It had been one of the greatest evenings of Ash's life. He remembered the thrill of walking down the steps to David's basement on a snowy February day. The joyous, familiar faces looking up. The talk in Russian. The old games.

Ash happily looked at a photo of a group of adults sitting in a circle, on a blue Oriental carpet. The camera, imprisoned in its fixed position, caught Corinna running around the outside of the circle. Just a flash of female calves and a white swishing dress, but it was her, he knew it. Ash laughed out loud. That game was, the girl passes the men, taps one on the shoulder, and the chosen one has to get up, run after her, and catch her before she reaches her place in the circle. But David's carpet had been slippery with worn spots and people had kept falling down. "Win and you get a kiss," David had said.

The old games, the Russian ones they'd played in the afternoons, when morning lessons were over. Here was a shot of Elaine Simms, wearing green as always, chatting with her chemistry genius husband Sam while David poured them California wine. And here was a shot of Bonnie Lutwick and Ed Tate imitating Dietz and DuChamp, Tate in thick glasses wagging a finger admonishingly, barely keeping the mirth off his face, Lutwick standing arms folded, foot tapping in Dietz's most famous posture of disapproval after a test where even one of them had gotten less than 100 percent. Ash remembered how they'd all roared, telling Dietz stories. And here was a photo of all of them, god, all of them, grouped by the ice cream cake with its nine candles, one for each year they'd been here, blowing them out, their anniversary of deception. Lifting fluted champagne glasses when the hidden camera snapped them.

What Ash remembered now, amid the lovely memories, was the exquisite yearning that night to know more. The way he had soaked up everything anyone said, automatically seeking clues. Traffic was backed up on the freeway to the airport, Howie Granger had said. Ash had thought, ah, freeway, he lives on the West Coast. Sarah Taylor had begun a sentence, before she caught herself, "Last Tuesday at Marshall Field's . . . ," and Ash, savoring it, having a place to put her, had thought, Chicago. Later on he'd given her a house in Evanston, a suburb he'd once visited for the paper, and a daughter, and constructed a life for her he carried around in his head like a snapshot or a letter. It didn't matter if it was a fantasy. It was good enough for Ash.

But of course it had been sad little Lewis Pell, the doomed one, the engineering genius, who had revealed the most. Lewis, who had headed for the bar the minute he and Glorie arrived, who hadn't left the liquor all night, a slumped, chain-smoking man in a sweater vest, drifting back and forth near David's little folding table covered with papier-mâché, peach-colored bunting, downing gin and tonic after gin and tonic, growing more slurred, more angry, more depressed.

"You're lucky, Jimmy. You probably live in a city. You can lose yourself in a city. You can have friends but not tell them anything. But in a little town you see the same people every day, go the same places every day, have the same conversations every day. From the company to the college. The college to the Snow Bowl. The Snow Bowl to Mr. Ups. People get to know you. And if you aren't all . . . there, if you know what I mean, if they sense something is missing in you, you feel it. You hear me? Even if they don't say anything. Those long winters, at Glorie's faculty parties, they're always looking at us."

"You're probably imagining that," Ash had soothed, thinking, Mr. Ups, intrigued at the name. Is that a person? A restaurant? He decided it was a restaurant because of the impersonal way Lewis said it. He'd given Lewis Pell a seat at a town bar called Mr. Ups, imagined him alone in the corner. Maybe a little neon flashing through the window from outside. Other people asking Lewis questions, but Lewis just drinking alone. Ash had made it winter. He'd given Mr. Ups big windows so flakes fell outside. He'd made it dark because it was winter and added skiers coming home on the street outside, college kids because Lewis had said "Glorie's faculty parties."

"Oh, my God," Lewis had said, "it's so lonely up there."

Ash and David stood over the desk, cradling the color snapshots in their hands, passing them back and forth.

"Look at this one, look at this one," David said. It was Minsky with a broom over his shoulder, goose-stepping in front of the bar. "Remember that big guard outside the gate on Tuesdays and Fridays? The one from Vladivostok?"

"He's imitating him!"

"It's perfect!"

"He's got the stance. Look at this one, my God," Ash said. "You kept these."

David, looking happy but chagrined, said, "See, I broke the rules, too. I could never throw them out."

"But if people ever found them . . ." Ash said, suddenly worried about the group.

"I should burn them."

"I know," Ash said.

"I can't," David said.

Ash said, "I'll burn them."

"I guess that's why I showed them to you," David said. "I could never do it. I just couldn't do it."

Ash located a steel waste bin by the desk, scraped the scraps of crumpled paper from it, put it on the desk. He ached as the photos slid out of his hand and clunked onto the bottom of the basket. He should never have come here two nights ago, he knew. He should have been able to control his urges. Just seeing the faces had made him ashamed, made him see how he could have endangered them. David pulled a gold lighter shaped like a dragon from a zipper pocket in his running suit. "From Shanghai," he said. Ash hesitated an instant, the flickering fire an inch from the edge of the first photo, the one showing Lewis Pell by the liquor table.

Then the fire quickly ate into the chemical gloss, the blackening picture curling into itself, the flame catching, flaring up on the other photos in the basket, the dogs whining across the room, smelling the smoke.

Neither Ash nor David said anything. It was all over in seconds.

Ash looked into the wastebasket at the ashes on the bottom. Already the metal rim was cool. He put the basket back where he had found it. "So long," David said to the residue.

"I never should have come here," Ash said.

"I should have known better, too," David said.

Ash couldn't believe Tyler was dead. He said, "What did he think he was going to do anyway, drive Minsky out of my house?"

"I told Price to leave your clothes in the living room," David said.

They gazed toward the wastebasket. "It was a good party," Ash said.

As they left the study, David threw his arm around Ash's shoulder. Ash had the actual physical feeling of being back in the forest. They were walking through the birch woods toward Smith Falls, Price and Minsky trailing behind. Ash actually smelled the steam.

"I should have known you'd never turn," David said.

The light was on in the living room. The fire was out and Price was gone, but the clothes were folded neatly as if they'd come from a laundry. Ash started to dress. All he wanted to do was go home, get in bed, sleep.

"You dog," Ash heard David say affectionately behind him as he buttoned his trousers, "you never left any letters at the *Post* about me. Did you?"

Only the fact that Ash was facing away when he heard it saved him. David had been good, so good if they had been looking at each other, he would have seen the truth in Ash's face. Ash used all his effort, all his concentration, to keep dressing smoothly, to choose his words carefully. "Of course not, at least not in the mailbox," he said. "Suppose someone came to the paper while I was here and found the letter? I left it in my drawer."

He buttoned his shirt, still facing away from David. It was such a ridiculous lie, especially in light of what they'd been saying a minute ago. It isn't going to work, he thought. He tried to keep from flinching. He envisioned Price standing there, with the gun. Or Minsky even. He was trapped. He imagined David commanding the dogs, "Lemon!" and then "Go!" or "Get him!" or whatever the attack word was. A lone bead of sweat chilled Ash's armpit. At least it wasn't on his forehead, where David might see.

The long pause behind him went on.

David's voice said casually, "Your drawer."

Ash turned and there was only David there, and the dogs, and he said, tucking in his shirt, "Well, I had to protect myself. I didn't mention the others, just you, you son of a bitch." Ash laughed like it was a big joke. He made his voice heavy in a bad imitation of a Mafia don: "I needed protection." They both laughed, but David was on the fence, Ash could see. It could go either way.

Ash said, looking around for his belt and thinking fast, "Besides, I have to go back to the *Post* tonight anyway. I'll rip up the letter." He hoped he was making himself sound distracted, like he was only paying half attention to what he was saying, "I've got the damnedest story. Mexico, bi-ig scandal, someone down there's ripping off USAID."

It was the sweetener and the doubtful look faded a bit from David's face. Something shiny and interested came into it. Mexico was one of his "clients."

"Mexico?" he said.

"Big payoffs to guys down there," Ash said.

There was something about having seen those photos. Like the others stood in the room with them. Ash found himself back on his original questions. What connected David's clients with Moscow?

"Well, what exactly is this Mexico thing?" David said, sitting on the armrest of the couch. "Payoffs to whom?"

"That's what I have to find out," Ash said, lacing his sneakers.

David walked a little in the living room. Ash saw he wasn't absolutely convinced yet. Then he said, "Don't come here anymore, but you'll be getting a call on this. Hold off telling the *Post* what you find."

"Okay," Ash said. He made himself look contrite. "David, I'm . . . sorry again."

"Ah, don't worry about it. You know my secret," he said, meaning the photographs. "I know yours. Get out of here."

David steered him to the door. Ash was dying to escape, but he had to do this perfectly or they wouldn't let him. He said, "I need my gun."

"Your gun."

"Yeh. Price took it." Ash shouted, "Price! Where's my gun!"

The hallway remained empty. David was staring at him.

After a moment David called out, "Price!"

He came out of the kitchen, a piece of pie sloppily in one hand. "Ash needs his gun," David said. When Price hesitated, looking confused, David said, "Give it to him."

Price pulled the silvery parabellum from his jacket pocket. He looked down at it a little too long. His index finger, when he handed it to Ash, brushed the back of Ash's hand. The skin felt clammy. Ash checked the gun; it was still loaded. He shoved it into his belt.

Ash said, "So long, Price, you pervert."

A clock chimed somewhere in the house. The last glimpse Ash had before turning his back was David, the rottweilers, and Price in a semicircle. Ash forced himself to walk slowly to the door, open it, turn back, and wave. He closed the door behind him. The car, parked only twenty feet off on the white gravel, seemed a mile away. They were probably watching. Inside, he rolled down the windows, started the engine, kept himself from glancing at the house.

Ash began the long descent down David's driveway. The cameras in the trees would be tracking the car. The question was, would the gate be open? His heart was hammering but he kept the car from going fast. He gripped the steering wheel; the gate wasn't open, but as he drew closer, it began to move.

Ash turned the car onto the highway and headed back toward Washington. His head reeled with what he had learned. There had been no doubt that David believed in his loyalty. Yet David had still been about to come at him.

The explanation was staring at him now. David was worried because he had something to hide *from the group*. It was Ash's loyalty to the group that bothered him. David, whose interests had always been identical to theirs, was suddenly afraid of them. Ash had been a reporter for fifteen years, and he knew when someone was frightened of him. David wasn't concerned about the others. He was terrified for himself.

Ash shook his head and turned the radio louder. He told himself it couldn't be true. His logic and intuition could take him only so far before smashing up against his loyalty. He was horrified for even thinking it. Think of David as me, Yuri had always said. Maybe I misinterpreted his tone, Ash tried to tell himself, since I wasn't looking at him. Ash turned onto the George Washington Memorial Parkway, staying in the right lane, checking the rearview mirror. No one followed. He yearned for Yuri's presence. Yuri would know what to do. But there was no Yuri.

David turning against the group? They operated under so much pressure, and within such a thin margin of safety, that even a slight deviation posed risks for them all. Had Moscow ordered David to put the group in greater danger than before? Pieces were missing. Who could guess what madness gripped their old masters with the government falling. Would David listen if they ordered him to do it? What if he had no choice? What if he was up to something Moscow didn't even know about?

Ash couldn't convince himself he was wrong any longer. He shut off the radio to think better.

Somehow, David was a threat to the group.

Which made it beyond David now, beyond any one person. Driving across the Roosevelt Bridge, toward the lit-up Lincoln

Memorial, the last bit of confusion coalesced into the realization
that Ash had to try to find the others, wherever they were.
Whatever David was up to was too much for Ash to piece
together alone. But together maybe they could do it. Ash's laugh
sounded loud to him in the car. Find the others. After seventeen
years. Find thirteen people scattered around the country, with
different names, jobs he didn't know, kids now, homes now,
lives he could only imagine. He shook his head. It was absolutely
taboo, going to look for the others. His heart was galloping. He
was so happy. It was for all of them to decide. I'm going to do
it, he told the photographs he had seen tonight in his mind.

David Kislak, back in his study, looked over the stack of photographs he had taken from the safe. They were copies of the ones
Ash had burned. He saw Corinna by the bar, beautiful head
thrown back, hair tossing as she laughed. He saw himself clinking a champagne glass against Danny Minsky's.

"As if I'd burn them," he said.

"But why'd you let him go?" Price said from the couch.

David didn't look up. On the wall, the photo of Kislak shaking Ronald Reagan's hand had been moved sideways so he could
open the safe. Then he'd reached past stock certificates and
jewelry to detach the back wall and work the combination of the
inner safe.

Price said, rebuked by the silence, "I didn't say it was a bad
idea. I just don't understand."

David looked up. "Come here."

What he held out was a single sheet of paper from the inner
safe. The neatly typed headline read ASH.

Of all of you Ash is probably the most loyal. This may
seem odd in light of his constantly mocking, questioning
plans, motivation, and systemics, but it is a veneer from a
man who wants desperately to belong. Ash may rebel
against his need but it is at his core. It is his desire for my
approval and Corinna's love.

"See, even Yuri thought he'd never go to the FBI," David said.

Price stood holding the paper, chewing his lower lip. David snapped, "You heard what he said about Mexico. Call Minsky off Ash's apartment."

David got up and began putting everything back into the safe. "At least for a couple of days. Have him watch him, if he can do that much. Until we get an idea of what he's doing." He locked the inner safe. He rearranged his stock certificates and jewelry in the outer safe, scattering them, then he closed that door and replaced the picture of President Reagan. He looked angry suddenly. "Corinna's love," he said. "That shithead really thought Corinna would stay married to him."

"Corinna loves you, everybody knows that," Price said worriedly.

David's cupid face was suffused with red. "Then what's bothering you? You think he's smarter than me?"

"No, I don't think that."

"Then what?" David demanded.

"It's that . . . well . . . he makes those guesses sometimes," Price said. "Out of the blue. I don't know how he does it. What if he goes to the others?"

"Just how would he *find* the others?" David demanded.

"You're right, it's impossible," Price said.

They fell silent and Price looked miserable as he always did when David reprimanded him. The dogs licked each other's ears. It was quiet in the house, and pleasant, and a clock ticked in the room. A panel had slid sideways on the wall, revealing two television screens that showed a raccoon nosing through the forest on the grounds. After a while David said, "But I thought of that. And if he did try to find the others, this is what I would do."

Price listened, and then he smiled, and then he said, "David, you always know what to do. I shouldn't have asked."

EIGHT

ASH BEGAN SWEATING within minutes of leaving the *Post*. His trousers stuck to his thighs, his shirt to his back. The driver of the cab he hailed looked like he'd been caught in a shower, dreadlocks wet down to his Caribbean shirt, perspiration shiny on his white face. "Air-conditioning's out, man," he warned. "The last passenger couldn't take it."

Ash gave the man a Capitol Hill address and they took off toward the Potomac.

Ash's heart beat fast. Since six this morning he'd raced through files at the paper, trying futilely to follow up clues Lewis Pell had given him eight years ago. At the same time he'd made sure to protect the facade he'd built up with reporters. "Take nothing for granted," Yuri had always said. "Especially the person who people think you are." Ash had joked with the librarian, stopped by Sheperd's desk to remind him of the Sunday barbecue, checked with the kid in metro for an update on USAID. Listen to what they're saying, he'd told himself. Act normal. Smile. Nod. Slap him on the back.

He'd found nothing useful. But then he'd had another idea.

Now the driver hummed along with Paul Simon's "Graceland" as they shot through light traffic on Rock Creek Parkway. Washington's dog days of August had arrived. Congress was out of session, the politicians had fled for home. The president was on vacation. Tourists were down. The city seemed to function through a brown, choking haze. Ash did not believe in higher powers. It was Yuri he tried to please. He thought, let the answers be on Capitol Hill. The Parkway spilled the cab onto Independence Avenue, where they passed the Russell office building. Ash remembered the crucial hints Lewis had mumbled eight years ago, drunk at a party. Small town. Glorie's faculty parties. Snow Bowl. Gyroscopes. Mr. Ups.

He hoped they'd be enough to find Lewis's widow. Even with Lewis gone she might have her job if it was important to David.

Beating the dashboard to reggae, the driver cruised past high-priced town houses that formed a buffer between government offices on the Hill and poorer sections of Washington. Ash checked traffic. Nobody was following. The windows were down and he smelled the driver's sweat, marijuana, Chinese food, gasoline, and roses. Roses made him think of Jennifer Knowles. When she came into his mind, he felt a clenching in his gut, a tightening all over.

When Ash worked on stories, he usually experienced a heightened awareness. Voices seemed louder, smells stronger, ideas came faster than usual.

But this was even more than a story. Once he'd decided to find the others, images flooded him. He saw the group as teenagers, around a campfire on a July night, singing "Home on the Range." He saw the big guard Posner, his only friend when he was ten, trudging away from the fence after being posted east by DuChamp. He heard DuChamp and Dietz in DuChamp's office where they didn't know he could hear, saying, "Do you know who his parents are?"

Who are my parents? Ash thought. Why were Dietz and DuChamp scared of them?

Ash shot up in the seat, stared at a man walking a terrier. He looked just like Yuri! But on second glance the man looked nothing like Yuri except for the curve of his back.

The street where the cab stopped was lined by two-story garden apartments on one side and an office building of smoky glass on the other. On the apartment side laughing black children took turns holding a water hose and spraying each other in small, well-tended lawns behind a chain-link fence.

The people going in and out of the office building were white and black, well dressed, carrying briefcases. The building seemed to float above a recessed alcove entrance of clear glass. On the architect's table it had probably looked futuristic, but it had turned out to be another squat glass office building within walking distance of the Capitol.

Ash's legs felt heavy as he got out of the cab. What if nothing panned out here either? Then something else will, he told himself. Glorie Pell is too smart to waste on a job that doesn't bring information. And with Lewis's old defense company nearby there's a good chance her college has a research contract with it.

The building didn't have a lobby, just the glassed-in entrance-way surrounded by parking lot, with an elevator going upstairs and a stairway marked EXIT going down. In the directory, behind glass, he saw DEFENSE WEEKLY. BASEMENT ROOM ONE. He checked the street to make sure nobody else was pulling up.

He took the stairs, footsteps echoing on the Formica floor-ways. There was a ticking in his head, a dry thrill in the back of his throat. In Washington some of the highest-paid, most-specialized journalists were ones most readers never heard of, Ash knew. They were owner/operators of private newsletters, publications available at great cost to subscribers interested in the inner workings of government. Ash knew lots of them. *FCC News* served telephone companies, broadcasting networks, computer manufacturers, and foreigners wanting to break into communications businesses. They could learn what contracts were up for bidding, what votes were scheduled in Congress, what regulatory-agency commissioners thought about issues affecting them in a more detailed way than any newspaper would provide.

SEC Week or *U.S. Treasury Weekly* served banks, real estate corporations, investment counselors, and brokers wanting a jump on the week's money machinations.

And contractors wanting to monitor the defense industry, or know where to send their lobbyists that week or learn what threats loomed to their businesses, read *Defense Weekly* or any of a dozen other private publications covering the Pentagon.

Good newsletter owners could retire in their thirties as millionaires.

The building seemed older inside than it had from across the street. Alone in the basement, pipes running overhead, Ash knocked at a rust-colored steel door with a plastic LEIGH PUBLICATIONS plaque screwed into it, and at a woman's muted "Come in," entered a long I-shaped cinder-block room lined with two parallel rows of old oak desks, all with computer consoles on top, most manned with reporters talking into phones, writing stories, reading papers or magazines, guzzling canned soft drinks. Just like the *Post*. More plaques on desks read DEFENSE WEEKLY, WHEAT DIGEST, SATELLITE REPORT.

The office had a mom-and-pop feel to it; sneakers, jeans, sports shirts, and especially the baby in the mechanical swing, automatically clicking back and forth beside the secretary's desk, weren't like the *Post*. Asleep, cheek squished against baby blue terry-cloth collar, the infant dribbled mustard-colored food on itself.

"Hi," the secretary said. The mother, Ash figured, eyeing the photos of mom and kid on her desk. No man in any photo. Single mother, he guessed. And beautiful. Short, blue-black, shiny hair. Huge brown eyes. Black beauty mark on one cheek, accentuating the cupid mouth. Tight, black tank top, which showed fantastic breasts as she leaned forward. There was an immediate sensuality, a heat that came off her.

"They let you keep the baby here?" Ash said.

She laughed. "I'm the owner. Nobody wanted the desk by the door. Big deal. This is Rolf." She nodded at the baby. Two more pictures of Rolf were on her computer. Rolf lying naked with a half-open diaper underneath. Rolf in a pink bath basin with a hand holding up his head. She had white, even teeth and Ash smelled her perfume. He flashed to the face of Jennifer Knowles.

"He pretends to be asleep when he doesn't want to meet people," the woman said. "Don't be fooled. I'm Angela Leigh. What can I do for you?"

She seemed impressed when he told her he was from the *Post*. He said he was trying to find someone who worked in the defense industry, for a story that had nothing to do with defense. He didn't want her to think he was stealing a story. Ash hoped she might have a list of contractors working on defense, flight issues in particular, maybe even gyroscopes. He said he didn't want to start at the Pentagon because you had to put requests in writing and wait for months for answers, and half the information that was public everywhere else was a secret there.

"Tell me about it," Angie said, laughing. "I tried to get a job at the *Post* years ago, when I was starting out. Not good enough." Then she asked if he knew which branch of the military he wanted. She pursed her pretty lips when he said, "Sorry," which Ash took to mean he had a big job ahead. "Rolf, talk to the man while I see what I can find," she told the snoring infant, and swayed down the aisle. Round ass. Tight, checkered cotton culotte that showed white ankles, rolled athletic socks, and tennis sneakers. Head inclined while she moved, the whole effect heightening her curves. Ash let out his breath.

Angie Leigh conferred with an older, fat man at the end of the room, the only worker here in a shirt and tie. The man studied Ash with a resentful glare. He shook his head at Angie. Ash knew the proprietary look. The man didn't want to share information. But finally he opened some drawers and piled loose-leafs as thick as telephone directories on his desk. Angie Leigh swept them into her arms and headed back toward Ash. She had to be stronger than she looked to carry the books so easily.

Again Ash flashed to Jennifer Knowles. "Call the Grand Dragon. Your hood is ready at the cleaners," had been the message on his desk at work this morning, beside another call from Horace Cragg. He'd returned neither, distracted by Detective Allegretti coming toward him with acting editor in chief Carl Lockheed in tow. The policeman grinning, dripping with thuggish jewelry: gold necklace, rings, watch, bracelet. Lockheed in a crisp white shirt and World Wildlife Fund panda tie. Ash thought, shit.

"Mister guy!" Allegretti said like an old pal, pumping hands.

"Feeling better today? Doc Gooden!" he said admiringly, spotting the cutout on Ash's computer. *"There's* a guy can burn a hole through a catcher's mitt. I used to catch a southpaw in high school. Earl Lord. Big skinny kid. But what a fastball." He shook his hand. "I still feel it."

Beyond Lockheed's worried face Ash spotted Sheperd on the run, coming toward them, proprietary as always when one of his reporters was in the spotlight. Lockheed said, "Allegretti and I go back. He told me you might be in trouble."

"Carl saved me from my life a crime," Allegretti said, grinning. He winked. "I was his cause."

With the two men standing there Ash felt the pressure building around him, mounting on all sides.

"I just wrote the story," Lockheed said modestly.

"Take some credit. Be human," Allegretti said.

"Detective Allegretti has a different view of what happened to you last night than you do," Lockheed said. "You can trust him. Anything you tell him stays here. I don't want you getting hurt for a story. It isn't worth it. *Are* you working on something that might have caused that break-in?"

"I told him last night, no." Ash shrugged. "I wish I could be more helpful."

Their acting teacher, back in Smith Falls, had always said, "Use props. Don't keep your hands at your sides. Don't look stiff. Look cooperative."

Sheperd banged his knee on a desk, hopped a few feet back, grimacing. Lockheed chewed his lip. "I'm serious. It's okay to tell him," he said. "You can work together."

"Tell him what?" Sheperd said, limping up to them. Reporters, copygirls, everybody was staring. Since word had spread about the break-in at Ash's apartment, they all knew this meeting concerned that.

Lockheed lowered his voice, asked Ash, "You want a bodyguard?" Ash was shocked. Lockheed was notoriously cheap, and hiring bodyguards for reporters was expensive and only done on rare occasions when editors were truly fearful about reprisals.

"A bodyguard?" Sheperd said. "He needs a bodyguard?"

"I don't need a bodyguard," Ash said. "Excuse me. I'm working on a story here."

"What story?" Allegretti asked. His glance swept over Ash's desk, but there was nothing telltale on it.

"Why does he need a bodyguard?" Sheperd asked Allegretti. "Ash, talk to me. Somebody talk to me."

"See?" Allegretti told Lockheed. "Nothing." Lockheed nodded at the detective. "We'll work it out. Say hi to Pat."

After they left, Ash gave his version to Sheperd, and Sheperd said, "Fuck them. You're not telling them anything." He looked excited. "Who do you think it was? Mexico?"

"Could be," Ash said.

"A bodyguard," Sheperd said in disgust. "Walking around with a bodyguard. Lockheed burns me up. You know why he's acting editor?" Sheperd lowered his voice. "He's a nephew. A bodyguard," he said again, shaking his head. "He'd probably give war correspondents bodyguards. Ha. Guns going off. You're interviewing someone and they say, 'Who's that?' 'Oh, no one, just my bodyguard.' " Sheperd glanced toward Lockheed's office. The editor was talking earnestly with the detective. "That pansy," Sheperd said.

"Sheperd," Ash had heard himself ask, his thoughts realigning, shifting, Ash not even sure why he was asking what he was. "What if you had a friend, a good friend." He knew Sheperd wasn't that, nobody was that. "And he told you he was into illegal, something he had to do."

"How bad?" Sheperd said.

"Bad."

Sheperd looked interested. "What is it?"

"If," Ash said. "I said if."

"Fuck the guy," Sheperd said, leaning over. "If he was a real friend, he wouldn't have hidden it in the first place. And he wouldn't put your ass on the line telling you about it." Sheperd winked. "Write it up," he said. "Make it personal. Readers like that."

Sheperd walked off.

Now, in the office of *Defense Weekly*, Angie Leigh unloaded her stack of loose-leaf files on her desk, beside the photo of Rolf with a tiny black Malcolm X cap on. The infant was waking up in the rocker. The eyes opened. They were huge and brown like Angie's. The baby looked at Ash. He started to cry.

"Pull up a chair," Angie said, hauling Rolf from the rocker, cradling him in her lap, reaching down to slide up her tank top to feed the baby. Ash couldn't help staring. Angie smiled at him. She said, "The other desks are busy, I don't mind if you work here. You've got about two thousand pages to go through, all contractors. One book for each branch of service. The bad news is, it's alphabetical by company name, not by what they do. Want to send out for some breakfast?"

"He looks hungry," Ash said, watching Rolf.

Her big eyes seemed to swim up at him, and he felt the blast of sensuality from her, which made his knees weak. "You like spicy?" she said.

Hours later Ash turned pages, eyes swimming. The roast beef she'd sent out for at lunchtime had been good, smothered in horseradish, crispy dill wedges on the side, fresh seeded kaiser roll, all washed down with sugared iced tea. Angie ate a fruit salad with a plastic fork. She was copyediting a story. Ash had finished the Navy book and was on the Air Force. Rolf slept in the rocker again, doped up with milk. The good news was, he'd been able to eliminate lots of pages right away. Each loose-leaf was organized not only by branch of service, but by specialties within the branch. Ash had been able to bypass sections on ships, weapons, ground transportation, health insurance, building contractors, food services, clothing manufacturers.

Most of the other reporters had left for long lunches after their noon deadline. The big electric clock over the fat man's desk said 1:12.

"Finished," Ash said, closing his book. He'd jotted down thirty companies working on military aircraft guidance systems. Ten were in hot or flat areas of the country, Florida or Iowa or Alabama or Texas. No ski areas there. Ash drew a line through them. Twelve others were located in or near big cities. But Lewis had said small town. Ash crossed them out, too.

That left eight businesses, at least eight that Ash had located, that might be where Lewis Pell once worked. "Go ahead, use the phone," Angie said. "Can you watch Rolf a minute? Ladies' room."

She swayed off and the office door shut behind her. Ash figured he'd better start on the East Coast companies first, since they'd close first and he might not get the information he needed from them right away. There were three, two in Maine and one in Vermont.

He dialed directory assistance in Dellum, Maine, and asked for the town's Chamber of Commerce. A woman with a twangy accent answered on the fourth ring. Ash said, "I'm calling from Washington. I want to take a ski vacation this winter, with the kids. I'm wondering if you've got hills there with beginner slopes."

"Sure thing, and not only that, it's new, not crowded," the woman said happily. "Brand-new hotel. No lift lines. You want me to send you a brochure?"

"Terrific," Ash said. "I might even have a friend who went to college there. You have a college there, right?"

Long pause. "Well, about a hundred miles away." Ash scratched Fiume Flight Corp. off the list.

The next town, Blake, Maine, had a community college but no skiing.

Ash hung up. Six companies remained on the list.

"Middlebury Chamber of Commerce!"

Ash asked the same questions. Yes, there was skiing near Middlebury, an older-sounding man answered. At the Middlebury College Snow Bowl, although frankly, he added, if he himself were planning a vacation, he'd try Stowe. The blood roared in Ash's head. Lewis had used the same words: *Snow Bowl.*

Ash said to the man, as Angie Leigh came back in, "I'm not sure if this is the right town, but I think I heard about a good restaurant there. Mr. Ups?"

"That's us all right," the man said. "Great lunches. Great

everything. Anything else I can do for you?"

Angie said when Ash hung up, "You found it, didn't you?"

Ash wanted to shout, to celebrate. They looked at each other, sharing the triumph. After a second, some of the heat dissipated and her smile became strictly friendly as she saw which way this was going to go. "I wondered if you'd really do it," she said to the clicking of the baby rocker. Were it not for Jennifer Knowles, Ash would have been in bed with this woman within hours. "Let me know if you find him," she said, unbuckling Rolf to take him home. "Or her."

He didn't trust Jennifer but he couldn't stop thinking of her. Packing, his plane to Burlington leaving in an hour, Ash's mind jumped from Glorie Pell to Jennifer Knowles. Glorie, the reedy girl back in Smith Falls who was perpetually in braces, the math genius and reader of romance novels who had married Lewis Pell. And years later, the tall, well-groomed woman at David's party, staying as far from her husband as possible through the night and then practically carrying him to the car.

And then Jennifer. It wasn't just Angie Leigh who had reminded him of her. A rose, a shadow, a bit of radio music, reminded him, too. I'm only seeing her until I find out who she really is, Ash thought. But Ash found himself imagining her hips. He'd been captivated by the voice, then the fingers, and now the hips. Jennifer was wedging her way into his unconscious in pieces. He made her hips pleasingly jutting, with the smooth white scoop of her belly in between. He put a brown beauty mark on one side of her belly button. He pushed her away and conjured up Corinna. Ash was shocked. He didn't want to think about Corinna. He imagined running his lips up the hard bones of Jennifer's hips.

The letter! Ash thought. The one he'd taken from her house but never read because the break-in had interrupted everything. It must be in the pants he'd worn that night.

The bell rang and instead of unlocking the door as usual he checked the peephole first. It was her. His warning bells were going off again. In the fish-eye lens Jennifer swam up at him out of a fun-house mirror. Cheekbones wide as a basketball, nose long as a pen. Smile like the Joker's in the Batman comics Principal DuChamp had given out in Smith Falls, saying, "Read them, you'll be tested." Superman, Archie, Sergeant Rock, the Hulk.

"Wanna buy a raffle for Pancake Tuesday?" she said when he opened the door. Pancake Tuesday brought back memories of Smith Falls, a series of snapshots DuChamp had handed out showing people eating breakfast at long tables outside a stone church. Second Tuesday in August, Miss Dietz had said. All you can eat for three bucks.

"I ate too much last year," Ash said.

Jennifer drew herself up and scrunched her face so he knew she was imitating someone, he had no idea who, probably someone associated with Pancake Tuesday, the two-hour holiday Smith Falls took each year to honor founder Charlie Smith. She said in the sonorous voice of an old man, "Pancakes for the Lord, folks. Pancakes for the Lord. And prizes for the congregation!"

"Don't you ever sleep?" Ash asked her, smiling.

"Does that mean you'll take two?" she said. She wore baggy white shorts that showed terrific legs, a body-tight T-shirt that said RAY●BAN with a surfer on it, and tiny tennis sneakers with rolled athletic socks.

"Okay, but I want to win the Ford, not the busted space heater," Ash said. Jennifer roared and said, "You remember that? That was a riot!" What he remembered was a report Dietz had read them in class about a prize blowing up in someone's house. Jennifer said, "You were there? I was there. I don't remember you there." Jennifer looked down at an imaginary roll of raffle tickets. "You won!" she said.

She bent out of view in the doorway and Ash guessed what was coming and grew angry. She straightened, cradling a cardboard box against her chest. "I know it's early for this," she said more seriously, "but I was worried about you. I went to the shelter just to look, not to take one. But they were going to gas him today."

The kitten was already in midair. It landed on his shirt and hung on and started biting one of his buttons. She said, "I asked for the meanest, angriest guy they had. One nobody else wanted."

Ash detached the mewing, struggling ball of rage from his shirt. It was a tiny black Angora with a white tip on its nose. He felt the heart hammering against his fingers. Ash thought, how come she knew I was home?

"Hey, Quincy," Jennifer said to the cat, scratching its head with her index finger, "this is the guy I told you about. He hates helpless creatures. He'll probably throw you in the bathtub when I leave."

"Quincy?"

"Tyler was a president. So I figured Quincy," she said.

"Quincy who?"

"John Quincy Adams! From Massachusetts! Let's not forget our roots!"

"Oh, that place," Ash said. He put the cat down. It leaped on his cuff, biting. He and Jennifer burst out laughing. Then they were quiet.

"I guess I'll go," she said. "Whoever I talked to at the *Post* said you'd checked in from here. I figured I'd take a chance and catch you."

Ash had called the office, about thirty minutes ago. He felt a little better. He was touched by the gift. The little animal was one of the most thoughtful presents anyone had ever given him. The kitten jumped on the couch and closed its eyes. Ash said, lying, "I'm going to California for a couple of days. Maybe you can watch him." From where they stood in the living room he saw Tyler's food and water dishes against a wall in the kitchen. He hadn't moved them and he didn't want to now. It was too soon. Jennifer followed his gaze and said, "Oh, no, you're not sticking Quincy with those things. A new cat gets a new dish. I've got one in the car."

"Thanks."

Jennifer shrugged. "You won the raffle. You got the prize." Then she looked a little uncomfortable, which made her nose

turn up a little, and a thin inverted V ran across her forehead.
"Did you think about what that detective said?"

"What detective?" Ash said innocently. He checked his
watch.

"I can take a hint," she said. Jennifer reached for the cat.
"But I'm not keeping him one day longer than you're away."
Quincy attacked her fingers.

"Clown," she said to Ash.

Dear Jennifer, thanks for sending the tapes of your show.
Everybody loved them. You were always fascinated by this
love stuff when you were a girl, all your questions used to
drive me and Mom crazy. Why did Uncle Frank leave
Cora if he loved her? Why do people fight if they're in
love? Who ever would have thought you'd make a business out of it. Make money out of it. Mom would have
been proud.

I wish you'd come home though. You always come
home when you're upset about something, and you always come in August, and here both are going on and you
stay there. Honey, I'm sorry about what happened with
Rick. People go their own ways sometimes. What the hell
do I know, blabbing. But I do know you're happiest when
you're hiking in the hills around here, and drinking Cokes
at the diner, and playing with the dogs. So why deny
yourself when you need it? There's no special reason to be
in Washington during vacation, is there? I got my selfish
reasons for wanting you here. Gus is knocking at the door.
He hurt his wrist and can't bowl tonight so he's driving.
Love, Dad.

Ash laid the stolen letter on his seat tray beside his half-empty
plastic glass of Coke. He folded the paper in threes and tore it
into small, long strips, feeling the gash of the paper beneath his
fingers. He stuffed the pieces in the airsick bag. Nobody sat
beside him on the plane. He pushed his seat back and looked out
the window. Who was Rick? Why was she upset? He felt dirty

reading her private mail, but this was a question of survival, not etiquette. The letter looked real, but he wished he had taken more of them. Everything about Jennifer Knowles unsettled him.

"We'll be starting our descent into Burlington airport in ten minutes," the pilot said. "The crew will be passing through the aisles, collecting trash." Below, Ash glimpsed the dark green Berkshire Hills becoming higher, older Vermont mountains. In blue gaps between fluffy white clouds, he saw cars, dots taking tourists to Canada, the Finger Lakes, the hiking trails of the Green Mountains, or home.

There's no special reason for you to be in Washington in August, is there? Jennifer's father had written.

But then Ash put the letter from his mind because they were landing, and in the airport he rented a Prizm. An hour later Ash drove into Middlebury, Vermont. The windows were open and it was so cool Ash had a sweater on. The town was beautiful, long winding main street, church spires under blue sky, a big inn with a long terrace by the traffic circle, prosperous-looking small shops with students going in and out. Newer cars with Middlebury College stickers in diagonal parking spaces.

He was breaking every rule, every order he'd been given over the last twenty years. Ash got directions to the campus at an Exxon station. The student union was open but practically deserted in August. He found a closed information booth, but there was a student/faculty directory chained to a wooden counter.

Ash was so excited he had to force himself to continue. He didn't want to be disappointed, didn't want to find nothing. He watched his finger run down columns of faculty names. Be here, he willed. He tried the math department. He didn't know what last name Lewis and Glorie used here, so he checked the whole department, looking for anyone named Gloria.

Nothing.

Talking Heads music blared from a loudspeaker. A couple kissed passionately on a couch in the hall. Ash flipped to the chemistry department. Almost immediately his heart started beating fast. Gloria Alvarez was the first name on the list. An assistant professor. Ash's excitement cooled. Glorie was too smart and had been here too long to be an assistant anything. Plus Alvarez was a Spanish-sounding name and David shied away from names implying ethnic origins. They invited curiosity. Ash would check Gloria Alvarez, but he had a feeling she wouldn't be whom he hoped.

Even if Glorie had moved after Lewis's death, she might have left a forwarding address. "Always be normal," Yuri had said.

Ash tried the physics department.

There it was.

Professor Glorie Winter.

Winter, Ash thought. Lewis Winter and Glorie Winter. The Winter residence. Hello, Professor Winter.

Ash laughed out loud. He said it. "Winter."

He copied the home number and office number and rural route 125 by Glorie's name. How many Glorie's, spelled "ie," could there be? Outside, on the quad, he asked a couple of girls lying on the grass if they knew where 125 was. They didn't. He tried a distinguished-looking man in a tweed jacket and maroon tie, walking with a cane. The man cupped his hand by his ear and asked Ash to repeat the question. Then he said, in a loud, quavery voice that carried and caused students on the grass to glance at them, "That's . . . by . . . the . . . Bread Loaf . . . campus. Go down seven and you'll see the sign."

Ash drove fast, out of Middlebury on the two-lane blacktop. He passed a commercial strip of supermarkets and scattered restaurants outside the town. At 125 he turned left and the road narrowed to bring him past two-story white clapboard houses, across a stone bridge, and up a zigzaggy route through mountainous state forest. Ash passed rocky icy streams plunging down on the right, a wall of Vermont pines blanketing the cliffs to his left. He passed through the pinpoint town of Ripton, just a general store, and the road flattened at a mountain meadow and sign saying ROBERT FROST HOUSE and then CAUTION—STUDENTS AHEAD.

SNOW BOWL—FIVE MILES.

Snow Bowl. Poor Lewis was in Ash's head again, propped on one arm against David's bar/table, mixing a little tonic into his lots of gin, squeezing the lime on the tablecloth instead of into the glass by accident, saying, ". . . from the college to the Snow Bowl . . . from the Snow Bowl to Mr. Ups . . ."

The mailboxes were spaced miles apart on the road. Sometimes he could see the houses they belonged to, set back in the sun. Other times there was just a long driveway through trees, or past rock walls. He saw DOWNEY.

He passed a mailbox by a dirt driveway that said LEECH and three more, all for "Rod." SIDNEY ROD. IRVING ROD. MELISSA ROD. He passed what had to be the Bread Loaf campus, whatever that was, well-kept three-story bungalow-style buildings near an inn, with lots of people walking with books in their arms as a bell clanged nearby.

KRAMER.

LEFKOWITZ.

WINTER.

Ash pulled the Prizm to the side of the road. There was a sense of culmination, of crescendo, in his head. The house was not visible from the highway, just a lovely looking dirt driveway disappearing beyond a stone wall and beneath arched willows planted as far along its length as he could see. He heard a stream bubbling over the idling of the engine. No other traffic was on the road. He didn't even know if Glorie would be here, if she would have children, be married, even talk to him.

But now Ash was turning the car onto the long, beautiful driveway. And now he stepped down on the accelerator and the car slid down the lane. Dust obscured his vision in the rearview mirror. The drive paralleled another rock wall for fifty yards, turned right, and spilled him onto a lawn where he saw the white Cape Cod–style house ahead, one and a half stories high, well kept with gables, a widow's walk, and a long porch with a double swing near the door. There was a maroon Subaru wagon parked on the grass where the lawn seemed worn. And a woman in a wide-brimmed straw hat was crouching in a flower bed beneath the porch, now straightening, wiping her hair, shielding her brow with one hand while holding a gardening spade in gloves.

She took off the hat.

Ash stepped out of the car. He stood by the door. They were twenty yards apart.

The woman's mouth opened.

"Oh, my god," she gasped.

How would he get her to believe him? And believe what, with no evidence? A feeling? A claim? Some sentences from a person she'd not talked to in eight years? Accusations going against everything she had accepted since she was a girl? Suddenly his whole task here seemed impossible.

Ash could scarcely hear his own voice over the thundering in his head: "Want to buy a raffle for Pancake Tuesday?" he said.

She had no children, had not remarried, so at least there were no interruptions. Ash poured them both another glass of her iced tea. He'd followed her inside when she got the pitcher, to make sure she didn't use the phone. He couldn't believe he'd really found her, couldn't believe he was really here. They sat on white wicker chairs on the porch. It was cool and blue jays flew to a bird feeder in the garden. Her little spade and hat lay on a round wicker table near the swing. The sun made halos around bees zipping in the air.

"I don't know how to say this without starting from scratch," Ash had begun, looking into her gray, terrified face, calming her down, convincing her he was alone, and nobody knew he was here. That nothing had happened to David. Praying he'd be able to convince her. Then he'd poured it out, the only way he knew it might make sense. The way it had happened to him, in pieces. The way the slow realizations had come to him. The way David had sent Minsky to his apartment. Whatever she decided, Ash felt relieved saying it.

From the garden they probably looked like a couple of old pals having a cold drink together, but up close her eyes quivered, locked on his face. Ash remembered all that had been necessary before he had accepted that David had turned against the group. And now if he failed with her, David would know within minutes, and his mission would be over before it began. But despite that, he felt alive and real. It was the same feeling he had experienced talking to Corinna. That she knew him. That everything else was false.

"They tried to kill you," she said, flat voiced, as if David, even after murdering her husband, could not do such a thing. He'd rarely talked to her in Smith Falls. Not out of animosity but because of different interests. She'd been more bookish, more introverted.

"It was Danny Minsky."

"Just because you asked a question," she said.

"I know it sounds crazy," he said. "I didn't believe it myself until after I went to David's house. I don't expect you to accept it blindly. In fact, what I'm saying isn't going to make sense to you unless you've had doubts yourself. But if you've been wondering the same things . . . if your work's been odd . . ." Ash fumbled for how to say it. "I thought if we get together, all of us, maybe we can figure it out."

Ash said, "You can call David when I leave. That's your choice." As if she needed his reminder to know it. He didn't say, "If you do, they'll kill me." But they both thought it.

Glorie slumped in the wicker chair, brushed her hand across her cheek. A whole range of emotions flickered across her face while he talked. Doubt. Fear. Thoughtfulness.

"Danny used to kill animals," she said.

"He was in my house," Ash said.

She surprised him. "Remember when we used to call you Moon Boy?" she said softly, fingering her glass. She had long fingers with nails painted red, dry skin with pallid color, despite her hours in the sun. Ash noted the muscles on her wrists and long neck. She kept in shape, too.

"Yeh," he sighed, remembering all right.

"But you were right about that bomb. I'll never forget it. We were laughing at you, thinking that was the stupidest question we ever heard." She seemed to be talking to herself. She had a faraway, unfocused look. " 'Why not put a camera in a bomb?' I couldn't breathe I was laughing so hard. I thought I would lose control of myself. And then last summer before Iraq I was working on theories for those bombs, guided bombs, bombs with televisions in them. And I thought of you, Jim. I really did. I wanted to find you and say sorry to you. It's funny how a scene can seem so clear to you after so many years. I remembered you walking out of that classroom. Head high." She shook her head. "You had guts. And you were right. Is it silly to say sorry now?"

"No," Ash said, feeling emotion well in him.

"Well," she said, smiling a little, "sorry."

"Does that mean you believe me?" Ash said.

"Your story today is the nuttiest thing I've heard since then. The only problem is, I've been getting odd assignments, too."

Ash, lifting his glass, stopped.

She said, looking away from him, looking at the bees, the tea, the sky, anything but him, "They killed Lewis a few years ago. Ran him over and made it look like an accident. He was getting afraid, losing control."

"I know they did," Ash said.

She said, as if he had not spoken, and she were talking to herself, "You know a person who has a talent. He sees things before other people. The first few times he does it you laugh, but his predictions come true. After a while he still doesn't make sense when he tells you things, but you remember the times he turned out to be right. Years go by and he shows up and tells you the craziest story of the lot. I'm talking about you."

She stared deeply into his face. "You hear what I'm saying," she said fiercely. "You remember the times he was right."

Ash knew when to keep quiet.

After a moment she said, "It was always—what they wanted from me—about defense. The college has a contract with Lewis's old company. For years I did research and passed it on. But for the last six months they haven't wanted to know anything about research. They've wanted to know about an exchange student from Senegal. A freshman rich kid; his father owns cocoa plantations. Kid's wild. Cocaine, everything. But Senegal? And the worst part is, at the same time the department's making real breakthroughs in laser guidance systems.

There's nothing like it in Russia. So why do I have to concentrate on the kid?"

"Senegal," Ash said. "Maybe Senegal is one of David's clients."

"You took a big chance coming here," she said.

Ash exhaled. "I figure whatever is going on has something to do with what's going on at home. But if he's gone private, if he's just selling information now, how could Moscow let him do it?"

"Oh, I know that," she said.

Amazed, he stared at her, didn't even follow when she said, "Wait," and walked into the house, returning a few minutes later with a *Time* magazine she tossed on the wicker table. It was folded open to a page where the headline said, "KGB Future in Doubt." "Read it," she said. The first paragraph said, "What will happen to the feared KGB in the wake of changes in the Soviet government? No one knows, especially in light of recent revelations that top KGB officials amassed millions in secret Swiss bank accounts, diverted KGB funds for dachas, private cars, and luxury goods, and even used agency operatives for private gain."

"Don't you see?" she said. "You keep wondering how David could hide it from Moscow if he was working for private clients. But what if it's his boss in Moscow who's ordering him to do it?"

As soon as she said it, it felt right. Ash thought about it. But then he shook his head. "It's almost right, but there's one thing that doesn't fit. If David's still working for Moscow, he's covered. He's not doing anything wrong. He's just following orders, and there's no reason for him to come after me once he's convinced I'm loyal to the group." Ash shook his head. "I don't think he's following orders. That's what I think he's nervous about. That's what I think he's afraid I'm going to find out."

"But it's impossible for him to go off on his own," she said. "They're monitoring him from home."

Ash shrugged. "Let's face it. We don't know who he deals with. We don't know what's happened back home. We have no idea what's possible or not."

Ash shrugged and blew out air. "We have to find the others," he said. "And piece it together. You must know how to contact at least one. I think there are thirteen of us left. David slipped that much out. Maybe if we put together our assignments we'll have the answer."

Ash watched her face close in on itself as he reached the crux of his plea. This was what the whole trip had boiled down to. The bottom line. Asking her to go against all their training. He was sweating despite the cool air. "Remember when David told us we couldn't depend on anyone else, except ourselves?" he said. But this was the place where logic flew out the window and loyalty remained. Suddenly he knew Glorie wouldn't tell him more. Then she said, "How did you find me?"

"Lewis told me enough to track you down."

"Lewis," she said, leaning back, her lips in a tight line. "Lewis was a good scientist, but he never should have been allowed to come here. Did you know Lewis and I were lovers in Smith Falls?" She smiled at Ash's surprise. "We were in love even then, but one of Yuri's assignments was to see if we could hide it from everyone else. Lewis had a hard time even with that. I begged Yuri not to send him here when we graduated. I told Yuri Lewis wasn't strong enough. You know what Yuri said? He said, 'Glorie, you make him strong. Read to him and make love to him and help him perform.' Yuri said, 'I can't waste Lewis's talent.' "

Glorie looked up from the floor. "You really think we're all in danger?"

He nodded. Then her lips pressed down tighter, and when she looked up, Ash saw anger. She said, so softly that Ash had to strain to hear, "They didn't have to kill Lewis. He never did anything bad to them. They could have taken him home." She wiped away a tear. Suddenly she looked angry. Glorie said, "Frances Rice. She's in Boston. A vice president at Ritchie Chemicals. She was the third in our group."

He was dizzy with relief. Ash had a flash of Frances Rice, a chubby girl with braces, in a white blouse and floral scarf, playing the violin in high school. A girl with racks of test tubes and chemistry books filling the dormitory room the other girls refused to share with her. A fat, perfume-doused matron in a sack dress at David's party eight years ago, eating a third piece of strawberry shortcake.

Ash knew Ritchie Chemicals. "Ritchie's into everything," he said. "Oil-eating bugs. Chemical weapons overseas. Breakthroughs in synthetics. There's plenty to be passed along."

"Formulas," Glorie said.

"What's the best way to get her to listen to us?" Ash said.

Glorie paced on the porch. Dusk was falling and the sun had sunk half above the trees across the clearing, shining directly into their faces. Ash didn't feel alone anymore. They were moving now. That's three, he thought. We'll find the others.

"I don't know," she said. "I have to think about it. We meet once in a while just to have someone to talk to, but bringing you along . . ." She laughed. "You'll sleep here tonight. You like summer squash?"

She took the spade and said as they walked into the garden, "I could call her and tell her to meet me. I could do that. You could come."

The sun cast shadows on the vegetables against the side of the house. "Grab some tomatoes." She pointed to fresh ones on a vine. Ash bent over. Her shadow behind him stayed straight, moved closer. She said, "But she'll be wary."

Ash plucked a beefsteak tomato off a vine. Her shadow was closer now. She said, "Or I could tell her . . . ," but the shadow hand came up quickly. Ash registered the spade shadow plunging at his back. He threw himself sideways, but felt a punch and tearing in his shoulder, a hot, slicing pain, and he hit the ground, rolling. The pain exploded.

She rushed at him. Ash kicked out. Glorie toppled sideways on the grass. "Traitor," she hissed. She gripped the blade.

On all fours they faced each other. Her face had gone white in a rictus of hate. She said, "They said you might come. I didn't even believe it."

"You *knew* I was coming?"

They stood up. A wave of dizziness made Ash sway. He felt

sick. They all were actors, all of them, and he could never believe anything that any one of them did. His vision clouded and she seemed to know it, coming at him in a blur. He reached up, felt her wrist, twisting it inward and down, but her right knee slammed into his groin. He doubled in agony but held on. The pain in his testicles exploded into his stomach. He wouldn't let go. He saw the blade on the grass. She must have dropped it. The sun seemed to expand on his head.

"No, I . . ."

The side of his shirt felt sticky and he had trouble balling his fist on the injured side. She would be able to kill with her feet or hands. A twig. A pitcher. A stone.

Ash roared, dropped his good shoulder, and rammed full strength into her chest. There was a crunching sound. She gasped and flew back. She groped in a dress pocket and he leaped on her, pulled her fist free, straddled her. She clawed at him, his chest, his wounded shoulder. She dug her nails into his shoulder. Ash screamed. He groped into the pocket, pulled out a switchblade.

Ash put the knife to her throat.

"You always were a freak," she gasped. "You never belonged. How much is the FBI paying you? Kill me," she said. "I'm not going to prison. But one of us will get you."

Ash looked down at the twisted, hating face. The eyes impaling him. His throat burned. "David's lying," he said.

"Who do you think I'm going to believe, you or him?" She spit at him and missed. He said, "None of us works at Ritchie Chemicals, do they?" She tried to kick him. Blood bubbled from her mouth. Smeared her lips.

"You're hurt," he said.

"You don't have the guts to kill me," she said. She coughed. "I used to be faster," she said. She gagged, choking. Ash couldn't tell what was an act and what wasn't anymore. But he scrambled to his feet, let her up so she could breathe.

Glorie Pell stood, swaying. She clutched at her throat, rammed her finger down her throat. She hooked a gob of red from her mouth, dripped it on the lawn.

"You better get to a doctor," Ash said. "I won't stop you."

"You were always a freak," she said. "If it weren't for your father, you would have been kicked out at the beginning. You never belonged. You were never one of us. We laughed at you all the time, you hear me? I don't care who your father is."

"My father?" The blood was pounding in Ash's head. A wave of dizziness swept over him. "What do you mean, my father? You know who my father is?"

She choked, stuck her finger in her mouth again, gagged, doubled over. But when she straightened, she gave a derisive leer. "You don't even know, do you?" she said. "You, and you were always guessing things about everybody else, and you didn't know." She laughed, but started choking. When she stopped, tears were streaming from her eyes.

"Come on, think," she said. "You should have been in a carnival with your guessing acts. Who was too nice to you all the time? Who always singled you out to spend time with? Who went to bat for you when DuChamp gave you things too hard for you to do?"

Ash suddenly understood. He couldn't breathe. "Yuri is my father?"

"Congratulations."

"But how do you know?"

"We all knew. Everyone knew. That's the only reason they kept you in the program. Why do you think he tried to give you Corinna? You were his favorite, that's why. He liked you best."

She started coughing again. This time it was harder for her to stop. She was gasping and Ash said, "Let me take you to a doctor."

"Get away from me," she said.

In an agony of aloneness he said, "But they killed Lewis. You loved Lewis."

She coughed but stood proudly. Blood dribbled from the corner of her mouth. He had hurt her worse than he'd imagined. "You don't understand anything," she said. "I killed my husband. I told David he was getting weak and then I killed him. You think I'm going to listen to you?"

*   *   *

Ash stood on Sixteenth Street, gazing at the Russian embassy across the street. The heat wave had worsened the short time he'd been away. In Washington the air was thick; buildings two blocks away were partly obscured by haze. Workmen tore up the street with jackhammers and the sidewalk vibrated. Ash crossed the street through stalled traffic, toward the embassy.

"If something ever happens to David, if they're closing in on you, if there's absolutely no other way, if the alternative is capture, go to the embassy," Yuri's voice, his father's voice, said in his head. "But once you go there, you can never work in the States again. Use the word *teenager*. Tell them you are in the teenager group. That will get the word to me, and I can get you out. You will be in trouble if you don't have a good reason. The FBI photographs everyone going in there. Everyone coming out."

But there was nowhere else to go. No place at all. Driving away from Glorie's, in a pained, dazed fog, he could only think, Yuri? Yuri is my father? And the images had poured in then. Yuri and Ash in DuChamp's office in school, Yuri saying, "Go easy on the kid." Yuri and Ash fishing on a Sunday, Yuri having gotten permission to take Ash from the compound. Yuri saying, "You hate me, don't you? Go ahead, get it out." Not like a scientist.

Like a guilty father.

Why didn't he tell me?

Ash couldn't believe it. Ash didn't know what to believe. But he couldn't go to the others now, after David had alerted them. He couldn't go back to David. He couldn't go to Corinna. He'd never go to Detective Allegretti.

What he had wanted to do, before Glorie had told him about his father, was just leave, lose himself, drive into America and make a new life. Or try to. But now he wanted to find Yuri.

My father.

He was doing it for Yuri, he told himself, walking across the street. Doing it for his father, he told himself, coming up to the iron gate, aware of the closed-circuit camera focused down on him from above. Feeling, as a physical presence on his back, cameras trained on him from windows across the street. Knowing he could never go back to his apartment after this, or the *Post* or Corinna or anything he had known. Knowing that even coming here was a double-edged risk, because if whatever David was doing was being controlled from this building, he'd never get out alive.

My father.

He'd not even returned to Washington by plane because David would be watching the airport. He'd taken a train to New Carrollton, north of the city, and transferred to a cab that had brought him here. His shoulder throbbed under the bandage the emergency-room crew had fitted him with at Middlebury Hospital. "I fell on a garden spade. Pretty stupid, huh?" he'd told the nurse.

A young, blond man lounged by the iron gate and Ash told him he wanted to talk to someone in the embassy.

"Who?" the man said.

"I don't know who," Ash said, opening his wallet, showing his *Post* ID. He just wanted to be inside, away from the cameras. In the shadows inside. In Russia. Home.

"Call for an appointment with the press attaché," the blond man said, handing back Ash's wallet. "But it's hard to see him with the trade minister coming to town. Maybe in a week or two, when the visit is over. But call."

"I have to get in now," Ash said.

The man shrugged.

Ash controlled himself and didn't grip the bars. But he whispered fiercely, "Listen to me. I work for you. Don't turn me away or you'll be in trouble. Let me in."

The man frowned and stared into Ash's face. He said, "Wait a minute," and disappeared up the white marble steps through the double doors of the building. He returned a minute later and unlocked the gate. He said, "Let me have that press pass again."

Ash heard the voice through the thunder of his own heartbeat. The doors were coming closer now; he felt a blast of air-conditioning sweep out into his face from inside. He flashed to Glorie Pell lurching to her car in his rearview mirror, clutching her chest. He hoped she'd made it to town all right. The man beside him guided him into a cool marble hallway beneath a huge oil of First Secretary Gorbachev. The building was big and empty inside, and the blond man said, "Wait here." Ash took a seat by the portrait and beneath a hall chandelier. Ahead, the marble hallway stretched into cool, dark recesses of the embassy. There were some antique tables with marble fawn statuettes, a carpeted stairway going up with a gold-leaf-covered banister. There was a big mirror in the hall and Ash figured he was being observed from behind it. A radio played light Chopin in the recesses of the building. Ash sat on the seat and heard a clock ticking. Ash glanced beyond the bright glass doorway to regular Washington traffic fifty yards away beyond the now locked steel gate.

Ash looked up at the portrait of his prime minister. His leader. His First Secretary. It did nothing for him. The building was totally strange, cold and far away. Ash steeled himself for whatever was about to happen. Wherever he'd reached, he told himself, he had finally come home.

NINE

MAJOR GREGOR VOLSKY, Afghan war hero, family man, world-class kayaker, ex-assassin, and Soviet assistant commercial attaché to the United States, sat in his embassy office at lunchtime munching one of his wife's homemade chicken burritos and finalizing security arrangements for the trade minister's upcoming visit. During his daily thirty-minute break the KGB officer ordered "no interruptions even if Lenin himself appears from the dead." Volsky's best ideas came during quiet.

"The minister's visit will highlight a crucial campaign to get loans from the U.S.," the coded cable from Moscow had read. With the economy in shambles, the wheat crop failing, bread lines growing, and even rumors of a coup in the air, nothing must go wrong with the minister's mission.

"Stop all espionage activity until the loan comes through," Volsky's superior, Col. Sergei Akromeyev, had snapped. "Shut it down, everything, especially that Montana plumber. Any scandal during the visit and you and I are finished." Akromeyev was unhappy with the liberal direction politics was taking at home.

Akromeyev had run the KGB in the United States for fifteen years. In public, when Americans were around, he was a dour, quiet background presence in the assistant ambassador's entourage. In private he had a much more violent personality. He was an ex-interrogator and archconservative whose appointment had appeased Kremlin hard-liners during the Brezhnev years, and he'd been kept on as a bone to the right wing under Gorbachev.

"Begging, that's what he'll be doing," Akromeyev had snorted. "Who ever dreamed we'd slink to Washington for money. Even reformers like you never thought it could sink to this, did you, Volsky?"

It was a polite gibe because Akromeyev respected Volsky's war record. Volsky had shrugged. "No, but even Lenin said Americans would sell us rope to hang themselves, so what's so bad about a loan? Besides, countries default on loans to them all the time. They never do anything about it."

Volsky was worried that without the loan the Soviet Union might explode this winter. Now he had shut down operations. The Silicon Valley vice president passing along designs of computer chips for cash. The Pentagon ensign selling Navy codes for call girls. The Montana plumber who had a contract to service toilets in the Minuteman missile silos and who brought along a tiny camera during trips. All were dormant, at least for two weeks.

"Gorbachev is selling out the country," Akromeyev had said. But even in these more permissive days the colonel knew how far he could go. He didn't add the phrase he usually applied to people he disliked: "He deserves a bullet."

"The generals who lost Nicaragua deserve a bullet!"

"The new leaders of Eastern Europe should get a bullet!"

"Don't release dissidents from prison. The bullet!"

Volsky finished the last delicious bite of burrito, closed the report, and ignored his intercom as it began beeping. He'd have to explain his lunchtime procedure to his new secretary for the fourth time. But it was a small matter to tune out noise. He'd ignored worse when he'd been captured in Afghanistan.

Volsky sipped iced tea and let his mind rove and it settled on Akromeyev. Something was wrong with the colonel recently. He was more touchy than usual. He spent too much time in the cable room. He locked himself up in his office for hours. His tirades against Gorbachev were growing more vehement. "Look at this, Gregor!" he'd ranted at the seven A.M. meeting today, waving dispatches. "MG's breaking up the country! A union

treaty? *A treaty with parts of your own country!* Two weeks from
now it will be the end of the country! CIA pacification!"

The buzzer screamed. Pacification to Akromeyev meant dis-
mantling the military. Akromeyev had paced back and forth in
his big office upstairs, from the Lenin bust to the French windows, from the Ivan the Terrible tapestry to the three TV screens
built into the mahogany-paneled walls. Up to now Volsky and
Akromeyev's differing political views had not affected how well
they worked together.

"He's taking the Party people out of KGB units! He's cutting
security budgets!" Akromeyev had cried, waving a *Time* magazine picture of the hammer and sickle on a Moscow bus stop
defaced by vandals' yellow paint. "Ten years ago this never
would be tolerated! And Western reporters wouldn't be allowed
to take pictures of it! You reformers will be sorry, Gregor!"

The buzzer screamed. Today, as usual, Volsky wore a double-
breasted Saville Row gray suit, not caring if it was in style or not,
a pearl-colored shirt and tie pin from his old unit. He reached
into the sack lunch he'd brought from home, unwrapped a Devil
Dog, and chewed slowly. The dough got stuck in his dentures.
His teeth had been knocked out or broken in Afghanistan. The
guerrillas had done a lot of damage. At thirty-four, Volsky wore
a patch over the empty socket where they'd gouged out his left
eye trying to get information. At least they hadn't played horse
polo with him as the ball, like they had with other prisoners.
Volsky shuddered when he remembered the live bodies torn
apart. Now women at parties told him he reminded them of the
Van Heusen model in shirt advertisements. They found the
patch sexy, but Volsky was in love with his wife. And he valued
loyalty.

In fact, on the right side of his office wall, opposite his
kayaking photos, he'd mounted color shots he'd taken from the
Nuristan area of Afghanistan, where he had been part of the
Soviet "pacification program." In that case, pacification had
meant assassination. Dirt on his face, alone at night, Volsky had
prowled the rocky passes and icy streams and gorges in the dark,
acting on informer intelligence, creeping into villages, slipping

into huts and past guards, slitting the throats of leaders of the guerrillas. He had killed two men responsible for supply caravans reaching the enemy. Had blown up an ammunition dump hours before a guerrilla attack was scheduled on a Soviet air base. But they'd caught him when a faulty timing device set off the blast too soon.

"When you were tortured, you revealed nothing. You escaped and led five comrades to safety," Premier Brezhnev himself had read, awarding Volsky the Lenin Star, the Soviet Union's highest medal, in the hospital. After the Tass photographer had left, the premier had asked, clearly hungering for a positive response, "When do you think we will win this war, Lieutenant?"

"I think we will lose and never should have gone there in the first place."

Brezhnev's advisers had gone pale, but the premier had just pulled his chair closer, looked thoughtful, and said, "Why?"

"Because they hate us and we don't care about winning as much as they do."

Brezhnev waved away the advisers. "You're brave in more ways than one," he'd finally said. "What do you want to do now, after the army?"

"I'd like to work for the KGB."

Brezhnev had looked surprised. "Why?"

"Because our own men are afraid of them," Volsky said, too tired to care about being polite or frightened. "Because you must have had bad intelligence to go in there in the first place. And because my friends, good Russians, are dead because of it. I want to work in intelligence to make sure it never happens again."

"All right," the Premier had said. "We'll start you out at home and see how you do. Now get some sleep."

Three years later Brezhnev was dead, and so was Yuri Andropov, the next premier, and it was Vladimir Kryuchkov, Mikhail Gorbachev's new head of the KGB, who promoted Volsky to major and assigned him to Washington after Volsky broke the Petrov spy ring. Alexander Petrov was a Kiev engineer altering a night-flying problem on the Hind attack helicopter and passing the information to the Americans. Volsky had no qualms about dealing with traitors. After questioning Petrov, he'd pushed the man out of a window. Under an unwritten code, counterintelligence people rarely killed foreign agents on their own soil. That could start a bloodbath of vengeance that would be unproductive to both sides, since many spies were diplomats, and diplomats made the rules. Capture, imprisonment, torture, exposure, were acceptable. But not execution except in cases where you killed your own people. Cleaning up your own problems was "allowed" if you did it quietly.

The intercom buzzed. Volsky glanced at his watch. The thirty minutes were up. He punched the black plastic button. "What did I tell you about my lunchtime?" he said wearily.

Instantly the door opened and Marta Yavlinsky, Akromeyev's latest lover and Volsky's secretary, rushed in. Today she wore an ankle-length skirt of drab green, a brownish sweater, below stringy dark hair, that revealed the shape of her breasts by inference only, since they didn't seem to be there at all, and a necklace of expensive pearls that had to be Akromeyev's contribution to the day's wardrobe. Akromeyev despised smart women. Volsky simply wasn't attracted to thin ones.

"Comrade Major, someone is here to see you!"

"Who?" Volsky asked.

"A *Washington Post* reporter! He wants to talk to you!"

"I don't have any interview with a *Washington Post* reporter," Volsky said, annoyed.

"It's not for an interview. He says he has to talk with you."

Volsky was intrigued. "He asked for me by name?"

"Not by name, comrade Major," Marta said as if it were Volsky, not she, who was unclear. "He says he wants to talk to the head of the KGB. He says it is important and he can only tell the head. The press attaché is not here. Serge . . . uh . . . Comrade Akromeyev says you should talk to him."

"Very well. Send him up." Volsky sighed, pressing the hidden button to activate the tape recorder in his desk. He put the security report in a drawer. Something must be up if Akromeyev was actually steering the man this far. A big, blond man whose face resembled Baryshnikov's walked resolutely into the room, looked around, and sat, at a gesture from Volsky, in the stuffed armchair facing Volsky's long birch desk. A flicker of pain crossed the man's features when his upper back touched the chair. Injury, Volsky figured. Volsky asked to see the man's *Post* pass and was disturbed when he recognized the name, James Ash. Volsky suppressed a frown. Ash was an investigative reporter. All Volsky needed with the trade minister coming was an investigation.

Volsky smiled like a bored bureaucrat interrupted on his lunch break. The Devil Dogs wrapper still lay on his desk. He'd only been in his post three years, and the one other time an American had wandered in off the street asking to talk to "someone from the KGB," the man had turned out to be an itinerant Boston painter who said he wanted to "help start a revolution." Volsky had sent him away.

Now Volsky said, as if amused by the visitor's request, "So! You are looking for the KGB." Akromeyev would be listening upstairs from any one of a dozen microphones planted in Volsky's office. Volsky hoped this wasn't going to be about one of their operations. "I'm sorry there isn't anyone from the KGB here. Actually, this is a misconception many Americans have, that we have 'spies' in the embassy. I'm the assistant commercial attaché. Perhaps I can help you."

"No, it's got to be KGB," Ash said.

Volsky had a good, fun-loving laugh. "Pretend I'm the KGB, just tell me."

Volsky looked into the angry, resolute face of the big blond man in a seersucker suit, who said he wanted to talk to the KGB. "What you're saying is you are KGB," Ash said.

"No, I'm—"

"Look," Ash said, leaning forward. "I'm not here to play games. I'm sick of these fucking games. If you're really KGB, who is Carl Donaldson?"

Volsky was shocked. Carl Donaldson was a top aide to the head of the Senate Banking Committee and a compulsive gambler over $200,000 in debt at the moment from monthly jaunts to Caesars Palace in Atlantic City. Volsky had never known how the KGB had first been tipped three years ago that Donaldson owed so much money. But in exchange for cash, the man was coming on line; he was still handing over innocuous information, public record. In a few weeks Volsky would ask Donaldson for something a little more classified. By then there would be photographs of their meetings, and Volsky hoped Donaldson would be dependent on the payments.

Except how did this stranger in front of him know about Donaldson?

"I'm waiting?" Ash demanded. "If you don't know, I want to talk to someone who does."

"What did you say the name was?"

"I know who Donaldson is," Ash said, his eyes blazing. "If you want me to tell you what I know, prove you're who you say you are."

"He likes to . . . play dice," Volsky said.

"Erma Benziger."

Volsky leaned back and looked bored and tried to hide the fantastic shock jolting through him. Ash stared straight into his eyes, like he could read what was inside him. As if he knew. Just a man walking in off the street reciting the best-kept secrets in the embassy. Secrets even most of the KGB men here didn't know. Akromeyev would be shitting in his pants upstairs. Ash was acting exactly as he would if he really were a Soviet agent. He was also acting like he might if he were trying to confirm a story for the *Washington Post*.

"She has a big appetite," Volsky said.

That would be enough information and still be circumspect. Erma Benziger was a secretary to one of the joint chiefs of staff, an ugly, mousy woman who typed top-secret reports and went home to a studio apartment in McLean and ate TV dinners and watched taped soaps, except three years ago she had begun a love affair with an assistant attaché from the Polish embassy after she'd glimpsed the man in the halls of the Pentagon. She was insatiable in bed. She talked nonstop. And she talked about what she was typing.

Volsky thought, I always wondered how we found out she had a crush on him in the first place.

Volsky stared at the man in front of him.

Suddenly Volsky had a premonition there was going to be trouble. It's that Montana plumber, he thought. He drinks too much and he talked. I knew we should never have used that plumber. But then Ash said, "I'm going to tell you a story," and for the next forty minutes the most incredible tale Volsky had ever heard poured out. About children brought up in a group in Siberia. And someone named Uncle Yuri and an orphanage in Massachusetts and an ex–assistant secretary of state named Kislak. Volsky even knew Kislak. He'd met him at parties. He recalled, as Ash kept talking, a confident, typically naive American with a beautiful blonde named Corinna on his arm. An argument at the punch bowl at the Italian embassy, he couldn't even remember about what. Kislak striking him as one of those ex–fraternity stars who wedge their way into American politics on good looks and abound in Washington.

Kislak was a SPY? Kislak ran a Soviet network?

It couldn't be true. It was too ridiculous to be true. It sounded like a paranoid fantasy, except if Ash was really a *Post* reporter, anything he said had to be taken at least a little seriously. *A whole facsimile town* in Siberia? A ring of agents who had been operating for *seventeen years* and Volsky had never heard of them? Incredible.

"They told me to use the word *teenager*," Ash said. "That's our group. Teenager."

Volsky remained impassive. He nodded, listened, lifted his brows. He knew nothing about any "teenager." Ash launched into the part about the group trying to kill him. It was too much.

"Why are you telling me this?" Volsky finally said.

"I told you. I'm afraid the group is in trouble. David's doing something he shouldn't."

"And just for the sake of argument," Volsky said, "who are you to question your superiors?"

Ash shrugged. The answer was obvious if the story was true, which it couldn't be, except what if it was? Volsky said, "Would you like a glass of water?" and went to the sideboard to pour from a carafe. That gave him a minute to think. It also enabled him to press a hidden button that let people downstairs know that this particular visitor was to be followed when and if he left the building. Volsky's mind raced. What if the press pass was false? What if this was some weird FBI entrapment scheme with the trade minister coming? And Kislak or Ash weren't KGB at all? There were plenty of people in the U.S. government who wanted to see the minister's mission fail. It was much more likely for a U.S. journalist to be an intelligence operative for the United States than the other way around. Lots of them were, despite what the American public believed.

Or was this some kind of reporter's joke? "I Fooled the KGB!" A funny article?

Worst case . . . what if Ash really was a reporter and he'd had a tip and this little charade was designed to get information? What if Ash's credentials were false and he was a nut?

Volsky looked skeptical when he put the drinks on the desk. Ash gulped his right away. "Can I see that press pass again?" Volsky said.

The picture matched the face. And the photo people downstairs would already have snapped him from behind the mirror and would be combing their journalist files for a match. "And your other identification?"

The driver's license matched. So did the library card. Health insurance card. American Express and Visa cards. Sprint long-distance phone card. They all matched. The pictures or signatures were Ash. Or at least this man, who said he was Ash.

"You're acting like you don't know anything about this," the man calling himself Ash said.

Volsky sighed. "I told you, I'm just the assistant commercial attaché, although I have to say, this is better than going to the movies! What a story! Mr. Ash, why did you come here really? Are you going to write a funny story for the paper? What do you want me to do about this?"

"What do I want you to do?" Ash was angry again. "Some-one's fucking around with us, endangering us. I don't even think we're working for the government anymore. Someone's making a profit from us. But every time we get you something, pass on information, make a call, find a contact, we risk our lives, families, each other. Do you really have to ask me what I want? I want it to stop. I don't know what's happening to the KGB, maybe we're falling apart like the country at home. Maybe someone, David's control, I don't know who, has him doing these things. Maybe he's doing them on his own. But I want it to stop."

Ash stood up. "I want it to stop."

Ash put both his hands on the lip of the desk. Angry, he seemed bigger. He laughed, a raucous, furious bray. "I want to be left alone. I want them to stop coming after me. I want to keep the people I grew up with from landing up in jail because someone is trying to make money off them. If it were just me involved, I wouldn't even have come here. I don't want you shipping me back. I want to tell you something. I have proof. I wrote it down. Something happens to me and the FBI will get it. Proof. Okay? I want out. I want to be finished with you. And if it's David alone, I want you to do something about him. Is that so hard to figure out?"

Mildly, Volsky said, "No. Calm down, down. Just a few questions, please. From what you're telling me"—Volsky leaned back, sounding relaxed while his mind raced—"David works for us. *You* work for us. There's a whole group of people I've never heard of out there working for us. Don't you think if David is doing something, he's following orders from us, if we are his superiors? Just for the sake of discussion?"

"No."

"And the part about trying to kill you. First at your house, then in a playground . . ." Volsky said it wrong to see if Ash would correct him.

"Rock Creek Park," Ash said.

"Oh, yes, Rock Creek Park. And then in New Hampshire . . ."

"Vermont," Ash said.

"Tell me," Volsky said, taking a new tack, looking amused.

"You say you've been here seventeen years? In seventeen years, what have you done for us?"

Ash stared at him a moment, which might have been ignorance, or just simple caution. Then Ash sighed and began talking, and Volsky really started to get a headache. Ash talked about passing information on about a gay engineer who worked for COMSAT. Volsky knew about the engineer, all right, since he had been the one to blackmail him. What Volsky had never known was how Moscow knew the man was gay.

Ash mentioned how Kislak had passed along secret information to him on cost overruns on a new U.S. missile the Soviet Union had wanted to stop, and using this information Ash had written articles that had raised an outcry and gotten work on the weapon canceled. Volsky had read the series in the *Post*. At the time he'd wondered how the reporter had come up with the information.

Now there was a knock at the door and Volsky said, "Excuse me," and answered it. The man on the other side wordlessly handed him three black-and-white, eight-by-eleven photographs. Volsky remained, back to Ash, in the doorway. He was looking at some of the standard pictures the embassy kept of important journalists, diplomats, and government officials. You never knew who was working for the American government, and you never knew when Moscow would want to verify someone's face. Volsky's mood dropped when he saw the first picture. He'd been hoping the man who called himself Ash would turn out to be someone else, but the picture he was looking at showed a tall, blond man on the *Post* softball team, on a day it played the White House. In the photo Ash stood in center field, waiting for a ball. He was crouched, in gym shorts, mitt resting on his knee, face riveted toward the plate. The embassy photographers took lots of shots during softball games by the Potomac. It was easy to pose as a tourist there and just snap away. There was no doubt the man was Ash.

Volsky returned to his desk. "Payroll problems," he said, rolling his eyes at Ash. Then he said, "If these people you're talking about are really after you, trying to kill you, why should you care about what happens to them enough to come here? Why not just run off somewhere? Escape them? I mean, for the sake of argument."

Ash sighed. "They're my family," he said. "I grew up with them. They're all I have. They don't know David's lying. And also"—he looked into Volsky's face, intense and resolute—"I don't want Corinna to be hurt."

Volsky glanced over at his photos-from-Afghanistan wall. The one of his unit around a smoldering fire, in a rocky gorge at dusk. There was Ivan Rutskoi, the Georgian who'd been machine-gunned to death in an ambush. Gennadi Khasbulatov, the corporal who told bad jokes and had drowned in a spring flood during an attack. Arkadi Silayev, the captain who'd shitted himself to death from dysentery during the escape. "I keep these pictures so I will never forget," Volsky told anyone who asked why such grim mementos lined his wall.

Suddenly Volsky kept tears from his eyes. Suddenly he had the worst feeling that despite the insane-sounding story, this man was telling the truth.

Then he remembered how oddly Akromeyev had been acting lately. Akromeyev had been in Washington fifteen years. And this Ash person was saying his group had been here that long, too. Volsky's heart pounded. It was entirely probable that Akromeyev ran spies Volsky knew nothing about.

Except if Akromeyev was guilty, why would he send this man to Volsky, so Volsky could hear the story?

Volsky was in a terribly tricky position. With the trade minister coming, and food for the winter dependent on U.S. goodwill, the slightest bad press could have disastrous repercussions. Volsky knew he could keep Ash in the embassy and question him, but he couldn't do it right now because if it turned out Ash was a reporter looking for a story, it would land up on the front page. Just the kind of stupid dirty-tricks setup the CIA pulled from time to time, and the CIA could have given Ash the information he was saying. They might already have taken photos of him coming into the building. If he didn't come out, that would make the story better. A story about the old bad

KGB in Washington, complete with interrogation techniques, could wreck the loan. It was crucial to the success of the trade minister's mission that the Soviet Union look like a crippled, endangered shell of its former self, not the old familiar enemy, or the American Congress would never give money that would normally go to their own people, anyway.

Volsky's mind worked quickly. If he let Ash go and Ash was telling the truth, Ash might go to the FBI, for protection. He seemed too loyal to do it. But it was a risk. If Ash felt betrayed by his own people all the way down the line, who knew what he might do?

Volsky could have Ash followed, but if Ash went to the FBI, there wouldn't be time to stop him.

Volsky sighed. The only half-decent part was if Ash was right about people trying to kill him, and they succeeded, the story would remain secret. Volsky had Kislak's name, so there was no problem of finding him later. In a way that was the safest option, although if Ash was telling the truth, it had taken amazing courage to come here. Kill Ash? That was the kind of thing Akromeyev probably used to do, in the old days. Kill the messenger.

He stopped. *Appeal to his loyalty*, Volsky thought.

He said, "One more question, you say that Koslik—"

"Kislak."

Suddenly, without missing a beat, Volsky switched to speaking Russian. "Yes, that Kislak may be selling information privately and sharing the profit with someone higher up, in the KGB. What if that person is here? What if that person is, well, me?"

"I considered that possibility," Ash replied in the same language. He looked utterly resolute. Volsky again had a feeling he was dealing with a brave man.

"And?"

Ash suddenly smiled. He was quite charming when he did. Volsky's fourteen-year-old son, Boris, was a film lover and always brought home old classics from the rental store to watch at night, and last week he had shown Laurel and Hardy comedies

all Saturday. Volsky realized Ash was doing a pretty good imitation of the thin one, Stan Laurel. He managed to make his
mouth rubbery, stretching the smile wide.

"I'll take you down with me," Ash said.

Akromeyev called out, "Come in, Gregor," but didn't turn
around when Volsky entered. He had slightly parted the gold-
brocaded curtains and stood with his thick hands behind his
back, probably looking down at Ash walking away below.

"You're sending me out of here?" Ash had asked, incredu-
lous, at the end of the interview.

"Leave your phone number," Volsky had remarked like a
bureaucrat ready to get on with his next task, like a man who had
already spent too much time on the issue at hand. "I told you,
there are no, uh, KGB agents here, but someone will check your
story. You have to understand, if you are who you say you are,
that we need time to check it. Just a day or so. Twenty-four
hours. You must understand that we have to be cautious. Come
back in a day.

"Thank you for coming in," Volsky had said.

"You don't believe me," Ash had said.

Volsky had smiled. "I have no experience with espionage
matters. But I'll tell our people what you said. Go home. Relax.
Go back to work."

"Go back to work?" Ash had said, half rising. "They're trying
to kill me."

At any point if Akromeyev disapproved of Volsky's decisions,
the red light under his desk would go on. It didn't. Three
followers were on the street when Ash left the building. One on
each corner, so he wouldn't be aware someone was behind. One
driving an off-duty cab.

Ash had strode briskly from the building when he'd left.

Akromeyev drew the curtains now, changing the light in the
room from natural to artificial, blocking the lip-readers and
directional microphones the FBI would be aiming at them from
the AFL-CIO building across the street. He turned. At fifty-five,

he'd lost none of the suppressed fury that had propelled him through the ranks of the KGB, from interrogator to investigator, investigator to administrator. He was smaller than Volsky but exuded wiry strength in each crisp, compact athletic movement. Pale blue eyes studied Volsky from lightly tinted steel aviator frames. Today he wore a boxy suit of light blue linen that had been tailor-made in Hong Kong. Akromeyev had been posted there briefly before coming to the U.S., and his tailor had his measurements. It cost the motherland less to pay for custom-made suits in Hong Kong than off-the-rack ones in the U.S. The KGB chief's face remained youthful in its smoothness, but it had a purplish tinge that suggested to Volsky high blood pressure or too much drink. Rather than implying dissolution, this added to the sense of force emanating from the man.

The delicate touches in the office—the crystal chandelier, the Ukrainian Flemish-style landscapes, all dark purple clouds, hanging low over peasant huts, the set of Chinese cups on the mahogany shelves—seemed endangered by Akromeyev's presence. Like the small, angry man could rampage through the space at any moment, destroying it.

"Well?" Akromeyev said.

Volsky fell into a hard-backed chair without being asked. "Craziest story I ever heard. Except I think he believes what he's saying."

"You have men on him?"

"Three."

"You think he's really who he says he is?"

Volsky let his silence imply that possibility.

"The trade minister is coming in two days," Akromeyev said, propelled back and forth behind his desk, filled with too much energy to sit. "Fifteen years. *I've* been here fifteen years and I never heard about this."

"You don't believe him," Volsky said.

"No, I don't believe him," Akromeyev said explosively. "It's a story, a fabrication. Listen to the man! Who put him up to it!"

"Except what?" Volsky said, knowing Akromeyev's different kinds of rages and guessing that more was coming.

Akromeyev groaned and fell into his chair. There was sweat on his forehead, below the thinning strands of brown, slicked-back hair. "Except he knows what we've been doing here. And except for the Yuri part."

He leaned back. Volsky perched forward. Akromeyev stared into space, toward the landscape, except he wasn't seeing it.

"Yuri," Akromeyev said softly.

"You know Yuri?"

Akromeyev glanced at Volsky. "I know a story," he said. "Rumor actually. A long time ago." Akromeyev burst out, "A bullet! That's what they should get!"

Volsky wasn't clear who "they" were.

From outside, car horns began blaring. There must be a traffic jam. A grandfather clock in the corner chimed. Akromeyev reached into a drawer and pulled out a half-filled bottle of vodka. Volsky shook his head. Akromeyev poured some into a large tumbler and put in ice. He seemed to inhale the whole portion. He leaned back.

"Vladimir Semichastny," he said, "headed the KGB from 1961 until 1967. He was a good man," he said, which Volsky took to mean he killed innocent dissidents. "He knew how to safeguard Mother Russia. But he had a weakness. Some of this is in the files. He had a son." With his thick, stubby index finger, Akromeyev pointed to his forehead. "The son was crazy. Sick in the head. Wild. Spitting, screaming. They drugged the kid up, but Semichastny didn't want a mannequin for a son, he wanted a real son. Psychiatrists, well, we weren't supposed to believe in them. But there was a professor in Kiev, Yuri was his name, who wrote articles about disturbed children. Who treated children of Party members, children who had . . . lapses. Semichastny sent his son to Yuri, and Yuri got him functioning. Yuri sent the boy back. . . . I wouldn't say he was normal . . . but he functioned."

Volsky was riveted. "Semichastny was tough," Akromeyev said admiringly. "But when it came to his son, he was weak. In the KGB, there was a name for Yuri. We called him Rasputin because of the influence he had. We never knew a last name. And you have to understand at this time, 1961, we were much weaker than now. The U.S. could have wiped us off the map. There were so many enemies, inside and out. More than we could deal with. The Whites were still around. The CIA had agents everywhere. Our nuclear capacities nowhere approached America's. They weren't in Vietnam yet. They were still a cohesive country."

Akromeyev blew out air. "Semichastny was interested in stopping treason before it began. In teaching children, you see? A terrific idea! And Yuri designed education programs to steer them in the right direction. These programs worked. He'd gone from dealing with single children to groups of children."

Akromeyev stopped. Volsky, heart pounding, said, "And?"

"That's the end of the fact part," Akromeyev said. He poured another half tumbler of vodka. He sucked it up in a single breath. He exhaled audibly. "Now for the rumor.

"You and I both know how frustrating it can be to find good people, to get good information overseas. Our own people can only get so much. We need helpers. We have to rely on who comes to the embassy. On who we can blackmail. We pander to perverts and traitors, people who disgust us, we give them things they want for information. The plumber. A man writes us a letter. We contact him. He goes to work for us. It's all so much . . . luck.

"But what if we had a supply of Americans available to us from childhood? People who would grow up loyal to us, from when they were children, smart people who would one day get powerful jobs, become influential, work for us throughout their lives?"

"Science fiction," Volsky said.

"Sure, sure, but Yuri's work was on conditioning children," Akromeyev said. "The rumor was Semichastny was diverting huge monies to a project in the East. Something Yuri was involved in. Semichastny was slavish when it came to Yuri. No matter how crazy, he'd give the man anything. He believed Yuri could do miracles. And maybe he could."

"And?"

Akromeyev shrugged. "Maybe he did."

"How do you know this?" Volsky said.

Akromeyev laughed. "It's easy to know rumors," he said, "because ninety percent of the time they are false."

"But Semichastny was out in 1967, you said," Volsky said. "And then Andropov ran things until the early eighties. And then Chebrikov."

"And now Kryuchkov."

"That's four administrations."

"I know."

"And fifteen years."

"I know," Akromeyev said.

"It couldn't have been kept secret that whole time."

"Who says it was?" Akromeyev said. "Maybe it's not a secret in Moscow. Maybe if this man was telling the truth, Moscow knows about it. They report directly to Moscow. It has nothing to do with us. All over the world operatives report directly to Moscow."

"Then we leave it alone?" Volsky said.

"No, it's us on the block." Akromeyev had a flushed, red complexion from his drinking. He was such an angry-looking man, and Marta was so thin, that Volsky envisioned the secretary cracking in two under the KGB man's assault. Akromeyev said, "If it's a legitimate operation, and this man Ash has gone renegade, there's one solution and we better do it fast."

"A bullet," Volsky said.

"A bullet. But if Ash is telling the truth and this Kislak has gone renegade, a bullet for him. And anyone cooperating with him. A bullet for all of them."

"Thirteen people?" Volsky said. "They have families. And Kislak is a former undersecretary of state! It's too many people to keep secret!"

Akromeyev's face hardened. "You went soft after Afghanistan," he said. Then he said, more kindly, "The problem with you reformers is you don't understand the mathematics of it, it's just numbers, Volsky. Do you kill one person to save a million? Of course you do. Numbers. It's for the greater good."

Volsky set his expression. "But if Ash told the truth, the other people don't know what Kislak is doing."

They stared at each other. Akromeyev smiled. "At least the difference between you and other reformists is that you do what you're supposed to after you stop arguing."

"I'm waiting for my turn," Volsky said calmly.

"You'll never get it unless you harden up."

Volsky said, "I'll take my chances."

"Anyway, it's early to do anything until we find out more," Akromeyev said. "But I don't like him. He threatened us. The part about the FBI, writing everything down."

"He's protecting himself," Volsky said. "Who can blame him, if the story is true? It might have even been a bluff."

"You don't threaten a superior officer," Akromeyev said coldly. "Let me tell you about whistle-blowers. They're unhappy people. They like to complain. They're unreliable in the long run. Useful, but in the long run they don't shut up. It's a personality type. They find other things to make problems about. Even if he's right now, he knows he can threaten us. I don't trust him."

Akromeyev's buzzer rang. Reaching for it, he said, "He threatened us. Us means me."

Akromeyev picked up the phone. "It's for you." Volsky got on the line and listened to the man on the other end, and a deep frown formed on his face. When he hung up, he said, "He lost them."

"Three of them?"

"He's a pro," Volsky said. "He saw them right away."

"Great," Akromeyev said. "Gregor, if MG doesn't get those loans because something goes wrong here, Kryuchkov will blame us. Never mind who knows about what's going on in Moscow. If something happens here, we're finished."

"There are worse things," Volsky said. "It's not like the old days."

Akromeyev got a hard, odd expression on his face. "At the moment, no. Gregor, pack your bags. You're going home tonight. I want you to find out what's going on with this Ash. Unofficially," the old infighter said. "Check the files you can see.

But don't push things so they find out what you're doing. Ash told you names, try to track them. And do it fast. A week or two."

Volsky had the feeling that Akromeyev wanted him out of Washington.

Akromeyev said, "Marta can work on the minister's arrangements. Get back here when you have it."

"Marta?" Volsky said.

"She's smarter than you think."

"I hope so."

Akromeyev smiled. "If you weren't a war hero, I'd put a bullet in you myself," he joked.

Volsky paused at the door. "But I told him to come back in a day or so. What happens then?"

Akromeyev said, not looking up, "Let me worry about that."

Volsky called his wife and asked her to pack his overnight bag. He asked her to cancel their appearance tonight at the Kayakers Club at the Potomac boathouse. He'd been looking forward to the drinking and story-telling for two weeks. He promised his wife he'd bring back two bottles of her mother's borscht for her. The embassy people would call Aeroflot and bump a paying passenger from first class to get a seat for Volsky. He wished he could figure out what it was about Akromeyev that had been bothering him before Ash showed up. But he'd think about it later. There was too much to do now.

Volsky sighed and locked the security report in his drawer. The arrangements were all made so Marta wouldn't have any problems. He wondered what Ash was doing out on the street. The man was a pro, and if he had been telling the truth about the rest of it, he would be going into hiding. Volsky sighed. Seventeen years? Volsky would try to sleep on the plane. He had a feeling it was all the sleep he was going to get for the next few days.

The cable room at the Soviet embassy is a small, cramped basement space filled with radios, satellite-monitoring equipment,

Teletype machines, and phones. It looks like an electronics genius's cluttered hideaway, a mass of gray machinery and blinking lights beneath fluorescent tubes and building pipes. Normally it is manned by a single radio/cable operator, but at midnight Col. Sergei Akromeyev had sent this man away and occupied what little space existed for moving around. The KGB man was squeezed into the small steel swivel chair, staring at the cable machine as if he could will the reply he was waiting for to spit itself out.

Whenever Akromeyev thought of the *Washington Post,* he remembered the column, now-deceased writer Manfred Light, "America's Cold Warrior," had written about him when he first arrived in the capital fifteen years ago. The column calling him an "old-style KGB butcher." Akromeyev had laughed back then because this was supposed to be a negative description. Americans despised their own fighting men who kept their country strong. They had no understanding of numbers. No comprehension of how you had to sacrifice a few people sometimes for the greater good. Of how it took a strong man, not a butcher, to pull the trigger against an innocent person in order to save many others. That's what Akromeyev had done back in the Soviet Union. Americans would throw a thousand men into battle if just one was in danger. Russians understood the value of strength.

It was just math.

I'll never forget what the fascists did to my father, Akromeyev thought, suddenly a small boy again, hiding in a closet, peering out in terror as a ring of Germans beat an already dead man on the bed, with the boy too frightened to move.

Volsky was gone, on the evening Aeroflot flight to Moscow. Akromeyev, watching his fleshy face reflected in the transparent glass over the cable machine, knew there had been no need to send him. But for all his liking of the young war hero, Akromeyev didn't trust his reformist tendencies. Not to mention that at this time in particular it didn't hurt to get all the credit for a big success for himself.

Akromeyev blew out air. He'd lied to Volsky. In all of the last

fifteen years Akromeyev had never received instructions mentioning any espionage operation like the one Ash had described
today. Which meant if it existed, it wasn't his responsibility. And
that meant if something went wrong with it, someone else
would be punished, not Akromeyev.

Since Akromeyev wasn't responsible for the group, he could
only get credit by telling Moscow about it.

Without high-level access to files, Volsky would be in Moscow
for weeks trying to get information. He'd fail. By the time he got
back, Akromeyev would have taken care of any problems here.

Akromeyev had labeled the urgent transmission he'd sent two
hours ago with double red-star coding. Get this to Kryuchkov
immediately, wherever he is!

Akromeyev raged inside while he waited. MG had gone soft!
Soft! Seventy-five years of struggle about to go down the drain
if MG managed to pull off the new union treaty. Yeltsin the
traitor already hinting he would pull the Russian Republic out of
the Soviet Union and form his own country. The other republics
were clamoring for release. Lenin would be turning over in his
grave.

The Teletype machine let out a long electronic hiss and the
keys began pumping and the printer ball swung to the right and
began typing out the coded reply. Akromeyev saw the words *red
star.* And saw them again.

It was the cable he was waiting for.

His heart pounded.

He decoded it as it came over the wire.

NO KNOWLEDGE OF SUCH A GROUP. NO CODE
TEENAGER. FIND OUT MORE.

The room fell silent as the printer stopped. The head of the
KGB was telling him that neither he, nor anyone close to him,
had ever heard of the people Ash had described to Volsky earlier
in the day. For a moment Akromeyev just stared at the words.

FIND OUT MORE.

It was the kind of assignment Akromeyev liked.

The KGB man went upstairs and poured a stiff vodka and
considered possibilities. Either Ash was a good reporter who'd

learned some tidbits of information and was fishing for more, for a story—or he was CIA. Or he was who he said he was, part of a spy ring that had somehow gone renegade or been kept secret from the head of the KGB himself. A group answerable to someone other than the head of the KGB. Terminating such a group would be a coup.

Akromeyev remembered how skillfully Ash had eluded his followers.

He's not just a reporter, he thought.

He asked himself what advantage the CIA could get from revealing how much they knew about KGB operations in Washington, apparently a lot.

Not much.

Akromeyev poured more vodka. He came to a decision. There were times in life when you had to take risks, and now seemed a good time to do it. He reached under the desk and pressed a button. Several moments later the door opened and the three men whom Volsky had sent to follow Ash entered the room. They were big, tough-looking men but they acted fearful and embarrassed. They hadn't even managed to keep sight of the journalist for an hour before the man disappeared. Akromeyev felt a little better. At least Volsky was out of the way. By the time he got back, everything would be different, not only in Washington, but at home. Plus, Akromeyev liked people to be frightened of him.

Akromeyev envisioned Ash from the photographs he'd seen. The big blond man in jeans and a cotton shirt.

The rage in his head was a red ball growing bigger and hotter. This was exactly what happened when leaders allowed the reins of government to go slack. People went off in their own directions. Anarchy was the result.

Ash might come back tomorrow and that would take care of that problem. Kislak was trickier. Akromeyev wished there was a way to meet the man, talk to him, gauge him. Then Akromeyev started laughing because the way was so simple, so ridiculous, that it struck him as funny. No matter how much time Akromeyev spent in America he would never get used to the openness here. Meeting Kislak would be easy, more than easy, it would be fun. And as for Ash, well, if we're lucky, we won't even have to go after him, Akromeyev thought. Ash will come back tomorrow, as Volsky asked. Only this time we'll question him right.

TEN

ASH STEPPED FROM THE EMBASSY into the broiling midday sun. The air was choking, like all oxygen had been sucked from it. He was furious. He couldn't believe he'd been sent from the building. He could feel the cameras on him from across the street, in the itch on his shoulders. The sweat in his shirt.

Volsky had looked blank during his whole story.

And now they'd sent him back outside. To David. After he'd told about his operations. Given the code that Yuri had promised would bring safety. Ash had harbored it for years, hoping he'd never need it, praying he might. The password to his father. To no more lies.

Well, fuck Volsky.

Ash started walking. Come back tomorrow? That was what clerks said when stores closed. What motor vehicle bureau guards said when they cleared the lines at four-thirty each day. Go home and sleep. Give it another try in the morning. Get a good night's rest.

Horns blared on Sixteenth Street. Ash pushed the dazed feeling away, there was no time for it. David might be coming. Through the crowds and almost by rote he picked up a movement out of sync at the far end of the block, a tourist in jeans and a black T-shirt pushing himself off a newspaper machine. It had been the flick of the head. The glance.

He turned his back on the man and walked south toward K Street. Making it easy. He shoved his hands in his pockets as if deep in thought, but he scanned the block for other followers. Ash passed two printers he recognized, heading back to the *Post* after lunch. A group of secretaries, giggling, and he heard one say, "It wasn't a ring, just a bracelet." The D.C. Gas men tearing up the street didn't glance at Ash. That didn't mean they were innocent. An off-duty Diamond cab was double-parked across the street and a Pakistani driver in a yellow cab pulled over and called, "Want a ride?" Ash shook his head. The man drove off. Ash told himself, anything special? Anything different? The Diamond cab's insignia was broken off at the tip.

DuChamp used to say, "If you're following a pro, sometimes it's better to use more than one man and let him spot one. Once he does that, he'll relax and stop looking for others."

Ash thought, I'll make my own rules now.

At K and Sixteenth he checked reflections in the City News machine. Superimposed over the headline "Soviet Union Breaking Up While Gorbachev Vacations at Black Sea," Blue Jeans was still coming, same distance behind.

Ash crossed K street, turned right, and walked to a small park occupying a square block at K and Connecticut, just green grass and an X-shaped walkway lined with benches where workers ate sandwiches or got tans. At two-thirty only late eaters remained, and a smattering of homeless people who slept on the ground at night and begged money between police roundups. Ash slumped onto a bench and lowered his head in his hands. He wanted to look upset. He was raging inside. Between his fingers he spotted the off-duty Diamond cab that had been across from the embassy, only now it was double-parked across from the park.

Ash thought, that's two.

"Got a dollar, mate?"

Ash recognized the homeless man standing before him, a lean, bearded Australian who slept on the steam grates in winter and had haunted the park for years, asking for money each time Ash walked by, without recognizing him. Some days the man just lay on the grass, twitching and talking to himself. Today he seemed stable.

"I'll give you five dollars if you do me a favor," Ash said.

The man drew himself up. His shirt was missing two buttons, and one of his pockets was turned inside out. He had a weathered, sunburned look. "I ain't gay," he said.

Ash said, "It's not that. Can you take a note to the pizza place on the corner and give it to the cash register girl?" He'd never met the cash register girl but saw her every day through the glass.

"That's all?" The man looked suspicious.

"You want the five bucks?"

The man twitched and scratched his beard while Ash pulled his pen from his pocket. He scribbled *I am a war veteran. Please give me a dollar for lunch* on a scrap of paper. He folded the paper and handed it to the man with the money.

"The checkout girl," the man repeated. "Who do I say gave it to me?"

"Mr. Volsky."

As the homeless man left the park, a man in a gray seersucker suit whom Ash had not noticed before pushed himself off a bench and fell in behind him.

The homeless man looked back at Ash when he reached K Street. He wasn't going anywhere Ash wanted. He dropped the note and kept going. The man in the seersucker suit stayed behind. Ash remained in place on the bench, staring at the ground, pretending to be deep in thought.

He would make his move in minutes. I did everything I could, he thought. There was a ticking in his head. Something important was coming. The feeling of oppression dropping away. The certainty rising out of seventeen years of bullshit. Ash saw himself at his *Post* job interview. He saw Tyler at his food dish. He saw a small, frightened engineer in the front seat of a blue Volvo, begging, "Please don't tell." He saw a KGB man with an eyepatch telling him, "Come back tomorrow."

Ash stood up. The blood roared in his head. Something burst inside him, the cells of his body gripped by a sudden, violent charge, flowing upward through him, exploding into a sense of liberty so powerful and delicious Ash physically felt the bonds breaking.

He was not going to do what they wanted anymore. It was finished.

Now there was just one last task to complete and Ash could get on to his own business. Finding my father. He struggled to his feet, careful to keep projecting the worried expression. The follower in jeans and a T-shirt was reading the *Washington Times* on a bench twenty feet away. Pigeons strutted at his feet, pecking at crumbs a woman with a shopping cart broke off a hunk of rye bread.

The Diamond cab with the broken insignia remained across the street. Ash trudged across the grass in the opposite direction. The cab started moving, but it would have to circle the block before it reached him. In the sluggish downtown traffic, the cab caught a light.

Ash strolled to the curb, spotted a yellow cab coming. He stepped into the street and flagged it and got in. "Go! Now!" he cried. Blue Jeans shot off the bench. Ash's driver turned to look at him. He was a middle-aged Oriental man with a wide face and a brushy mustache. "What you say?"

The man in the jeans pounded toward them. Ash threw twenty dollars on the seat. "I said go!"

"But . . . where?" the driver said. Ash shouted, "Just go!" and the man hit the accelerator, nudging Ash back, and they sailed across K Street up Connecticut. If he didn't get away this time, they'd put an army behind him.

Ash turned around. Too late. Blue Jeans was getting into another cab.

Ash leaned forward over the front seat. "Straight up Connecticut. Fast." The driver looked nervous in the rearview mirror.

"My girlfriend's brother is following me," Ash said.

"Girlfriend brother," the driver said, craning his neck and looking beyond Ash in the rearview mirror.

"I have to get away from him. He's crazy."

The driver said, "Why?"

The other cab was gaining a little. It was two cars back in light traffic. Ash said, "Under Dupont Circle. Come on! Make this light!"

They shot through a yellow light into the tunnel. Ash turned around. The other cab ran the red.

Ash had a sudden suspicion. "You speak English, don't you?" he said.

The driver snapped, "How drive if no speak English!" The driver muttered something in Korean.

Ash made his voice urgent, but reasonable. "I'm not kidding, the guy is nuts. He's after me. He might have a gun. So I dropped her, big deal. Get me away from him, will you?"

The driver's eyes widened. They shot out of the underpass. Ash let another twenty drift onto the front seat. The driver saw the money but looked as if he would rather Ash would leave.

Ash told the man to speed up and make a quick right down T Street.

"No, get out of cab! No dollah! No trouble! No trouble!"

Ash leaned over the seat. "Please."

The driver slowed and veered toward the curb.

Ash suddenly understood. He grabbed the man's shoulder. "Look, asshole. I work for Immigration. If you don't get me away from that nut, I'll make sure they send you home, understand? We'll investigate you and your whole family!" Ash read the name on the man's license in a clear, accusatory voice. "Kim!"

The man looked terrified.

Ash barked, "Faster!" The driver really hit the accelerator now and the cab leaped forward. The other cab picked up speed, too. Ash's driver stared at him in the mirror, and Ash shouted, "Watch the road!"

Ash gave quick directions. "Make a right on Sixteenth!" They roared past town houses, D.C. College, Jack Anderson's office. The other cab nearly sideswiped a postal delivery truck at a corner as it came after them. It plunged through an intersection, veering to miss a messenger on a bicycle. It was fifty yards back, which would give Ash about five seconds to do what he needed when they reached the alley he was heading toward.

The driver whimpered, "Don't send me back! I go quicker!" He shot the cab through traffic and Ash said, "Stay to the right! The next alley! Now!" They nearly slammed sideways into a garage as the car made the turn. Ash shouted instructions as he kicked the door open, but instead of getting out he lay out of sight on the backseat. He hoped the man understood. He said, "I'll find you if you run, Kim." The driver jumped out as the second cab appeared at the head of the alley. "It coming!" he told Ash.

"Now!" Ash hissed.

The driver stood by Ash's open door, faced the other way, down the alley, shook his fist, and screamed, "Come back! You owe me money!"

Ash heard a car door slam. He heard running footsteps receding down the alley.

He straightened up.

The other cab was backing out of the alley. The man in jeans was at the far end of the alley, turning a corner at a run.

Ash gave the driver an address on Nebraska Avenue in northwest Washington, half a mile from where he was really going.

The driver looked miserable.

Ash settled back as they drove off. He hadn't even realized the radio was playing. An announcer was saying, "Fighting continues in the Soviet republic of Azerbaijan. Troops have been sent to quell the rebellion."

"I keep green card, right?" the man said. He looked near tears.

"Sure, sure," Ash said. "That guy was always crazy."

Ash walked into Beltway Savings & Loan with ten minutes until closing time. The air-conditioning had to have the temperature below forty. The sweat froze on his arms.

He had to get out of Washington tonight. They'd be watching his apartment and the *Post* and the car rental places and the hotels. They'd be making phone calls and saying they were him, asking questions to see if he'd done business there. They'd be cruising the streets. They'd be watching his regular bank. They'd be checking with Corinna and maybe even Jennifer Knowles, if they'd figured out what her name was. Unless of course she was one of them. Unless she'd been with them all along.

Ash regularly banked across the street from the *Post,* but his emergency stash, false documents and one of his extra parabellums lay in a safe deposit box here. The documents would be useless with his own people looking for him. They already knew the false identities with which he'd been supplied. But the fifty thousand in cash was what he needed.

Martini's voice, in his head, barked, "Extra money! Extra arms! Twenty years'll go by and you won't need it. Then one day everything will depend on it." Ash had another spare gun in a rented box on McArthur Boulevard.

He sauntered past a smattering of customers toward the back area of the bank where the manager's desk was, automatically scanning the tellers and customers for an out-of-place glance. Anything special? Anything different? You weren't even supposed to tell your own people where you kept your stash, but you never knew. Everything looked quiet. Everything seemed okay, except it was freezing in here.

The bank seemed to be remodeling. Workmen in coveralls clustered near the big, closed safe. Only eight minutes to closing. Ash recognized the manager. A large, happy-looking man in a charcoal gray, close-cut Italian suit, who looked more like a designer than a suburban banker.

The manager shook Ash's hand, but did not recognize him.

"I'd like to get into my safe deposit box," Ash said, pulling out identification.

The smile faded. The manager suddenly and unconsciously began playing with the dial of his watch.

"I told them," he said. "We've been working on this all day. Mr. Ash, this has never happened in twelve years here. It's the humidity. I *told* them. Testing the timer in Minnesota is useless. They don't have humidity like this in Minnesota. I used to vacation there when I was a boy, that's how I know."

"Are you telling me the safe is broken?" Ash said. "You can't get in?"

The manager twisted the winder on his Seiko. "It's not broken. It's just jammed. Like my Datsun. When it gets humid, moisture gets in the points, I can't start it. But I use my wife's hair drier, hook it up to the garage outlet, and half an hour later, car starts right up." He smiled as if he expected Ash to be amused, and when Ash didn't, he began twisting the watch dial again. "We paid so much money for this safe, you wouldn't believe how much, and then a little humidity and the timer jams. Customers have been at me all day, I mean *weeks* go by and nobody uses the boxes. And of course, on this day, everybody has to come in. I'm not blaming you. It's just funny how things work, isn't it?"

"I'll wait," Ash said.

The manager looked sheepish. "But . . . um . . . we close in six minutes. I can't have anyone here after that." He sighed deeply. Ash could pull cash from the automatic tellers around the city with his bank card, but with a $400 daily limit on withdrawals he couldn't get enough. And once he was gone he did not want to leave a trail of withdrawals in other cities. He had his credit cards, but credit cards also left a trail of where the user had been. He could leave anyway, but he would run out of money in less than a day.

The manager was saying, "I'm sorry for the inconvenience. Maybe you could come back tomorrow. We've been playing with the air conditioner in here all day, hoping the climate would free up the lock.

"I hope it's not an emergency," he added.

"It is an emergency."

"I see. There is one thing you can do."

"What?"

"Write a letter," the manager said. "That will make them test things right the next time." A little irateness crept into the man's voice. "Humidity, Mr. Ash. I'm sure none of us want a repeat of this during the next heat wave."

"What time will the safe be open in the morning?" Ash said.

"The bank, eight-thirty," the manager said, looking relieved that he wasn't going to get an argument. He leaned close. He glanced with disapproval at the workmen pouring coffee from a thermos instead of working on the safe. "They're union," he said conspiratorially. "They'll quit at five. And they spent half the day on breaks. I told the management. I *told* them to use nonunion."

"What time will the safe be open?" Ash said.

"Noon maximum. Who knows? Maybe they'll get lucky and open it up now, ha ha ha . . . we have five minutes till closing." Ash didn't laugh. The man said, "Would you like to leave a number? I can phone you when the safe is open?"

"That's okay, I'll come back."

The sun went down but the heat got worse. After he'd gone out to McArthur Boulevard to pick up his extra gun, it seemed to swell from the earth, buildings, air conditioners, cars. "Don't go out, especially if you're elderly," the radio said in the cab that left Ash four blocks from Corinna's apartment.

He waited in the woods along Tunlaw Road, across from her condominium. There were the rotting smells of heat and vegetation. A bar of streetlight penetrated the shadows a foot away. The seventeen-year cicadas were coming out. In the dark, he could feel and hear them all around him. The waxy leaves were coated with humming, crawling insects. Cicadas covered windshields of parked cars. Their black, chitinous bodies lay crushed on the street. Whenever a vehicle passed, headlights illuminated masses of dark, slug-shaped insects on leaves, twigs, trunks. They had wings but were so heavy they preferred to sit.

Through the foliage and across the street, lights came on on balconies as condo owners came home for the evening. They strolled through the yellow-brick gate toward the uniformed doorman in the glassed-in lobby. They drove Mercedes into the underground garage. A congressman Ash recognized walked a Shar-Pei near the building's tulip garden and used a plastic glove to pick up after his pet.

Corinna's building was positioned to give the impression of country living. In this part of northwest Washington, Tunlaw was a two-lane, countrylike blacktop dipping past copses of oaks and park. The only way into the front entrance was through the lit-up gate beneath wrought-iron floodlights. There was probably a back entrance, which involved going over the surrounding brick wall.

Couples ate on balconies, candles lit between them. Ash saw two women in terry-cloth robes toasting each other after coming back from the pool on the roof. A party was in progress up there. Ash glimpsed Christmas lights and heard faint beats of Willie Nelson's "Moonlight in Vermont."

Corinna's unit stayed dark.

She would have been warned about him, might even be waiting for him, be guarded. But Ash had to see her. It was ceremony. Good-bye.

Six inches from his face, on a bare twig, a cicada squeezed from its egg-roll-shaped cocoon. Albino on emerging, it took on capillary-thin red lines along its translucent wings. It had brooded in the ground for seventeen years. It would live in the open for a month and then die.

Ash's pulse sped up. A silver Mercedes convertible turned into the driveway. But it wasn't her. A teenager drove.

The cicada, taking on black color on its back, seemed to vibrate before his face. It took a step on the leaf.

Beyond it he saw a beige two-door Nova cruise down Tunlaw and slow, looking for a parking place. It wedged into one on Ash's side, practically brushing a big oak near the curb, and Ash stood straighter when Corinna stepped out. She wore a light gold business suit, high heels, and no stockings. Her hair, bound at the nape of her neck, fell down her back in a braid.

A short, bullish-looking man got out of the driver's side, spoke to her while she nodded, and got back in.

It was Minsky.

The heat always brought out more sensualness in Corinna. More fluidness in her sway as she disappeared through the brick walls. He could smell her even though she was far away. Ash stayed behind the tree. The cicada in front of him seemed to hang at the end of a leaf that bowed from its weight. The light went on in Corinna's condo. She opened the sliding-glass doors and appeared on the balcony. She leaned over the railing. Minsky's arm came out of the Nova. He signaled he could see her. The trap was set.

Ash slid through the woods to the hum of the cicadas and the swish of tires on Tunlaw Road. When he'd moved far enough away so Minsky wouldn't see him, he emerged and crossed the street. He was quite happy Minsky was here, with the way things were going. He headed back for the building through the woods on this new side of the street. The yellow-brick wall came up quick.

It was ten feet high and more of a retaining wall than a protective one. It had little exposed chunks of brick sticking out along the side, decorations for the architect, toeholds for Ash. He was over in seconds. He dropped down to a driveway/trash area behind the condo. A steel door said SERVICE ENTRANCE. It smelled like the back of a Chinese restaurant out here, with the heat whipping up the stink, and the roar of the building's beehive-shaped cooling pump overhead.

A rat fled from the trash bin into a drainage grate. Its tail whipped sideways and disappeared.

Ash tried the steel door. It was locked. He walked to the trash bin and opened it. There were piles of black Hefties inside. He pulled one out. After a few minutes the service door opened and a man carrying a trash bag came out. Ash dropped his bag in the garbage with the other man, wiped his hands, said, "Hotter than hell," and followed the man into the building when the man used his key. The man left the fire escape at floor two. Ash hiked to four.

Ash thought it was funny because in all these years he'd never been in her apartment. He'd driven her here once, dropped off a hat she'd left during the divorce. Left little items, a cassette player, a birthday present, with the doorman once or twice. But he'd never been inside.

The hallway had imitation gas lamps glowing above a crimson red carpet with polished marble floors on both sides. It was cool from rushing air pouring from overhead vents. And empty.

Ash pulled his gun from the ankle holster. He could hear a

Chopin sonata playing lightly inside her apartment. He kept the gun at thigh level. The question was, would she open the door right away or give him an excuse and wave Minsky up? That would depend on whatever the two of them had decided.

Or maybe Minsky was just a backup. In that case she'd use her own gun.

"It's me, Ash," he said when he heard her voice. There was a sliding sound at the peephole and he saw her blue, blue eye. Then an unlocking noise. He moved in fast when the door opened, throwing his shoulder into it and knocking her back. "Don't move," he said, shutting the door with his back, groping behind him, finding the lock, but Minsky might have a key.

The Chopin was bright and airy, fingers bouncing over ivory keys. She wore a nightgown of solid white that ended at her calves. Her toenails were peach colored. The way the light struck her, Ash could make out the shadow of her body beneath.

"Minsky's outside," Corinna said.

"I know."

"He's in a white . . . not white . . . what do you call that color?"

"Beige," Ash said. "I saw him."

The apartment seemed an extension of the hallway. More artificial gas lamps coming out of the walls. Glass coffee table, kitchen table, stereo shelf, bookshelves. Red pile. White leather couch and armchair. Calder-style mobile hanging by the balcony. Abstract oils, lots of powder-blue and black slashes against a field of white. When they'd been married, she'd had one work by this artist, an Italian. Now half a dozen were on the walls.

Corinna rubbed her arm where the door had hit her. She looked at Ash's gun. Her face was blotchy as if she had been crying. "Oh, Ash, he's as bad as I remember him. They want to kill you. You didn't go to the FBI, did you?"

"No."

"I told David that. I told him he was overreacting."

"Overreacting." Ash laughed. "Yeh. I'm going to tell you something. I want you to know it, and then I'm going to leave, okay? I'm not going to hurt you."

"You would never hurt me," she said with a feminine disdainful logic. "Sit down." She glanced at the balcony. "You didn't come in the front, did you? He's supposed to spot you coming in. If not, I'm supposed to go to the balcony, just stand there. If I show up on the balcony, it means you're here."

"I saw the rehearsal."

"You want something to drink?" she said.

"No."

"Eat?"

"Corinna," he said.

She sat on the armchair, Ash on the couch. Ash told her the whole story. About getting suspicious of David. David trying to kill him. The trip to Vermont and Glorie Pell and Volsky, who Ash believed had never heard of their group. He told her about the code word that hadn't worked. All of it.

Corinna's blue eyes remained locked on his. One time she shook her head as if something he said had triggered something she remembered. She crossed her arms. Her lips tightened. She said, "Glorie Pell. With a garden spade."

Ash accompanied her across the living room to the bar. He checked inside before she made herself a drink. No weapons there. Corinna poured a Dubonnet, dropped in ice. Frowned. And brought it back to the chair. The Chopin switched off and ice tinkled in the glass when she drank.

It occurred to Ash that there could be another part of her arrangement with Minsky. Like if she didn't appear on the balcony regularly, that meant Ash was inside.

Corinna said, "You came here to warn me."

"That's right."

"You were always good to me."

Ash said nothing.

"You're going away," she said.

"No," he lied.

She laughed. "I'm glad you're leaving. And there's something else." She smiled in a warm, new way that had knowledge in it. "Something you aren't telling me."

"I told you everything," he said.

"Who is she?"

"Excuse me?"

"Ash, you met somebody, didn't you? There's something different about you . . . something freer. You met somebody you love finally. I know it. A girl knows when something's missing. Come on, who is it?" She actually giggled. "I'm glad for you," she said. "I hated how lonely you were. But what will you tell her about who you are?"

Ash shook his head like there was a tick in his ear he needed to be rid of it. "Corinna, he's dragging everyone down. I just wanted to tell you that."

Corinna drained her Dubonnet. "Oh, I know that. It's been getting clearer. You tried to protect him when we had lunch, but I could tell even then." She shrugged. "But I love him."

They stood up together. "Good luck," she said. Her hands were cool when he held them, but they were just normal hands now, their touch didn't jolt him. "Are you taking her with you?" she said.

Ash said, "I have news for you, Corinna, even you aren't right about this."

"Fine," she said. "Good-bye, Ash."

Her face slid closer and he felt the softness of her lips. His cheek tingled where she'd brushed it. A minute later he was back in the hallway, back at the fire escape, outside, and over the wall. He retraced his steps until he was where he had started. Minsky was ten feet away in the car. He had the engine off so Ash wouldn't be alerted by a sound. Which meant the air-conditioning was off, both front windows open.

Ash made out Minsky's form, half-turned toward the condo. The block-shaped head and sideburns upraised as he never took his eyes off Corinna's balcony.

Ash stuck the parabellum through the front window. "Don't move," he said.

Minsky's head swiveled toward Ash slowly.

"Hands on the roof," Ash said.

Minsky's eyes glittered at him. Then Minsky's gaze moved over Ash's shoulder.

"Forget it," Ash said. "There's nobody there."

"Price!" Minsky said.

Ash laughed. Minsky's frown returned. Ash said, "Give me a break. Get out of the car."

There was the sound of a car coming up the street. Ash saw through the windshield that it was a D.C. patrol car. "I'll shoot. Hands in your lap." Ash leaned into the car as if talking to a friend inside, the gun lowered to the seat.

Minsky watched the white squad car roll past, up the hill.

A voice in Ash's head said, "If you're going to shoot someone, do it fast, don't give them time." Ash ordered Minsky from the car. He chose a spot where the streetlamp penetrated the woods and made the backs of the crawling cicadas slick with light. He made Minsky lean against a tree, unbutton his pants and drop them to his ankles. Gun pressed to Minsky's back, he frisked his hair, armpits, shirt. Minsky said, "I don't have anything. It's in the glove compartment of the car." Ash found a wire, an ice pick taped to his back, a holster strapped to his ankle.

"Where we going, FBI?" Minsky said. "I won't tell them anything."

"Pants up," Ash said.

Minsky did it.

Ash hurled the wire, gun, and pick into the trees. He released the clip on his parabellum so it slid into his hand.

Minsky looked surprised. Then he grinned, gathering himself.

"Here's your chance," Ash said.

The rage was pumping in his head. A cicada flew wobbling into the light as Minsky launched himself across the clearing, head down, but it was a fake and he straightened, the kick aimed at Ash's knees. Ash parried it. The bar of light slid back and forth across Minsky's face as they circled. The cicada sound seemed to grow thunderous. There was the whishing noise of a car moving past.

"Feint, feint, always remember, feint," the defense instructor Martini had said. They'd been trained the same. They'd be thinking the same.

Ash came in fast, started striking with the left palm, started to pull back, and suddenly and viciously continued through with the attack. Fuck the feint. He connected.

Minsky looked surprised going down. And then Ash was on him. "Make every blow count," Martini had said. Ash drove his knee into Minsky's groin. His fury seemed to grow. The ground near Minsky's head crawled with cicadas. Ash felt one land on his neck. He'd immobilized the man with the first blow and now he took his time, punishing him. He couldn't stop punching Minsky. The face below was becoming pulpy and red. Ash turned Minsky onto his stomach. He yanked Minsky's arm, heard the dislocating snap. He snapped the other arm. Minsky was whimpering, "Stop."

Ash stood up. Minsky's face was in the dirt. His arms looked twisted and dead, like they'd been glued onto him the wrong way. He was moving his head, groaning. His shoes pushed back and forth in the dirt, leaving a thin impression in the dead leaves and soil.

"Tell David I'm leaving. Tell him to stay away from me. I'm no threat to him. It's his business what he wants to do. I'm finished here. Tell him if he comes after me again, I'll kill you, all of you. You hear me? Say it."

"Oh, god," Minsky groaned, unable even to roll on the ground, his black hair alive with crawling insects. The night buzzed. Minsky tried to get up but his arms were useless. He tried to rise by propping himself with his forehead on the ground. He fell back. He didn't seem to have a nose anymore, just a fleshy blotch in the middle of his face. His shirt had ridden up and a cicada landed on his bare back.

"Say it."

"I'll . . . tell . . . him."

Ash kicked him in the kidneys. Minsky rolled on his side, tears streaming down his face. His face was unrecognizable.

Ash retrieved his gun.

"That's for my cat," he said.

At one A.M. Ash exited the last train to Vienna, Virginia, and stood in the night. The air was finally cooling. Without the

concrete of the city there was a few degrees' relief out here.
Suburban Virginia was heavy and still.

Cars picking up the other passengers pulled out of the parking
lot. Ash left the metro station and walked out onto the street
until he found an all-night Mobil station across from a closed
Toys "R" Us. He was in an ugly suburban strip of shopping
malls and gas stations. He asked the attendant for a map of the
area, then checked street names until he found the one he
wanted. It was ten miles away, in Reston. Ash called a cab
company, gave his name as Jackson, and asked for a ride to a
street a quarter mile from where he wanted to go.

By the time he reached his destination on foot it was after two.
He was on a quiet suburban block where all the houses looked
the same. They were two-story colonials with green shutters,
flower gardens up against the bay windows, and two-car garages
with imitation Amish good-luck charms on the gables.

Ash walked up a curving walk and rang the bell. There was a
heavy metal bumper sticker on one upstairs window. After a
minute a light went on in another. There was the sound of
footsteps coming downstairs. A man's voice said, muffled with
sleep but wary, "What is it?"

"Horace?" Ash said.

"Who is it?"

Ash said conversationally, "James Ash, from the *Post*, Mr.
Cragg."

The door swung open. The little State Department bureaucrat stood in a robe and light blue pajamas tied at the waist with
a white string. He was barefoot. His hair was tousled. There was
a plaster-cast black jockey by an umbrella stand behind him,
instead of in the garden, where those things usually stood. It was
under a chandelier where little light bulbs were shaped like
flickering candles.

"Oh, God," Horace Cragg said.

"You've been phoning me," Ash said.

"Who is it, Horace?" a scratchy, irritated woman's voice
called from upstairs.

"In a minute," Horace called back.

"Well, what did you want?" Ash said.

"I was just . . . I was . . . what are you doing here?" Horace said. "It's three o'clock in the morning."

"I decided not to run the story on you," Ash said.

Cragg sagged against the doorjamb with relief. Then he said, "You came here to tell me that?"

Ash held up a hand. "Remember you told me you'd owe me a favor?"

"Now?"

"It's easy," Ash said. "I want to sleep here tonight. And I want to borrow your car tomorrow. I'll keep it a secret. You'll keep it a secret."

"My car?"

"For a day."

"Sleep *here?*" Horace Cragg said.

"You have a problem?" Ash said.

"What'll I tell my wife?"

"Horace," the voice upstairs called. "What is going on down there!"

"Tell her," Ash said, "it's State Department business. You can't talk about it. They gave you something important to do."

"They never give me anything important to do," Horace said. His eyes widened. "There's blood on your shirt."

"Yeah. I need to borrow a shirt, too. A big one. Your size is too small. You have one of those Hawaiian shirts?"

Horace hesitated and Ash said, colder, "Been down to Fourteenth Street lately, Horace?" Horace went white. A woman in curlers came into view behind him. She stomped up to him. She smelled of cold cream. She glared at Ash. "Who are you?" she said.

"I am so sorry to get here this late," Ash told Horace. "Your directions were terrific but Amtrak broke down. They made everyone wait. Ma'am, I hope I didn't put you out. Horace said you'd make a special dinner. I tried to call but it's impossible from the train."

"What is he talking about?" the woman demanded.

"Horace, you said she was pretty but she's beautiful," Ash said.

She said, "I never been beautiful in my life. Horace, did you forget to tell me a guest was coming?"

"Uh, yes."

"What is it with you, Alzheimer's disease?" she said.

"I hope I'm not causing an argument," Ash said.

"You going to make him stand out there all night?" the woman said, looking like she'd kill Horace once they got upstairs.

"Come in," Horace Cragg said, turning to introduce them. "This is . . . I bet I told you about him from Berkeley . . . this is, uh, James . . ."

"Jackson," Ash said. "All I need is a couch, ma'am." Cragg closed the door behind him. Ash was suddenly exhausted. He needed to sleep. "I know it's late. Don't worry about the linens. Just a couch'll be great. Hey, Horace, what was the name of that girl in chem?"

In his dream Ash walked by the banks of a stream in a forest of Russian birch, with Yuri beside him. Ash unwrapped a Chuckles candy. Yuri packed his pipe. A big raven in a branch made a hooting sound like a monkey. It was winter but green leaves were on the trees. Ash tried to chew the Chuckles but he couldn't, it was stuck in his mouth. There was snow on the ground but it was hot, like summer. Large, black insects crawled in the snow, crunched beneath Yuri's sneakers.

"Here's the code. Here's the code. Call me if you need me," Yuri said.

"Why didn't you tell me you were my father when you were alive?" Ash said.

Yuri just smiled and packed the pipe. It was so hot and snow began falling. Then Ash saw what was falling was insects, pale white insects with translucent wings.

"Get up," Horace Cragg was saying. His face looked huge and terrified above Ash. "Who's Yuri?" he said.

"Is it morning already?" Ash said.

Cragg's wife and punk-rocker son glared at him at the breakfast table. In the car, on the way to work, Cragg said he told
them Ash was an old friend who'd gotten out of prison.

"Prison?" Ash said.

"In the old days people I knew at Berkeley were pretty radical.
You know the Symbionese Liberation Army?"

"Don't tell me you were in the Symbionese Liberation
Army," Ash said.

Cragg looked exhausted. Ash figured his wife had kept him up
all night. "A guy in my geology class was."

At the State Department Cragg handed over the keys, looking
worried. "Just for a day, right? Don't you have your own car?
Doesn't the *Post* give you a car? What are you going to do with
this car anyway?"

Ash just looked at him. Horace slumped. "You're not coming
back tonight, are you?"

"I'll call and tell you where I leave the car. Thanks, Horace."

Cragg disappeared into the building and Ash called the bank,
but the vault wasn't open yet. "An hour, they promise they'll
have it open in an hour," the manager said.

Ash went back to the car and sat and thought a minute. He
was wearing one of Cragg's old Hawaiian shirts and a baseball
cap that said BUETI'S DELI and the Honda had Virginia plates.
"Never take things for granted," Dietz had told them in Smith
Falls, but the truth was, to hell with her, he wanted to drive
around while he waited. He was sick of hiding and he knew he
would only be spotted through a fluke.

Ash drove into downtown Washington through rush-hour
traffic. Around him commuters in suits listened to their morning
radio shows, munched rolls, drank coffee, tried to rouse themselves to get interested in the day's work. Ash remembered
covering Jimmy Carter's presidential inauguration. Only what he
thought of now was the outgoing president, Ford, and the way
Ford had left town. Ford had gotten into a Marine helicopter on
the west lawn of the White House. Then the helicopter had lifted
off and made a circle around the town. Then the helicopter had
done it again and finally flown off.

Ash was saying good-bye to Washington.

Ash drove the battered gray Honda along Massachusetts Avenue, past the embassy where he'd watched the Japanese diplomat carry David's message inside. He drove past the *Post*, seeing the sun glint off the orange windows on the upper floors. He passed through Georgetown, where he'd lived with Corinna. He found himself downtown in front of the FBI.

How many times during the last seventeen years had Ash thought about the FBI? Feared they might catch him? How many times had he passed this building on his way to the theater or a friend's house or Capitol Hill or a story in Virginia. All those people trying to track Soviets in Washington, all those people who would come after him if they ever guessed who he was. Ash double-parked across from the FBI and looked at the building. At the secretaries and bureaucrats hurrying in for the day. A little driveway entered the grounds, past a guard building, where a uniformed man checked IDs.

While Ash watched, a Diamond cab pulled up to the driveway. Jennifer Knowles got out and walked inside.

Ash started the engine and rolled up Twelfth Street. There was a deadness inside him, a heavyness in his arms and throat. At Dupont Circle he turned onto Connecticut Avenue and traffic picked up because it was heading away from downtown. Ash felt utterly empty.

Fight it, he thought. You knew there was something wrong with her.

He turned on the radio. "There's been a blackout of news from Moscow," the announcer said. Ash switched channels and rock music blared from the car. She'd been wearing a peasant dress and sandals and a white cotton blouse. Her pageboy hair had bounced when she'd run up the driveway. She'd carried a little black purse strung over her shoulder. She'd been in a hurry. Moving fast.

Ash found a parking space near the bank, and when he got inside, the vault was open. He signed the right papers and waited for someone ahead of him to come back out of the vault. The $50,000 was in hundreds and fifties, bound with green rubber bands. He put most of it in a lunch bag he carried. He put some in his pocket and took his false IDs outside.

In the street, he ripped the false passport, driver's license, and other ID cards into tiny pieces. He dropped them into a corner wastebasket. Then he continued up Connecticut Avenue, to the Beltway, and took Route 95 north, and the city was gone.

Ash kept to the speed limit passing through Maryland and into Delaware. He would leave the car in Wilmington and phone Horace Cragg to find a way to pick it up. He would buy a used car and pay cash for it, then use the temporary registration to get him to Massachusetts. He didn't know what he would do after that. First he had to get to Smith Falls.

When he turned off the interstate, he stopped for lunch at a diner. The waitress was cute and spoke with a French accent. She told him she was a student at the University of Delaware. He said he was a lawyer in Philadelphia, working in the office of an assistant DA. She lingered at his table when she brought his cheeseburger, joked a little, asked if he was sticking around, asked if he had relatives in Delaware, asked if he had cases involving "dangerous criminals." Ash mindlessly turned pages in *USA Today*.

When the waitress brought the check, she'd taken off her apron and just wore jeans and a university T-shirt. "I get off now," she said. "I guess I'll go back to the campus and work."

He looked up at her. She looked a little like Jennifer, the way her nose turned up, the streak of dirty blond in her brown shiny hair. "I guess I should head out of here also," he said. She looked hopeful, smiled. Ash said, "I have a long way to drive," and she just said, "Business or pleasure?" Ash had to think about that.

"Both, I guess," he said as they strolled out of the diner together. The sun was dazzling on the pavement. There was a used car lot across the four-lane street. There were little colored flags on poles in front of the cars. Even at this distance Ash could make out thick black lettering in cardboard signs in the windows. "A Honey!" "Drive It!" "Wowwww!"

"I'm going home," he told the waitress as he headed for his car and she walked off toward a bus stop. He hoped it was true. It felt true. "I have to see my father about a few things," he said.

ELEVEN

MAJOR GREGOR VOLSKY RODE the Moscow metro to Dzerzhinsky Square and strode through rush-hour traffic toward the massive, gray, marble-trimmed headquarters of the KGB. A lone militiaman directed cars around the unmarked building. Crowds streaming past the statue of founder Iron Feliks kept their eyes on the ground. Even in these more liberal days they feared being noticed by the KGB. Volsky passed beneath the white bas-relief of Yuri Andropov and pushed through the tall oak door. The entrance guards glanced from his eyepatch to his ID, stiffened with respect, and let him pass.

On the ground floor, headquarters might have been any of dozens of diplomatic posts he'd visited in his career. Men and women in uniform or suits hurried along white marble hallways on red carpets, through double oak doors, up wide, winding stairways under glowing chandeliers. Volsky rode the packed, silent elevator to the fourth floor. The veneer of statecraft dropped away and the hard military aspect dominated. Those important enough to work here carried themselves with the confident, straight-backed demeanor of top-echelon leadership in a totalitarian country. The brisk pace reminded him of preparations for a military campaign.

Volsky had a list of names Ash had given him. He planned to check them against the KGB's computerized file of current employees. If that didn't work, he would try pensioners. But even if records existed, they might be too classified for a mere major to access them. That's why Akromeyev's dispatching him to Moscow didn't make sense. Akromeyev had higher clearance than Volsky. He could check the names from Washington. Volsky didn't like the way Akromeyev had said, "Let me worry about it," when Volsky had asked what would happen to Ash.

Volsky had slept almost the entire flight to Moscow, but in his dreams he'd been back in Afghanistan, unable to help his men. The stewardess who had laid a blanket over the handsome man with the eyepatch hadn't known he was on a high mountain, in a snowstorm, trying to keep a wounded private from drifting fatally to sleep. The American fur trader across the aisle, sipping scotch and envying his neighbor's ability to doze on a plane, had never dreamed that beneath the peaceful countenance the major was squatting in a smoke-filled hut, pulling bandages from the pack of a dead medic, trying to stop blood spurting from the neck of a sergeant who screamed in agony.

Maybe if I would have tried harder, I could have saved that man, Volsky thought when he woke. Then his attention was caught by a line of tanks moving toward Moscow while the Aeroflot jet descended over the western Soviet plains. Maneuvers, he thought. Now, in headquarters, the memory of the dying sergeant flashed back to him. And made him angry. Although Volsky had visited this building only briefly during his rise through the KGB, he shared the field officer's condescension toward bureaucrats who never left their offices and sent other soldiers to fight. Desk jockeys, Volsky thought, remembering the expression he had learned in the United States. These are the desk jockeys who sent my friends to die in Afghanistan.

If Ash had been telling the truth, he was like those friends. Ordered to do a job and forgotten and left in the cold.

Records turned out to be a long, drab room lit by overly bright bulbs in copper fixtures above rows of desks where uniformed women typed at computer screens. They kept track of KGB recruits, retirees, and everything that happened in between. Commendations and disciplinary marks. Transfers. Inquiries. Observations from officers about loyalty, trustworthiness, potential.

Volsky knew it was a massive job. The KGB had 555,000 members, 265,000 of them border guards, with their own tank units, artillery, ships, and air force, 230,000 in other military units, 40,000 assigned to spying on the Russian people, and another 20,000, the elite division of which Volsky was a part, working in intelligence abroad.

"Captain! Captain Volsky! I thought that was you!"

Volsky turned. Limping up to him in his crisp brown uniform, grin on his face, was one of his men who had helped in the Petrov case. Dimitri Ageev, then a junior lieutenant, and veteran of Afghanistan, now, from the green band on his cap, a proud captain. Ageev was an eager comer, a fine investigator back in Kiev, a hard worker, youthful ladies' man, an enormous drinker, and now, he said, sweeping his hand to encompass the massive room, "the man who makes sure the men get their rubles."

For Volsky such a meeting was a stroke of luck. Otherwise it could take hours or days to get access to the computers. "I heard you were posted to Washington, Captain," Ageev said. "Ah! Major now! Congratulations! How is it? Here things are tough, tough. You can't even get a carrot in the shop."

They chatted for a few minutes, catching up, then Volsky said he was trying to track people who worked for the KGB twenty years ago. They might still be active. Ageev said he would check the files up to clearance-level orange, which was Volsky's level; high, but far from red.

Ageev waved a pear-shaped, sullen-looking redhead off the nearest computer and took the seat himself.

"Okay, chief," he said merrily, "what directorate do you want to check?" The KGB was broken into nine directorates, or divisions. Volsky said he didn't know.

But Ageev just laughed. "Starting from scratch, eh? Just like Petrov. You'll get them! Back on the hunt!"

They went through Border Guards, Internal Security, Surveillance. Volsky gave Ageev names. DuChamp. Dietz. Martini.

Kazanjian. Posner the guard, who Ash had said had been his only friend when he was a boy.

Ageev lost none of his cheeriness.

"Twenty years is a long time," he said, shrugging when they came up empty. "Why don't you check pensioners across town, although they don't have computers yet. They're still using paper files." Ageev laughed. "What am I·saying? Me telling *you*? I'll write you a note."

Ageev scribbled something on a slip of paper stamped with the KGB shield. "Give this to Captain Nazarbayev. Big stomach." Ageev held out both hands, forming a circle to indicate girth. "Tell him you're the captain I always talk about. He's a good fellow. Probably ask you questions about American women. Did I tell you I got married?" Ageev rolled his eyes lasciviously. "Want to see a picture of the baby?"

From outside in the hallway came the heavy tread of someone running. "What's all the activity today?" Volsky asked.

Ageev looked surprised. Then he said, "Of course, why would you know? You just got here. The big rehearsal is today. Countercoup."

"Countercoup?" Volsky asked.

"Yes, a rehearsal. If there is ever an attempt at ousting our beloved MG," Ageev said with a wink, "we all must be ready to repel the plotters."

Volsky remembered the tank columns he had seen from the plane, crawling toward the capital. An uneasy feeling inside him grew.

"Countercoup," he said.

David Kislak arranged the plates and wineglasses on the mobile dining cart. He'd sent the waiter back to Chez Daphne and told the man he would serve Corinna himself. For this lunch everything had to be perfect. The white wine breathed in its silver bucket. The blackened redfish simmered on a hot plate beside the long white candles. There were bottles of cold Perrier by the fresh-cut roses, and lemon tarts warmed on the lower level for dessert. He lit the candles with the gold dragon lighter he'd been given by the Chinese premier in Shanghai.

"No calls during lunch," he'd instructed his secretary. His office door would be locked and Corinna would stay until late in the day.

Kislak would tell Corinna the truth today. He had been putting it off and he had no choice. It would be tricky, but she would understand, he told himself. If she didn't, with a little time, patience, and loving, she would.

Kislak poured the wine, imagined her walking into the lobby, all the male heads turning. He envisioned her slim white finger pressing the button of his floor. He was hard already. He loved when she asked to have lunch in the office. It meant she was randy or upset, which turned into the same thing after they talked. After twenty years they were still like animals ripping at each other, in heat.

Then he thought of Ash and the rage made him dizzy. He remembered Price coming to the house last night to tell him about Minsky. Minsky was in Georgetown Hospital, after being "mugged." He'd told the police he didn't remember his assailant. Minsky was useless now. Ash was gone.

Or was he gone? Kislak drank wine without waiting for Corinna.

"David."

He advanced toward her, arms outstretched. She looked beautiful in a plain dark blue business suit, frilly lace bow tie by her throat. He drew her close, felt her hips against his groin. She just stood there, a little distant. Whatever it was, he'd talk her out of it and then things would be fine.

"I am your waiter, Emil," David said. "Let me 'andle your menu today." The shades were drawn, the office dark. Sometimes they made love on his leather couch. He loved when she rode him and the metal studs on the leather dug into his back, and he could feel the sharp, smooth bones inside her raking his prick.

He pulled the chair out for her.

"I 'ave taken ze liberty of ordering your favorite, Louisiana fish with very spicy ingredient," he said, smiling his best smile. "Some wine? A very good white!"

"Ash came to my apartment last night," Corinna said.

He kept the smile on his face with the supremest effort. But he was stunned. She hadn't phoned him. He poured the wine and said, "Um-hmm," and inside he screamed with rage.

Once again Ash was ruining what was supposed to happen. They were supposed to dine and make love and then he would say, "Corinna, have you ever dreamed of leaving here? You and me going, never coming back?" And she would say, "But we can't do that," and he would say, "We can. They've shut us down," which was the small white lie, but only Ash could guess that. She would look happy. Then he would say, "When you finish this last job, it's over." He would say, "When can you tell me what evidence the Justice Department has on Manila Refineries?"

What he wouldn't say until months later, when they were settled in the new place, with their new passports, villa, servants, and she understood why he had done it, would be, "I'm getting five million in cash."

"He said you were lying to us," Corinna said.

Us. That bothered him. Us meant all of them, the whole group. He didn't like when she thought about the others. It complicated things. "You could have been hurt!" Kislak said, coming around the cart, stroking her cheek with the back of his fingers. His gold Yale ring slid down her flesh.

"David . . ."

"If something happened to you, I don't know what I would do," he said.

"He didn't hurt me," she said.

"Glorie Pell," he reminded her. "He attacked her." There was a spot below her left ear where she was sensitive. Brushing it, he saw the barest relaxation of the outline of her shoulder blades. He was thinking, I can send Price. Price knows how to shoot. He isn't as quick as Minsky, but he'll do the job.

"Tell me where he is," David said.

"I don't know."

David said, "Ze fish, it is magnificent." He lifted the silver cover and the spicy aroma of Cajun cooking rose with the steam. She was so beautiful it could stop his heart. She wore small turquoise earrings in gold, teardrop-shaped frames. Flesh-colored lipstick that caught the light. The severely cut business suit gave a delightful sense of body underneath. Like she sat utterly naked, as she would soon be.

Then she wrecked the mood again, starting on Ash. "David, he said there's something wrong with you. He thinks you're selling information." David burst out laughing, fork poised, dripping with hearts of palm and Béarnaise sauce. "What an imagination. He's never changed."

"That's what I'm afraid of."

This was going to take a while, Kislak saw. She'd given him an argument yesterday when he sent Minsky with her, to watch her apartment. He thought, wait a minute. What if Ash came to her apartment *before* he attacked Minsky. What if she pointed out Minsky to him?

Suddenly Kislak envisioned her in bed, with Ash. Like when they'd been married. He couldn't stand thinking about it. Kislak wanted to scream.

Kislak chewed. "Very good. Try it." The food tasted like cardboard.

"Even when we were kids he was right. We just didn't realize it," she said.

"You're serious," Kislak said, using his stunned look. Once, at a news conference before Reagan sent troops to Grenada, a reporter had asked Kislak if an invasion was imminent. Kislak had used the look. Later Reagan had said, "You should have been the actor, not me."

"Madame, you are not even trying ze fish. Pierre will be very upset."

"Stop it," she said.

Kislak put the fork down, wiped his mouth with his linen napkin.

"Tell me now," she said. "Stop pretending it's nothing. Stop treating me like I wouldn't have figured this out. Why do you want this Philippine information? *What is going on!"*

He laughed and threw up both hands in mock surrender. "Okay, you win," he said like it was no big deal. Ash never should have come here, he thought. I told Yuri not to send Ash. Told him he'd mess things up. I always hated Ash. I tried to keep Minsky from saving him in the forest that day. Tried to screw up our direction in the woods. But Yuri said it was an act and we had to save him so he'd start liking us. And Minsky wanted to fight more than he wanted to watch Ash get beaten up.

Yuri had said before he'd left for America, "You're a sociopath, David. Do you know what that is? It's someone who doesn't believe in rules. Someone who believes he makes the rules. It's why I love you, David. It's your special talent. It's a very, very good thing. But it can get out of control. It's why you are such a good leader. But it's why Ash has to go along."

"All right, I'll tell you," he said smoothly.

She started eating. Good sign. "Good," she said.

David said, "Corinna, have you ever dreamed of leaving here, you and me?"

"What?"

"Never coming back?"

His buzzer hummed. That stupid secretary, he thought. She never buzzed him during a Corinna lunch.

"But we can't do that," she said.

He nodded. "We can. They're shutting us down." Despite her anger, hope leaped in her face. "That's right," he said. "Yuri said it would happen someday. They just want one last piece of information." She looked doubtful. He leaned forward. "You may have noticed, in the last few months, I've wanted different sorts of information. Business things." She nodded. Her eyes were enormous. He said, "It's the changes at home, everything revamped. Like your Philippine case. Ten years ago Moscow would never have wanted information on a court case, a trade case. But now *we* want to trade. *We* want to be in that market. We're setting up our own companies. *They* spy on each other's companies. We're being used differently now, Corinna. You can't imagine the changes going on at home. New people. New orders. New jobs for us." He drank wine. "We're already inside American companies." He laughed. He was doing well. "We've turned into industrial spies," he said. "Capitalists. Part of the transition to a new economy. Why, in Silicon Valley—"

"Why are they shutting us down if we're so effective as industrial spies?" she said.

"What?"

"Well, if this information is so crucial to the new Soviet Union, why disband the people providing it?"

Kislak chuckled. "It is pretty stupid," he admitted. "They don't tell me everything. I'm just the messenger boy when it comes to them. But if I had to take a guess, I'd say—"

"Shut up," Corinna said.

They stared at each other. He was shocked. Never, ever, in twenty-five years, had she told him to shut up. The buzzer hummed and Kislak just unhooked the wire and the room fell silent again. Less steam rose off the blackened redfish. The Béarnaise sauce smelled sour to him.

I'll kill him. I'll figure out a way and kill him, Kislak thought.

"David, leave Ash alone. He's never done anything to you. He let me go to you. Tell me what's going on, now!"

The knocking got louder. "Go away!" Kislak yelled.

The knocking stopped. Kislak shook his head in admiration, his your-mind-works-really-fast look. "I was going to tell you," he said. "Today." He laughed. "But you wrecked my presentation. Look at this, the wine, the flowers. You beat me to the punch! We really can go away. Don't you want that? Aren't you sick of the way we've been living? I have IDs. And money. When you get that Philippine information, we're out of here." He gazed into her eyes. "Name the place. Mexico? You want to live there? Is that too hot? Ecuador. I know it's far away, but if you have money, you can live like Rockefeller. It's cooler in the mountains." He'd said too much. Corinna looked horrified.

The knocking started again, more timid now.

"So Ash was right," she said. "You're selling it. I can't believe it. I can't believe you've been using us, all of us."

Kislak sighed. "Look at me, Corinna. You think I'd do that?

I take orders. I only have so much leeway. Yes, I'm selling it, but that's what I was ordered to do. And I questioned it and they threatened me, and then"—he laughed—"they said I could keep some. The carrot and the stick. They said if I did it for three years, I could stop. They're crooked, Corinna. Thieves." He said, "The very top. And I mean very. I couldn't fight them."

"You went after Ash to protect yourself," she said.

"Stop talking about Ash. We can go away!"

"That's all you can think about? Going away?" She was staring at him like he was a different person. He said, "I didn't try to kill him. I just wanted to scare him. I love you."

"You're disgusting," she said. There was something in the look that stopped him. And then he understood. She actually didn't believe him. Kislak went cold. She's going to leave me, he thought. She's going to go with him. Never, in all Kislak's years, had such a thought occurred to him. The room seemed to sway. The angry lines stood out on her face. The most incredible rush of panic flooded him. He said, "Listen to me," but it was just words, he was talking without an end in mind, saying anything while he tried to think of another lie. But he was collapsing inside. She was the only person he loved. Life without Corinna was the most terrifying thing he could imagine. He heard a voice that couldn't be his, it was too high, it was a man's voice, not Corinna's, it couldn't be his yet it was, and it was saying, "Don't leave me."

"Leave you?" she said. "Who said anything about leaving you? I hate you, but I'm not leaving you."

She pushed back from the table.

Kislak said, almost weeping with relief as the knocking grew loud, "We're free. I'll leave Ash alone. I promise. *Just get that information and we can leave!*"

Kislak stomped to the door, swung it open, looked into his secretary's irritated face, and barked, "What?"

She said, "Mr. Kislak, I'm sorry, I know she's here, but there's a client, a new person. I *told* him your lunches run late, but first he said he'd wait and now he's becoming annoying." She pursed her lips. "He just walked in off the street, but he's a big client. A new client. I'm sorry if I was wrong in interrupting you."

"Who is it?" Kislak said, feeling the daring of escape, success, completion. A soaring feeling. She wouldn't leave him. Kislak pulling triumph from the fire.

The blood pounded in his head he was so giddy. He set his face in a businesslike expression and tried to concentrate over the raging celebration in his head. It didn't make a difference how angry she was. With time he'd wear it down and things would be the same as always. He'd tell Corinna the real truth someday. That there wasn't any boss anymore. That Moscow didn't even know they were here anymore. That he kept all the money for himself and for her. Right now Miss Harris's words came to him faintly, from a distance. He had to ask her to repeat them. And when she did, the blood rushed from him.

She said, attentive to his mood, "His name is Akromeyev. From the Russian embassy. . . .

"Are you all right? He wants to hire us," Miss Harris said.

If the condition of this building is any indication of how pensioners are treated, they're in bad shape, Major Gregor Volsky thought. A fat KGB officer waddled toward him across the filthy lobby of the pre–World War Two converted warehouse. Volsky had taken three buses through seedier and seedier areas of Moscow to reach here. The guards at the entrance had had their tunics unbuttoned, their shoes scuffed.

"*You* are Captain Volsky! Dimitri always talks about you," the fat captain said. Volsky smelled alcohol and garlicky sausage. It seemed impossible an officer could be allowed to get so heavy. The man hadn't even properly shaved. But if Captain Nazarbayev was Ageev's friend, there was probably some substance to him. Despite the size difference between the fitter Ageev and the corpulent mountain in front of Volsky, both captains had an easygoing grin.

"You want to track down pensioners?" Nazarbayev laughed. "At least you're not here for money! That's what visitors to this place usually want. Well, I want something from you, too! A question! Do American women really always wear perfume, even under the covers? If you can't smell the woman you're with, why be with her? And anyway, don't they all smell the same if that's the case?"

"I'm sure you could find differences," Volsky said. Nazarbayev roared, drunker than he looked or more easily amused. "He said you were quick!"

Nazarbayev led him up three flights of stairs—"Our elevator broke in 1982"—through a waiting room packed with old men and women staring hopefully at bored, uniformed clerks sifting through volumes of records at a snail's pace, past the counter, and into a gigantic room, big as a ballroom. It encompassed most of the original warehouse, only now it was packed with musty-smelling, brown, leather-bound volumes of records lining gray steel shelves. There were no windows, only sickly light from bare bulbs. Volsky heard the creak of rolling ladders in the aisles. A few clerks having a tea break in a corner sprang to their feet when the officers walked by.

Nazarbayev sighed. "Get to work. Those people out there are waiting." The clerks fanned out from the table briskly, so Volsky had a feeling Nazarbayev was stricter than he looked. Nazarbayev held out his hand. "The names."

Then he said, with interest, "Let's narrow things down. You've only got a rank for two of these people. Kazanjian the lieutenant rifle instructor. And Posner, the corporal guard. You have no first name for Kazanjian. But Posner, hmmmm. Their records could be unimportant enough to be here. 1967. We hit the indexes. Posner. Posner," he said, strolling down an aisle that barely allowed him movement. "Posner. *P. Pr. Pos.* Ah!"

In tiny, barely legible, hand-scrawled pencil letters were at least four hundred Posners in the KGB Border Guards in 1967. But only twenty-one Viktor Posners. Only five of them had been corporals at one time or another. Only two listed birthplaces in the Ukraine.

"This is a very positive sign," Captain Nazarbayev beamed. "Now to the dungeon."

Volsky followed him back down the stairs to the basement.

The second room had a ceiling so low that Volsky stooped, even though he probably didn't have to. He smelled mouse droppings. This time the steel shelves were piled with white cardboard boxes. "These," Nazarbayev said, "are the actual files.

"Not all the files are here. *A* through *M* were just moved to Leningrad."

With the shelves at their backs, they sat at a rickety table of plain Russian birch, beneath a bare bulb, beside a barred window overlooking an alley where vandals had scrawled HEAVY METAL in blue paint. Volsky opened the first file. There was a snapshot of an unemotional-looking man, fleshy face, a little old to be a corporal, bald on top, a birthdate and a town in the Ukraine. A good-conduct commendation. A decent rifleman. A mechanic, too. It looked promising. Volsky turned to the second page.

DECEASED was stamped over the back of the form.

Volsky opened the second file. This man also seemed old to be a corporal. He checked the back before going on and there was no deceased stamp. There was a birthplace in the Ukraine and a mailing address in Odessa, the Black Sea resort town, a good place to retire. The man had served in the East. An unspectacular record. Decent marksman. Twenty-five-year man. One commendation for good behavior. Loves music. Volsky copied down the address where the checks were mailed.

"I hope that's him," Captain Nazarbayev said. "Why are you looking for him anyway?"

Volsky said nothing. Nazarbayev said, "Why do I even ask?"

An hour later Volsky was on the Tupolev 124 one-o'clock flight to Odessa, looking down at the wheat-field-covered steppes of the Ukraine as they headed south. The flight was smooth, and planes to Odessa tended to be filled with happier passengers: foreign tourists or Party officials going on vacation. Behind him were a couple of travel writers from Manhattan, cooing to each other and sipping champagne. Again he saw tank columns below, this time moving south. He tried to read the paper. Tass reported MG was vacationing near Foros, writing a new book for the American publisher HarperCollins.

Volsky was too anxious to read.

Outside, Air Force Tupolev fighters swept past, also heading south, with the citrus farms north of the Black Sea coming into view ahead. The fighters easily outdistanced the slower passenger jet. Volsky wondered if they were also on maneuvers for the countercoup.

By the time he landed it was late afternoon. KGB troops lined the runways, concentrated around one hangar far across the tarmac. "Looks like more troops than usual. Someone important must be here," a knowledgeable, professorish-looking passenger said to his seatmate as they waited in the aisle to exit.

Volsky splurged on a cab. The driver wore a souvenir T-shirt from Kabul and claimed his meter was broken. The man chain-smoked cigarettes, honked his horn a lot for fun, and pointed out sights. The opera house. The open-air theater. The stadium. The shoe store where his brother worked. The road to the "very good Arcadia spa."

"You seem to be driving in a circle," Volsky said at one point. The man touched one finger to his shirt. "It just seems that way because the streets are crooked," he said. They cruised up poplar-lined Primorsky Boulevard past tourists in shorts and sandals strolling, shopping, coming back from the beach. Bells rang on the trolleys. The summer heat was cooler than Washington's, the smell of salt water invigorating, yet Volsky was gripped by a strange sense of urgency. He could not get Ash out of his mind. He could not stop thinking of his dream on the plane last night.

The Lada taxi took the winding streets back out of the city and began threading narrow streets overlooking the harbor, filled with yellowing block-style Soviet-workers housing, limestone buildings, identical squarish, seven-story units with balconies strewn with wash, tricycles, little palm trees, lawn chairs. Boys played soccer in the street. The tourists were gone. As they drew closer to his destination, Volsky's excitement grew.

Finally the driver eased to a stop in front of another yellowing building. He named a ridiculously high fare. Volsky pulled out money but let the man see his ID. The driver turned white. "I thought you were tourist. Please. No charge," he said. Instead,

Volsky handed over a fair amount. The man looked surprised, but quickly left.

The mailbox said POSNER—14. Volsky mounted green linoleum stairs, hoping he'd found the right man. The hallway echoed with the sounds of a man shouting, "Kick it!" over and over again over the crowd and announcer noise of a televised soccer match, radio news, American rock-and-roll music, a dog barking, and bad coughing. A woman carrying garbage downstairs glanced fearfully at Volsky; the suit and eyepatch probably meant KGB to her.

The smell of good borscht made Volsky hungry. No. 14 occupied the end of the fourth-floor hallway.

The coughing grew worse behind the green door.

Volsky instantly recognized the man who opened the door at his knock as the man in the file he had seen this morning. The years had grayed the man's hair, thickened his nose into a drinker's bulb shape, and lengthened his earlobes a little, but the heavy, squarish face was the same, and so was the placid look directed at him from pale blue eyes behind wire spectacles. Viktor Posner was wearing a sleeveless undershirt torn at the chest, charcoal black cotton pajama bottoms, and worn backless slippers. Over his shoulder, Volsky took in the neat, tiny apartment, which didn't seem to go with the rotting odor and whiff of rubbing alcohol coming to him. The coughing started up from a figure on a couch in front of a black-and-white television. A black man played jazz trumpet on the set, but the sound was barely audible. The figure lay under a heavy blanket of purplish wool even though the room was hot. Volsky couldn't see the face, couldn't tell from the hacking if the patient was a man or a woman.

"Mr. Posner," Volsky began, uncomfortable with *comrade*. "My name is Gregor Volsky. Please don't be alarmed. I am a major for the KGB."

The placid look remained in place, and Volsky saw it was not calm but weariness. The blue eyes took in his suit and tie.

"I can see I'm here at a bad time so I must apologize, but I want to talk to you about something that happened, well, many years ago. It's nothing to be worried about."

The man snorted. "They send a major for nothing." The trumpet music was Miles Davis, "Blue in Green." Posner said, irritated, "I told the others who came! How many times are you people going to come!"

"Papa," a girl's voice called from the couch. The youth of it shocked Volsky. He'd been speculating wife. "Don't get excited this time," the voice said.

"Other people came here?" Volsky said.

Apparently, Posner was not going to follow the sick girl's advice. Crimson color was seeping into his face. "You see I'm alive, can't you?" He plucked the chest of his undershirt so it snapped. "My wife is the one who died, not me! No wonder this country is falling apart if so many people have to work on a pension for one retired corporal. I worked for you twenty-seven years."

"Oh, it was just a pension matter," Volsky said.

"No, not 'just,' because that pension pays for a good doctor for her," the old man snapped. "You want to see my papers again? Ivana's death certificate again?" The coughing exploded behind him. Posner whirled and rushed to the couch.

He cradled the girl's head in his hands. Volsky, who had followed, was shocked at the red eyes boiling out of the skull. From the face, Volsky guessed her age at twenty-five or twenty-six. But close up the body beneath the covers looked as thin as a ten-year-old. "Papa's here. Shaa, shaa," Posner crooned.

On the television, Miles Davis told an interviewer, in raspy English and above Russian subtitles, "I love the French people. I love Montreux."

Volsky waited until the coughing subsided. Posner rocked the girl. "I'm not here about your pension, Mr. Posner. I want to talk about something else that happened a long time ago. Somewhere you were posted."

Posner didn't look back, but Volsky knew the man listened.

"A little town," Volsky said. "In Siberia."

"Lay on the soft pillow. Isn't it a soft pillow?" Posner told the girl.

"The town of Smith Falls," Volsky said.

"Look how he holds the trumpet, see what I was telling you? The crook of his arm?" Posner said.

"Mr. Posner?" Volsky said.

Posner sighed. Like he'd been hoping Volsky would vanish. A thin, skeletal hand emerged weakly from under the blanket and patted his bald head. Posner said, without turning from the girl, "I was never in Smith Falls. What kind of name is that?"

Volsky moved around so he could see the face. He contained his hope. If there had ever been a Smith Falls, and KGB troops had been stationed there, they would have been warned never to talk about it, would have been given a false story to tell if they were questioned about it, would be insane to blurt it out to anyone, let alone a major asking about it after twenty years.

"I'm not here about the town, but a boy," he said. "James Ash." Posner laid the girl gently back on the pillow. Her red eyes shut. Her hand slid back under the blanket. Posner had tears in his eyes.

Volsky went on, "He would have been a small boy when you knew him."

"What are you talking about?"

"I work in Washington. In the embassy. A man came in and said his name was Ash. You either know this or you don't." Volsky let his eyes rove a little and take in the cheap photos of Posner on the beach, at a happier time, the teenage girl in a red bathing suit, a lean black-haired woman holding Posner's hand. There was a glass mineral-water bottle filled with daisies centering the four-seat eating table, and a freestanding bookshelf unit except instead of books it had piles of newspapers and magazines, a ceramic angel in billowing robes with golden, streaming hair, a heart-shaped photo frame with a photo of a white, shaggy dog in it, a little wooden box on hinges with tiny figures of Christ in the manger inside.

Nothing in plain view reminded Volsky of Ash's story.

"This man Ash is in danger. Like your pension, I guess. We have no record he ever existed. But if his story is true, I can help him, get him back to Russia. Otherwise he's stuck there. This will make no sense to you unless you know it already." Volsky studied the lined face. "Do you know what I'm talking about?"

Posner stood up. He looked back at his daughter. "I'll never get the pension in time. They think I'm someone else," he said miserably.

Suddenly he started shouting. "She's sick! She needs help! I can't pay for it without the pension! I can't pay a good doctor. Sure, there's the government doctor, but it isn't the same! Can't you see how sick she is?"

Posner rummaged in the piles of magazines and thrust crumpled-up discharge papers in Volsky's face. "It's me, me, *me!*" he shouted in agony. "Do I *look* like a woman? My wife is the one who died! My god, I don't want to lose Dina, too!"

Major Gregor Volsky stood in the middle of the studio apartment, looking down at the sick girl. Her hair was stringy from perspiration. Her face was all jutting bones and had a washed-out pallor he had seen in Afghanistan on men soon to die.

A crucifix was above the television where Miles Davis played, eyes closed, floating with his music. Christ was pretty bloody on this particular cross.

Volsky said, not ready to give up, "I'm sorry about the pension. I work in Washington and know nothing about your pension. I'm trying to help this man Ash, and if he was the boy you knew, please tell me. I hear everything you are telling me. But comrade, you know how the KGB works. If you really knew this boy, you would have been asked not to say it. But he grew up and remembers you and he's in trouble now. I can't help him unless I find out more about him."

Volsky wondered what Ash was doing. If Ash had gone back to the embassy. If Ash was in hiding somewhere. "I know you are saying that you didn't know him," Volsky said, "but if you did, if you were that boy's friend, tell me so I can help him. We have no record of him. No way of knowing if he told me the truth. I know you have better things to do than listen to me. I'm sorry your daughter is sick. I hate to be here bothering you. Look at me. What I'm saying is real. Once I leave I can't help him anymore."

Posner fell into the armchair. "Like talking to a rock," he said. "At least she's sleeping now. Go away."

Volsky knew if he hurried back to the airport he might make the evening flight to Moscow. Maybe Ageev or his friend Captain Nazarbayev would have another idea.

Volsky left the apartment and walked downstairs and saw a taxi. He told the driver to wait. He went back upstairs, and when Posner came to the door, said, "Get her dressed. We're going to the KGB hospital." Posner looked stunned but didn't ask questions. Together, they helped the sick girl to the car. She weighed practically nothing. From the looks of the sticklike body Volsky feared cancer. He hated that after years of service the KGB was ignoring Posner. Volsky remembered that during the worst days in Afghanistan, it had been thoughts of his own family that got him through.

The hospital was small and well furnished and just outside of town. In a land of socialized medicine, officers could get special treatment for themselves and their families here. It was clean and bright and the nurses wore starched white uniforms. Volsky flashed his ID in the emergency room, which was crowded, like every emergency room in the Soviet Union. A nurse tried to explain that even Posner, let alone his daughter, couldn't use this facility. Volsky used what he thought of as the KGB stare. Three minutes later the chief doctor, another major, came out in surgical whites.

He took one look at Volsky's suit and eyepatch. Checked the ID. His eyes widened at the word *Washington*. He looked down at the girl.

"We need this girl healthy," Volsky said coldly. The less you said, the more cooperation you got. Beside him, eyes wide in terror and hope, Posner wrung his hands.

"Get her inside," the major told the nurses. To Volsky he said, "You didn't have to threaten me. I would have done it anyway." He smiled.

Volsky left the hospital and strode through the small parking facility to the gate where he'd had the cab wait. Maybe there would be a Kazanjian in Moscow. Maybe Kazanjian would confirm what Ash had said. Maybe if not Kazanjian, he'd figure out something else.

There were running footsteps behind him. A hand gripped his shoulder.

Volsky spun to look into the white, heaving face of ex-corporal Viktor Posner, sixty-eight years old.

"It isn't me, I told you," he said. "I'm not the person you want. I can't do anything for you! There's nothing I can tell you later. Why did you do that?"

Volsky said, "I hope they make her better. I can see you love her very much."

Volsky turned back to the cab.

Behind him, he heard Posner whisper, "Bastards! They told us those children were dead!"

Colonel Sergei Akromeyev felt wonderful being ushered into Kislak's office. It was like being in the field again after years behind a desk. The feeling of anticipation tingled in his fingertips and made his pulse race.

"Mister Akromeyev," Kislak said, pumping his hand, steering him like a favored client to a maroon leather chair. A beautiful woman had left as Akromeyev came in the room. Maybe that had been Corinna Hanson, Akromeyev thought. Did Akromeyev want a drink? Kislak said. Something nonalcoholic like apple juice? Had he been waiting too long? Secretaries, Kislak said, sighing, could let an important man waste hours in a waiting room.

In the old days, questioning had often started in an office and usually ended in a cell. Now Akromeyev accepted a small vodka with ice, reveling at the ease he had had in just coming here. The great thing about America was that everything was for sale. A Russian, the head of the KGB in Washington, could breeze into the office of a former undersecretary of state *to hire him as an employee* and it would be commerce, not politics. Kislak might even already know who he was. What a laugh.

Kislak took the swivel seat behind the desk. Akromeyev had decided on the image he would project. The one he usually used with Americans, the bland, unimportant bureaucrat, wouldn't work here. Any half-intelligent lobbyist would know the Soviets would only entrust a private meeting like this to a high-level operative. So Akromeyev reached into the past for a persona he'd never needed in Washington and never shown Volsky, who saw him as utterly humorless. Today Akromeyev would be the back-country bumpkin outclassed by the sophisticated intellectual with whom he had to deal. A powerful man, but so coarse as to miss the more subtle aspects of a situation. Akromeyev would start out as jovial and avuncular in a faded tweed jacket, open-necked shirt, and light V-necked sweater against air-conditioning. He'd shaved last night instead of this morning to add a hint of shadow to his cheeks. He was a man you'd see whiling away afternoons in a Crimean-island coffee shop, fingering worry beads. No threat.

In the old days, even prisoners who knew Akromeyev's rank would often relax a bare fraction when he walked in like this. Just enough to make breaking them easier when Akromeyev turned nasty.

Akromeyev appreciated the expensive leather sofa and took in the room. There was the vista of the Capitol outside, implying an intimacy between the occupant and the government. And supporting photographs of Kislak with Ronald Reagan and George Bush. Akromeyev noted the obligatory mounted presidential souvenir pens and thank-you notes found in better Washington offices. Kislak had even included a rakish modern-art oil, lots of powder blue slashes against a field of white, showing his interests were broader than mere politics, that he was cultured and knowledgeable in art, too.

Akromeyev said, "We never met when you were in office but I heard many good things about you." Kislak acknowledged the compliment with a smile. Akromeyev laughed. "It is funny how things can turn out, isn't it? That my country would even think of hiring an American consultant to help with our aims."

Kislak laughed heartily; it sure was funny how the world worked, he said. All his attention on the potential client, smile warm and attentive as if Akromeyev were the most fascinating person he had met in a while. They chatted about the changes in Russia, "remarkable," Kislak said. The new administration. "Oh, I still have one or two friends there." Kislak dropped some impressive names to let Akromeyev know the extent of his contacts. An undersecretary of state. An assistant to the head of the Treasury Department. The head of the Senate Subcommittee for foreign loans.

"Perhaps we can do some business," Akromeyev said.

"I hope so!" It was a joke and they both laughed. Kislak beamed. "That would be a pleasure, but I should caution you. Sometimes potential clients come here expecting me to do miracles." He chuckled. Obviously Akromeyev wouldn't turn out to be one of those. Kislak said, stretching his manicured hands wide, "All I am is a conduit. You have something you need. I can help you reach the right person to ask for it or make your case, or just tell them what you think. All I do really is help the system work a little smoother. No miracles. And of course, I always protect anything I knew when I was in office, that is classified."

"Of course."

"I couldn't do anything different. You have to understand that up front."

"No one would expect you to do otherwise. All we want is a fair hearing." Akromeyev edged forward, setting his trap. What he had loved as an interrogator was dealing with a person like this. An overly confident intellectual who believed he was smarter than Akromeyev. A man who addressed Akromeyev as if he were some ex-peasant buffoon. Akromeyev loved the moment they saw the opposite. Then they would try to bluff their way out of their situation, becoming more desperate, and then they would give out a tiny portion of the truth, thinking this would satisfy Akromeyev, when in fact it would whet his appetite.

At the same time, one of Akromeyev's best traits was that he had no trouble accepting the possibility that not everyone was guilty. Akromeyev had never confused getting a guilty man to confess with making an innocent one look like he was guilty. You had to do both for the greater good, but right now only the first possibility mattered.

Akromeyev said, "Sometimes it is hard just to get the right people to listen to you in Washington."

Kislak nodded sympathetically. "I know what you mean."

"People are afraid of us. They don't trust us. They see a Communist conspiracy when all we want to do is business."

Kislak laughed. "That's right," he said. "For seventy-five years we want you to go capitalist. Then you do it and we don't want to deal with you."

"Exactly," Akromeyev said.

"It's funny," Kislak said.

"But there are so many important issues, trade, defense, treaties. Why shouldn't we have the same kind of access to your government that other countries have? Just to make our position known. You, well, they trust you."

"Absolutely. You only want a fair hearing, there's nothing wrong with that." Kislak stood up. He projected a fatherly quality despite his youth. He came around the desk, pulled a chair closer. At least he didn't touch Akromeyev to show he was sincere. This was a trait Akromeyev had noticed many Americans thought made you trust them, touching. Akromeyev had learned that when an American touches a stranger, he is going to screw him.

Kislak did not touch him.

Kislak said, beaming, "If we're talking about getting access to people, I can open a few doors." Akromeyev sipped the vodka. Kislak raised his brow a little. "We are expensive, though." Akromeyev waved away money. It was not an issue. Kislak nodded, pulled his chair a little closer, clasped his fingers above his knees, and said, "Maybe you can give me an idea of the sorts of things you'd want. That way I have a better idea if we can help you."

"Yes, certainly. The Kremlin, as you know, is getting more interested in private business. As a government we've done business with companies since Lenin. But as individuals, Russians are new at it. We have markets we'd like to open for ourselves. As you know, sometimes, even if the markets in question are overseas, you have excellent statistics or experts on these areas here in the United States. People we could learn from." Kislak nodded his understanding. Akromeyev detected no nervousness in the man. It didn't really make much of a difference how Akromeyev set up what he was going to do, as long as it made sense enough to keep going. Once Kislak heard what Akromeyev wanted, it would become obvious whether Ash had been telling the truth.

"What markets are these?" Kislak said.

"Uruguay is one," Akromeyev said, noting that Kislak just nodded when he dropped the first country Ash had mentioned. "There are some armaments contracts coming up there. We know they are shopping here. We would like to meet the buyers and assess their needs. Perhaps we can offer them a better deal."

"Um-hmm." Unfazed.

"The Philippines," Akromeyev said pleasantly, mentioning Ash's second country. "Your Justice Department is suing Manila Refineries." Akromeyev noted a slight drooping of Kislak's grin. "We're very interested in following the way the American government conducts a restraint-of-trade case. With our own country opening its markets to overseas corporations, we need to see how better to protect our fledgling companies. Perhaps you know some of the attorneys involved. Corinna Hanson, I think she's very important."

Kislak had edged forward slightly in his chair. The smile was gone.

"Also," Akromeyev continued as if he had not noticed, "we are thinking of setting up a logging business in Malaysia, yet the Japanese seem to have a lock on that market. Our own satellite information is sketchy there, but I understand the NORAD shots are quite impressive. We're curious as to the Japanese penetration of that area.

"And then there is a small matter with Somalia," he said.

Kislak was staring now. It was time.

Akromeyev barked in Russian, "You are in trouble!"

If Kislak were innocent, he wouldn't understand. He spoke

no Russian, according to his file. Akromeyev had broken no laws in coming here. The worst that could happen was that Kislak would refuse service and send him away.

But a lone bead of sweat had collected at Kislak's hairline, not even large enough to roll down his face. Kislak rose with an ease Akromeyev knew he was not feeling and began moving toward the desk. Akromeyev got up, strolled to intercept him. Akromeyev's right hand slipped into his jacket pocket.

Kislak said, "I think I'm going to call my lawyer."

Very quick, Akromeyev thought, impressed. He's hoping I'm FBI.

What he said was, "If you touch that phone, I will kill you."

David jolted to a stop and Akromeyev let his facade fall away, let David see his rage. He opened his face up and the truth was there, streaming out from him so forcefully David's eyes grew huge. He saw the incredible reality. That even in this office, with his secretary outside, and the police down on K Street, despite his assumption that at this moment he was safe from physical harm, which seemed unassailable from his standpoint, despite the insanity of it, Akromeyev would kill him. Akromeyev could not afford to let him call anyone.

Both men were two feet from the phone, which formed the third point of a triangle with them. The shock jumbled David's features. Akromeyev said, low and reasonable, "You think I'm the FBI? I'm not FBI. I'm not advising you of your rights. I'm not arresting you. You think you're going to walk out of this office and pick up airline tickets and fly away? You really think we'll let you do that?" Akromeyev hardened his voice slightly. Just a little. "Collect the money you've stolen? Reach the airport? Or call the Americans? Even reach the lobby of this building? Do you actually believe you can pick up that phone?"

It was the crucial moment in Akromeyev's gamble. But he was thrilled. If he were wrong, his career would be over. He would have to kill this man. Have to use the chemical in his pocket. Inject him right here. And he would do it. He was poised to move in fast, wrap one hand around the throat, cutting off a cry, use the other to smoothly press the little hypo into the skin. To run into the waiting room crying, "Heart attack!" sixty seconds later, and after silk-glove handling by the police to return unimpeded to the embassy because no one would believe he had actually sauntered in and murdered a former undersecretary of state. He would hope the autopsy didn't reveal the needle mark or signs of struggle, which it probably would. But by then he would be back home in shame while the government let the CIA know that David had worked for them. That would close any investigation. Prevent an outcry. But terminate Akromeyev.

I'm right, Akromeyev thought. His pulse was roaring.

David's hands fell to his sides. The shock turned his tan white. He had never been talked to this way. He may have been a professional, but he had never faced this kind of threat. Now it was important to finish up quickly. To move in and take over fast. David said, "Who are you?"

Akromeyev said angrily, "You know who I am. Sit down."

He hid the delicious triumph as David moved away from the desk. Akromeyev let the silence stretch out. He kept sight of the fact that there was still a ways to go here. But the initial collapse was always the sweetest. A man could deny things for days and then cry, "Yes, it was me, me!" Or he could start breaking right at the beginning. The really smart ones knew when to give up, knew that resistance beyond a certain point was useless. In movies the victim could gain the interrogator's respect by holding out. In real life, questioners were like everyone else. They wanted to finish the job and go home to a wife, a movie, a meal, a bed.

Get the questioner angry, that was a big no-no.

Now there was the soft whoosh of air-conditioning. A horn honked out on K Street.

So softly, so that Akromeyev had to strain to hear, Kislak said, "What are you going to do?"

Akromeyev knew that if David was any good, which he had to be, however pliant he looked on the outside, inside he was thinking, maybe there is a way out of this.

"That depends on you," Akromeyev said. "I have men outside. Around the office." Inspired suddenly, remembering Ash's words and the furious look on the face of the blond woman he had passed storming out of this office, Akromeyev added, "And at Corinna's house."

The threat did it. The agony leaped into David's face. "Oh god," Kislak said in Russian. He sank down. Akromeyev had found the hook. Akromeyev had been perfect.

He could feel the juices flowing in him, bubbling hotly out of the past and running through his veins. This was real power, one-on-one, breaking a human being and holding his fate in your fist. Sitting behind a desk was success. But crushing a life was power. Akromeyev adjusted the angle between them so Kislak had to look up at him. The handsome facade had broken into pieces. Kislak's shoulders had slumped.

Akromeyev moved to the arm of the couch.

"Tell me everything," Akromeyev said.

And the story rolled out. Just like that. In broken sentences that picked up speed, while Akromeyev nodded as if he already knew it. Kislak repeated everything Ash had said. About the town and Yuri and the trip to the United States. But there was more. "Only fifteen of us made it . . . two broke down, they couldn't take the pressure. . . . I only use thirteen now . . . four in San Francisco . . . two in the Navy . . . one at the *New York Times* . . . two in research at universities . . . but you know that." Akromeyev nodded and memorized it all.

"It . . . it got out of control," Kislak said. "I didn't mean for this to happen. But . . . they . . . just stopped contacting me. I don't know why. Three years ago they stopped picking up my messages. I never knew who the contact was in the first place."

Akromeyev was thinking, Volsky arrived three years ago, after the man he replaced died.

Kislak said, "At first I kept collecting information. Yuri had told me never go to the embassy unless I had to leave."

Bullshit, Akromeyev thought. Kislak could have contacted any of dozens of people in Washington. He had chosen not to.

Kislak said, "At first I took on one client. It paid so much. I was going to turn the money over when you contacted me." Akromeyev gave him the stare. Kislak said miserably, "I was doing the same job I'd always done, collecting information, only for different clients. They never asked how I found things out. They assumed I had contacts. They were grateful to get it. They paid well. I could do it right out in the open. Nobody questioned it. Lots of people do it. It's even expected of you, that you'll go private. Comrade, it's incredible."

Akromeyev said, "Don't call me comrade."

Kislak flinched.

The traitor should be executed, wiped away for what he had done.

Yet a more prudent, mathematical part of Akromeyev's mind appraised the scene differently. Akromeyev had dealt with low-lifes for thirty years and you had to take the larger view. A KGB officer who managed to recruit one agent in the United States was awarded one of the highest medals the Soviet Union gave its soldiers. A KGB officer who could bring in, intact, an entire spy ring of thirteen well-placed people would be treated like a king.

"But if you knew what I was doing all along, why did you wait until now to contact me?" David said.

Akromeyev stood, went to the window, let him sweat. You never answered a question unless you wanted to. You let them think they had done something wrong by speaking to you. You made them understand that there was absolutely no equality between you. You reduced them to the point that they became slavish just for the opportunity to live. And when they were broken completely, you gave them something, something they wanted, something that bound them to you by more than fear. Sex or money or something that fed their weakness. You made them understand that to disobey you would mean death.

Akromeyev understood he was more than just an interrogator here, he was a potential case officer. A good case officer knew that to make someone fear you transformed them into a hard worker. But a great case worker knew that to make them love you, too, would bind them to you forever. To be God to a person meant you had the capability of making them happy as well as afraid.

Akromeyev unfolded a piece of paper from his breast pocket.

Kislak could not see that it was a cocktail party invitation from the French embassy. Akromeyev said, "The names."

He got them.

"I will want the records."

They were in Kislak's home, in Virginia. In a safe.

Akromeyev was jubilant. So his own old number two, Blitsky, had been the go-between, reporting to someone other than Kryuchkov in Moscow. And with Blitsky dead the person in Moscow had stopped the contact. Which meant it had been too risky even to send a replacement. Which meant whoever had been running Kislak had been hiding the group from the top management of the KGB. Probably using the information to advance his own career.

Akromeyev had already pulled off the greatest coup of his career. He could go to Kryuchkov now with the information. Or he could try to identify the person in Moscow.

"You disgust me," Akromeyev said. "You actually thought we were so stupid?" Kislak said nothing. He knew Akromeyev was deciding his fate.

"Even your own people deserted you," Akromeyev said. "Your man Ash came to us and—"

"Ash?" Kislak said, jerking up. "Ash?" His face flooded with blood, the hatred so intense it drove even fear from the man. Both Kislak's fists were clenched. Akromeyev wondered if some sort of power struggle was going on between Kislak and Ash.

Kislak repeated, "He went to you?"

"He's a patriot, he could see what you were doing. But he didn't tell us anything we didn't know."

"He went to the embassy," Kislak repeated in a trance. "To the embassy!"

If there were a power struggle between the two men, that was bad. Akromeyev didn't want to bring in a group in turmoil. He wanted one that functioned smoothly. Kislak or Ash? he thought. Which?

Kislak seemed to remember where he was. The hatred cleared out of his eyes. He looked up.

"You will return on the next plane to Moscow," Akromeyev

said softly. "You will report to headquarters. We will decide what happens to you there!"

"No!"

Akromeyev walked to the window, turned his back, gazed down at traffic below. Kislak could see the noose all right. Stay here and we kill you. Or expose you. Or go to the FBI and live the rest of your life in fear, or jail. Kislak would have to take the last step himself, would have to offer himself for what Akromeyev wanted. Come on, Akromeyev thought. Get it over with. Do it.

"Don't send me! Please! We can go back to the way it was before! Thirteen agents in place! They do whatever I say! Anything I want them to! We can use them, I can run them! Please, please, I am sorry for what I've done. I'll do anything! Please don't make me go home!"

Kislak put his head in his hands. He was sobbing.

"I don't need you for that," Akromeyev said. "We can run those people without you!"

"But they . . . they work better for me. They are used to me. I'm the only one they ever worked with."

It was possible Kislak was right. If he wasn't, he could always be removed later. He could have an auto accident. Or get a piece of chicken stuck in his throat. The KGB never carried out hits in the United States, but under the unwritten rules, cleaning your own house was "allowed" if you did it without fuss. Akromeyev let him cry. Pitiful, slimy traitor that he was. He let him sit on his fine couch and slobber. He let a few minutes go by.

"That is an idea," Akromeyev mused.

David's face was shiny with tears. "I can get so much for you! Armaments! Research! Anything you want! Let me stay here! I'm very valuable, you'll see! What the group is loyal to is different. You need one of us to run things."

"I would have to make a case for you in Moscow," Akromeyev said.

"My god!"

"They are very angry with you."

"I'll get things . . . you won't be sorry."

Akromeyev assumed the attitude of a man deep in thought. He would have to demonstrate to Kislak what happened to people who did not do what he wanted. "You would give all the money back to the KGB?"

"Yes."

"One dollar kept from us, one order disobeyed, do you know what will happen to you? You won't be sent home. Do you hear what I am telling you?"

David was shaking.

"Please compose yourself."

David looked away from Akromeyev, down at the floor. He wiped his eyes. His shoulders seemed to square. After several seconds he looked up again. It was fantastic. His eyes were rimmed from crying, but the jaw was set again, the cocky smile showing. The hair was perfect. Akromeyev knew he had a perfect little sociopath in place.

And with Volsky gone, the credit would be all his. First impressions were everything. By the time Volsky returned, Moscow would know.

"There's some information you may be able to help us with," Akromeyev said. "You get this, it will help you. The Americans are working on a new missile shield, not Star Wars, something more expensive. A way of detecting incoming missiles seconds quicker. I have a list of some companies working on the components. Perhaps one of your people is affiliated with one of these companies."

He showed Kislak the list. Kislak said, "Someone in Vermont is working on these systems."

"Excellent."

"I can get you the plans, the blueprints for the system."

"That is a good start," Akromeyev said.

Kislak said, "May I . . . may I ask a question please?"

Akromeyev considered. Breaking Kislak further would be counterproductive. "What?"

"Ash," Kislak said softly. "What will happen to him?"

Akromeyev glared. Kislak said, "I'm sorry." But Akromeyev

was thinking. Ash is the loose end. It was true he had performed a patriotic service by coming to the embassy. But he threatened me. Threatening us is threatening me. And now he had disappeared. He might have gone to the FBI, in which case Kislak would be rounded up. Akromeyev, with diplomatic immunity, would go home. No coup for Akromeyev.

On the other hand, if Ash were sent home in triumph, it would be he, not Akromeyev, who got credit for bringing Kislak back into the KGB. Akromeyev would be the bungler who hadn't even realized a Soviet spy ring was operating under his nose for fifteen years. Instead of getting the highest reward in the Soviet Union, he would become the butt of jokes.

He threatened me.

"What do you think I should do with him?" Akromeyev said.

Kislak's eyes blazed with hope.

Akromeyev was amused. Not only was Kislak recovered, he was bartering! Staring at Akromeyev with a kind of fanaticism. The bald hatred streaming from him. Akromeyev had misjudged the man. He was cooler than he looked. He'd sensed that Akromeyev needed him in place. And now he wanted something in return.

Akromeyev knew that in a perfect world Ash would be rewarded.

Akromeyev mused, I could blame everything on Ash. Or report, "Ash and David were in it together. I killed one of them. Now the others will stay in place."

He told himself, it's a question of math.

"He's not reliable," Kislak was saying. "He always asks questions. He doesn't follow orders. He never should have come."

"You're hardly the person to judge that," Akromeyev said, feigning annoyance. Akromeyev checked his watch. While Kislak waited, he would ice the cake. He asked Kislak, "Do you have a radio in your office?"

"Yes."

"Put on the news."

Kislak went to the sideboard. He did what he was supposed

to do. The radio was built into the stereo unit. Kislak found the news.

". . . tanks, reportedly sealed off the Foros airport where President Gorbachev is staying. He is rumored to be sick, but we repeat, there has been a coup in the Soviet Union. Hard-line Communist elements have taken over the government."

Kislak stared at him, awe in his face now. Good. "A . . . a coup?"

Akromeyev, grinning, said, "The good old days are back."

Akromeyev had to get back to the embassy. His job had been arranged weeks ago. It was special because most KGB staff in embassies had no idea the coup was planned. But Washington was too important. He would make sure the diplomatic staff stayed loyal to the new government. That they made no statements damaging to the trade minister's visit, which would be hard enough with a coup happening. He would have a little chat with the ambassador, would advise him what to say and remind him that his mother and father were still in the Soviet Union. And Akromeyev wouldn't have to worry about that reformer Volsky, with the man out of the way.

A colonel could climb quickly to general in this environment.

Akromeyev decided to give Ash to Kislak. First we have to find Ash, if he is still available. Then you'll go along with my people, David, and finish the job yourself.

TWELVE

ASH DROVE NORTH through western Connecticut, singing golden oldies to the radio with the windows rolled down.

He was free. He bellowed "You've Made Me So Very
Happy" and "Bad Moon Rising." He beat the steering wheel
like a snare drum. Played imaginary guitar with one hand. The
sun was brilliant above the southern Berkshire hills, fields,
horses, woods.

"Where were you, July 1974?" cried the deejay, his gravelly
bass anywhere from twenty-five to forty. Ash flashed to the
foredeck of the Soviet freighter *Bulganin* easing into the Montreal harbor in the rain. Ash at the bow beside Glorie Pell, soaked
as they eyed the Canadian customs boat speeding toward them.
Glorie had said, "I'm scared."

"Nineteen seventy-four!" said the deejay. "Watergate's about
to knock Richard Nixon out of the White House! *The Beast
Must Die* is at the Pittsfield Drive-in! The Boston Pops plays
show tunes at Tanglewood! *Gigi! Brigadoon!* 'Aw, dad, shut
that stuff off!' "

At the graduation dance Ash had spun and twisted till he
sweated, while DuChamp rolled his eyes, hating the Rolling
Stones. Then Ash had taken Penny Rae Moody behind the
school, slipped off her lace bra, and kissed her breasts while
"Riders on the Storm" blared from the windows. He remembered the lovely shock of a girl's fingers on his penis for the first

time. Seeing red fingernails stroking him. Penny Rae Moody had come to Canada with them, but had not been at the reunion. He wondered if Penny Rae Moody was still alive.

Route 8 meandered through valleys smelling of the paper or Naugahyde mills that kept their towns from disappearing. The interstate shrunk to two lanes at Winsted, rising through woods and past trout streams, reservoirs, blasted-out sections of granite cliffs. Ash crossed into Massachusetts. The back of the used Cavalier was littered with empty cake boxes and sandwich wrappers and bags of plums he'd bought at roadside stands. Ash was ravenous. He couldn't stop eating. He was free.

"Now the news," the announcer said. Ash switched off the radio. When Route 8 hit Route 20 Ash saw the sign that said SMITH FALLS—8 MILES. His heart beat faster. He flashed to the black-and-white aerial shot Miss Dietz had tacked to the bulletin board in fifth grade, by OUR PRESIDENTS and HEADLINES THIS WEEK.

The photo, from a low-flying plane, showed an L-shaped village clustered along both sides of Route 20, the only road of consequence to flow through it. Bigger buildings such as the paper mill, bowling alley, and gas stations hugged the longer stem. Town offices and historical homes occupied the base.

"Home," Ash said out loud, driving into Smith Falls. Then he laughed. "Whatever." It was a weekday, a workday. At Ed's Texaco, still there, two men in dungarees worked on a jacked-up Cutlass near the high-test pump. Beyond the Shell and McDonald's was the Cumberland Farms grocery 'n' gas up, only now there were homes on both sides of it instead of the dirt/grass sandlot field. Antonio Pizza was closed till night. That didn't stop teens in cars from grouping in the parking lot. But the cars were foreign now. And the teens had shorter hair. There was even a video arcade and shopping mall.

He checked into The Happy Pilgrim motel, at the sign of the familiar grinning Puritan that Ash remembered from his youth. Ash distracted the pimply clerk from his Rubik's Cube long enough to let him know he'd stay at least two nights. The boy said, "Your room's by the pool, Mr. Rice."

He'd hardly slept but he wasn't tired. Ash left the overnight bag he'd bought in Wilmington on the bed. He strolled into town, turned right at the War of 1812 monument, and stepped onto the raised sidewalk marking the two-block-long Main Street, where shoppers steered cars into diagonal parking spots. Two cops stepped from Smith Falls Hall, the red-brick, Civil War–era building housing town offices. One told the other, "You call that a pension?"

Through gold lettering across the plate glass of McKay's pharmacy across the street, Ash saw customers at the fountain, beyond the stuffed bears and Russell Stover candies on display. He'd spent lots of afternoons at McKay's. Well, the other McKay's. He remembered the cutout of the smiling farm girl saying, "Chocolate's my favorite!" Except due to Soviet shortages, the old McKay's served only vanilla.

Drifting in a cloud of nostalgia, Ash paused outside stores, nodded to shoppers, remembered. In his mind the two towns, the replica where he'd grown up and the real thing, merged. He let it happen. It was a harmless, gratifying game. Here was The First National Bank of the Berkshire's, where he'd started his first savings account. Nine dollars. The Price Chopper. The library where he'd done homework, across from Ben's Barbershop, with its rotating candy-cane pole. DuChamp had gotten a haircut there every Thursday from the Azerbaijani barber in the KGB.

Ash turned off Main Street onto the patchwork residential lanes near the heart of town. He hoped David wouldn't try to come after him. But he figured he would. There were no sidewalks now. Kids in polo shirts rode by on bicycles. Older houses dated as far back as 1845, but zoning must be light because they alternated with newer ranches or colonials.

My god, Ash thought. The Johnson house. He looked over the turreted Gothic gables and twin towers, which the kids had called "The Addams Family" house, where Mr. Johnson had put up a wooden cutout Santa in a sleigh each Christmas, waving, pulled by reindeer taking off.

He stopped in front of the Topaz house, where Nina Topaz

had sold lemonade when they were nine and held pajama parties on hot nights at thirteen. The clapboard sides were still a washed-out lemon. Gingerbread molding still surrounded the widow's walk from where the giggles of Corinna and the other girls had floated down to the boys in the street. Except when Ash passed the mailbox it said NEWTON. And the Newton house was supposed to be next door, the brick Cape Cod coming up on his right, with the spruce in the front yard and the tricycle half-crashed in the flower garden. And that mailbox said TOPAZ.

He laughed. It was nice to know the KGB wasn't perfect. Ash envisioned Jack Newton, the skinny political-science major who'd built a computer in the dorm. A clunky machine blinking with lights that could add, subtract, and multiply up to five integers. Newton had been the baseball statistician who had invited the boys for bologna-and-mayonnaise sandwiches and spread his baseball card collection over his mother's thick white pile. Roger Maris. Gil Hodges. Little Russian kids looking at baseball cards.

Some mother.

Newton had flunked out with a week to go. He cries too much, DuChamp had said.

Ash walked to the edge of town. There was no barbed wire, no tundra stretching off, gouged with cart tracks. Just Massachusetts Route 20 climbing north, toward Pittsfield.

It would be nice to trace how he had gotten here, maybe even find a way to contact Yuri, but that wasn't the main point. Being free was.

Back at McKay's counter he ordered apple pie and coffee. When he asked for a second piece, the waitress crowed, "My god, more!" She was an elderly, bustling woman beneath a forest of red curls, and a name tag that said "Lynda." "That's the kind of eating I like."

They all smiled at him. The old man in the red cotton shirt and square glasses, reading the *Berkshire Eagle*. The two teenage girls holding long spoons dripping with sundaes. The bald man in factory khakis and shit-kicker boots, finishing up a roast beef with potatoes.

Propped on her elbows, Lynda said, "Dottie makes the pies herself. This your first time in Smith Falls?"

There it was. The opening. Between mouthfuls Ash said, "I lived here a few weeks once. At DuChamp. Then it burnt down and we got sent away."

She looked sad. "Oh, your parents . . ." She didn't finish the thought. She felt sorry for orphans. "I remember that place. Now it's just woods."

"Sheeee, that fire," piped in the old man. "Went up like papier-mâché! Never saw a building burn like that. I was a fireman then. We got there quick but late." His half grin carved circles on one cheek. "Eddie got plenty of insurance for it, though. He did all right."

Ash ignored the inference. "He rescued us," Ash said.

"Yep. Got the kids out. That's what I mean. Something goes up so fast, you expect a little injury," the old man said, and winked. "But he's okay. Pretty good bowler. But a little nutsy now."

Ash's pulse quickened. "He's still around?"

The old man got off his stool and dropped a five on the counter. He folded the *Eagle* but left it for the next person. "Well, physically. But try to have a conversation with him you got a little problem. Alzheimer's. He's over at Gus's."

"That's for old people," Lynda said helpfully. "More coffee? Refill's included."

"How about a piece of blueberry with it," Ash said.

"Where are you putting it?" the waitress wondered.

"I saw a man eat ten pieces of pizza on 'David Letterman,' " one of the teenagers said. "It was gross."

"What were you doing up so late?" the waitress asked.

"That fire," the old man said. "Where'd they send you after that?"

"Pittsburgh." Don't give people hooks to find out who you are, Yuri's voice came in his head. "I was driving through, figured I'd visit."

"A lot of crime in Pittsburgh, I bet," the man said.

"My neighbor got mugged," Ash said. "But they didn't hurt him."

Ash changed into gym clothes and jogged for an hour, up Route 20. Martini's drillmaster voice in his head shouted, "I don't care if you just ate! Faster! You think if someone's after you, they're going to wait for you to digest your food!" Ash was breathing hard when he got back. He did eighty push-ups. He worked on his stomach awhile.

He'd have to be ready if David came after him. But it was so peaceful just now. He'd treat himself to Tanglewood tonight.

At the Price Chopper he bought California red wine, French bread, grapes, fresh cheddar cheese, olives, figs, and homemade brownies. He couldn't believe he was hungry again. He drove to Lenox with his picnic, joined the stream of music lovers carrying their food onto the complex's lawn. Couples and families lay on blankets around him, eating or talking quietly as the music started, their dinners half-finished, their champagne bottles leaning sideways, little candles flickering on blankets beneath a full moon.

An all-Mozart program tonight. "Haffner" and "Linz."

Ash closed his eyes and felt the warmth of the evening. He sipped wine. Tanglewood nights in Smith Falls had been thirty children in a classroom listening to taped music to a slide show, while Dietz lectured about the decadent rich in the United States. Beethoven's Opus 1 would play while Ash gaped at slides of rioting blacks in the slums of Memphis against fat white women on lawn chairs at Tanglewood, dripping with jewelry, drinking wine. He'd see photos of hungry coal miners' children, nine in a bed in West Virginia, beside shots of conductors in tails bowing to applause.

He drifted with the music. He could stay in Smith Falls a couple more days. "And now something much more lively," the conductor said.

As the concert ended and a slightly drunk Ash weaved toward his car, Colonel Sergei Akromeyev strolled up a curving stone walk toward a one-bedroom Tudor cottage in suburban Chevy Chase. After an hour of careful driving he was convinced nobody had followed him here. Kislak had picked a good meeting place. Price's house was separated from its neighbors by copses of spruce and weeping willow trees.

Akromeyev frowned though, turning over knotty problems in his mind. How much to trust Kislak's subordinates. And how to find Ash.

As for Kislak, there was no other way to gauge the situation besides coming here. Akromeyev hated exposing himself but the reward was worth the risk. David's group was too important to trust to anyone else. And he certainly could not count on Kislak's word.

Akromeyev's eyes burned from strain and irritation. All afternoon, in the embassy, he'd gotten unexpected opposition to the coup. Nothing overt. Staffers were too smart for that. But there'd been sluggishness in the way they were performing. It wasn't just shock on their part, but genuine opposition. He'd needed an hour to get the ambassador from condemning the coup on American TV.

We'll replace him soon, Akromeyev thought. And Volsky and the other reformers. One or two days more and everything will be under control.

Akromeyev banged the gaudy top-hat knocker and Kislak opened the door as if he had been waiting behind. Good. He wore a fresh suit and was freshly shaven. He oozed deference, stepping back to create a path.

"Where are they?" Akromeyev demanded.

"The living room."

But Akromeyev didn't go in. He stood on the step, lit a Camel, said, "You wait. They go," and Kislak seemed startled as Akromeyev's men materialized from the darkness. They were the three who had lost Ash earlier. They were eager to make up for the lapse. Akromeyev thought of them as the Boxer, No Eyebrows, and Riga Soccer Star. The Boxer had enjoyed a slight fame in the KGB ring when he was younger, and the nose that seemed glued to his otherwise bland, unremarkable face extended one way, then the other, then straight. His hands were enormous. No Eyebrows actually had eyebrows, but they were so thin and light colored, like his hair, that they blended in with his flesh. He was a superb shot. Akromeyev considered both men to be controllable nut cases every country used in low-key violent work. Riga Soccer Star was smarter and read a lot and tended to run the group when they were on their own. He had a possible future as a replacement for Volsky.

Akromeyev blew smoke and flashed to the photos he'd seen of Ash as the Boxer frisked David for wires, and the others disappeared into the house to check for cameras or mikes.

Where is he? Akromeyev thought. Between the coup and the trade minister's coming Akromeyev was short on staff. He had scattered as many people as possible around the city. At Ash's apartment and outside the *Post*. He'd tried the hotels and car rental agencies. Hertz. Avis. Dollar. Rent-A-Wreck. Akromeyev's men would phone, say they were Ash, claim they'd had a breakdown. And ask for help. That would be enough to find out if Ash had rented something. But each agency had claimed to have no car rented to any Ash.

Now the smallest guard, Riga Soccer Star, came back to the hallway. "Clean," he said in English. "No cameras. No wire."

"Wait outside, all of you," Akromeyev told them. To Kislak he said, "I'll meet them now."

He would forget about Ash and concentrate on these people. He must not make an error at so crucial a time. Akromeyev told himself they would probably cooperate. After all, they were seasoned agents who had been operating superbly for seventeen years. They were on Akromeyev's side. Except for David, they followed orders. It wasn't as if they were an unknown factor. They'd been loyal to the motherland since they were kids.

In the long, white rectangular living room, Akromeyev took in the video screens embedded in the walls, all silently broadcasting different pictures at the same time, casting light from their images on the faces of the others present, on the chrome and glass table, on the chrome and tan leather chairs. It's not what he would have expected in a little house in the woods. One screen showed a blond man in a red flannel shirt, just staring, blinking every few seconds, but the blink was always the same. The screen was showing repetition, not time lapse. There was a shot of soldiers in battle gear marching, three steps then back to the beginning, three steps and back again, except their faces were blocked out by distortion, making the scene more mechanical than human. One video showed a hand endlessly turning a *New York Times* front page, just fingers with hair on them and a bit of newsprint saying NEW. YORK and lower, in smaller letters, MURDE . . . then back to the beginning. The eerie repetition gave Akromeyev a sense of claustrophobia and unfulfillment.

The only picture not moving was an eight-and-a-half by eleven framed black-and-white photo of Kislak on a boat with President Reagan. Reagan had his head thrown back, laughing unabashedly. It was a terrific shot of Reagan, and anyone who didn't know better would think it was on the wall because the President was in it, not the other man in the boat. Kislak.

Intrigued, Akromeyev directed his most effective stare at the sick-looking man sitting, hands folded, on one of the chrome chairs. This would be Price. Akromeyev knew, remembering Ash's description of the man to Volsky. No chess sets around, but Price had been a childhood chess genius, Ash had said. Eyes averted, Price looked at the floor. Not the kind of man Akromeyev would associate with this kind of art. He must understand the motivation of the three who had turned on their friends: David, Minsky, and Price. David wanted power. Minsky loved violence. Akromeyev looked at the lean gray man in the corner. What drove Price? Akromeyev grunted to himself. Twenty years of self-sacrificing unrequited love? Or more?

"Here they call Price, Granger," Kislak was saying.

"And this is Corinna," Kislak said, lowering himself beside her on an uncomfortable-looking couch. A long piece of tan leather stretched between thin armrests of plated chrome. The video screen over the couch broadcast coral-colored shapes that might have been bare legs, or might have been a desert landscape, from the slow long contours. Nothing moved on the screen.

Akromeyev switched his look to Corinna. She was attractive in a brassy way that did not appeal to him. She didn't compare to his sexy secretary Marta. A woman should know that she doesn't have to flaunt herself to be provocative, Akromeyev thought, taking in the tight linen suit, the long white heels half-buried in the pile, the silver earrings dangling too far down. Very ostentatious. She met his gaze without rancor, without nervousness. She wore too much perfume, he thought.

But he felt strength inside her. That made him like her more than Price, but be more wary, too. The question was, had David lied to him? Had Corinna been with him all along?

"You are the attorney," Akromeyev said.

"That's right."

"For the Justice Department." She didn't seem to mind the stare. He said coldly, "You know what Kislak has been doing?"

David said, "She just found out today."

Without shifting his body Akromeyev flicked his eyes to Kislak, who froze. Akromeyev repeated dryly, "Today."

"He told me," she said, looking disgusted. "Actually Ash told me last night. David confirmed it today."

"And what did you think of what you found out?"

"It made me sick," she said without change of expression. Personal problems didn't concern him except when they could affect how well agents worked together.

Akromeyev told Kislak, "You aren't very popular with your own people." To Corinna he said, "I find it hard to believe you didn't suspect earlier. From the directions your assignments were taking. Didn't you think something was wrong?"

"I did what I was told."

Right answer. "And when Ash came to you and told you the truth?" Akromeyev said.

She glanced at David. "I didn't want to believe it." She grew contemptuous. "Not of David."

Akromeyev strolled in the room a little. Let them sweat while he took his time. He knew the fear that his silence inspired. It had been that way since boyhood, when the other children called him "Little freak," because of his coldness.

He paused by artificial cattails in a vase on the floor. There was the vaguest sweet odor of incense in the house.

He barked, in Russian, "You knew."

He saw that for all his techniques, to her he was just a desk officer querying a field agent who had done nothing wrong. "You're testing me," she said. She adjusted position on the pillow, giving more back to Kislak, but her discomfort was from the seating, not her reply.

Akromeyev said, "You expect me to believe he didn't tell his lover what he was doing?"

She said arrogantly, "Oh, do you tell your lover all your secrets?"

He liked her courage. He switched tack. "And now, returning to the fold," he said. "What do you think about that?"

She shrugged. "That's where I thought we were all along."

"And what do I do with David for his lapse?"

He'd gotten to her finally. Suddenly she had tears of fury in her eyes. "That's your business," she said. But Akromeyev saw she didn't want David hurt. That gave him some hold on her. A hold always made him feel good.

Now for Price, while he let her stew and think she'd passed the test. "And you?" he said, fixing the bug with a glance. Price looked at David for help. Akromeyev wondered at the extent of their relationship. The three of them? A one-way crush? Later he'd have Riga Soccer Star solicit David, to see if he was gay. And Price, too, to see if he talked in bed.

Price told Akromeyev, "I do what I'm told, too." The faggy little parrot. But after a few more questions Akromeyev decided Price probably told the truth.

"Why do you hang this trash on the wall?" Akromeyev asked Price. It wasn't part of the interview. He just didn't understand it.

"I like it."

"Wait outside," he said. He wiped Price from his mind. Akromeyev didn't want him to hear what he said next.

After they heard the door shut, Akromeyev told David, "You will keep being a private consultant. You fell into a good thing. Now you can get secrets from your clients, too." And to Corinna, "You'll help us find Ash. You can find out things that would be hard for us. Call the *Post,* say it is an emergency. He may have left a forwarding number, or they'll know his friends. . . ."

Akromeyev stopped. She was shaking her head.

"Ohhh, no," she said. "I'm not helping you with this."

Akromeyev stepped closer to her. A little throbbing began in the back of his head.

"He's not doing anything to you," she said.

David said, terrified, "Corinna."

She turned on David. "You want him to pay for what you did. Well, I'm not going to be part of this. You hear me? He didn't do anything to you."

"We're not going to hurt him. We only want to talk to him," David said.

"That's right," Akromeyev soothed, paving the ground in case she ever passed along this conversation. She'd never know the difference in the end. "But I may have to send him back. He's not entirely loyal."

To Akromeyev's surprise she stood up. She was taller than he was, which he didn't like. Her fists clenched. She was so close he could see the pores on her face, the shades of turquoise mascara.

"He's more loyal than any of us," Corinna said. "You want to kill him. Well, I won't help. And you won't hurt me." There was a quaver in her tone.

Akromeyev picked a piece of lint off his lapel. He kept his voice calm. "Why is that?"

"Because you're smart," she said. "Because I'm good at what I do. I bring information and I'm no threat. There are thirteen of us and I couldn't do anything to hurt the others. But mostly because the police already know someone tried to kill Ash. So if he disappears, and his ex-wife does, too, who's the suspect? David," she said fiercely. "The whole world knows I'm his . . . was his . . . lover.

"Do you want them to investigate David?" she mocked. "Dig

up his past? Three people from the same orphanage? Maybe they'll want to know who else went to that orphanage."

She was in Akromeyev's face, unafraid or too angry to care. "Ash worked for you," she said. "He did a good job. He's no threat. He told me he went to you. He did it to protect us. He risked himself to warn me. You go to hell. I hope he gets away from you."

"Corinna!" David cried.

Akromeyev laughed. He wanted to crush her right here, do it himself. That slender cartilage on her neck where her Adam's apple rose. "Well, that's that," he said, containing his fury. "You can go now."

"Go?"

He waved a hand casually, dispatching her. "Yes. Go home. We'll call you. Forget the Manila Refineries job. David will give you something else to do."

"Just go?" she said, looking around the room, his acquiescence more frightening than a fight.

David said, "She doesn't mean it. She'll do what you want."

Akromeyev eyed him coldly. "Oh, she means it." He would move on her later. But at the moment she was right. He said, to Corinna, "Don't you?"

She nodded, not trusting herself to speak.

"Believe it or not," Akromeyev remarked, "Ash has approached the FBI." Akromeyev nodded. "Ash may have a special feeling for you personally, but he's against the others. I have evidence."

"What evidence?" she said.

It was the evidence he would manufacture to send to Moscow. He said, shrugging, "You're angry at David. I understand. I'm angry at him, too. We'll decide what to do. Later, you'll see we were right. But Corinna, you better understand something. If I find out you even tried to contact Ash, it won't just be you. It will be David who gets punished."

She was quite ugly when she was furious, all her features twisted out of alignment, an unladylike rush of blood suffusing her face. Her red lipstick looked masklike. "You'll decide," she repeated. Tears sprang to her eyes. She glanced from Akromeyev to David.

"I can't believe I loved you," she said.

She slammed the door when she left.

The phone rang.

David said, "She'll get over it."

"You think so?" Akromeyev said. "I thought you were smart." At least David's humiliation had eclipsed his own. He flicked his hand to indicate David should answer the phone. "If they ask for Rosenberg, hand it to me," he said, wrapping his hand in a handkerchief so he'd leave no prints. David said hello and held the phone to Akromeyev. "Yes?" Akromeyev said. The voice on the other end, which he recognized, said, "We've been at Petitos for an hour. When are you coming?" The voice said a name then. Akromeyev said, "My watch must have stopped."

But it was excellent news, and as he hung up, he felt better. Kislak still stood, frightened and uncertain, in the middle of the room. Akromeyev realized he could use Corinna as a hold on him, too. Perfect, Akromeyev thought, starting toward the door, expecting his new underling to follow obediently, which David did. Akromeyev told David, "We have a lead on Ash." David's face leaped. Akromeyev said, "I think you should make some phone calls. To Smith Falls."

"Ash is in Smith Falls?"

"He may be."

David seemed uncertain, like he was building courage. Then he actually built up enough to say, "You won't hurt Corinna, will you?"

Akromeyev looked offended. "What do you think I am, a butcher?" he said.

Ash saw from the digital clock that he'd slept eleven hours. A peaceful, dreamless sleep. He couldn't remember the last time he'd woken as late as ten. The motel's curtains were pulled back; sunlight formed rainbows on the ceiling above Ash's king-size bed.

Ash did push-ups, then jogged out of town in the direction

he had arrived from. The day was warm but lacked Washington's humidity. He had good stamina in this kind of heat. By the time he got back, showered, and shaved, it was eleven-thirty. He strolled to McKay's. The waitress called out, "Dottie, it's the guy I told you about!" when he walked in.

"What's for breakfast?" Ash said, seating himself at the counter. "And where's Gus's, the old-folks home you told me about."

He took his time on his double egg portion, mopped up the yolk with wheat toast. The orange juice was fresh. He had more blueberry pie for dessert, and an extra cup of coffee.

Time would be slower from now on. More the way he dreamed it could be. But he still felt a dryness in his throat as he paid and strolled the hundred yards up Main Street to Gus's, an aqua-colored Victorian mansion behind a waist-high wrought-iron fence.

He doubted DuChamp had ever met Yuri. Probably he'd never heard of him, but there might be something to learn here. A contact. A name to help Ash track his past.

Ash mounted the gray wooden stairs. Nodded to an old man and woman playing Monopoly on the porch. Pushed through double swinging doors beneath cut-glass panels of tulips over the entranceway. The lobby was a converted octagon-shaped parlor with high ceilings, empty chintz armchairs near a glassed-in fireplace, Mexican pottery pigs on the mantel. Lush ferns hung by the bay window. Hidden speakers pumped violins playing "There's a Place for Us." From upstairs, he heard footsteps, and a woman's voice called, "Mr. Osborne, stop that please!" Ash smelled perfumed flowers, Lysol, sachet, Windex.

"May I help you?"

She'd come out of a white swinging door under the freestanding winding staircase. A young, moon-faced woman in Birkenstock sandals, jeans, and a small gold necklace that said Karen in script over her plain white T-shirt. "Are you here to see a relative? Everyone just finished eating."

Ash said he was looking for Mr. DuChamp. He told Karen he used to live in DuChamp's home for children. He said he was passing through town and heard DuChamp was here.

She seemed pleased that DuChamp had a visitor. But she sighed. "He's got Alzheimer's, I don't know if you know that. He might not be too communicative. I don't think he's having a good day."

"He's not in pain, I hope," Ash said as he followed her up the winding stairs, eyeing a little panda she'd stitched in red and blue thread on her back pocket.

"No. Mr. Carver, his friend, can get through to him," she said over her shoulder. "But you might find he doesn't remember you. Sometimes he doesn't say anything for hours. Sometimes he just talks about movies."

"Movies." Ash, who had known Duchamp a total of six days, had no idea what he liked or disliked. He tried to put together the big, nervous man who had driven him across the border into the United States with popcorn, previews, Cokes guzzled from a straw.

"He's probably playing cards with Mr. Carver in the Greenhouse Room."

They went up another flight and down a wide hallway curving past private rooms. Ash glimpsed, through open doors, an old man in an undershirt on a bed, an old woman with a walker, an attendant carrying a bedpan emerging from a room marked STAFF ONLY. Copper, knee-high cuspidors served as ashtrays. The runner was worn but spotless. The floors polished to a glow. There was not much money here, but whoever cared for the place lavished attention on it.

The Greenhouse Room turned out to be an upper porch converted to glass walls, heavy with condensation from plants inside. Orchids. Bougainvillea.

Ash was sweating. It had to be ninety degrees in here.

DuChamp had shrunk. His shoulders folded inward over his cotton sweater vest, his head jutted birdlike, over the white rustproof table where he and another man held cards. The other man wore a yellow cardigan despite the heat.

Up close, a few wisps of cottony hair remained where DuChamp's brown mop had been. His skull was thickly freckled and Ash could see a throbbing blue vein.

"Mr. DuChamp?" Karen said softly. "You have a visitor."

DuChamp stared at his cards.

"Mr. DuChamp?"

The other man lifted his hand to his throat, so Ash saw he was pressing a speaker box to his larynx. He was dapper with a mane of longish white hair, shiny-shaved skin the color of corned beef, pleasant and alert pale blue eyes, and the yellow cardigan that seemed too big for him and had once probably been just right.

Throat cancer, Ash thought. The words came out flat, metallic. "He's forgetting today."

"But he was talking at breakfast," Karen said. To Ash she explained pleasantly, "Mr. Carver is his best friend. He lives in town but visits every day." And to Mr. Carver, "Mr. Ash used to live at the orphanage. He came to visit Mr. DuChamp."

Mr. Carver had a bony, strong handshake.

Mr. Carver touched the biggest liver spot on DuChamp's yellowing wrist. "Ed?" he said, the box converting his concern into robotlike tones. There was a small click from the box after Carver stopped talking. "Emphysema," he told Ash. "Ed? Someone is here to see you. You'll like this. One of your kids."

DuChamp stared at his cards.

"Ed."

DuChamp looked up. Frown lines wrinkled his head where the hairline used to be. He peered at Carver.

"Who are you?" he said.

Karen sighed. Ash hoped if he ever grew senile, he'd have someone like her taking care of him. She said, "Mr. DuChamp? What was that movie you were telling me about yesterday. Remember it? You remember it. There was a girl in it. There were police."

"Movie," DuChamp echoed softly. Ash could barely hear him.

"Remember?"

DuChamp looked at the cards again.

"How about his wife?" Ash asked. "Is she still alive?"

Carver shook his head. Karen said, "Heart attack two years ago. That's what put him in here."

"Any children? Relatives?"

"Not that we know of," Karen said. "Mr. Carver, does Mr. DuChamp have any relatives in town?"

"No relatives," came the flat voice. Carver smiled, showing teeth severely stained from nicotine. "I pulled a flush, Mr. Ash. He does this on purpose when I have a good hand." He sounded like a robot making a joke.

"Let me try," Ash said.

Karen stepped back as Ash leaned over the table. The trick was to say enough so that, if DuChamp was lucid, he would understand who Ash was, but not enough to alert Karen and Carver. If he could get through to DuChamp, they could make an excuse to be alone and then talk. But now he wished the other two weren't here, so he could really ask what he wanted. "Mr. DuChamp?" he said softly. From somewhere above, hammering started. Someone was fixing something in the house. "I used to live at the home." Ash watched the expressionless face for any sign of comprehension. "I was there the night it burned down."

"He stole my cereal," DuChamp told Ash. "Carver ate my cereal."

"You knocked the bowl on the floor, Ed," Mr. Carver said.

"I want my cereal."

Carver said, "Ed, I have a flush. I win."

"There was a fire," Ash said. "Flames were coming out the windows. Remember? We got out. Firemen came. Remember?"

"He's like this a lot more lately," Karen said, leading Ash back toward the door. "They've got this new drug for Alzheimer's, I wish the FDA would let people take it. I see them come in, they're so vibrant. A few months later they're like him." She brightened. "Maybe he'll be better in an hour, or later this afternoon. You have to be positive. I know he'd be so happy to see you. If you have time, why don't you come back then." She looked at him hopefully, distressed that Mr. DuChamp might miss the chance to see an old friend.

Ash said sure, he'd come back later. DuChamp had put his

cards down and was staring at the foggy pane as Ash left the greenhouse. Carver waved good-bye, holding up his queen-high flush for Ash to see.

Ash retrieved his car from The Happy Pilgrim and headed for Pittsfield, ten miles north. There were other possibilities to check while he waited.

Driving, he passed a lake and woods and he entered the strip of retail outlets south of the town. He asked directions to the *Berkshire Eagle* at a Shell station. The newspaper occupied a larger building than he would have imagined, a converted warehouse with a clock tower on top. He parked in the employees/visitors lot and found the city room. It was quieter than the *Post* but the feel was the same. Beyond a receptionist crocheting a Haitian flag he saw reporters at green computer screens, typing.

Ten minutes later Ash was at a microfilm machine, scanning for the date of the fire: July 23, 1974. The machine hummed, the front pages of the *Berkshire Eagle* began rolling across the screen in the yellowish light. Ash leaned forward. July 21. July 22.

"Blaze Destroys Orphanage. Dramatic Rescue Saves Kids!"

It was a bad photo but it brought Ash back. He was standing outside in the trees, with the other kids, watching flames shoot from the windows. They hadn't reached the roof yet. DuChamp saying, as they heard sirens, "Nobody talk to the police, if you can help it." DuChamp white faced with nervousness, even in the dark.

The *Eagle* quoted DuChamp in the article: "It's all gone, everything. The building. The records. At least we saved the children.

"We'll send the kids to sister institutions," DuChamp said.

But there was no other clue. No quotes from other people. No history he could use.

I wonder who paid for that orphanage, Ash thought.

Ash drove to the library looking for books on local history. In *The Berkshires: Past, Present, and Future,* there was no mention of DuChamp. In a 1974 *Leisure Time: The Summer Magazine for the Berkshires,* the blaze was mentioned in a one-paragraph write-up in "News This Month."

But again, nothing. By the time he left the library it was four-thirty. Tomorrow he'd try city records in Smith Falls, to see who paid for the orphanage. Now for DuChamp again. Karen was still on duty. She seemed tired but happy to see him.

This time the old man was in his third-floor bedroom, in a wooden rocker by the window, looking down at Main Street as the curtain buffeted him with each late-afternoon breeze. On a birch dresser was a photograph showing DuChamp and the woman who had brought Ash over the Canadian border. They stood in front of a stone church in a foreign country, which Ash could tell from a bit of writing that seemed Eastern European on part of a wooden sign in front. A camera was around DuChamp's neck, and he and his wife, or whoever the woman had been, held hands.

Karen said, "Mr. DuChamp, this is Mr. Ash. He was here this morning."

The old man looked up without expression. But then Ash grew excited as DuChamp said, "Hello."

Ash eased onto the hard, narrow bed, facing him. There was a sink and a throw rug and a poster saying SANTA FE on the wall. He wished Karen would leave.

"I talked to you in the Greenhouse Room," Ash said.

DuChamp shrugged. He had a slight druggish monotone to his voice, and a quaver. "I don't remember. But I have Alzheimer's disease. Karen said someone visited me. I'm a little kooky sometimes."

"I was at the home," Ash said.

DuChamp nodded. Because of the angle of the setting sun blazing into the window, Ash found it hard to see DuChamp's eyes. "It burned down."

Ash kept his voice calm. "Right, I was there. One of the kids. We took a drive once in Canada. Remember?"

Ash couldn't tell if DuChamp remembered or not.

"Fire, everywhere," DuChamp said in his wavering voice.

"The bell went off. I was sleeping. I was asleep. The bell went off."

DuChamp was repeating the story he'd used with the papers. Ash said, "But before the fire we had fun. We drove in Canada. To Montreal."

DuChamp blinked up at him. Ash thought he saw a glimmer in the watery blue eyes.

DuChamp looked sly suddenly.

"Carver eats my cereal. Hide my cereal from him."

Ash pulled in a deep breath and let a little of it out. Behind him, he heard Karen say, "You two talk together. I have to check Mrs. Roth." She closed the door as she left and Ash said, more urgently, "I was one of the Russian children. The Russian children. You brought us from Canada. You started the fire. It's okay to tell me. Do you hear me?"

Saying it, Ash realized if DuChamp did understand him, he would probably alert whoever had arranged the arrival so many years ago. Ash saw he had lied to David. He wasn't going to just fade away if he got a lead here. He was going to be a pain in the ass. Which meant David would try to come at him again if DuChamp understood what was going on.

Try it, Ash thought.

DuChamp peered at him, the billowing curtain brushing the parchmentlike wrinkles making up the side of his face. "You told me not to tell," he said.

"*Who* told you not to tell?"

"They speak English," DuChamp said.

Ash's heart thundered. He said, "Do you remember Yuri? Someone named Yuri?" He thought, she'll come back soon. "Who told you where to pick us up, Mr. DuChamp? Who told you to go to Canada and bring us to the United States?"

From down the hallway, Karen's voice called, "Mrs. Roth. What did I tell you twenty minutes ago? Your son visits *Tuesday* nights."

"Mr. DuChamp."

"Don't trust Carver. He took the bicycle, too," DuChamp said.

In Russian, Ash whispered, "Tell me the name."

The knob turned. Karen walked in.

"How are you getting along?" Karen asked cheerily. "Sorry I had to leave. Mrs. Roth gets upset sometimes."

"Yeah, it must be tough," Ash said.

DuChamp was looking away, out the window. "We took a vacation in Czechoslovakia," he said.

Oh, god, not now. Not with her here. Ash said, "That's nice." DuChamp picked idly at his trousers, said, "Russian children. Diplomats' kids. Just for a few nights. That's what they said."

Ash said, "What is he talking about?" Karen came close and made a sucking sound with her lips. She said, in an amused, chastising tone, "Mr. DuChamp, are you talking about that movie again? You have a visitor. Don't you want to talk to your visitor? You can talk about that movie later."

Ash stared at her. "This is the movie?"

"Mustn't have an accident. Get across the border. Mustn't let police see. Very important," DuChamp said.

Karen sighed. "That must have been some movie," she said.

DuChamp went waxy. The pale blue eyes wandered along the walls. Suddenly he didn't seem to know where he was.

"Mr. DuChamp?" Ash said.

DuChamp's eyes slowly lifted to Ash. "Who are you?" he said.

Ash had to know. "What happened in the movie?"

DuChamp shrank away from him. He looked terrified suddenly. "You took my cereal," he cried. "And gave it to Carver."

"That's it for today," Karen told Ash. "Tomorrow we're taking them on a trip, to Mt. Greylock to watch the hawks. We won't be back until evening and no visitors allowed then. But I'll tell him you came, or if you're around in two days, come back. Maybe he'll be better."

"I don't trust Carver!" DuChamp cried as they left the room. "Carver isn't what he seems!"

* * *

Outside it was cooler. At dusk a steady stream of cars headed out
of town on Route 20 toward Tanglewood and the Pittsfield
movies, or the dancing at Jacob's Pillow. Or *As You Like It*,
tonight's Shakespeare on the Mount.

So close, Ash thought as he slipped into the hunt room at
Lester House for a drink. He'd come back for DuChamp tomorrow night and try to talk his way in even though visitors weren't
allowed. Try one more time. But after seventeen years his pri-
mary purpose wasn't to track down the father who had sent him
here, and who was probably dead anyway by now. If nothing
happened tomorrow, he'd keep going. Start his new life. It
should be easy enough. They'd taught him how. He'd use the
obituaries to get the name of a man his age. He'd find a copy
of the man's birth certificate. It was tricky but possible. People
in the life did it all the time. He'd write social security and send
the certificate and say he'd lost his card. He'd use the card to get
other ID: credit cards, license, passport. He'd waited seventeen
years so far and a little more time wouldn't kill him.

Who knows, Ash thought, amused. Someday, if the Soviet
Union keeps breaking apart, maybe I can go back as a tourist and
do some looking myself.

The hunt room was a small, dark alcove off Lester House's
fine steak restaurant, with bear and deer heads on the wall, and
old flintlocks held in braces. He could smell the meats starting
to sizzle in the kitchen in the back of the place. A color TV
mounted in a corner broadcast a Red Sox game, where the Sox
were winning for once. Most of the swivel chairs were empty,
but a couple of town cops drank Cokes, or what looked like
Cokes, at one of the tables nearby. An Oriental man in a tie and
jacket, a salesman maybe, ate peanuts from a copper tray, sipped
beer, and watched the game. A young couple at the far end of
the bar were arguing in muted tones over Budweisers. He heard
the girl say, "I'm sick of your brother!"

Outside, through the bay window, Ash saw a power company
truck pull up.

"Vodka. Stoli if you have it," Ash said.

"A twist?"

"No."

"We interrupt this game for a special announcement," a voice said. On-screen, Fenway Park disappeared and in its place Ash saw an angry crowd screaming, shaking fists. A line of yellow-brown tanks with red stars on the turrets, with the spires of Moscow's St. Petersburg Square behind. Lettering flashed. "Soviet Coup." His blood went cold.

No, it can't be possible. They didn't really do it. He felt sick. Violated. He'd read in his own paper that a coup was possible, even imminent, for months. But it seemed unreal that it had really happened. Moscow, beautiful Moscow, Dietz used to say, showing slides of flower gardens, skating rinks, happy people holding hands. Museums. Moscow, where his orders had come from.

What am I even thinking? Ash thought. Beautiful Moscow? Precious Moscow? I never even saw the damn place.

Ash drained the Stoli and must have signaled for another because the bartender was filling his glass, and they gave nice portions in Lester House. "It is believed that one of Gorbachev's own appointees, KGB chief Kryuchkov, is behind the plotters," the announcer said.

Is this what David had been into? But that didn't make sense when Ash remembered his work over the last few months. How could such scattered assignments have had anything to do with this coup?

The Oriental in the sports jacket said, still munching peanuts, "There goes the peace dividend." He had a Boston accent, dragging out the *ea*. The Moscow correspondent from ABC said, "Will Soviet troops fire on their own people?" The cops at the little table were getting up, ambling toward the bar for a better view of the news.

"I should have kept my stock in Lockheed," the Oriental said.

Ash lifted his glass. "Call your broker immediately."

Then a vague smell of roses came to him, and behind, an unmistakable voice said, "I don't believe it. Baryishnikov! Is that you?"

There was the sense of air going out of the room, seeping away, draining into a vacuum. Ash went cold. "All over the

Soviet Union, workers are going on strike," the announcer said.
It took an eternity to turn, and when he did, she was standing
with the cops moving around behind her, smiling with her
mouth only, sadness there. The whole bar smelled of roses now.

The cops looked him over with an open, easy curiosity. The
man in the sports jacket half swiveled toward him, one hand
holding his beer stein, one under the bar.

The funny thing was, seeing her, he knew how much he'd
liked her. Not since Corinna.

She slid onto the stool beside him with a little sideways rump
movement, head cocked as if she were actually waiting for him
to look glad. Her crimson Georgia Tech T-shirt torn at the
shoulder. He saw a small flash of white beneath. Her hands on
the glossy bar were as small and slender as he remembered them.
She wore the thinnest plain gold ring on the right index finger.
The denim on her knee brushed his trousers, where they hung
off his calf. She would have backup outside in the power company truck. And more outside in back.

"You're late. I've been waiting since three," Ash said, lifting
his glass.

The tanks on-screen headed right at the camera. His gun was
in the car outside. She said, "I thought you were going to
California. What happened? The plane get lost?"

Within reach he saw possible weapons. The glass. A magazine.
A pen on the bar.

"One crucial question is, who controls Soviet nuclear codes?"
said a State Department expert on TV.

"Well, what should we talk about?" Ash said, examining the
crystal. "The ball game? The coup? Any ideas?"

"Grump."

"Coincidence, there's a good topic," Ash said, draining the
Stoli. "As in accident. Karma. Meeting out of the blue."

"I don't believe in coincidences," she said.

"I didn't think you did," Ash replied.

The cops leaned closer, the distance to the nearest gunbelt a
foot and a half now. What the fuck. Ash signaled for a refill. "Are
you going to get all gushy on me?" said Jennifer Knowles.

THIRTEEN

GREGOR VOLSKY SPED from Dulles Airport onto the Dulles access road in suburban Virginia, racing toward the capital in the back of a yellow cab. He pored through the *Washington Post*, desperate for news of the coup. "Soviet Leader Feared Dead," read the lead headline. "Miners Strike in Vladivostok." The eight-hour flight from Moscow had been torture, starting just after takeoff. Volsky had looked down to see tanks surrounding the airport. Then clouds obscured the tanks and the Aeroflot crew had tried to make it a normal trip, smiling and serving drinks as if the world weren't turning upside down behind them. Aeroflot flights to the U.S. tended to be boisterous, but the Soviet passengers had been silent and grim.

Volsky demanded to see the pilot, showed his ID, asked for information. But the pilot claimed there was a blackout, and from the suspicious appraisal he gave Volsky, Volsky guessed he was KGB, too.

It was unbearable. Everything he had worked for, hoped for, being crushed while he was strapped into a wide-body jet beside a Chicago University history professor drinking straight gin and laughing at a movie. The shades down. The engines throbbing. The flickering lights emanating from the screen where a poor black American slum dweller inherited a fortune from a racist and cantankerous white man. A cute stewardess offered him back issues of *Soviet Life*. They were filled with boastful articles on

"The New Era of Openness." Volsky tried a *London Economist*. "Coup Rumors Persist," it said.

Volsky thought, my own people, the KGB, did this.

He bought every paper he could when he landed. And now, feeling sicker by the minute, he scanned the *Post*, *Chicago Tribune*, *USA Today*. But he didn't need American reporters to tell him what would be happening at home. There would be troops at intersections. Citizens half pushed, half dragged from their flats at night, stuffed into Black Marias and driven to their death. Cells filling up in the Lubyanka. Printing presses smashed. Students arrested. Fresh barbed wire going up at borders. Train cars with no windows rattling north, toward the prison camps.

Volsky couldn't stand it. He could hardly believe such horrors could happen in 1991.

He grabbed the *Atlanta Constitution* off the seat. On the front page a crowd of enraged, unarmed Muscovites defied a row of tanks outside the Russian Republic's palace, standing screaming at the gunners, unprotected. Blocking the path to the new republic's headquarters with their bodies. Flesh against tanks. Volsky closed his eyes at the bravery of these people. He had a vision of a T-34 tank firing into charging rebels in Afghanistan. The body parts bleeding, twitching on the ground. The smell of cordite mixing with that of death.

The cab took Route 475 to the George Washington Memorial Parkway, and headed along the Palisades. Volsky squeezed his eyes shut. He might even know some of these people. His cousin Alexandra lived in Moscow; a chubby, bubbly woman he saw once every five years when he came to town. Volsky searched the tiny faces for familiar ones. Members of his old unit. Anyone he knew. The faces were strangers' faces but also faces he would see anywhere in Russia. An old woman in a scarf. A middle-aged man in a beret. A boy, his older son Ivan's age, fists in the air, mouth open, screaming.

Thank god Ivana and Boris are safely in Washington. But Ivan is in the technical institute outside Kiev.

The cabdriver, glancing at his passenger buried in the paper, said, "I knew it was too good to last."

Volsky crumpled the paper and let it fall to the pile. He glanced out the window at the Key Bridge, which they were driving over. But an image of Ash came into his mind. So many revelations on this trip, and none of them good. He'd never been so ashamed of his own people. "He's still alive?" the old guard Posner had said eagerly, in the parking lot outside the KGB hospital in Odessa. "What does he look like? Is he married? Does he have a family? Will you give him a message for me?"

Yes, I'll give him a message, Volsky had said.

The old man had gripped Volsky's sleeve, like a child. "Tell him I never stopped thinking of him."

The burning in Volsky's intestines grew worse. His jaw clenched and his teeth ached.

"They said we'd be killed if we talked about it," Posner had said. "That boy used to sit for hours, share my lunch, beg me to let him out. He was lonely. But he was lonely because he was smart. And then they sent me away for talking to him. Can you help him, Comrade Major? If he's still alive, he gave his whole life for this shit."

The cab headed down M Street in the District. The sun was shining, the sky blue. To Volsky it seemed unreal that life proceeded normally here as his homeland was being crushed. Volsky saw mothers wheeling strollers on M Street. Laughing workmen in dungarees unloaded steel beer barrels at Clyde's, for the afternoon crowd. A couple, hand in hand, walked out of Georgetown mall carrying brown shopping bags. A trio of gray-suited businessmen lurched from The Guards after lunch.

Akromeyev's mocking voice echoed in Volsky's head: "The difference between you and other reformers is that after you stop complaining you do what you are told."

So that's why Akromeyev had been so quiet lately, Volsky thought. He knew what was going to happen. Shutting himself in the wire room, pacing in his office late at night. He probably had instructions. He's probably got the embassy terrified, if they don't do what he says.

The driver asked, watching him again, "So what was it? Vacation? Business? Where'd you go?"

"Moscow."

"You're Russian? Congratulations, you just got out in time," the driver said.

In Afghanistan, he'd been able to shut out his surroundings and direct his attention toward tasks at hand. Concentrate on your rice, not the maggots in it, he'd tell himself. Savor the sunset instead of looking at the bars in between. "Don't look at a cockroach as an insect but as protein to sustain you," he'd tell the men. "Be glad you can feel cold. It is proof you are alive."

The taxi pulled up to the embassy and the newsmen outside caught sight of Volsky. They surged his way.

"That guy works here!"

"Gregor, is Gorbachev alive!"

"How come the KGB hasn't arrested Boris Yeltsin!"

Volsky pushed through the screaming newsmen, their faces swimming close. Whatever human qualities they possessed disappeared when they got into a pack. He saw a blur of khaki raincoats and linen summer suits. Someone grabbed his arm. It was the *Washington Post* Embassy Row reporter, a pale, overly made-up New Yorker with a tiny tape recorder in her fist. He had the urge to ask her if she knew Ash. She cried, as microphones were thrust between them by other reporters, "Will the ambassador make a statement today?"

"Ask the press office." Volsky broke free, strode through the iron gate and into the embassy. Volsky noted that the usual guard, the blond man who generally seemed to be idling by the gate but in fact was posted there, the one Akromeyev called the Boxer, had been replaced.

Inside, the embassy was as silent as a tomb. He passed the secretary from public relations on the stairs, and she murmured hello but averted her eyes. A plainclothes man who had replaced No Eyebrows on the first landing nodded at Volsky, but his lips pressed together, and his gray eyes looked bleak. Volsky had seen this expression in his soldiers in Afghanistan, directed at the KGB political officers. Now the embassy staff looked at Volsky that way.

"Comrade Volsky!" Marta crowed as he reached Akromeyev's outer office. "What a surprise! Comrade Akromeyev said you would not be back for weeks!" I bet, Volsky thought grimly. He had not cabled Akromeyev, following Akromeyev's orders to avoid alerting Moscow about Ash. "Report to me personally," the colonel had said.

That was fine with Volsky. He wanted to be present when he told Akromeyev about Ash. Ash had made a mistake by threatening to go to the FBI, idle threat or not. Volsky knew that to Akromeyev, a subordinate should never threaten a superior, no matter how severe the provocation. And especially if that superior was Akromeyev. Threats would never be tolerated by Akromeyev.

Did I ever really think I could change anything by joining the KGB?

Marta smiled radiantly, her outfit surpassing even her usual hideousness in taste today. Her pink cashmere sweater clashed with the ankle-length brown tweed dress, frumpy turquoise ankle socks, low-heeled leather flats. She looked like a bad imitation of a character in the American theatrical show *Grease,* which Volsky had seen with his wife at the Kennedy Center last year.

"Comrade Volsky, it is so exciting," Marta said, coming toward him to greet him. "Things were so dark at home and now they will be all right."

"Where is Sergei Akromeyev?"

"Busy, busy, busy! So many things to do! He is at a luncheon with the trade minister! Have you seen the stilted reports in the press here? What is it really like at home? All they show here is the negative! They want us to be weak!"

She parroted Akromeyev. Volsky said, "Did that American, Ash, ever come back?"

"No, comrade."

"Where is Riga Soccer Star?" he asked. "I didn't see him on the landing."

"Out of town, and will probably be gone for a few days."

Out of town during the trade minister's visit? During a coup? Little warning pinprick itches brushed the back of Volsky's neck.

Volsky thought, act calm, look calm. She tells Akromeyev everything.

"And the Boxer and No Eyebrows?"

"Also."

Volsky said, making a little finger mark on a dust spot on her desk, "Where are they?"

Marta shrugged. "You must ask Sergei Akromeyev that."

In Afghanistan once, Volsky's troops had accompanied Afghan units seizing a town from rebel forces. But the troops had been from the same town. As soon as the village was secure, they went on a rampage. They shot rebel soldiers and their wives and children. They arrested landlords they didn't like. Or neighbors who'd offended them. They would say, that man was a rebel, and then nobody would ask questions. It was a free, savage time of retribution. A brief moment when civilized restraints disappeared. An opportunity for barbarism without punishment. Volsky felt afraid for James Ash.

"Comrade Colonel Akromeyev will be back soon. I will tell him you've returned," said Marta.

Volsky reached his office. The day's *Pravda* was on his desk. The pages filled with hearty proclamations about the future and veiled warnings against dissent.

He fell into his swivel chair and looked with loathing over the expensive quarters he had been rewarded with for being KGB. There was the red private phone and Sony stereo unit and artwork and wet bar. The photos of him, kayaking on the Potomac on weekends. The three-bedroom apartment in the Soviet compound in Glover Park. The chauffeur at any hour he wanted it.

"Volsky!"

Akromeyev stood in the doorway, looking weary but triumphant. He advanced into the room with his bearish, dangerous gait, blue suit rumpled as if he had worn it for days. "You are back! Wonderful! Wonderful news at home! What did you find out about Ash?"

"He was who he said he was."

"Ahhhh."

"The town, the story, all of it. True. We must bring him in."

Akromeyev nodded eagerly, fixing Volsky with his red-rimmed eyes. "And how did you find this out?"

"Records," Volsky lied.

"Yes, it is true, I found also," Akromeyev said. "Fantastic! A whole spy ring and we've turned them back! They are working for us again! Only Ash, he was a problem," Akromeyev said, nodding sadly. "The story he told you was not entirely true."

Akromeyev looked shrewd. "It was almost true," he said delicately. "But he left out that both he *and* Kislak were selling information. Not just Kislak. They fell out. He figured he would come to us, we'd get rid of Kislak. But Ash was selling satellite data to the Japanese. I have a copy of the report he sold. He kept the money. The two of them went private."

"But why would he come here?"

Akromeyev held up a hand. "I have it under control," he said. "I've made adjustments. Kislak will stay on for the time being. The group responds to him. Don't concern yourself with it anymore."

"What kind of adjustments?" Volsky said. "If Ash was selling information, why come to us? He had to know we would make him stop."

Akromeyev stood, yawned. "Yes, well, he wasn't very logical. He feared for his life. And anyway, that is no longer your concern. You're on trade minister duty, Volsky. There's a dinner tonight at Congressman Raban's . . . if he doesn't cancel. Raban's worried about the Jews. Take care of security, eh?"

Akromeyev turned, walked toward the doorway. "By the way, he likes cheeseburgers," he instructed. "Make sure you know, wherever he is, where there're good cheeseburgers. Not Mc-Donald's, he doesn't like that. Burger King is okay. So's Clyde's. He hates White Castle. And he likes those white cheeses, Monterey Jack. Swiss. Not cheddar. He likes pubs."

"How does he like them cooked?" Volsky said dryly.

Akromeyev said, staring into Volsky's face, "I have evidence."

When he left, Volsky blew out air and made his decision. He used a long, skeleton-style key to open a long drawer on the left-hand bottom corner of his Russian-birch desk. Akromeyev is not my officer anymore, Volsky told himself. Akromeyev is a traitor. I don't take orders from him.

His mouth was dry but his heartbeat was steady. Inside the drawer was a combination safe he opened with four numbers. And inside that was a red, leather-bound book with inked-in coded numbers inside.

Nobody in Moscow would ever doubt Akromeyev. To those bastards he would be a big hero who brought in a spy ring. And even if they doubted it, nobody would care. Thousands would be dying in Russia now, and the important thing to the new government would be the spy ring, not one unknown man who died.

Volsky used his red phone to dial Riga's beeper. In America everyone had a beeper. Doctors. Car salesmen. Crack dealers. Assassins.

He let it ring twice, hung up, and dialed again. This time it rang once before he hung up.

Five minutes later his red phone buzzed. Volsky heard the high-pitched whoosh of highway traffic in the background on the other end. No talking. He said, "Volsky. Fourteen eleven," and hung up. He reached back into the safe and removed his Walther PPK, registered in the U.S. He put it in his belt, in the small of his back.

Volsky checked his watch, fought through the newsmen outside again and caught the fourth cab outside the embassy, after waving off the first three. He told the driver to take him to Fourteenth and T. I never helped my men in Afghanistan but I will help this man, he thought. The list of booths used by Intelligence for incoming calls was changed each month, and once a booth was used, it was not reemployed for at least five years. Even if Volsky was watched, there would be no time for the FBI to tap this booth. And he would keep his head down when he talked, to block the view of any lip-readers.

When they reached the phone, which was on a corner near a Texaco station, he told the driver to wait. Except a boy in baggy jeans and old Reeboks was using it, hopping from one foot to the other while he talked. The kid couldn't be more than eleven. He barely reached the phone. He had a beeper snapped to his right hip. When he saw Volsky waiting a few feet away, he snapped, "Yo, man, I'm using this."

"I'm waiting for it."

"Wait somewhere else."

The kid glowered. Volsky noticed a long scar across the top of his forehead. The kid said, "Fifty! Each one's fifty!" But he didn't like somebody being within earshot of his conversation. He said into the receiver, "I'll call you back."

The kid slammed the phone down and stomped up to Volsky. He was about three feet shorter than the KGB man. He had a fat, leather notebook in his breast pocket, and a shiny ballpoint pen. "Yo, man, this is my phone."

"May I borrow it?"

The kid saw he wasn't intimidated. "What happened to your eye?" he said, tilting his head to see better.

"I was shot. In Afghanistan."

"You're Russian?" the kid said, impressed.

The phone rang. Volsky and the kid lunged for it. Volsky was closer.

"Volsky," he snapped when he picked it up.

"We're still a half hour away," Riga's voice said while the kid made signs for him to hang up. "Kislak had cramps and we stopped on ninety-five. Want me to call back when we arrive?"

"Where are you exactly?" Volsky snapped. The kid listened with professional interest.

"Winsted. The last place in Connecticut. Smith Falls is about thirty minutes, forty. Then we have to find the Knowles house."

Smith Falls, Volsky thought. He's gone to Smith Falls. He's gone home. Every soldier's dream in battle. Tears sprang to Volsky's eyes.

"Return to Washington," he told Riga in his most imperious tone. "There's something else for you to do."

He wished the man on the other end had been the Boxer or No Eyebrows. They would have listened. Riga, who was smarter, hesitated.

"But Mr. Bliss told us—"

"He told me to change that. We have an emergency. Your trip is canceled. Come home."

From behind him, the kid said, "Hurry up, man."

Riga said, firmly and with deference, "Please excuse me, but tell Mr. Bliss we will come home when he tells me himself. Those were his instructions."

"Then wait by the phone," Volsky ordered, figuring the delay might give Ash another hour. "I will get him."

"No need for that. I have my beeper," Riga said. "We have to go."

The connection was broken.

"You finished?" the kid asked. "Don't you have a phone where you work?" The kid rolled his eyes. "Aw, don't use it again."

Volsky dialed his home number and sagged with relief when Ivana answered. As always, hearing her gave him a warm, soft feeling inside. He had to keep the urgency from his voice because all lines at the compound were tapped by Domestic Surveillance, KGB. But he had to let her know how serious this was. "I got back early, rabbit. I got the borscht but never got to see Cousin Irma. She was away."

"Cousin Irma" was code between them, dating back more than ten years. Neither of them could stand Ivana's cousin Irma. Whenever one of them wanted to escape from a dinner party conversation, they'd bring her up. They'd say "I saw Cousin Irma" or "Did you hear from Cousin Irma" or "That woman looks like Cousin Irma." Anything with the words *Cousin Irma*. Then the other one would know the speaker needed help.

"She'll be disappointed," Ivana said, playing along perfectly.

"Well, next time," he said. "Why don't you go over to Eddie's place and pick up a couple of steaks. I should be home in a few hours."

He heard the intake of breath on the other end, but didn't think it severe enough so that anyone who didn't know would understand she was alarmed. "Eddie's place" was code, too. When Volsky had just arrived in Washington, a State Department attaché named Eddie Frank, a man everyone knew was CIA, had invited Ivana and him to dinner several times. "Come out to my place, we'll grill steaks," he'd say. Akromeyev never let Volsky go. But over the years, in their jokes, "Eddie's place" had come to mean American intelligence.

Volsky had just told his wife to get out of the compound with their son. "Great idea," she said. "I'll bring Boris. We'll stop at Lettie's on the way back, see if she wants to eat with us, too." Lettie was the name of a woman who owned a motel they had stayed at in the Shenandoah, two hours away.

"Take all the time you need," she said. She was telling him, you want to defect, that's fine with me. I'll think of a way to leave the chauffeur/surveillance man. I'll meet you at Lettie's.

"Love you," Volsky said. His heart was thundering. They hung up.

The kid was standing directly behind him, looking impatiently at his Rolex watch. "You got any quarters?" Volsky said.

The kid shook his head but smiled in a way that made Volsky know his pockets were filled with change.

Volsky pulled out a twenty. "Keep it. Just give me four quarters."

The kid laughed. "Yo, man, I'll give you quarters if you get away from my phone." The kid handed him the money. The kid said, shaking his head, "Big deal. Twenty bucks."

Volsky found another phone two blocks away at a gas station, which also had road maps, and he tried TWA, Delta, United, and American. Smith Falls didn't have an airport. But in western Massachusetts there was a Springfield-Hartford airport, the Delta operator said. And a flight in three hours. The flight took two hours if there were no delays. Renting a car would take half an hour, if he could find one. From the airport to Smith Falls would take another hour, he saw on his map.

Seven hours to Smith Falls if I fly, if there are no delays.

Eight hours if I drive.

Volsky climbed back in the cab and directed the driver to Anacostia. There was a garage in Anacostia and a car he could use. Officially, Soviet diplomats weren't allowed to leave the city without State Department permission. There were many places in the country they weren't allowed to go even with permission. For instance, Soviet diplomats were not allowed to drive across the Mississippi River on any of the bridges there. They were not supposed to have close-up knowledge of the bridges. They could fly across the river, but not drive.

The truth was that on emergency occasions it was possible to leave the city and drive anywhere. The Americans managed to do it in Moscow sometimes, and it was much easier for the Russians to do it here. You could not do it often, but it was done. If the Americans found out, they followed you or protested. There were cars, identities, and driver's licenses stashed in lockers and garages around town.

Volsky got out a block from his destination, tipped the driver, and waited until the cab disappeared around the corner before continuing on foot. He was on a seedy block within view of the Anacostia River, filled with old clapboard houses with wide porches, half collapsing in on themselves. There were old cars on blocks in driveways. Bars on windows. Cats fighting in uncollected trash on a stoop. Boys in the middle of the street playing rubber ball.

Volsky located a one-car garage in front of a boarded-up house, used a key, and slid the door up. He'd never personally met the man who had rented the space and serviced the car monthly and made sure the lock was fast.

Eight hours, he thought, heading onto the Baltimore Washington Parkway fifteen minutes later. He was desperate to hurry but made sure to be the second-fastest car on the road.

He thought, Ash will think I'm coming after him if he sees me. He thought, *what* house was Riga talking about? This time I'm not going along with them. This time I'll fight them. If I can't fight them at home, I'll do it here.

Volsky thought, I hope I get there in time.

Ash drained his second Stoli and watched Jennifer joke with the Smith Falls cops in the brightly lit Heublein mirror behind the Lester House bar. She playfully swiveled back and forth on the seat beside him, sipping orange juice from a cocktail straw. The cops hung over her shoulder, guzzling RC colas, laughing. They seemed to be having a gay old time.

The bartender wiped a shot glass with a rag and said, "Call me Larry." The cops said call me Ken and call me Fred. The Oriental businessman moved over to be closer to the conversation, lit a Camel, and the smoke drifted across the TV screen, where Kansas City went ahead of the Red Sox in the eighth.

"Say it, say it, Jen," the younger, louder cop, Fred, said. The younger one smelled of garlic, the older of Paco Rabanne. They were so close to Ash, each time they paid they brushed his biceps.

Jennifer shook her head. "No way."

"Say it or we won't stop bothering you," said Ken, who was fitter. Both cops wore crisp black uniforms like the uniforms in Smith Falls when Ash had grown up. But unlike police then, these two wore their .38s in Sam Browne belts, not hip holsters. The younger cop and Jennifer seemed the same age.

Jennifer sighed and rested her glass on the inside of her jeans, so it left a smudge mark from condensation on the faded denim. She wore a crimson Georgia Tech T-shirt with a Yellow Jacket in front, and the tiniest rip on the right shoulder showed a slit of white skin. Her bare arms were freckled under her tan. The bronze made her eyes greener. The sun had turned her hair a lighter shade of blond.

Jennifer said, in her husky, radio voice, "This is Jennifer Knowles, Lenox High School. All classes to the auditorium please."

The cops burst out laughing. "Every Thursday, I'll never forget it," Fred said. The Oriental ordered a bottled Anchor Steam, working his way through the beer brands lining the top of the mirror. The bartender said, "Ash, that's your name. Isn't that his name, Jennifer?"

"That's right," said Jennifer, who had told them all his name.

The bartender poured himself more house red. "She was wild, Ash. *Wild*. I thought she'd end up smashed into a tree in the middle of the night. Cars. Boys. You should have seen the losers she hooked up with."

"Hey," Jennifer Knowles said, blushing. "They were more interesting than you guys."

"Whoa! We thought . . . we all thought," Larry the bartender said, pouring another vodka for Ash, waving off the no-thanks, "she'd be dead by twenty. I had a crush on her." He shook his head. "But when Jennifer liked a guy, no one could change her mind." Larry looked sad, then burst out laughing. "She was even in a motorcycle gang," he said.

"I was not!"

"You went out with that Hells Angel guy for two years," the cop Ken said. He laid his hand on Ash's shoulder. It felt cold through the fabric, and pudgy. "Ash, I'm telling you," he said, and seemed to forget what he was saying. "Ash, I'm telling you."

Ash thought, if they're going to arrest me, why don't they do it?

"And now she's in Washington," Larry said proudly.

"Our famous Jennifer," Fred said.

"Are we off duty now? Good. No more Cokes, Larry," Ken said. "Hit me, baby."

Ash swallowed the Stoli and felt it in his stomach and it spread through him, like it flowed through his veins. He would have one chance to get away and he would have to pick it perfectly. Larry said, "Hey, let's drink to the *Washington Post*. The way you got Nixon!"

"The country would be better off if we still had Nixon," Fred said.

"Amen," Larry said.

"Republicans," the Oriental said. "How about a Hood ale now. Were you really nominated for a Pulitzer Prize?"

"I shouldn't have told you about the prize. He's shy," Jennifer said.

Ash put a big tip on the bar and got up. Maybe I was wrong, he hoped. Maybe it's really coincidence. Maybe I could stand up right now, pay, walk out. Other people run into people from their hometowns. Maybe I'll get out of here, get out of Smith Falls.

Jennifer stood up when he did.

"Where we going now, Baryshnikov?" she said.

She linked an arm with his and they walked outside where the daylight had faded. In his mind he still saw her walking into the FBI. The cars making their way down Main Street toward Tanglewood had their headlights on. Her skin against his arm felt warm and satiny. It made the inside of his forearm tingle, and his forehead hot.

Despite the vodka Ash's senses seemed magnified. He saw the street in precise, clear pieces. The way two girls in shorts coming out of the Cone Joint waved at them. The way a janitor with keys on his belt locked up the town hall across the street as the brick clock tower chimed eight. The way the wrought-iron streetlights, at dusk, created small, emerald-colored halos over the one-story storefronts. Jennifer smiled up at him with an impish look.

"Not that way," she said, tugging him away from his car and toward the workmen from the power company truck. "I want to show you something. You feel tense."

How did she know I was here? he thought. He'd taken a different car and different clothes and he'd not used plastic to pay for anything. Only his shoes and the parabellum he carried were the same. Could they have put a sender in his shoes? In shoes? That was impossible. Senders, electronic tracking devices, didn't exist that small.

And anyway, where could she put a sender in a shoe?

The men in coveralls realigned themselves on the sidewalk as Ash approached. The back door of the truck slid open. He thought, none of it makes sense. They could have snatched me in the bar with less fuss. A worker with a beer belly got out of the truck. A gray-haired worker held a wrench, standing on the sidewalk. A tall, pale one with long sideburns watched Ash coming, hands in the pockets of his coveralls. Anything else? Anything special? The overalls looked faded, like overalls on real workmen, unless it was just an extra touch.

Jennifer led him past the workmen. She unlocked the door of her Mustang.

She said, squeezing his arm before letting it go, "A trip dowwwwwnnnnn . . . memory lane!"

"Kidnapping," Ash said.

She giggled. They rolled up Main Street, out of town. Back past the gas stations, bowling alley, Cumberland Farms. Into the darkness. Out of the light. There were woods on both sides of the road.

"Once I saw Baryshnikov in Boston in a performance," she said, driving. "It was the first time I saw him in person, not on TV. The way his muscles filled those tights, I couldn't breathe, watching him. And I never knew a human being could stay in the air like that. Like he defied gravity, floating. He would go up and not come down."

"Yeh, he's quite a dancer," Ash said. In the mirror, no cars followed.

"When he defected, I was thrilled. I used to save up and go to New York to see him dance. I mean, what kind of life did he have in the Soviet Union? As soon as he stopped dancing, they'd take his privileges away. Here he could have anything he wanted and keep it. He could be a king."

"Ah, defection," Ash said, looking at her driving now, getting it finally. They were giving him a different option first. A soft option. "I didn't know you were such an expert on life in Russia."

"Sure. Me. Life in Russia," she said, smiling. "Ask me anything about it. But look at the life he has now. Houses. Women. Did you see that movie he made with Gregory Hines?"

"The one about the defector?"

"That's right. When they danced together, that was incredible," she said, taking her hands off the wheel to make the point. "That tap-dancing scene."

They headed south on Route 8, back toward Connecticut. It was a two-lane road and in the dark the headlights picked out sporadic homes, dark trees, an occasional sign indicating a severe curve ahead. They passed a pub that said GREAT EATS. They came around a long curve circling a reservoir. In a sky studded with fast-moving clouds, the rising half-moon gave the surface of the water a silvery sheen.

"With what's going on in Russia now, I bet a lot of people would like to come here," she said.

"I bet."

"Scientists. Artists."

"Maybe we should charter a boat," he said. Ash checked the rearview mirror. Nobody behind. All he would have to do was reach over, grab the wheel. Shove his foot down toward the brake. "When you use your hand to strike," Martini had said, "one swift blow to the neck or the bridge of the nose. Do it right, it drives cartilage into the brain. You kill the person instantly."

"What are you thinking?" Jennifer said, driving.

"Talking about Baryshnikov reminded me of Doc Gooden. From the Mets." I can't kill her, can't hurt her, he told Martini in his mind.

"The Mets?" she said.

Do it now. Right now, Martini's voice in his head said.

"One time I went to Shea Stadium, in the bleachers, during his rookie year. People used to hang off the banisters up there, put up these little cards, strike-out cards, K cards they called them, when he fanned a guy."

"You're thinking about baseball?" she said.

Her Adam's apple bobbed on her throat.

"Well, you were talking about Baryshnikov."

"That's what Baryshnikov made you think about? The most romantic . . . baseball?" She sighed. "Here's an idea for a show," she said. "Why is it every time a girl asks a guy what he's thinking, he says baseball?"

"Because girls only ask men what they're thinking when men are thinking something they don't like."

"Who are you? Dr. Ruth?" she said.

They climbed through the blasted-out granite sections Ash remembered from the ride up. The headlights picked out a sign saying RESERVOIR ROAD and Jennifer swung the wheel a little too fast so the Mustang screeched as it skidded left, off the highway, onto a one-lane blacktop that took them along a dike crossing the edge of the lake. There was no other traffic. On one side, woods. On the other, a high cliff and water. Ash thought, FBI parked in the trees with their headlights off will be invisible.

"We used to come here on summer nights," she said. "Swim. Drink. Skinny-dip."

"Is this the seduction part?" Ash said.

"I hope so," said Jennifer Knowles.

Inside him the pressure mounted. I won't do it, he told Martini in his mind.

She parked on a natural overlook jutting over the reservoir. They were forty feet up. The clouds came in faster. The moon cast a long, patchy lance across the water to wooded hills two miles across the lake. It was pleasantly warm with the smell of piney woods. Ash heard stillness punctured by the cry of a bird. Trees would give him the best chance of cover he had had since she showed up.

"My god, I love this," she said. "I go down to the Potomac at night sometimes, around Great Falls. It's not the same, though. You ever go down there?"

She took his hand. Twined his fingers. "The water is so cold here," she said. Almost time, he thought. "Like ice," she said. "We used to come out here till October, bring big blankets, make a fire. Jump out and wrap in the blankets and drink brandy by the fire."

"With your motorcycle gang," he said, heart pounding.

She laughed. "Now you know everything about me," she said. "All my secrets."

"So long, Jennifer," Ash said. He ran.

He headed south across the parking area, swept into the woods and pumped up a hill, waiting for shots or footsteps. He dodged, bumped into a tree, tripped, but kept going. "Ash!" came her cry behind him. It was like the old exercise where Martini used to make them run blindfolded. Or make them run at night through woods where the soldiers had suspended flood-lights. The soldiers would switch the lights on, off, on, as the kids ran. Blinding them as they crashed into bushes, trees, rocks. Martini shouting, "Memorize the landscape. Don't stop!" as their little knees pumped.

Ash ran into sticker bushes, felt thorns tear at his face. And now he heard the footsteps behind, to the right. They were coming after him.

Ash ran harder.

Except he realized there were no footsteps behind.

Ash stopped, heaving. He felt a drop of rain. And the hot flow of blood from cuts on his cheeks. He smelled his sweat over the odor of the forest, and a new odor, humid and electrical, ozone.

Some animal, a raccoon or skunk, scurried away in the dark.

Ash squatted in the forest. There was nobody all along, he thought. I was afraid of nothing. And then Ash saw that he had not left anything behind by leaving Washington. He had taken it all with him. The others were still inside him, tearing at him.

The greatest rage seized him.

He heard Jennifer's voice, small and distant sounding. "Ash? Where are you? Ash?"

"Ash? Ouch!" he heard. "Ash? I'm lost!"

Ash walked downhill in the direction he had come from. He used the gradient of the slope to retrace his steps. It had actually been a coincidence, a fucking coincidence, he thought. I guess I can have a real coincidence once in my life.

The car was still parked on the overlook. From behind, Jennifer looked tiny and helpless sitting on the cliff, legs dangling over the side, in the rain.

Thunder cracked.

She didn't turn even though he knew she heard him. Ash sat beside her. The electrical smell was almost overpowering now, and a blue haze formed a foot above the surface of the water. She'd been crying. There were deep lines on her face. When she jutted out her lower lip, she looked like an eight-year-old.

"What do you want from me?" she said. "Why did you come here?"

Ash said, "Who are you?"

"Who am I?" she said, whirling on him and heating up.

"Who am *I*? Who are *you*?" She emitted a short, derisive grunt. "Oh, Jennifer," she said, shaking her head. "What is it about you? Always the crazy ones. Always the nuts. You have the knack, kid. Maybe Fred was right."

"I saw you go into the FBI," Ash said.

"You saw me what?" she said, not getting it right away. "You saw me," she repeated, processing it. Her eyes widened. "In Washington? *You were following me?*"

"I wasn't following you. I was in a car." Ash looked at the water. There was a vague drumming sound as the drizzle grew more steady. "I was passing the building when you were going in."

"And?"

"I saw you."

"So you saw me," she repeated, frowning as if she didn't get it. Ash's head started to throb. Jennifer said, "What do you care if I went in the FBI?"

"You're not in the FBI?" Ash said.

"Oh, my god," she said, and the lip went back in. She showed dawning comprehension. "This is a riot, just a little riot. I don't believe what I'm hearing. I'm a radio host," she said fiercely. "You reporters are so paranoid. I hate Washington," she said. "Puffed-up, self-important assholes. Wha'd you think? The FBI is trying to figure out what you're working on? I'm a little spy for the government? Looking at big, important reporter James Ash? Is that what you thought?" She laughed. "Oh, Rick would get a kick out of this. Someone thinking, me! Working for the FBI."

Ash said, "Something like that."

Jennifer shook her head bitterly. "What is it about you, Jennifer? Even when they don't come on to you, you find them." To Ash she said, staring out at the water, "It's not your fault. I didn't have to go over to you in that bar. I didn't have to call you. I didn't have to give you the cat. I asked for this. My ex-husband is in the FBI, are you happy now? Rick. Remember I told you about Rick? The guy who judges everybody? Who dumped me? Who won't sleep with me? Or maybe you think that's my 'story'? My 'cover'? Me in the FBI. Do you think that's my 'cover'? Ash?"

Drops hit them, heavy and warm, smearing his face. She looked furious. "That's why you stole my letter," she said. "From my house."

Ash started. "I saw you do it. I came out of the kitchen to surprise you, and you were in the drawer, and later the letter was gone. And I can't believe it, I didn't even say anything. I'm *such* an *idiot*."

"Why didn't you say anything then?"

She looked small and slumped and alone and hurt.

"I'm stupid, that's why," she said. "I spend my nights giving advice on the radio to other people. What a joke. I had a feeling about you." She rocked a little. "Wishful thinking. I saw you in Lester House and I was so happy. I thought, 'He followed me to Smith Falls.' What an idiot."

Ash's heart pounded. The blood roared in his head. He was free. There were no FBI. All he had to do was stand up, drive back to town, get in his car, leave. Free to do whatever he wanted. He had really escaped.

Except Ash heard himself say, "You were talking about defection."

Ash thought, Do. Not. Say. This.

"So?" she said.

He stood up. I'm leaving, he thought.

"I'm the spy," he said.

He was getting soaked.

"You're not funny," she said. "I'll drive you back."

"I'm serious," Ash said.

"Jennifer," Jennifer said. "Get out of Washington. Go to a normal place, with normal people. Dad was right."

"Jennifer?" he said.

He took her hand and she shook it off. Let it go, he thought. "Look at me," he said. "I mean it. I've been a Soviet spy for seventeen years."

"Shut up, okay? Stop joking and let's go. It's raining."

He grabbed her. "Jennifer!"

The rain picked up. He let her see it. He put it into his eyes. Let her see everything. He wasn't going to be able to do this with words. He put the truth of it in his face. He willed the truth of it into her. She was really looking at him.

Yuri's voice, Martini's voice, all the fading jumbled old voices inside him, crying from far away, stop this. You can't do this. You mustn't do this. Stop.

"You're not kidding," she said. "Really not kidding."

"No."

"My god," she said. "You actually believe this."

"It's true."

She looked at the sky. "He believes this."

Ash released her and let his hands fall to his sides and the rain soaked him. He said, "Remember in the bar you said you had feelings about people? Remember the feeling you had about me? Nothing. You said you trusted your feelings."

She sank down. *"Spy,"* she said, "is a word for movies. You're telling me you're a spy. Like you pass on secrets to people. Little minicameras and things. Passwords. I'll be carrying the Dickens. The Eagle flies at midnight. Stuff like that."

"That's right."

"And then you just tell me. Isn't that sort of thing a little frowned upon?" she said flippantly.

"I don't want to hurt you."

"You can't hurt me." She was quiet, then said, "You're serious," again. Then she laughed. "Boy, Fred thought the motorcycle gang was bad."

"Look at it from my point of view," Ash said. "Just imagine, for a minute, that I'm sane and I'm telling the truth. Just for argument, okay? A stranger comes to me in a bar. Keeps telling me I look like Baryshnikov. Talks about defection. I see her go into the FBI."

Jennifer started laughing. Great whoops of mirth in the rain. Her voice came to him over the steady drumming.

"And I thought I liked you because we were from the same town. Because we had the same roots. What am I saying? You have me actually discussing this. It isn't true." She cried out, "This is stupid!"

She started crying again.

Ash said, "I'm sorry."

"*You're* sorry," she said. Now there was disgust in her voice. He hated hearing it. "You're telling me you're a reporter, but when you learn things, you pass them to the Russians. That's horrible. A traitor. Like that Walker, in the Navy, who sold the Russians secrets. You're telling me you do things like that."

"I am Russian," Ash said.

They were soaked.

"They trained me. They sent me here when I was seventeen. I never really came from Smith Falls."

"Stop this," she said.

"I took the letter because I didn't know who you were."

"No, no, no, no," she said, slapping her hands against her ears.

Ash said, "Jennifer, remember the man who was in my apartment? Remember what the cop said, that I was hiding something? Remember what he did to the cat? They wanted to do that to me."

Ash sat down in the downpour and gave up and waited to hear the car start as she drove off. After a few minutes he felt her sitting next to him.

She said, "You wouldn't tell me this if it were true. I could turn you in."

"I know that."

She screamed, "Then why are you saying it?"

Ash told her everything. All of it. He looked into her up-turned beautiful face and started talking and the whole story came out. He didn't care if she knew. He wanted to tell her. The town. The other kids. The arrival in the United States. He didn't feel the rain. It was like there wasn't any rain even though it was pouring. He didn't see the lake or the night. In his mind he was back in Smith Falls. Then he was completing his assignments. Telling her about them. Putting it to rest.

As she listened, her expression went angry, shocked, sad,

furious. She said, "This is crazy," and then, a few minutes later, "You're making this up," and then, "You must have felt awful. What am I saying?" And then, "You're saying your own people are trying to kill you?"

"Yeh."

"Your own people."

"Everything is breaking up."

"That's why you lied about going to California. That's why you quit the *Post*."

Ash went cold. "How do you know I quit the *Post*?"

"Don't start again," she said. "Because I called them. I wanted to surprise you when you got home, so I phoned and asked them when you were coming back from California. And they told me you'd quit. Walked off the job. They couldn't understand why you would . . ."

Her mouth hung open but no words came out.

"See?" Ash said.

"I hate you," she said. "I hate what they did to you. I hate that they treated you like that. I think you're lying and I think you're telling the truth. I hate you had to live like that. You must have been afraid all the time. I hate that you're the enemy. I don't know what to think. I can't believe you told me. Why did you tell me?" she said, leaning toward him.

"They used to tell us, telling someone only makes it harder for them."

"What are you going to do?" she said.

"Leave."

She stood up. The rain pounded down steadily. There was a hard edge to her voice that he had never heard before. "You're not spying anymore though, right? That's what you said."

"No."

"You should go away," she agreed in a monotone. "I won't tell them. I'll take you to your motel. No. You didn't have to tell me. Come to my house. I have a couch you can sleep on. Leave tomorrow."

"Tell me one thing. Why did you come over to me at Au Pied de Cochon that first night?" Ash said.

Jennifer said, looking at the mud as they trudged to the car, "I used to believe in love at first sight."

They did not touch each other in the car. Jennifer kept the radio off. The downpour worsened. Rain made it hard to see. After a while they were near Smith Falls again. But just before they reached the town she turned off Route 20 onto a dirt road that rose into the mountains. She drove more slowly on the rutted surface. There were no lights, and they bounced through puddles and around bends. Once she laughed wildly, but the rest of the time just looked sad.

Ash blocked everything out except the quiet, the sense of truth, the feeling of her small, beautiful body beside him. He was exhausted but at peace. His little concentrated love affair bordered by two ends of a drive.

At an unmarked intersection the headlights caught a big deer bolting into the woods. Jennifer turned onto another dirt road that bounced higher, past a log house, where floodlights lit a deck, a picture window, with a color TV showing a western inside. They passed a half-bulldozed lot for construction. The silence seemed deeper up here.

"My house," Jennifer said finally. "My grandfather left it to me. I use it when I'm here."

In the flashing lightning Ash glimpsed a Cape Cod of weathered shingle, centering a small lawn surrounded by woods. There were no streetlights, other houses, or cars visible. They were in the middle of the forest. Jennifer parked the Mustang on the lawn. They ran across the sopping grass and Ash splashed into an ankle-high puddle at the front door while she fumbled with the key. She pushed the door open, stomped inside, and switched the light on and alarm off, punching numbers into a keyboard by the door. "We had vandals a couple years ago."

The house was dry and warm and smelled of maple wood. The combined living/dining room took up the whole ground floor, with a balcony and doorways leading to bedrooms above, and stairs by the far wall. The kitchen and back door were behind a counter that also served as a dining table. It was simple, rustic, and comfortable; Ash saw polished maple walls and floors, throw rugs, a stone fireplace with long mantelpiece and two shotguns over it in racks. Posters of Baryshnikov. A long, low, worn, but comfortable-looking couch. Photographs of Berkshire scenes. A shot of the reservoir. A deer in the woods, antlers up, alert.

"I let my dad use the place for hunting. My mom wouldn't let him keep guns in the house. Even with her gone, he does what she wants."

Rain drummed on the roof.

"He's got clothes upstairs, first room on the right. Some shirts might fit you. There's a shower. I'm going to change."

"I can stay in town," he said.

She was crying again. "Why did you have to be you?" she said.

"I'm always me," he said.

Ash walked to her and put his arms around her and kissed her and felt her hands come around the back of his neck. She clutched him. She was so light he didn't believe he'd actually already lifted her. She kissed his nose, forehead, cheeks, hands. He was lost in the kiss. He couldn't believe it. It was the greatest sensation he had ever felt.

When they pulled back, all he saw were her enormous green eyes.

"What are we doing?" she said.

She unbuttoned his shirt. He pulled off her sweatshirt. Then they were on the couch, her shirttail sliding up to show white hips and belly button he kissed. He slid his tongue over her breasts, ribs. Up the lines of her clavicle. Her whole body seemed to be burning. She helped him with her zipper, her legs appearing, her smell of roses filling his head.

Ash kissed her knees and parted them and sucked at her. Her juices flowed down his chin onto the couch. She arched, pulled his hair. Drew him to her. She slid down his body, encircled his penis with her mouth, sucked, and ran the inside tips of her fingers along his shaft. She stroked his thighs as her head bobbed. He couldn't believe how satiny she felt when he pushed inside. Her legs came around him and they clutched each other.

"Ram me," she said, surprising him. "Ash, ram me."

The couch shifted. The little end table by the couch rocked, the ashtray on it wobbled. She straddled him. He turned her backward so his thighs pressed her rump. There was a tart, earthy odor. She reached around, stroked him with all her fingers. He was going to come. He couldn't stop it. He gritted his teeth and strained and her back was arching like she'd break in half.

"Ash, ram me."

The blood seemed to rush out of Ash's body.

They lay on the couch, unmoving. Ash heard the rain again. It had never stopped.

"Ash," she said. Her finger twined his hair.

He saw what he had gained in coming here. It was more than he had known existed in the world.

Ash kissed her shoulders, ran his lips up her neck. Around her lips slowly. Her fingers, faster. It was starting again. He pulled at her nipples. She kissed his chest. Ash was slick all over with sweat and the juice of her and his come.

This time it went slower. When they were finished, she reached past his shoulders, pulled a blanket off the top of the couch, spread it on them.

The storm grew worse outside.

She said, "Is Ash your real name?"

"As real as anything else."

"Do you know why I came to Smith Falls?" she said, not in her usual voice, but a softer version, a catch in her throat.

"To arrest me because you are an FBI agent," he said, kissing her neck.

"Because you were gone." She kissed his chest. "I called the *Post* to surprise you, meet you when you got back, and they said you'd quit. Gone away."

"I hated not seeing you," Ash said.

She said, massaging his shoulder with one hand, "I figured, Jennifer, go to the cottage. It's vacation anyway. I left a message on your answering machine. If you called in and wanted to find me, I would be here. But I didn't count on it. Then I saw you in town. I thought you'd heard the message. I thought, he *did* come. Funny, huh?"

"No," Ash said, tracing a line down her spine. Then her words penetrated. He propped on one elbow and looked down at her on the couch. "You left a message on my answering machine?" he said, his heart picking up,

"Yes. Is something wrong with that?"

"Saying you'd be in Smith Falls?"

She said, wary, "They couldn't get the message off your machine."

"Did you leave your last name or just say Jennifer? Did you say any part of your name?"

"I . . . I don't remember."

Ash stood up. He was filling with rage against them. The lights in the cabin flickered but stayed on. Without her body beneath him he was chilly. The wind rose, the rain was a roar. Those fuckers. Those fuckers. They'd be coming at him again. He didn't want to alarm her but had no choice. "Jennifer, you have an answering machine. You phone in for messages. How?"

"I call and push seven and it plays everything back."

"So if you want to hear the messages on someone else's machine you call them and punch one and see if it plays anything. Then you try two and three until you get the right one. Then you can call whenever you want and hear the person's messages."

Jennifer sat up, horrified. "When you say it like that, it makes sense, but people don't think that way," she said. "And even if they heard me, it doesn't mean you're in Smith Falls, too."

The house creaked upstairs. "We better leave," Ash said, handing her her clothing. What he was thinking was, then I'll come back alone.

"You're giving them a lot of credit," she said, but she was frightened. Trying to make herself feel better. "I might not have left my name at all. I might have just said, 'It's me.' "

"But you're not sure," he said, putting on his pants. "Anyway, they don't check my machine because they think you left a message on it. They're trying a hundred ways to find me. It's just one more way." The soaked, clammy shirt clung to his skin.

"Even if you didn't say your name, once they hear 'Smith Falls' . . . they don't believe in coincidences either. They'll send someone to check it. They may be in town now."

"In town?" she said. "You mean here."

"Yes. Here."

"At least you don't have to wear those clothes when we go," she said. "You're soaking. What size are you? I've got a men's extralarge shirt I use as a nightgown." Ash looked over the living room with a different eye. At the shotguns. The alarm system. The breaker box for the wires.

From upstairs, her voice called, "Just take a minute!"

She came out of the bedroom in panties, pulling a yellow T-shirt that said MEL'S BEST over her head. She threw a big T-shirt over the banister. It fit Ash just right. She said, dressing fast, "But if I didn't leave my name, they can't find you, can they?"

He shook his head. "Once they know there's a girl they'll call the *Post*, to try to find out who you are. Phone reporters, secretaries, the librarian. It's what I'd do."

He made his voice the imaginary caller's. "I'm trying to track Cousin Ash," he said. "His brother Ed is sick or Ash won money or his father is trying to reach him, or I'm an old buddy from where he went to school. He's not at home and I'm wondering if you know how to find him? Is he married? Does he have a girlfriend I might be able to try?" Ash made his voice friendly, grateful. "I really appreciate your help.

"The *Post* is a gossip mill," he said. "It only takes one person to say, 'I heard he goes out with Jennifer Knowles.' "

She looked guilty and miserable. He kissed her. "You are the best thing that's happened to me," he said. "How could you know? Besides, they might call the *Post* even if you'd never left any message. Smith Falls is small. Everyone in that bar knew you. How long do you think it will take a persistent person to find out you own a house here, and you have a friend in town named Ash. And then the spotter calls Washington. 'I found him,' he tells David. 'He's here.' "

He padded across the room toward the phone. "I better call my machine and erase the messages. At least we'll find out exactly what you said."

Whom had Ash been kidding, thinking he could just walk away? David wasn't a spy anymore. He was just a criminal trying to protect himself. And what about that man with the patch? Volsky? The man who had sent followers after Ash after he left the embassy? Maybe they were involved together.

There could be a whole group of people.

He said, lifting the receiver, "You drive back to Washington. Sleep somewhere else tonight. Not here, and not at your father's."

"What are you going to do?"

"Something in town," he said. "I'll call you tomorrow." It was a lie. He would not call her again. It was too dangerous for her. He would go after David. But if Volsky was involved, the links ran all the way into the Soviet embassy.

"You're doing this for me," she said. "You got screwed up because of me. If it wasn't for me, you would be away from them."

She stood in the middle of the floor crying. "You said you weren't working for him anymore. And the horrible way they brought you up. It isn't fair. You were protecting your friends. They won't see it that way. I know them. Like Rick. They'll put you in jail for a hundred years."

Ash was stunned. How did she guess it?

"I'll turn myself in, too," she said.

The depth of what she was saying rocked him. But he laughed. "For what? Anyway, if I wanted to turn myself in, I would have done it in Washington. You think I'd come up here to turn myself in?"

"I'll tell them I knew about it. They'll arrest me, too."

"You're being silly," he said. "I won't turn myself in. I mean it." He put all his persuasiveness into his voice. He gazed into her eyes. He was going to make David pay somehow. He lied softly, "I promise."

Then Ash put the phone to his ear and went cold.

He said, "The line is dead."

It was probably the storm, he told himself. Just a line down. But the rage was building. Just having to think about it all the time. "Get on the floor," he said. He crawled to the front door and drew the bolt that locked it. He pulled the hinged shutters down and locked them, too. They were frail, though. And the back door had only one lock. Someone could break in through the shutters. Jennifer was saying, "Oh, my god." He said, "Get the shotguns down."

"The shotguns . . ."

"It's *dead,*" he said. "Where are the shells?"

He kept the heavier shotgun for himself and loaded the lighter Remington five-shot automatic for Jennifer. They held pellets, which meant she'd have a big radius when she fired.

"Do you know how to use this?" he said.

"No." She was shaking.

"It's easy. Hold it like this, against your shoulder. Tighter. If someone tries to come in, fire. *Don't hesitate.* You get five shots. You don't have to reload or cock it. Aim for the middle of the chest. Remember, hold it tight. What did I say?"

"Hold it tight," she said, her slim hips thrust forward to compensate for the weight of the shotgun. She looked pregnant.

"Nobody's outside probably," Ash told her. "But we have to be ready." He felt them out there. He said, "There are things I can do to make the house safer." He slowed himself, spoke more calmly. "It takes five minutes. I'm going to cut some of your wires. Then I'll go to the car. When I reach it, I drive to the door and get you. And we leave and go have dinner and you kill me when we find out the whole thing was a bad phone line. Tomorrow an electrician can fix the wires."

"I'll go with you to the car."

"It's better if you don't."

"This is my fucking house," she cried suddenly. "You're turning me upside down and you're telling me there's people outside with guns and you're ready to put yourself in jail for me. I'm in love with you. I'm not staying here and letting them hurt you."

Ash said, "They've got a better chance of hurting me if we both go outside. Believe me, if they're out there, they're waiting. At least I have a little training in this."

He had not seen her so fierce before. Her eyes had reduced themselves to hard black points, and the blood, coursing to her face, turned it blotchy with fury. "My grandfather gave me this house," she hissed. "You know what he would do to someone trying to get in? Shoot them! That's what you do to burglars around here! I'll go with you!"

"If I go out and I get hurt, I might make it back here. We can fight them from here if the house is ready. If we both go, we're stuck."

What he didn't say was, if they kill me and you stay here, maybe they'll turn around and leave you alone. But he had no intention of letting them kill him. He was the raving angel of retribution. He was drawn by violent gravity out into the storm.

"Do you have a breaker box?" he said through the pounding blood in his head.

"What?"

"A breaker box that controls electricity for the house. Or are there fuses?"

It was a breaker box. The lights were flickering again. It was near the alarm panel. Ash, working fast, found each breaker labeled with a hand-printed paper. LIVING ROOM. UPSTAIRS BEDROOM. BATHROOM. HALLWAY. "Good, good. Candles, Jennifer? You have candles?"

"In the drawer next to the knives."

Ash took them and lit them. He shut off the breakers. The house went from bright to a vague yellow glow, an intimate aura more suited for a romantic dinner party. If David or Volsky was out there, they would be circling the clearing, looking through the storm at the house, taking time to do it right with the phone line out. Eyeing the windows, Mustang, appraising the strength of the shutters, which wasn't much. Saying you take the front door, I'll back you up.

He worked faster. He used the scissors to cut the wire that went to the television. Quickly he shaved the rubber insulation off both strands of the exposed wire, so the copper conductor was visible. He pulled the two strands of wire apart. He ran one strand under the door, so he knew it went into the ankle-deep puddle just outside. He looped the copper wiring of the other strand around the metal doorknob.

She asked if she could help and he said, "Watch the door."

"You know where I've always wanted to go?" she said, talking fast but clearly. Her way of making herself calm. "The Pacific Northwest. Washington or Vancouver. I heard there are little towns there, in the rain forest. It's peaceful. Lots of hippies move up there, change their names. Sunshine and Sky and Moonpuppy. There's a good name for you. Moonpuppy. Nobody asks where you come from."

Ash said, flat, "Us."

"Just a vacation," she said. "I have comp time coming. Or are you a welsher? You sleep with a girl and turn yourself in to the FBI? That old trick."

Ash said, "Remember to keep it against your shoulder, tight." She looked natural, sitting on the arm of the couch with the shotgun cradled sideways over her jeans. Like they were just talking about anything. Like none of the bad part were happening. She said, "You don't have to turn yourself in immediately, do you? You owe me a weekend in a bed and breakfast. After scaring me to death."

"Keep the gun on the door."

Jennifer said, "You're giving me an idea for a very interesting show. Fun things to do after sex."

He kissed her on the mouth. Felt her trembling. Fear jumbled her features, drooped one eye and slackened her mouth. Tightened the cords on her slender neck. He said, "If they're here, they'll try to get in a few ways at the same time. If I'm on the front door, you stay by the back. And we both have the windows. If you have to shoot somebody, be ready for another one right behind."

"If you have to shoot somebody," she whispered. "They're really out there, aren't they?"

He actually hoped David was out there. It was beyond logic

or protection, it was the pure desire to fight.

Thunder rumbled and made the house vibrate. Ash said, stepping back, surveying the wires snaking across the room. "I don't know, but they might be. We've made a trap here. This is what they taught us in Smith Falls." Despite her fear she seemed interested. He said, "Remember I shut the power that goes to the living room? If someone outside touches the door-knob and you turn the breaker back on, the current will hit his hand through the knob, his feet through the puddle. If he's in the puddle, it will blow the breaker and electrocute him."

"That's what you learned in high school? That's sick," she said.

"In shop," Ash said. He smiled. He felt a little better with the wires up and the shotguns loaded. He looked at the front door and thought, one last precaution.

He found the alarm sensor unit Jennifer had switched off when they arrived here. It was a simple plastic box nestled in a corner, linked to the main breaker box and coded alarm panel by wiring behind the wall. A standard home alarm that shot infrared beams around the room. If a person broke a beam, it triggered a bullhorn and sent a signal to the police. The bullhorn would go off in the cottage, Jennifer told him. The police would receive a message over the phone, "which is dead."

Outside, Ash estimated, the unit would probably detect movement for twenty feet maximum, the length of a big room.

"It will make an infrared arc from the front door," he told her. "And warn you if someone approaches the front of the house."

Ash unhooked the small plastic wall unit and tugged at the wires behind until they pulled free. There was extra wire, which gave Ash slack to carry the unit to the front door.

This was the most dangerous part, but it would give her added protection. I've got to open the door sooner or later, he thought. Ash swung the door open, swung the shotgun into the storm. He hoped if they were out there, they weren't prepared for it. It only took an instant. A flash of lightning illuminated sheets of rain pounding the clearing, and the dark, sopping woods beyond the parked car twenty feet away. He could dash for the Mustang now, but if they shot him, he wanted her to have some kind of warning if they came at her. Ash propped the unit against the doorjamb, away from the puddle, ran the wire under the door, slammed the door, and relocked it.

He switched on the breaker that said ALARM.

"Fort Knowles," Jennifer said, watching, sounding lighter since nothing had happened when he opened the door. "Actually, this is exciting in a perverted kind of way. Much better than the motorcycle gang."

"So you were in a motorcycle gang."

"I was never fully initiated," she said. "So I don't know if that counts. Hey! What are you doing with my grandmother's lamp!"

"Where's the bullhorn the alarm triggers?"

"In the laundry closet. In the kitchen."

Ash cut the wiring for the antique cut-glass lamp on the table beside the couch. He separated the two strands of the wire and shaved off the insulation on each, exposing the copper conductors. He carried the lamp to the laundry closet. He cut the wire connecting the alarm system to its bullhorn. He reattached the alarm system to the lamp.

"Now we have a warning system they can't hear outside," he said. "If a person comes toward the front door, the light will go on. At least you'll know where one of them is."

"You're extremely destructive, you know that?" Jennifer said.

"I thought it was inventive," Ash said.

The candles flickered. The acrid sex smell still lingered. The rain let up slightly but there was fresh thunder and the house shook.

"Okay," he said. "The Pacific Northwest. But afterwards you don't know me. We didn't go there. Better yet, if they ask you, tell them I told you who I was at the end. No! *You* call them and tell them who I am. Get some credit for turning me in."

"Do you actually believe people do half the things you think of? Can we go to the car now?"

The light on Jennifer's grandmother's lamp came on.

"Oh, shit," Jennifer said.

Ash exhaled and eyed the door. Come on, you bastards, he thought. The panels over the windows rattled from wind, but stayed locked. "It could be a raccoon. A deer would do it," he said, not believing it. "Do deer come near the house?"

"Yes."

"It could be a deer, but I'll hold off on the car for a few minutes."

"I never shot a gun," Jennifer said.

Ash whispered, "Go to the breaker box. You see the breaker labeled 'living room'? If I say to put it on, do it fast."

"I'm scared," Jennifer whispered.

"Me, too," Ash lied. He didn't feel afraid. He felt ready.

If it wasn't them, he would go look for them.

Ash unscrewed the warning bulb. It went off and he screwed it in again to set the alarm. This time it stayed off. Which meant whatever had passed through the beam had turned around or arrived at the door.

Ash thought, try it, you bastards. Come on. Jennifer said, "I didn't hear a car outside. It was a deer. I'm sure of it."

"Give it a few minutes."

"Yes, sir, Vladimir Moonpuppy!"

Ash aimed at the front door, Jennifer at the windows. He envisioned David and Price and the half-blind one, Volsky from the embassy, in the rain. Converging on the house. Come on, you bastards, he thought. Let's do it. Now.

"Hello?" a voice called from outside as knocking started. "Hello?" It was a man's voice, not David's or Price's. Not accented. An American voice. Ash had never heard it before. He had to restrain himself from pulling the trigger, just blowing a hole through the door.

"It's pouring out here!" the voice cried. Jennifer stared at Ash, looked terrified. He aimed at the door, but couldn't fire.

"Hey! Somebody!" the voice cried. "There's a car here! There must be someone in there! It's cold!"

Jennifer looked at him, not knowing what to do, shaking her head to say, I don't know that voice. The wind picked up. The rain battered the windows. The knocking grew louder on the door.

FOURTEEN

"**M**ORE CHAMPAGNE?**"** Corinna giggled, backing from the swinging double doors of the Pell kitchen, wobbling and almost dropping the silver tray. Ash couldn't take his eyes off her. She'd dressed in her graduation presents: cotton, frilly, low-necked blouse from Dietz; red leather mini from DuChamp; calf-high, fringed, white boots of soft leather, Yuri's contribution.

Their last night in "Smith Falls, Massachusetts." The dining room had been cleared of furniture to make a dance floor. Strung with red, white, and blue bunting. Pasted with color photos of the students being honored tonight. Their yearbook. The "parents" had already shipped home. Tomorrow the graduates would leave for the United States.

"Drink more! What's wrong with you?" Lieutenant Martini cried, happy-drunk himself, circulating with a fluted plastic glass in hand. He'd be heading for his new post tomorrow, too. They'd never see him again. "No more tests! No more late nights studying! A good soldier knows more than fighting! He knows how to celebrate! Drink!"

Ash drained his glass. The champagne was lukewarm and sweet for his taste. But he liked the floating feeling. By the fourth serving the back of his teeth throbbed and any sensation in his skull seemed concentrated above his left eye.

"We made it, you bastard," said Howie Granger, the statistics whiz, pumping Ash's hand and gripping his wrist, American style, the way DuChamp had taught them. "I never thought we'd get this far!"

They all wore graduation "presents" for their new posts. Howie in a brown box jacket and Weejuns. Ash in a Barney's suit of soft gray twill, Italian style with vents down the sides, not the back, like Kislak's conservative British tweed. Yuri, puffing his pipe, chatted with Glorie Pell. Ira Stowe, the electronics expert, offered a tray of pesto pastries to Ash.

"I hope they send me to California," Ira said, his normally bass voice weirdly high from drink. "Remember those pictures Dietz showed us, girls on the beach? I want to try surfing."

Ash chewed the doughy pastry roll at the window and looked out at a line of dejected teenagers piling into a canvas-topped Soviet Army truck at the foot of the suburban street. They were the washouts, the kids who would not graduate, already stripped of American clothing, and they inched toward the truck and piled American transistor radios, rock-and-roll cassettes, *Sports Illustrated* or *Glamour* magazines on a table while a bored-looking KGB sergeant checked off names.

The rejects looked like war orphans. They lugged bulging suitcases or duffel bags. They shared a glazed, terrified look that marked them as victims, even though they'd been assured they were not being punished, just being moved to a new job. Every few moments one glanced wistfully beyond the row of KGB troops flanking the line at the house where the celebration was taking place.

"DuChamp didn't have to load them where they could watch the party," Ash told Price angrily as the smaller boy joined him, sipping a quarter-filled champagne glass he held with three fingers. Price wore a crimson bow tie and double-breasted blue jacket with silver buttons with anchors on them, pressed charcoal slacks, and leather loafers with tassels on top.

Price rolled his eyes theatrically. "Just be glad it's not you. Why do you always have to ask about everything?" he said.

But looking out, Ash met the gaze of his old friend Billy Curtis. Gripping his suitcase with two hands, the lean red-haired boy looked directly into Ash's eyes. Ash had never seen him so sad. He'd been sure Billy would make it. Billy had the most amazing memory Ash had ever known. Say anything to him once, he'd never forget it. As a game the kids would yell numbers at him, rapid-fire. Whole series of integers. Fifteen in a row. He would repeat them in order, never missing one.

"Billy, you talk in your sleep," DuChamp had told him when he cut him from graduation.

Ash waved. Billy waved back, then shoved up his hand to order Ash, stay away. You'll get in trouble. Ash told Price, "Dietz always tells us how great it is outside. Then what's so bad about them going there?"

Price shuddered. "Without David?"

Then David pulled their attention back. "A toast!" he cried in the center of the little circle of winners, basking in their adoration, glass in hand. The room was hot from packed bodies. "To us! Everyone!"

Corinna's face swam up at Ash. She was taller tonight from the boots, and her blue eyes glowed with extra intensity. "Champagne, gentlemen?" She giggled. "We have seven hundred bottles in the kitchen. We have to drink them all tonight."

"I'll take the whole tray," Ash said. Screw DuChamp. He'd bring it to the kids outside. He reached for the drinks and the dining room windows blew in behind him. Corinna screamed and dropped the tray. The glasses shattered. To Ash, the smoking gas grenade skidding across the floor looked like a giant beetle, but then gray clouds of hissing smoke obscured it. Everyone started to scream.

Ash heard sirens outside.

Kislak was yelling, "The stairs! Upstairs!" Ash shouted, "No. The basement! Gas rises!"

From the street, a voice on a bullhorn bellowed, "FBI!"

The kids ran in all directions, choking. The smoke blinded Ash. Holding his breath, he pictured the door and groped toward it. He saw the outline of the swinging door. But then he glimpsed Corinna through the smoke. She was down in the corner. Curled up, coughing, shattered glass around her. It must have sliced her hand because a red line coursed down her knuckles. He was going to have to breathe to reach her. He spit on his handkerchief and pressed it to his mouth, but when he inhaled, his throat caught fire and the pain coursed into his lungs. Ash gagged.

Ash fought his way to where she sat, stunned and doubled over. He pulled her up by her wrists. The gas burned into him, made him nauseous. He could barely see through tears of pain.

"FBI!" the bullhorn roared.

"Down . . . downstairs," he hacked, pulling her toward the kitchen, toward where he remembered the basement steps.

"Always memorize escape routes when you enter a new place," Martini had said.

Ash thought, so we're free of tests. So we should drink more. So we should relax, you bastard. He wanted to drag her out the front door, to the truck, to fight his way to that line of dejected children. The two of them, bouncing toward punishment but together at least.

Ash thought, I'll find weapons in the basement. A pipe. A magazine. The furnace I can start a fire in, blow up the house. Hell, it's my last night here. Blow up the gas main. Get away in Martini's stupid game.

"Corinna! Move. We're almost—"

Ash found the door, pushed, but it flew at him, driving them back into the room. Gargoyle faces, soldiers in gas masks, rushed at them. Corinna tried to scream. Ash tried to hit them but had no strength, he couldn't breathe. They were lifting him, picking him off the floor, carrying him fighting out of the dining room.

They put him down on the lawn outside. Ash went down on his knees. He heaved, puking. He smelled his own bile. He tried to breathe but his lungs burned like he would never draw air naturally again. Martini, furious, swam down at him.

"Why didn't you find the exit?" the defense instructor shouted. "You can never relax when you're over there!"

Soldiers carried other kids from the house. Ash saw Kislak on the lawn, throwing up.

Corinna crawled toward Kislak.

Their new clothes would have to be dry-cleaned.

Martini hollered, "You're worthless!"

Ash forced himself up. Corinna was sick a few feet away. Kislak, suit torn and ruined, gripped her shoulders from behind, made ragged breathing sounds when he tried to comfort her. Kislak couldn't talk.

Ash stumbled toward Martini, glimpsed the other kids scattered on lawns, in driveways, on the black tarmac, puking. The truck with the rejects was driving off. The soldiers lifted off their masks. They watched with shiny, excited expressions.

Martini raged, "You had time to get out of that house! You should have been moving when the window broke! You should have headed for the basement, not upstairs! We left gas masks in the basement! It's your fault you ended up this way!"

Ash drew in breath, fighting the fire in his body. Martini cried, "You shouldn't drink so much your judgment is impaired! *You* decide how much you can drink! Not me! Not David!"

"Ash!" the lieutenant barked, bending down, hands on hips like a drill instructor, to the puking sounds around him. "Why did you go back for her? What good did that do you? In real life you would have been dead!"

Ash sucked in a full breath. Martini's voice was the loudest thing he had ever heard. "How many times do I have to tell you? *First* protect yourself and *then* save others. Secure position first! What do I always tell you?"

Ash straightened and winced and saw Martini blurred through tears. He used all his self-control to ignore the pain coursing back up his throat into his nostrils. He forced himself to his feet. Martini was glaring at him.

In one savage motion, Ash slammed his knee into Martini's balls.

"I'll remember," Ash wheezed while Martini writhed in the dirt, cupping himself. "Never trust anyone. Always be prepared."

Ash pressed back against the wall of Jennifer Knowles's cottage and aimed her father's shotgun toward the door. From outside, the stranger's voice called urgently, "My car blew a flat! My kid's sick! Can you let me use your phone!"

A ridiculous ruse. The most basic ploy imaginable. Except suppose it wasn't a ruse? How could Ash shoot blindly at a stranger through a door?

Ash had never shot a person. Never watched a person die from his own hand. Martini had talked about it, instructed them how to do it. Drawn diagrams showing positioning and logistics. Tested them on information on vulnerable points. Had them fire at dummies. Ash had blasted holes in sheets of paper hanging from wires. He'd gone to shooting ranges in Washington to keep up his skill. He'd shot clay pigeons. He'd been a superb information gatherer. But he'd never pulled a trigger in anger.

He kept the barrel aimed at the door. Whoever was speaking wasn't directly behind it, but to the side, with the thicker wall separating them.

"She has the flu!" the voice said with a slight New York accent. "I'm trying to reach the Walkers." Ash remembered the mailbox that said WALKER down the road. The voice said, "If I call them, they'll pick us up!"

"Go away!" Ash said. He slid a foot from his position, just in case.

He heard a soft curse outside, the kind anyone might give standing in a storm.

Then he heard Jennifer say, behind him and across the room, "Ash?"

What she meant was, it sounds real. Ash waved for her to keep quiet. And what about the warning light that had gone off a minute ago, by the front door. Nobody had blown any flat.

"Whaddaya want, my driver's license?" the voice cried. "What is this, New York? Open up! My kid's sick! I'll pay for the call!"

"Ash, you're being paranoid," Jennifer said.

Ash called, "Go somewhere else!"

"Oh, really," Jennifer said. "The kid is sick."

Ash yelled, "I'll call the police!" If David's people were outside, they'd know the line was out anyway. If they weren't they'd leave. But Jennifer was coming now. She'd had enough of this game and she wasn't going to let a sick kid sit in a broken car. A sick kid was much more real to her than some kind of spy story. She was going to unlock the door. The voice outside said, "So phone 'em. Tell 'em I broke down! Come on! Two minutes!"

She was ten feet from the door and closing. Ash yelled, watching her come, "What's Mr. Walker's first name?"

No answer.

She stopped.

"His first name," Ash said. "I'll open the door if you say it!" A lie but Jennifer backed up a step. He shouted in Russian, "What are both their first names?"

The force of the blast drove the doorknob through the air with a piece of door still attached to it. So much for Martini's trap. Splinters of wood burst inward, shredding the sitting chair and knocking one of the Baryshnikov photos off the wall. Ash was moving, yelling, "Get down!" laying down rounds through the door.

The couch, hit, moved two inches to the left.

A lamp on the end table shattered.

No time to see where Jennifer was, and the second and third blasts from outside blew chunks of wood into the room. Jennifer was screaming. Ash hollered, "Watch the back!" Less than two seconds had passed. What was left of the doorframe swung in at them violently and someone was behind it, bulling his way in, and Ash fired. He glimpsed a big round face and the face disappeared, and the body hurled backward into another person. Ash kept firing. He laid down shots outside right and left. He fought the recoil and rain blew in through the shattered door. He kept his panic down and his worry for Jennifer and concentrated on what he was doing. There was smoke everywhere. He stepped around spent shell casings. Two attackers lay in the mud pool outside, rain battering their inert bodies.

In the ringing silence he thought, the back door. And a shotgun went off behind him, in the house.

Ash threw himself back into the house, landed hard, rolled

left, and came up ready to fire at the kitchen. What he saw stopped him.

The back door was open, swinging on its hinges, rain pelting in. The light fixture above the door was shattered. As he looked, an icicle of glass tumbled down and clattered on the floor. He heard pounding footsteps running away outside.

Ash thought she had screamed, "Daddy!"

Jennifer stood near the sink, amid curling blue smoke, her cry having subsided to a series of guttural sounds corresponding to the jaggedness of her breathing. She'd dropped the shotgun, or at least she wasn't holding it. She stared at the ceiling, which was riddled with pellet holes. Her face, turning to him, was white and her eyes were huge, and he thought she might start screaming again.

"He was coming in," she said.

She'd scared them off, he thought, triumphant. Heard them come and fired and missed, but they ran away. They didn't think anyone would be armed, and they found two people with shotguns. He started toward her. "Are you all right?" he said, but *get out of here now now now now* exploded inside him.

Jennifer said, "I didn't really think they were coming."

"It's me they want! Get to the car after I go!"

He turned and she called him to stop, but this was best for her; to stay would turn the house into a death trap. He had no idea how many attackers were outside. "Burn the building down if there's no other option," Martini's voice said in his mind. Ash ran out the front door, over the two bodies. He screamed as he ran into the rain. It wasn't fear. It was a challenge. A battle cry so they would know he was outside. Come and get me. Try to get me. Come on, I want you, he willed.

In the dark something moved to his left, and charging, Ash blasted it, but in flashing lightning he saw only a waving bush.

Then suddenly the air filled with whining noises and the ground ahead burst into a line of fragments coming his way. He swerved. Something stung his ear. Moving low he ran for the forest. He could not see more than six feet in the storm. He realized there was no gunfire sound coming with the bullets.

Where are you? Then Ash saw flashes from the side of the house, where they'd been getting ready to try the window.

In the dark the trees came up so fast he almost ran into one, but he swerved and heard the bullets carving the bark on the other side of the trunk. Hit the ground. Crawled back circling at whoever fired at him. *One shot left*. Fuck you, he thought, letting the rage fuel him, lift his senses, drive him toward them. All of you. I'll kill you. I'm the angel of death and I'll kill you, David, Price. I don't care if there are a thousand of you. I'll get all of you.

Lightning flashed but only illuminated rain. Thunder boomed, and there were the trees in front of him. Branches to his right seemed to be spitting wood chips at him. They knew he was coming. He ducked, rolled left in brush, the sopping ground sucking at his back and legs. Ash felt a kind of wild joy rising in him, cresting, and he was thinking, with accumulated fury, come to me, come to me. Crawling, he thought, come to me. He worked his way around the side of the house. The corner of the building blocked whoever had been firing at him. *Now*, he thought.

Ash stepped onto the lawn.

He yelled, "Jen, I'll get help!"

Instead of going anywhere he dropped down to one knee.

He heard pounding footsteps coming around the house, in his direction. He raised the shotgun.

A figure loomed, coming fast.

Ash fired.

The man blew back, spread-eagled, silhouetted for a moment, a small object falling from his fist. Ash, even without checking, knew he'd hit the man in the chest. He crawled to the man. He raised the butt of the shotgun. But the man on his back was dead.

Ash looked down into the face of one of the three men who had followed him when he left the embassy. The one who had followed the tramp out of the park.

Volsky, Ash thought. David and Volsky. Together.

I'll go back. I'll get him, too.

There was no sound except rain falling.

Three of them, Ash thought. Three men followed me from the embassy. I shot three of them. That's all of them. *Is it* all of them? I can't be sure it's all of them.

Ash groped on the lawn, found the man's automatic. From the weight it felt like a 9mm. He checked the man's pockets, found a fresh clip, shoved it in his pants. To switch clips would be too much noise. Never assume, Martini had said, but fuck Martini. If the attacker was a pro, he wouldn't run around the house unless he had at least some bullets in his clip. Ash crouched, pivoted slowly, strained to listen.

No footsteps. No voices. No other car. Just rain and creaking forest and a faint sound of water drumming on the roof of Jennifer's Mustang. The wind was picking up, and he was more adjusted to the dark so he saw the treetops blowing. There was no sound from inside the house. He could see a bit of candlelight flickering in a jagged, undulating shadow outside the front door.

Ash switched to a fresh clip.

Maybe I did get all of them, he thought.

The gun was a 9mm Ruger, which he had not fired even at a shooting range. Time to check on Jennifer. Ash moved at a fast crouch toward the flickering light at the front door. Rain smeared his hair over his forehead. *Don't relax.*

He took in the first man he had shot still sprawled in the storm, leg in Ash's direction, cuff up showing the black lines of the ankle holster around the exposed pale and rain-washed calf. Steel automatic on the grass inches from the curled fingers.

Ash blinked rain out of his eyes. The second man was gone.

Ash cursed and hit the ground, rolled right, into the flowerbed beside the house. He can't be alive. I know I hit him. He has to be superhuman to still be alive. Ash lay in the mud behind the hedgerow, listening, heard only his own breathing and the rain, and from somewhere in the forest, the heavy, ponderous creak of a branch moving in the storm.

Clinging to the side of the cottage, Ash looked out and broke what little he could see into quarters, infantry style, and swept the area. There was the house and the bushes and the dim form of the car twenty feet off. The rain fell so hard he barely made out the dark line of forest thirty feet away.

Ash wriggled toward the door.

The scream seemed to come from right above him. He tried to bring the Ruger up too late. A big form lunged down at him, hit him like a linebacker, and Ash was big but this man was much bigger. Something heavy struck Ash's chest, he heard a crack inside. An enormous pain exploded in him. The man was yelling in Russian, "Boxer!" He was very strong. His thighs seemed clamped against Ash's biceps. Ash tried to get the gun up. He saw the finger strike starting for his eyes and used a forearm to parry it. The gun went off and a window shattered above them.

Now the man swung his big head down, trying to butt Ash's face. Ash got his free hand into the neck but felt his chest bubbling. His eyes bulged with strain. Ash struck the neck a cross blow and the man showed the slightest weakening where his thighs clamped Ash. Ash heaved violently, freed the gun hand, whipped his head right to avoid a nose strike, and brought up the Ruger and pulled the trigger. Two muffled reports in the rain. All strength seemed to go out of the man.

The man lay across Ash. He hiccuped once. He let out a long fart.

Ash felt the sticky itch of blood spreading along his chest. It was a different kind of liquid sensation from the rain. He pulled himself free and saw the face of his attacker and was awed by the man's strength. Half the man's face seemed to have been blown away by the earlier shotgun blast. When the attackers had first stormed the door, Ash must have knocked him unconscious with the shot. The other attacker must have absorbed the gunfire, dying and shielding this man with his body.

The garden smelled of roses but the shit smell from the dead man was strong. The rain whipped up a rotting odor from the mud and mulch. Mud and leaves clung to Ash's face. When he inhaled, he felt a sharp pain inside.

Silence.

Maybe I got all of them.

Ash fought down hope, slipped from the bushes, and made for the front door. He was amazed because so little time had passed that the flickering candles weren't even half-burned down. Ash moved out of the doorway, backed against the wall. The house sounded utterly silent. His face stung from the cold rain.

"Jennifer?"

Moving carefully, he slid through the room. Around the couch and along the mantel wall. The cottage was how he had left it; front door shattered, back door open, light fixture smashed over the kitchen, rain slanting in to hit the fringe of polished floor by the doorway. Shattered plasterwork inside the door, the glass shards still embedded in the windowsill over the sink, the pellet holes on the couch and coffee table.

"Jennifer?"

Maybe she'd run outside, too.

"It's Ash," he called softly. He forced himself to look on the floor behind the counter. He yanked the kitchen closet open. Saw mops inside.

His chest was really starting to hurt now.

Ash called, "I think they're gone. If you're here," he said, yanking open the pantry closet, seeing shelves of string beans, baked beans, brown sugar, hot sauce, packaged soup, oatmeal, spaghetti, Ragu—"come out."

At least there was a flashlight that worked in the closet. He took it but kept it off. He didn't want to pinpoint himself upstairs.

Ash looked up the stairs. He heard a creak up there. It might have been the storm.

Be upstairs, he willed her. In a closet. Be so freaked out you can't talk.

Be unhurt.

Blood seeped into Ash's mouth, filled it with a sick, sweet taste, and he felt blood trickling down one side of his chin. He kept the flashlight off.

In Smith Falls, old Smith Falls, the kids practiced assaulting Howie Granger's house. Attack up the *side* of stairs, Martini always told them. You make less noise. The center creaks, alerts the enemy.

Ash went up the side of the stairs. They creaked.

He went up slowly, against the wall. At the top he came up fast, gun out.

Nothing. No candles were lit up here, so the hall was darker, but he could still see. Ash breathed hard. In front of him were three open doorways on the balcony. It was darker inside the rooms. If he used the flashlight, it would pinpoint him in the hall, but if he turned the breakers back on, anyone outside would know he'd gone back into the house.

"It's Ash. Jennifer?"

A crash came from downstairs. Ash whirled but the sound hadn't been in the house. It had been a heavy noise like a tree falling. A lot of blood was on his shirt.

Ash heard a groan from the middle bedroom.

"Jen, are you all right?"

A groan.

Ash crept against the wall. Waves of pain washed through his chest. He had to pass the first darkened doorway. He swung the flashlight into the room and turned it on. He saw just a single bed and open closet and wooden statuette of Don Quixote on the sill, in front of drawn blinds.

Moving again, he passed a small oil painting he couldn't make out. There was a little cherrywood night table with a crystal vase filled with half-drooped daisies. From the ground floor, huge shadows undulated up the walls.

Ash reached the next room. He kept the flashlight off. He whispered, "Jennifer, I got the phone working. The cops are coming. I got them all."

Kislak's voice answered from inside the bedroom, "You don't even know where we cut the line."

Ash went dizzy. Gripped the barrel. Ash tasted blood in his mouth.

"I'll kill you," he said.

There was the softest laugh from inside the room.

Kislak's voice said, "He wants me to send you out. Should I

send you out?" Jennifer moaned, a sound of pain, not terror. Kislak called, "I don't even know why you want her. She's the one who got you in trouble. If she hadn't left that message on your answering machine, we never would have found you."

"Send her out, then I'll come in," Ash said. He'd come in all right. He'd shoot the bastard.

"I already have you," Kislak said. "I mean, I'm assuming if you got up here, you got the other two. You got them, did you?"

"Yeh, I got the other two," Ash said.

"Only it wasn't two, was it?" David said wryly. "No, you got them. You got lucky again." David made a sucking sound. "I'm not stopping you from leaving. The car's out there. We took wires, but I didn't hear you try to start it. Are you still there?" he mocked.

Ash said, "I wasn't kidding about the cops." He doubled, coughing.

David sighed. "I warned them. I told them never to take anything for granted with you. But no, they were the professionals. They figured you wouldn't be ready, they could just come in. How did you know we were here, Ash? One of your little guesses?"

Ash wondered if there was a ladder he could use to come in from the outside. Or an attic he could come down from. Jennifer groaned. David said, "You have to keep talking or I'll think you went away. She's not as pretty as Corinna. Remember those little pain spots Martini showed us?"

Ash heard a shuffling noise from inside the room. A creaking, like people were standing up, from a bed. Jennifer's voice said, "Ash, he wouldn't let me answer," and then there was a hard, thudding sound and she moaned and Kislak said over her grunt of pain, "No, no, darling. I told you not to talk. Ash," he said impatiently, "I think you should come in now. First slide in the gun. Are you still there, Ash?"

"I'm here."

"I never used one of these before. I always sent someone else. There's a real feeling of power. You can get carried away." Kislak sighed. "At least you did me one favor. I ran away when the shooting started, but now Akromeyev won't know that."

"Send her out," Ash said. "I know where you cut the line. I fixed it. The police are coming."

Kislak laughed.

"You cut the line like Martini taught us," Ash guessed. "You climbed up the pole and disconnected it." After the hit they would have reconnected it.

"I'll shoot her," David said. "Everybody else has fun around here but me."

Ash couldn't think of another way to get into the room. He kept his voice calm. "Jen, he won't do that. If he does that, I'll still be here."

"You're right," David said. "I won't kill her first. I'll shoot her little ear, right *here.*" She moaned because he must have shoved the gun against it. "Her elbow. I'll drag it out. One . . . two . . ."

Ash slid his Ruger on the floor in the doorway.

"The other gun, too," David said, sounding bored.

"I don't have another one."

"I don't believe you."

Ash charged the room.

He saw them outlined in the darkness, man behind woman, and a light exploded as something slammed into his shoulder hard, spinning him, but he drove forward sideways. The figures struggled and David fired but it was wild. Ash reached them. Another shot. Jennifer clawed at David. The gunhand was swinging again. Ash hit David with his shoulder, the pain ravaging him. He was almost out of strength but pulled David toward him, yelled, "Run . . ." But he was weak and David's fist came toward him. Plowed into his belly.

Ash let go.

Something smashed the top of his head. Ash was falling.

From miles away, he heard David's voice. "Stand still, Jennifer."

Ash's vision cleared. David, very high, a hundred feet up, stood looking down at Ash, pointing the gun.

Ash thought, don't give up.

"Oh, Ash, I'm sorry," Jennifer was saying. Blood was pouring from Ash's shoulder, where he'd been hit, and he heard ringing in his ears. The whole floor vibrated, or was it just his body? The end of the room was a tunnel, dark on the edges, and getting smaller and more concentrated the farther away he looked, where Jennifer was impossibly far away. Like in a telescope held the wrong way.

Jennifer said, "I just stood there when the shooting started. He just came in. Oh, Ash."

"You smell like roses," Ash said.

Jennifer spun to David. "The police! They'll find the bodies!"

David was dragging it out now, savoring it. That gives me a chance, Ash thought. "You really think we don't plan for this?" David told her. "I call a number. Medical! Removals! I never needed to use it before, but I've had it for years.

"Good-bye, Ash."

The explosion rocked the room. Ash felt the bullet smash him in the chest, driving him back toward the floor like it was pinning him. Jennifer launched herself at David. Moving in slow motion. He swung toward her.

Ash thought "now" and raised his gun to shoot, but there wasn't a gun, his hand was miles away, and Jennifer was screaming and David knocked her sideways. Ash was an infant, a baby with no muscles. The whole room was shaking. Jennifer screamed, "No!" and the muzzle swung at Ash to finish him and a voice shouted in gibberish, in Russian, "Stop!"

Ash, confused, heard sporadic words. ". . . down and . . . changed orders you . . . give me the . . . bed . . ."

The lights went on.

Jennifer's face, huge, looked down at him.

Miles away, tiny and getting smaller, a man with an eyepatch. A man who looked familiar. A man holding a gun. The pain eased in Ash, he was floating.

Ash looked up into a single blue eye staring at him.

A woman's voice said, "Oh, god, it's my fault. I didn't listen to him!"

"I demand to know what exactly is going on here!" Kislak's voice said. A warm, lovely feeling enveloped Ash. It started by his feet and seeped upward, into his thighs. "I have orders," Kislak said.

"He's still breathing," someone said.

"Call a doctor!"

Ash surrendered to the feeling. Ash felt it numb his chest, neck, head.

A light touch at Ash's wrist. Ash knew he was dying. His lifeblood pumped from his body. He wanted to tell Jennifer something but couldn't think what it was. A wave of pain smashed through the numbness but disappeared. Through a film Ash was barely aware that the man with the eyepatch looked up at Kislak. His voice was so muffled Ash could barely hear. "You are David Kislak?"

"David Kislak." It was the old annoyed voice. The imperial voice. The I-am-the-boss-and-you-listen-to-me voice. "This is a sanction by Sergei Akromeyev. Who are you? You will be in trouble for stopping this."

The man in the patch moved his mouth but no sound came out. Then Ash heard, "You're the one who ran the group? You are the one who took money for himself."

"I went over this with Colonel Akromeyev," Kislak snapped. "Show me orders. I don't think you have orders to stop me."

"Sergei Akromeyev is a traitor to our country," Volsky said, still kneeling by Ash. "And so are you."

Kislak brought the gun up fast, but against Volsky he was nothing. The bullet caught Kislak in the neck, driving him backward, exploding bits of bone against the windows and white lace curtains and paneled wall. David fell onto the bed neatly, bounced, and was still.

"Stay with him," Volsky told Jennifer, who needed no prompting. He ran to the top of the stairs. Men stood in the living room below. "Quick!" he called. The men ran up with medical equipment. Volsky walked back into the room with the pounding on the steps behind him. Jennifer rocked Ash. Gently Volsky pulled her away; the movement was bad for Ash.

"My name is Gregor Volsky," he told her. "I'm sorry I got here late." Men were opening steel cases, pulling out machines with wires, hypodermics, medicine. Volsky told them, "The one on the floor." They knelt by Ash. One said, "Breathing. Glucose." Another handed him a prepared shot.

Volsky told Jennifer, "Let's let them work." She said, "I'm staying." Volsky said, "It's easier for them and better for him."

Outside the rain had slackened. Volsky led her downstairs. "You drink coffee? Or tea?" he said, gentling her. She shook her head. She was shaking now, the shock coming fast. She said, "Who are you?"

From upstairs they heard people talking urgently in Russian.

"They don't look like doctors but they are the best at what they do," Volsky said. He put a blanket on her, on the couch. "They've got blood for him, antibiotics, painkillers, the best of everything. We wait. And there's nothing to fear from me, Miss Knowles. You can even turn me in if you want. The phone will be working momentarily. I called these men on the way up, but I hoped you wouldn't need them."

Jennifer still looked scared of him. "He said the men trying to kill him were Russian, too."

Volsky sighed and poured water into the kettle. "They are very good doctors."

A man hung over the banister.

"Major," he called down in English. "Bad."

Volsky waved for him to try harder. "Now what kind of tea do you like, because I see there are several kinds here," Volsky said softly. "Sleepy-Time? Orange? Maybe Sleepy-Time would be nice."

She stared at the ceiling, listening to the men trying to save Ash.

"Who are all you people?" Jennifer whispered.

"Removals. Medical," Volsky explained.

FIFTEEN

ASH OPENED HIS EYES and Jennifer sat on the bed and the room smelled like roses. Sun streamed in through the panes. He saw the lush green canopy of oak trees outside. He didn't recognize the room. She said, "He's awake again." Ash said, "Jennifer." He thought his voice sounded throaty and tight.

Jennifer said to herself, "He's talking, Jennifer."

She started to cry.

Ash's neck hurt. His hand felt heavy and there was a sharp throbbing in his shoulder. He was in her bedroom, he saw. Above her head was another of her photos of Baryshnikov, this one with the dancer in a gray suit, in a restaurant. Baryshnikov sat behind a table, the linen strewn with empty plates and mineral-water bottles. Baryshnikov was gesturing passionately at someone not in the photo.

"I want to hug you but I'm afraid I'll hurt you," she said.

Ash grinned. "I'm a masochist," he said.

When she grabbed him, it hurt, but he wrapped his arms around her. He felt his shoulder scrape against something tight around him, a bandage. A man moved into his field of vision. Volsky. Ash tried to push her away.

"No, he helped us," she said.

Volsky said, "Mr. Ash, are you feeling all right?"

Ash struggled to get out of the bed.

"He saved you," she said. "They worked on you for days,

doctors. Brought in machines. They fixed up the house, too, like a little hospital. Major Volsky said if we called the real doctors, the police would arrest you."

Volsky said, "You are a very strong man, but you should rest here a few weeks. I've taken care of your motel bill, although you'll have to pick up the car yourself. The rules." He smiled. "And I've told Moscow you are dead, Mr. Ash. You and Mr. Kislak killed each other. As far as they are concerned, neither of you exist anymore. In fact, with the coup collapsed, our country seems to be dissolving anyway. Do you understand what I'm saying?"

Ash said, "The coup collapsed?"

"We beat them," Volsky said proudly.

Jennifer said, "Don't move so much."

Volsky drew closer. He held himself with the stiff posture of a lifelong military man. He said, "Mr. Akromeyev, my boss, is recalled to Moscow. He's the one who sent people after you. I am in charge as long as there is a Soviet Union, which I do not think will be long. I don't mind though. Whatever happens will be better than what was. I didn't want to defect anyway." He winked at Ash with his one good eye. "I don't like your fast food."

"David?" Ash said. He expected him to be here.

"Dead."

Ash was surprised to feel a twinge of sorrow. But it was for the past, not for what David had become. "And Corinna? The rest?"

Volsky sat on the edge of the bed, the sagging of the mattress making Ash wince. He said, "They are fine. We have the list of David's people. We contacted them. No need of your services anymore. We got along without you for the last few years." Volsky smiled. "We can muddle through. If you want, you can come home. We'll just say you're alive, you didn't die." He smiled at Jennifer. Because his normal expression was so severe, the impression a smile gave was of sincere warmth. "You can come with him. But you do what you want."

"Why did you help me?" Ash said.

He couldn't read Volsky's expression for a moment. Then he was surprised to see the major was near tears.

Volsky seemed to be looking far away, thinking of something else. "You deserved it," Volsky said.

"Soon you'll play the piano again," Jennifer said.

"Clown," Ash said.

Volsky stood up. "I think you want to be alone. Your old friend Posner gave me a message for you. He said, 'Tell him I never stopped thinking of him.' Good-bye, Ash."

Volsky turned and walked off. They heard his crisp, steady footsteps down the stairs. "You can go home," Jennifer said when they heard a car start up outside.

"Yeh. Home," Ash said.

She said, smiling happily, "What part of Russia do you come from anyway? I never knew half the names I hear now. Belorussia? Moldavia? I read an article in *National Geographic*. They're supposed to be beautiful. I read a lot about it while you were asleep."

"I'd rather be with you," he said.

"Jennifer," she said, "don't start crying."

"Maybe we could visit it sometime, though," he said.

"I forgot," she said. She held a folded piece of paper toward him. "I didn't tell Volsky about this. But when I paid for your room at the motel, the clerk gave me this. He said an old man left it."

Ash got a dry feeling in his mouth.

He unfolded the note.

Mr. DuChamp told me something you may want to know. Come to my house. 14 Suffolk.

The note was signed, in a shaky hand, *Carver*.

She helped him across the lawn to the car two days later. "Maybe now you'll stop badgering me," she said. The sky was blue and cloudless, the afternoon warm. Carver was listed in the phone directory but had never answered when they called. They'd left a message for him at the old-folks home. No response.

"Volsky ought to hire his men out as gardeners," Jennifer

said. "This place looks better than before the fight."

Ash pulled his leg into the front seat. Despite the painkillers that "Removals, Medical" had left for him, his chest burned and his shoulders ached. She drove slowly, so he wouldn't be rocked by bumps. In Smith Falls they found the address on Carver's note, up the little street where Ash had taken a walk when he'd first come here.

Ash's heart was hammering. She pulled up in front of a small Cape Cod cottage with a steep roof and a ten-year-old blue Plymouth parked, rear out, in the separate garage. The bumper sticker said DISNEY WORLD.

"I still don't think you should come in," Ash said. "Why didn't Carver answer our calls?"

"Because he's old. Because they don't hear the phone. Because he forgot. Because he never got the message. You heard what Volsky said. You can relax." Her look softened and she squeezed his arm. "That must be a hard habit to form after so long. You want to go back?"

"No."

Jennifer said, "The whole town knows we know each other. If he was going to trap you with FBI, they would have come to the house."

Ash limped down the small, curving walkway. Half a dozen rose bushes flanked the stoop to the house. A black Persian cat was in the window looking back with yellow eyes. Silvery wind chimes hung limp beside the door.

When Ash knocked, Carver opened it himself, in the yellow cardigan he remembered. "I was afraid you wouldn't come," Carver said in his flat, electric voice, pressing the larynx box to his throat. "I hoped you'd call. You had an accident?"

"Car crash," Ash said. "We did call."

Carver grimaced. "It looks painful." Then he rolled his eyes. "I'm out a lot," he said. He seemed smaller than Ash remembered without all the plants around him. Despite the noon hour he had not shaved. Ash remembered a slightly more fastidious man and detected, from the hint of strain in Carver's smile, that something burdened him.

Carver took Jennifer's hand and led them to the lumpy couch. "I never get a chance to be lecherous anymore," he said, smiling. "Sit down. Not over there, the spring is loose. Old-man furniture," he said as Ash lowered himself slowly into a stuffed armchair and Jennifer chose the chintz couch. The place smelled of mothballs. "I rented this place. It came with the furniture. Believe me, I have better taste than this."

"You sent me a note," Ash said. "What did DuChamp tell you?"

Carver waved a hand meaning, hold on a minute. He liked visitors. He said, "It's a pleasure to have a visitor who really talks, not like DuChamp. I just made a Bloody Mary. You know my secret." He winked at Jennifer. "Morning drinker. Want one?"

Jennifer said yes for both of them.

Carver said, "The secret is the Worcestershire sauce. Never skimp on the sauce. And I am a Bloody Mary expert."

Ash said, "Mr. Carver, you said in the note that DuChamp had told you something."

"Yes. But I lied," Carver remarked, turning his back on them and shuffling out of the room, humming, not any tune in particular, just a low, flat, broken note. Jennifer stood but Ash waved her down. In the stillness they heard Carver humming and clinking glasses in the kitchen.

"DuChamp doesn't remember anything," Carver said, returning with a tray holding three Dixie cups, a red plastic pitcher, and a jar of white horseradish. He set the tray on the maple coffee table in front of the couch, over coffee stains.

"Is it cold in here, or am I older than even I thought?" he said.

"It's a little chilly," Jennifer said.

Carver smiled, showing tobacco-stained teeth. He pressed his box to his larynx. "Bad liar. Pretty girl."

Carver's hand trembled with slight palsy as he poured. "DuChamp never knew enough to tell you anything anyway. The trick to pulling off a big operation is to do it in pieces. This piece for you. This little piece for the other person. Nobody knows the whole thing except for one or two people. Everybody just knows his part."

It was like the air had been sucked from the room. Carver smiled and held the first Bloody Mary toward Jennifer. "Tell me if it needs more horseradish," he said.

Ash leaned forward, his whole body hammering with his pulse.

"You tell each person just enough to keep them going," Carver said, starting on the next drink. "You say to DuChamp, 'These are diplomats' children. Take them for a few weeks. We'll take it from there.' You tell the captain of a ship, 'Never mind who these children are. If you ever talk about it, you will be killed.' You tell the instructors in Smith Falls . . . well"—Carver chuckled—"the other Smith Falls, 'They all died. And if you ever mention it, you will, too.' "

He handed Ash the second Dixie cup. He bent over and spooned more horseradish into the third cup. "I like it really hot," he said.

Ash sipped the Bloody Mary. He didn't taste it.

Carver brought his hand out of his cardigan pocket. He held three Chuckles candies in his palm.

"How about a candy?" he said.

The room went still. Ash watched his fingers take one of the candies off the yellowing, liver-spotted hand. The wrapping paper retained a little heat from Carver's sweater. Ash stared into the old man's face.

Jennifer gasped. Dust motes danced in a beam of sunlight slanting through a window behind Carver's head. "But . . . Chuckles . . . you said . . ." Jennifer said.

"I shaved the beard off years ago," Yuri said in his flat, science-fiction-like voice. "That pipe gave me cancer. They cut out my throat." He grimaced. "It hurt. My hair went white. I shrank a little." For a moment he looked impish. "Well. A lot. More Bloody Mary?"

Ash couldn't breathe. He couldn't ask what he wanted. He was choking inside. He heard Jennifer to his right, from the couch. "You're his father?"

Yuri frowned. "No," came the lifeless voice. To Ash it was like tumbling down a hole. "You were orphans," Yuri said to Ash. "I told David you were my son. It was what he needed. To have a reason why I liked you. David told you I was your father? Hmm! He wasn't supposed to!"

"You told him that? That's awful," Jennifer said.

Carver sipped his drink with a slurping sound and wiped his mouth with the back of his hand. "Now I've disappointed you," he said. "I looked forward to this so much and you're hurt. Ash, I'm so sorry. You weren't supposed to know. But I felt like your father. I missed you."

Ash must have looked skeptical because Yuri said, "I did. I didn't even want them to send you, all of you, away in the end." He smiled sheepishly. "It hadn't occurred to me I would get attached to you. I was never married. I had no children of my own. You were my children. But it was too late to stop. When you left, I was so alone."

"Who were our parents?" Ash said. In his mind he flashed to the office of the principal, so many years ago. To himself sitting on a chair listening to voices from the room next door. Dietz telling DuChamp, "Do you know who his parents are?"

"You were orphans, all my children had no parents," Yuri said. "Dietz and DuChamp, they knew it, but it was a way of getting you to work harder. To please these people. Don't you see? To make yourselves able to survive! My boys and girls, my lovely, lovely children." He fell into his old speech pattern, except without intonation it sounded hideous. "All of you gathered from public homes around the country. Horrible places. Special children," he said, a glow coming into his watery green eyes. "Genius children. Tested for intelligence when you were babies. My special test because babies, well, develop at different rates."

Yuri turned to Jennifer, as if she would be more interested in this part. He said, "A child could do marvelously in the test if he got it too early, and then slow down in development. But by one and a half it worked over fifty percent of the time. Ash, you scored so high. You can't remember how splendidly you did. A little boy on a floor with blocks, with a little book, with pencils. You were magnificent, James. You would have had a hard life without me. I took you in. Gave you a good life. Remember I told you knowledge is power? I gave it to you."

"You really believe this?" Jennifer said. "How could you do that to children?"

Ash remembered an old man walking with him by a river. He said, "You think we had an easy life?"

"If you saw where you came from . . . if you remembered that filthy place, you wouldn't have to ask. I think you had an interesting life," Yuri said.

"This is sick," Jennifer said.

The throbbing in Ash's chest subsided into a dull ache. He pushed it away. There was more he wanted to know. "But from what you're saying, how special you were, how did you ever get permission to leave the Soviet Union?"

Yuri tilted his head back and opened his mouth to laugh, but no sound came out without the box. Then Ash saw the expression was more bitter than happy. Carver/Yuri brought the little box to his throat. "I didn't say I was special. I said the program was special. After a while they didn't need me."

"But you knew the secret, whether they used you or not."

Yuri held up a hand. He looked for an instant like the old Yuri, ready to make a point. Small folds of cardigan drooped off his belly, where he had lost weight. He said, "You have to understand about a secret, a *real* secret. Not just classified. Not just something stamped secret but a dozen people have access to it. A true secret. That's what my children were. The greatest secret in the country." His eyes gleamed. "First the KGB kept you secret because the program was new, and Semichastny feared it would fail. He didn't want to be laughed at. Then Andropov kept it secret because it worked, and whoever knew about my children could command great power in the KGB.

"Imagine it. Andropov could tell the big bosses, the apparatchiks, without reservation, that the U.S. wouldn't fight if we invaded Afghanistan. And be right. They could bring in the entire blueprint for a new missile. And they did. And if the big shots asked how they got it, he could say, 'We pieced it to-gether,' or, 'It's a highly placed agent, I can't tell you who. I can't compromise him. Do you want to take responsibility if something happens to him? Because if I tell you, I have to tell all these other big shots.'

"And it worked. The last thing the big shots wanted was that kind of responsibility. As long as the information was right, they were happy. They made right decisions. They wouldn't be the ones to be punished if something went wrong."

Yuri smiled wistfully, remembering. "When my children sailed off to America, I was so proud of you. So proud I cried. You don't know how magnificent you looked boarding that ship, eighteen of you. I never doubted you. And Ash, you, most of all."

Ash said, persistent, "So over the years as the KGB chiefs changed, the secret got passed on."

"At any time only three people knew the whole picture. Others knew pieces. But only three knew everything. Semi-chastny passed it to his number two man, Yuri Andropov. Then Andropov became premier and couldn't run the ring himself anymore. He had other things to do. But he didn't want the new head of the KGB to know about it. Whoever knew about it had too much power. So he gave it to Yevchenko, the new number two. Who would bypass his own boss and report to Andropov. That split power just a little in the top in the KGB. Kept the KGB people against each other instead of united against An-dropov."

Ash stood up. His shoulder was throbbing. The room was too bright with the sun pouring in, and hot with the windows closed. He heard a car drive past outside blaring rap music. And the sound of children playing. A girl's voice cried, "You're *it!*"

Yuri drained his Bloody Mary. Licked his upper lip and drew his forefinger across the wet mark. "Andropov came from the KGB and he knew that too strong a security apparatus could topple him when he became first secretary. He'd done too much plotting himself when he ran the KGB. He wanted a strong KGB at the bottom, where it controlled the people, but a weak one at the top, where it vied for power with him."

"So he kept his own head in the dark."

"When Andropov died only I knew about you and Yev-chenko, and Billy Curtis, remember him? He washed out of the program but years later we used him in the embassy in Washington. With his memory we couldn't let him go. We just used him through regular channels. He was the one who passed orders to David and information back, although David never knew it. All in Billy's head. When Gorbachev took over, Yevchenko and Billy decided to go directly to him and tell him. With me. To get it out. To bypass the KGB and be rewarded. And they would have been, except their plane crashed. I was delayed on a train getting to that plane."

"But how did you get out?" Ash said.

Yuri poured another Bloody Mary, offered the pitcher to Jennifer, who held out her glass. To Ash, who shook his head. In the gestures Ash saw bits of the old Yuri he'd missed at first. The way he dipped the right shoulder when he leaned toward you. The way he flicked his hand when paying attention. The stoop of the back, even though the body was smaller. In Ash's mind he could even fill in Yuri's natural intonation, never mind the box. The gentle, soothing cadence. The sense of knowing things.

Yuri said, "I was old. For years I'd been a consultant, that's all. Unofficial. No salary. No title. No office. Just somebody Yevchenko might visit. There were no records of the program, Andropov had destroyed them. There was nothing written down. Nothing in computers. Without Yevchenko and Curtis, nobody knew about me.

"Of course when I heard about the crash, I knew sooner or later David would come into the embassy in Washington when he realized no one was contacting him anymore. I had to get out before that happened. Under Gorbachev it was easier to emigrate from the Soviet Union. I wanted to see my children before I died. I have nothing there. And money here, in the West, I mean. All big KGB people do. It was easy for an old, unimportant man to get a visa out. And if you have money, believe me, you can get a visa in. I came to Smith Falls hoping someday one of you would come, too. I wanted to see the place. It was amazing. I'm happy here. It brings back the happiest memories. I stayed. It's like being home again. That's why you came, too, isn't it? We feel the same way. We must."

Yuri reached out and Ash felt the parchmentlike fingers wrap around his wrist. Yuri smiled warmly into his face. Yuri said, "I hoped DuChamp would tell me things. But he was in the home when I got here. And I don't think he ever knew anything important before I came."

Ash stared at the bent old man on the couch. The decrepit wreck with his shaking hand and red skin and trembling limbs and voice box. It was impossible to think that this man had ever wielded such power over his life.

"You don't like Chuckles anymore?" Yuri said.

Jennifer, sitting next to him, said, "Oh, my god."

Yuri unwrapped his candy, sat back. He looked radiant. "Now I will have someone to talk to. DuChamp, even when he's coherent, is not very smart." Yuri winked. "And he cheats in games. But James, you and I can take walks like we used to. We can visit. Where do you live now, Ash? I want to hear everything, all of it. I want to know about all these years. What you did. The assignments. The thrill of it. And this girl! You told someone! Amazing! I am so happy to see you."

Yuri's eyes watered.

"Look at me," he said. "The truth is, sometimes I felt like I had done the wrong thing."

"I know," Ash said.

"But now we are together again. My child and me. You and me and this woman who I see loves you. A woman who is not one of us. And she loves you. I never would have envisioned it. Ash, you are an American."

The word *us* seemed to sear Ash. Yuri or Carver, or whoever the old man was, said, "You have to tell me. How is David? Tell me about David. There is so much I want to know."

Ash saw himself with Yuri by a river, on a spring day. Walking in the warm sun. A fish jumped. Ash saw Yuri standing between him and DuChamp, outside the school, telling the principal he was too hard on the boy. Telling the principal to ease up.

Ash stood up. His shoulder was burning.

"Where are you going?" Yuri said.

Ash said to Jennifer, "Let's go."

The old man looked bewildered. "I don't understand," he said. "Did something I say disturb you?"

Ash looked down on the palsied old man who looked back at him, frightened, on the couch. Ash said, "Do you really believe, in your heart, what you're saying? That you did us a favor? That you made our life 'interesting'? You treated us like a bunch of dogs, like Pavlov's dogs, with candies instead of bells. Lewis is dead. David is dead. You took away our chance of having any life, any kind of real life. You sent us to an enemy country. You threatened us with death if we tried to get home. You made sure we could never have friends, never feel at home anywhere. You made us afraid for our whole life. That's 'interesting'? Do you really think that was better than anything that would have happened if you'd never existed at all?"

Ash trudged toward the door, Jennifer beside him. Yuri, behind them, said, "Don't leave me!" Outside the sun was warm on Ash's face. He didn't look back. The red Mustang grew closer. Jennifer didn't talk and they buckled themselves in. On the small, quiet street two boys rode by on bicycles. A girl with a tennis racket ran toward Main Street, her little pleated skirt swishing as she moved. A Plymouth Voyager passed with a woman driving, and children in back. It was all the scenes in the little films Ash had watched, over and over, to learn this place, when he was a child. The cars a little different now. The hairdos longer. The kids dressed in higher socks. But somehow everything was the same.

"I love you," Ash told her.

"Where to now?" Jennifer said, starting the car.

"Beats me," Ash said. "I always wanted to try the strawberry shake at McKay's. You know how crazy it used to drive me, looking at that sign, wondering what the kids were doing here, when we only had vanilla?"

"One strawberry shake coming up, Baryshnikov." She was laughing.

EPILOGUE

ROUTE 112, THE TWO-LANE HIGHWAY meandering along the northern tip of Washington State's Olympic Peninsula, is one of the prettiest roads in the United States. In late autumn, when the summer tourist rush has abated, it carries a trickle of late-season travelers through lush, rain-washed valleys dotted with tiny towns, vineyards, and views of the Strait of Juan de Fuca or the blue Pacific Ocean beyond. It curls through the last remaining temperate rain forest in the continental United States. And ends at Neah Bay, the northwesternmost point in the country.

Late in November a white camper trailer with Oregon plates pulled into a log cabin Mobil 'n' Snack shop just outside the farming and fishing village of Clallam Bay, in the misty rain.

The driver was named Wayne Armstrong. He was a shift supervisor at the Union/Sapporo steel plant near Youngstown, Ohio. He'd always wanted to see the Pacific Northwest. He'd rented the camper in Seattle for his two-week, all-expenses-paid, performance-reward vacation, just instituted by their new owners in Japan. His daughters wanted to visit the Indian reservation at Neah Bay twenty miles ahead. Wayne was up for hiking in the rain forest. His wife, Barbara, just wanted to read magazines and eat out.

Wayne chatted with the attendant, a big, amiable blond man, while the man filled the tank and checked the oil. Wayne's twin daughters, Karen and May, went inside to use the rest room and get a Coke and Cheez Doodles.

"The kids want to see whales," Wayne told the man, who wiped the window with slow, comfortable movements, and whose blue garage overalls had a nametag that read FRANK.

The attendant said it was late in the year for whales, but still possible to see them. He had the easygoing movements of a man at home with himself. He advised Wayne to buy plastic garbage bags or waterproof ponchos inside for the hike, "if you don't want to get soaked," he said, "garbage bags'll do it, if you don't want to spring for ponchos." Wayne asked the man if he'd been born in this part of the country, and the man said, no, Florida. He and his wife had moved here a year ago after a trip.

"I have to ask you a question," Wayne said. "Does the rain all the time ever get on your nerves?"

"No, it's peaceful."

Barbara came out of the cabin with Karen and May and a woman so tiny she looked about the girls' age at first. She had one arm around Karen and one arm around May. None of them minded the steady, light drizzle. The three of them were laughing. Both girls ate Cheez Doodles from a bag. Barbara had bought a *People* and a *Bon Appétit*.

"What do you say we close up early today and try for some pike," the small woman told the big blond man.

"Good idea," he said. They smiled at each other in a private way that made Wayne think of newlyweds.

It started to rain harder.

Wayne liked the woman's voice. It was low and liquidy and it made him think of quiet nights and logs burning. It was funny that a voice could do that to a person. It was a very sexy voice.

"Daddy," May said, "Harriet said we should visit the Indian museum at Neah Bay." She talked with food in her mouth. "She said it's in-credible! There's all this stuff they dug up! Like clothes made out of plants!"

"You're not supposed to call them Indians. You're supposed to call them indigenous people," Karen said.

"Indigenous people?" the small woman said. "Where'd you learn that?"

"School."

"Twenty-one dollars," the blond man said, topping the tank off. "Go past the reservation, to the point. There's a parking area and it takes about thirty minutes to hike. You'll drive past clear-cuts so watch the part of the road that's washed out. Cut down that forest and the mountains slide down. But it's beautiful."

When Wayne started the engine, the couple moved together. He liked the way their hips slid against each other, nestled there. Liked the way they looked, the big man and tiny woman, arms around each other. He had a good feeling about this place. To be a prize-winning shift supervisor you had to know people.

Wayne leaned out the window before he rolled away.

"Excuse my question," he said. "I'm just nosy. But it never gets too quiet for you here? You don't ever feel stuck in the boonies?"

The man smiled. "I've had enough excitement in my life."

"Well," Wayne complimented the woman, putting the camper in gear, "if you ever want to switch careers, you could go on radio, with a voice like yours."

Corinna climbed from the yellow cab at Dulles airport and waited while the driver struggled to wedge her biggest suitcase, the Louis Vuitton, from the trunk. After that came the floral bag. The little suitcase. The on-board bag with flowers on it. Corinna didn't even have to wave a porter over. Three waited for the chance. She was booked on an Aeroflot jet with a five P.M. departure that would get her into Odessa around dawn tomorrow.

A little vacation by the Black Sea.

"I wish I could tell you where you were born, or who your family is, but I don't know. I tried to find out. There are no records," the man with the eyepatch had told her when they met on the towpath near Great Falls. It had been a shock. First the coded call that she had assumed was from David. Then the instructions barked over a pay phone near the mall. The realization, on the towpath, as she shook with anticipation of seeing him, that he wasn't going to come. That he would never come. That the man strolling purposefully toward her was the contact.

Corinna had known then, without anyone saying it, that David was dead.

"I am contacting all the people left in the program," the man with the eyepatch said. He gave her a list of names. "You can call them yourself. It doesn't matter anymore. Some of them will go back. Some don't know. Or you can just go on the way you are."

Without David. Without Ash. Without anyone she knew.

"I expect to be called back myself," the man with the patch had said. "Unless things change again. I suppose I'll work for my own republic. Belorussia."

Corinna joined the first class line at the counter. There was a little problem getting business space for all the new airlines, each republic wanting its own, so the new governments shared Aeroflot so far, agreeing on new timetables to balance trips to distant parts of the old empire. The new capitals all wanted direct flights, not links through Moscow.

I just want to see home, any part of home, Corinna thought. I never even saw it. She wondered if she would feel anything special there. She wondered if there was a way to find the town where she had grown up. But of course it wouldn't be there. It would have been torn down by now. There was probably a big empty field there. Or a housing unit. Or the same old dirt-cart track.

Corinna picked up her first-class ticket and followed the smiling counter attendant's directions to the Republics Club, where she could relax before the flight. It was a converted Aeroflot parlor with a rolling bar, canapés, and maroon-jacketed attendants pouring soft and hard drinks. Corinna fell into a couch in the no-smoking section and asked the attendant for a brandy Alexander.

"Czekist," a voice joked. She looked up and and leapt to her feet. Threw her arms around the small, fat, grinning man who had spoken to her.

"Ira!" she said.

"Walter here," he said. He backed a step, cocked his head, and said, jovially, like a celebrant at a convention, "Walter Mears! Pratt Engineering! Omaha! Margie and I . . . oh . . . Jayne to you . . . we wondered about you!"

"He found you too?"

"Somebody came to the house. What a shock. First I thought it was FBI. The kids . . . do you have kids? I can't believe we can just talk like this. It feels so wonderful."

Ira lowered his voice. "I'd like to move back. Offer my services. An engineer can never starve over there."

"I'll stay here," she said. "My friends are here. I like Washington." She laughed. "I've been at Justice so long I can retire in five years, with a pension."

Ira thought that was funny. "A pension from *them*."

They both laughed.

"Who else do you know about?" he said.

"Glorie Pell's in Vermont. Danny Minsky's gone to the Georgian Republic."

"Figures. They're fighting there.

"What about . . . well . . . ," he said, old habits dying hard, "you know who I mean."

Corinna set her lips. "I don't know about David," she said.

In her mind, the man with the eyepatch said, shaking his head, "I'm sorry. I don't know anything about Mr. Ash or Mr. Kislak. I haven't been able to find either of them yet."

The smile went out of Ira's face. He said, "You look so sad suddenly. Nothing happened to him, I hope."

Corinna shrugged. She didn't trust herself to speak.

"Oh. You split up," he said.

"Yes," Corinna said.

"I'm sorry. That must have been tough." Around them, passengers lined up at a table for pastries, or read *Wall Street Journal*s or *Tokyo Times*es in plush chairs, or sat at swivel seats at the bar and ordered drinks from the well-stocked supply. Ira said, "After all he did for us. The way he sacrificed for us. I hope they give him some kind of special reward. If they have anything to give, that is."

Corinna said, "Excuse me a minute."

She went to the bar and ordered another brandy Alexander and sipped the sweet, syrupy concoction. Two men, she thought, and I didn't pick either of them. And Volsky was lying. I hope they both pulled through.

Then Corinna shook off the feeling and turned and she was used to men watching her, it happened all the time, but the big one pushing through the lounge seemed to have purpose in his stride. His hand came out of his pocket. She knew he was a policeman even before she saw the badge.

She felt dizzy suddenly. They were arresting her now? Now? She wanted to laugh.

"Washington, D.C., police?" she said, staring at the gold shield.

"Well, I'm not here officially. I'm just showing you the badge so you know I'm not a crackpot," the man said. Close up, with his flashy clothes and turtleneck and out-of-date sideburns, he reminded her of the cheap natty dressers she saw at the racetrack or Atlantic City the two times she'd gone. He didn't dress like a cop. But he looked at her like a cop.

Corinna dealt with Justice Department investigators all the time. Official or unofficial, it was all the same. He's checking me out.

The big man drew her into a corner. His name was Allegretti, he said. He was a detective for the Washington police department but he was a close friend of people on the *Washington Post*. In fact, he'd investigated a break-in at the apartment of her ex-husband, Ash, just weeks ago. "I owe Carl Lockheed a big favor. I told him I'd look into Ash, where he's gone," he said. "He just quit, quit and left," he said, watching her carefully. She remained expressionless, waiting for more, looking interested, concerned. He said, "Sorry to bother you on your way to . . ." He looked around the lounge and said, "Boy, everything sure changed over there, didn't it?"

She was not thrown off guard. "You mean he's gone?" she said.

"Have you heard from him?"

"We don't really talk. I mean," she corrected fluidly, remembering that he'd called her for a minute from his apartment last month, "a few minutes every once in a while." She frowned. "Did something happen to him?"

"That's what I want to find out. Phone records. He called you shortly before he left. Do you mind telling me if he was upset about something? Antsy? Anything alarming?"

Corinna's senses as a lawyer were offended. "This is unofficial and you got his phone records?" she said.

Allegretti grinned. "Unofficial on the disappearance. Official on the break-in," he said.

She could see Ira, worried, looking away, burying himself in a *Times* on the couch.

"Well, he was a little tired of work," she said.

"Did he mention quitting?"

"No. We were on a minute. 'Good morning.' That's it."

Allegretti's eyes never left hers. "Just gets up and calls, 'Good morning,' " he said.

Corinna said, "It was a friendly divorce."

"Thanks," Allegretti said, and turned away, and she thought, relaxing, that was easy, but he said, turning back, "What about David Kislak?"

"Excuse me?" Now her heart started beating faster.

"Well, I ask around about you, you know, the ex-wife, and people say, 'She's with Kislak, the lobbyist.' And he's gone, too, his secretary says. Both gone."

Corinna took a step closer to him.

"I'm glad you're getting into this," she said in her prissiest voice, "but you're irritating me the way you're doing it. You want to ask questions? Fine. But be polite. You don't have to be an asshole. David and I broke up."

Allegretti smiled. Fair enough. He eased his bulk down onto the arm of the couch. He said, "Two guys. What's their connection? Job? No. You. And actually, if we count Jennifer Knowles,

Ash's girlfriend, the disc jockey who quit, too, that's three. I mean, no crime. All the rent's paid. No law broke. But what's going on here?"

He didn't say anything else.

After about twenty seconds she said, "Are you going to ask something or just look at me?"

"We can talk later," he said, getting up. "They'll be calling your flight soon. You'll be back on the twenty-sixth, right?"

"That's right." She was rattled by the fact that he knew it. She reconsidered coming back. She said, "Come to my office anytime."

"Okay," he said. "I will."

He turned. Turned back.

"I told Ash the night of the break-in, he should watch himself. I promised Carl Lockheed I'd find out where Ash went." Allegretti smiled. "Promised."

Corinna waited until he'd left and Ira came over to her, watched the door, and said, "That was a policeman?" When she nodded he said, "Are you all right? I was afraid they were going to arrest us. That would have been terrible. Of all times. Look," he said, brightening and holding up a ticket. "I changed my seat."

The intercom announced boarding and in first class they settled in, took champagne from a smiling stewardess with a pageboy haircut and a winged shoulder pin.

"An engineer can always find work back there," Ira said. "Margie agrees. Here we'd always be frightened. That Volsky said he would help us. I'm going to scout a few cities, decide. Marge is selling everything in Omaha."

The engines revved and the stewardess collected glasses. The jet began rolling down the runway, picked up speed. Washington slanted below, grew smaller as they climbed. Corinna looked down at the mall, the White House, Connecticut Avenue. She saw her own apartment house. She saw the Potomac, and south of that, McLean, where David had lived.

Corinna blinked back tears.

"That's the last time I'll see that sight," Ira said, settling back, easing the big seat back, sliding the footrest forward, squeezing off his shoes. "What do you do anyway? Justice Department, you said?"

Corinna said, "Lawyer. But sometimes I play with the idea of"—Corinna blushed—"writing a book about us. Maybe after I quit." And especially if I can't come back, she added in her mind. "It's just something I think about. Some book. I don't know if I'd really do it."

Ira laughed, unsure whether to take her seriously. "Nobody would believe it," he said. "And if they did, we'd be in trouble."

"I would make it a novel. Change a few things. Wait a couple of years. Or find someone else to write it.

"Like I made it up," she said.

- On a calm night off the Florida coast, a fishing boat vanishes without a trace. Something deadly is hiding in U.S. waters, and the Navy brass would rather bury the truth than face it.
- Brash and unconventional, Mike Montgomery is hardly regulation Navy. At his side, Diane Martinson, the Chief of Staff's wife—smart, tough...and his lover. Under his command, the USS <u>Goldsborough</u>—a WWII-era destroyer thundering toward a showdown of water and fire.
- With the arrival of P.T. Deutermann—retired Navy captain, former arms control negotiator within the Joint Chiefs of Staff, and ex-commander of a destroyer squadron—today's naval thriller just climbed to a whole new level.

P.T. DEUTERMANN
SCORPION IN THE SEA

"**Realistic with fast-paced action that carries the story to a crashing, pounding climax.**"
—*Florida Times-Union*

SCORPION IN THE SEA
P.T. Deutermann
_____ 95179-5 $5.99 U.S./$6.99 Can.